THE DOG IN THE CHAPEL

A Novel

ANTHONY MCDONALD

Anchor Mill Publishing

Anthony McDonald

Anchor Mill Publishing

4/04 Anchor Mill

Paisley PA1 1JR

SCOTLAND

anchormillpublishing@gmail.com

The cover illustration shows a detail from *Ruby, Gold and Malachite* by Henry Scott Tuke. Cover design by Barry Creasy.

For Steve Gee

Intro

The summer of 1962 was one in which nothing seemed to happen. Or rather, it was the summer before everything happened. The Cuban missile crisis was still three months away, the death of Kennedy a full year off. That next year would see the Beatles' first string of number one records, the first TV appearance of the Daleks, and the start of *That Was The Week That Was*. The Second Vatican Council would not publish its deliberations until three years later, and homosexuality would not be legal in Britain until two years after that. But it is not true that, as Philip Larkin wrote, sex began only in 1963. This is the tragic-comic story of two young men, one aged twenty-one, the other eighteen, who fell in love during that previous summer, but who had the misfortune to be working as teachers in a Catholic preparatory school at the time.

ONE

The room was bare and cell-like. Tom had expected nothing else. A cheap reproduction of Giotto's Annunciation hung on one wall. There were faded green curtains which Tom somehow knew would not quite meet in the middle, no matter how tightly drawn across.

Socks went into a drawer. Toothpaste… On the windowsill for the time being. The window at least offered a view. Framed on either side by a pair of nearby trees in full spring leaf, one ash, one lime, was a broad expanse of playing field, marked out in readiness for cricket: a scene which would be a-buzz with boys tomorrow but was today empty and still. Beyond the far fence the ground dipped down through rows of vegetables to where a huddle of suburban roofs jostled in the dip. Past that and the land rose once more, was open country, a green plateau on which could just be seen the approach lights to an airfield, though its hangers, control tower and other buildings were out of sight.

A boy appeared from the middle of the lime tree, stepping out of the green. At least that was how it appeared to a surprised Tom. In fact the boy was walking along the far edge of the playing field, following the line of the fence that divided it from the kitchen garden beyond. The boy wore a light blue short-sleeved top above jeans, was lithe and slender as a Siamese cat, and had a shock of wheat-blond hair. Too old to be one of the pupils, none of whom would be more than fourteen at the most – and who were not due till tomorrow in any case – and too young to be a colleague. Tom wondered who he could be, as he disappeared into the middle of the other tree.

Tom left the room, turned right along the bare corridor and, when that had run its course of blank dark doors, headed downstairs. The chapel stairs. They were of light and highly polished wood and smelt too clean for comfort. On the half-landing a statue of the Virgin Mary stood on a plinth. She stood cradling the infant Jesus in her arms, a crown of stars threaded through her veil, one dainty foot protruding just far enough from under the hem of her robe to crush the neck of a puzzled-looking serpent with an apple in its jaws. You'd have to be careful not to send that flying if you took the turn of the stairs too fast, Tom thought. He made a mental note, against the time when he might be late for something, or a little drunk.

Along the chapel cloister. Past the offices of the bursar and the assistant head. Past the two doors of the prep room and, on the other side, leaded windows that had buckled slightly and looked blearily out into a court of climbing plants and hedged-in shrubs. Above his head the ribbed cross-vaulting did have an elegance that Tom grudgingly admitted, if eighteen-nineties Gothic admitted elegance at all.

'Sanders.' Tom had reached the intersection with the main cloister and turned to look along it in the direction from which he had been hailed. The old man was coming towards him. The empty main cloister receded behind him, bay beyond vaulted bay, a study in perspective. The old man advanced on him with small quick steps that gave the impression of a glide, an impression heightened by the polished tile floor and by his nearly floor-length black habit of tunic and scapular, which effectively concealed the motion of his legs and feet. He stopped, face to face with Tom. 'Sanders.'

'Yes, Father.'

The old man looked up at Tom with fierce blue eyes which shone through round, wire-rimmed spectacles. Beneath them were cheekbones so high and so sharp that they whitened the taut skin that was stretched over them. The cold eyes travelled downwards, taking in the whole of Tom's front elevation and then shot back up to peer into his eyes once again. 'This will be the last time we shall see you without a jacket and tie for a few weeks, I imagine. Shall we be seeing you at supper?'

'Yes, Father,' Tom answered.

'It's at seven thirty tonight. On school nights at seven o'clock. Don't be late.' With some effort the old man arranged his mouth into a grin that might have been borrowed from a death's head. 'Kippers.'

'I beg your pardon, Father?'

The grin vanished. 'Supper. Supper is kippers. Never mind. Sanders, while I have you on your own for a moment, I want to ask you to keep a watchful eye on a young colleague. Name of McGing. He's also new this term, but even younger and less experienced than you are, if such a thing can be imagined. He may need a little watching. And no doubt a few helpful hints would be appreciated, from someone with two whole terms' experience.' The grin almost made a re-appearance, but in the end did not.

'I'll do what I can to help him, Father.'

'Good.' The priest headmaster dismissed Tom by turning abruptly up the main staircase, a broad sweep of polished wood that stood handily beside him, but looked back when he reached the first half-landing to say, 'See you at kipper time.' Whether that was a joke or a slip of the tongue there was no means of knowing.

Seven kippers were served by Cathy the cook in the staff dining room that evening. Five people were already seated at the table when Tom entered the room on the dot of seven thirty, and Cathy was already fussing around with hot platefuls. The headmaster, Father Louis, glanced briefly at Tom from the head of the table, though without acknowledging him, before returning to his conversation with the dark-haired woman next to him. But his deputy, Father Matthew, a burly man with iron-grey hair and glasses, rose to greet him and offered his hand. 'Sanders, it's good to see you. I don't think you've met the rest of us. Sister.' He turned to address a cleaver-nosed lady who was obviously the school matron, already in starched blue uniform and a grand white headdress that formed a huge diamond-shaped background to her white-haired head. 'May I present Mr Sanders, who is joining us for the summer and perhaps beyond.' The matron dipped her head and murmured something that Tom did not catch, but she did not get up. So it was a surprise to him when the other two occupants of the table, the dark-haired woman next to Father Louis and a taller, older and greying woman who sat opposite, bobbed to their feet and introduced themselves as, respectively, Miss Coyle and Miss O'Deere.

At that moment a latecomer entered. The only latecomer, to judge from the seven kippers and place settings. 'Sorry I'm late.'

Tom almost fell into his seat. The contrast between the dowdiness around him and the youth of the newcomer had struck him with a physical shock. This was obviously the young McGing. And was the young person Tom had glimpsed from his window earlier, seeming to walk out of one tree and into another. Tom had thought of him as a boy then, and the idea of him as a boy was failing to fade from his mind even now that he was revealed to be a colleague. He was of a little less than average height, and slight and supple in build. His head of thistledown-blond hair Tom had already seen from a distance, but Tom hadn't guessed at the elegance of his features: the eyes of brilliant blue like scilla flowers, the smooth white of his cheeks, just now flushing with the faint pinkness of the late arrival. None of this gave any hint of femininity to his appearance, but rather an elfin kind of maleness. There was something about his walking into the room, something which Tom did not pause to examine just there and then, that precipitated in him a feeling, oddly, of relief.

'McGing,' the young man announced himself with an attempt at a conciliatory smile which he did not quite pull off. The others introduced themselves in turn in the smallest possible number of syllables, perhaps unconsciously taking their cue from McGing himself. The exception was Father Matthew, who offered a broad smile and a sentence or two of welcome.

Father Louis then rose abruptly from his chair, which caused everyone else to do the same – everyone except McGing, that is, who hadn't yet had time to sit down – and fired off a short sharp Grace in Latin. Then he sat down again, as did everybody else, and all began the task of dissecting their bony supper.

Father Louis used the occasion to conduct a progress check on preparations for the new term. Bath rotas, the allocation of lockers and the timetabling of music practice sessions all featured prominently in the discussion, which involved not only the matron and Father Matthew but also the two women teachers; Tom deduced that they made an additional contribution to the running of the school in a secretarial capacity. This left the two young newcomers, ignored for the moment by the others, to talk between themselves.

'Your first teaching job, is it?' Tom asked McGing, though he already knew it was.

'You're right there.' McGing flashed anxious blue eyes at him. 'A bit nervous about it, to tell you the truth.' Was there the ghost of an Irish accent?

'Well, don't be,' Tom answered reassuringly. 'As soon as you get stuck in it'll be a piece of cake.' Nothing in his own experience had indicated that this would be the case, but he wanted the younger man to feel comfortable.

Indeed, McGing's face brightened at once and he said, 'Well, if you say so, that's very encouraging.' That McGing should have such touching faith in the anodyne words of someone he had hardly met made Tom feel unexpectedly humble, induced in him a feeling almost of guilt at having spoken so lightly, and he found himself thinking that he would need to weigh his words more carefully in future with this person so young and trusting.

Those words crystallised in his mind. So young and trusting. That took his thoughts back in a direction he didn't want them travelling. To head them off, he said, 'What time did you get here, then?'

'Around three.'

'I saw you walking on the playing fields. When I got here.' Walking out of one tree and into another.

'You can see the sea from the end,' said McGing.

'Yes you can,' said Tom, who knew.

Father Louis gathered them back into the fold of the others' business conversation. There was much to do on the morrow. Father Louis had a way of saying the word *tomorrow* that loaded it with harmonics of dread and overtones of terror. Tom had never heard anyone pronounce it in quite this way: with a heavy, pausing tread on the second syllable, then a sinister drum roll on the double R. *Tomorrow*, as enunciated by Father Louis, would always sound somehow more threatening than today. Day on day would tomorrows grow more daunting till the march of time ended at eternity's gate. Today's *tomorrow* would begin in earnest with a staff meeting at nine o'clock. But before that there was something else. 'As from Wednesday the boys will be serving the morning Masses. Welcome though you'll be, Sanders and McGing, there'll be no need for the two of you to put in an official appearance until the start of school. Breakfast is at eight, of course. Here. But I wonder if, *tomorrow* morning, one of you two would serve at my Mass in chapel at seven thirty? And if the other would be kind enough to accompany Father Matthew over to St. Ursula's?' He turned to Tom. 'Perhaps you'd like to go with Father Matthew, Sanders, since you presumably know the drill. If you remember it, that is.'

'I'll do that, Father,' said Tom meekly. And McGing nodded his head, his mouth slightly ajar, to indicate that he too would be willing to rise before seven thirty, and serve Father Louis's Mass in the school chapel.

The meal ended with the clearing away of plates by Cathy, and the rising of all for Father Louis to say the final Grace. Then everyone filed out into the main cloister and began to disperse. Father Matthew laid one avuncular hand on the shoulder of Tom and the other on McGing's. 'Use the television room any time you want in the evenings. Any evening.' Then he slipped away.

Tom and McGing looked at each other. 'What do you say to a wander down to the local for a pint?' Tom said.

'Pub? I didn't know there was one near.' McGing looked a bit flustered by Tom's suggestion. 'I was actually thinking I might pop into the chapel and pray for a bit. I mean, with a new term coming up and me not having done any teaching before. I'm thinking I could do with all the help I can get.'

Tom felt his heart beginning to sink at this, but refused to let it go altogether. He had another try. 'You're in a bit of a funk, that's all. Half an hour in chapel will make you worse, not better. Anyway, there is a pub. It's just a bit tucked away, that's all. You can turn right outside the main gate, then right at the bottom of the road, or else turn left out of the gate and left again. Either way you get to the same place, the same pub. And same distance.'

McGing screwed up his face with the effort of making a decision. 'Well, all right then. Just a quick one.' He added, 'You were pretty quick to find the pub, though. If you only got here at five.'

'Well,' said Tom, 'I've been here before actually.' He sounded diffident as he added, 'I was once a pupil here.'

They made their way out of the Gothic-arched front door. It was set in an imposing three-storeyed gabled porch whose topmost floor, Tom knew, housed the headmaster's bedroom. And the window of that bedroom, broad and latticed like the captain's window at the stern of a galleon, commanded a grandstand view of all comings and goings beneath. Under Father Louis's presumed watchfulness, then, they crossed the front courtyard, a gravel sweep that formed a rough circle round a central lawn, and exited the grounds via the main gate: another pointed archway, some twenty-five feet high this one, surmounted, like every gable of the sprawling building behind them, with a big stone cross.

'You were here as a boy? At Star of the Sea?' McGing's tone was surprised. He clearly hadn't picked up on Father Louis's reference to Tom knowing his way to St. Ursula's to serve Mass. 'And did you go on to the big school? St. Aidan's?' He meant the public school, four miles along the coast, to which Our Lady Star of the Sea was a gate of entry. Both schools were owned and operated by a Benedictine abbey which stood adjacent to the public school.

'No, I didn't,' said Tom. 'I left here when I was eleven, when my father's finances took a knock, and I was sent somewhere a bit cheaper. I haven't seen the place since then. Eleven years ago.' A thought struck him. 'Which, in my case, is precisely half a lifetime.'

'Which makes you twenty-two,' McGing observed.

'In a few weeks' time.' He paused, then asked, 'So how old are you, then?'

'Nearly nineteen. My first name's Christopher, by the way. If you'd like to call me that.'

'I would. And call me Tom.' Then, rather awkwardly because they were walking side by side down a suburban pavement, they shook hands.

A moment later, a question occurred to Christopher. 'If your birthday's in a few weeks' time, when exactly would that be?' He had reason to ask: his own birthday was just six weeks away.

'June the twenty-first,' Tom said. 'Longest day of the year.'

'But that's incredible!' Christopher said in the excited tones of a rather younger boy. 'So's mine!'

'Well,' said Tom in more measured tones, 'that'll give us something to drink to when we get to where we're going.'

The pub, which was called the Admiral Digby, was a substantial, heavily built Victorian structure that had once been a hotel. It had a flower-filled front garden which faced the sea across a narrow lane. On the other side of the lane the land tumbled precipitously towards the unseen edge of the chalk cliff. Tom opened the gate, and they made their way between beds of aquilegia and Canterbury bells and then in through the open front door. After a second's indecision they chose the saloon bar. 'I'll do this,' Tom said, chinking coins in his jacket pocket. They faced a choice, among draught beers, of mild, or Trophy, or Tankard. Christopher chose Tankard, without naming the size, and Tom ordered two pints. 'That'll be four and sixpence,' the barmaid said.

Only a couple of tables were occupied. Without discussion they made for a vacant one in a bay window which offered a still day-lit view across the lane and out over the sea. Along the high horizon a line of ships trailed like snails on the top of a wet wall.

'So what is it you're afraid of?' Tom asked once they were sitting down and had said cheers to each other, but seeing confusion in the boy's face he added, 'I mean about the first day of term.'

Christopher took a thoughtful swallow of beer before replying. Then he looked into Tom's eyes and said, 'It's having to teach everything, I suppose. My subject's supposed to be history. I was quite good at English, and geography, and French. But when it comes to maths…'

'Look,' said Tom, 'I've been through all that. All you have to do – the trick is – you just have to keep one day ahead. Bone it up the night before and then go in with it. It's what I do. Remember that however little you think you know, they know a hundred percent less.'

'But supposing they don't? Know a hundred percent less, I mean.'

'Tell them they ought to be in a higher class. Then go to Father Louis and let him sort it out.'

Christopher took another thoughtful swallow. 'Did you know Father Louis before? I mean when you were a boy here. I mean, a pupil. Did you know all those people at supper?' He giggled at the oddness of his next thought. 'Were they your teachers?'

Tom laughed at the idea. 'No. None of them were. Things change in eleven years, even in Catholic prep schools. I never met any of the women before today. But I knew Father Louis, and Father Matthew, very slightly.

Father Matthew was something at the abbey – procurator or bursar, I think – but he used to come here once a week to hear confessions … including mine. As for Father Louis, he was at the big school as head of French – in the distant past he'd been master of discipline, which sounds a bit horrendous nowadays. And I only know that because he came down here once to give us a talk about public school life. That's the only time I ever saw him. Until he interviewed me for this job, of course. How he ended up as head of Star of the Sea I don't know. Monastic discipline, I suppose. 'Do this' and it has to be done.'

'Discipline.' The word had come up twice and now it was Christopher's turn to use it. 'How am I going to manage that? In the classroom, I mean. At my age.'

'You may be young,' said Tom, 'but you'll be twice as old as they are. And you're not exactly weedy or small.' Christopher looked as if he doubted this. Tom went on, encouragingly, 'They'll see you as a giant, remember. Half as big again as Father Louis. I don't imagine he has any problem. He had a reputation for being quite handy with the cane, so the rumour from the big school ran. A firm believer in corporal punishment. So he'll probably cut you a bit of slack there too.'

'How do you mean?'

'I mean taking the law into your own hand when necessary. Striking while the iron's hot. Use a gym shoe. That's what we did with the juniors in my last school. Works a treat.'

'Use … like … you mean, applied to …'

'To the bum. Double them over the back of a chair and give two or three hearty whacks.'

Christopher looked apprehensive. 'Which end?'

'Of the boy?'

'Of the gym shoe.'

'Hold the heel and whack them with the sole. It only hurts for a second or two, but the noise is quite something. Works as a deterrent to the whole class for upwards of forty-eight hours.'

'Well, thank you,' said Christopher. 'I'll remember that.' Tom thought he looked a bit shaken as he reached for his Tankard.

***

From John Moyse's diary: Monday May 7th 1962

Martha had 3 pups. 1 m, 2 f. Real shame I won't see them for weeks. Did a sketch of phone box at end of road. Spent rest of day packing and tidying up. How much more people wd acheive if you didn't have to spend time prepareing and then tidying away everything you do.

TWO

Christopher woke up at seven twenty-six. His head pounded for a few seconds. He wasn't sure if this was connected with the beer he had drunk or with the fact that he was due to be in chapel and serving Father Louis's Mass in four minutes' time. He catapulted himself out of bed and then hopped about like a sparrow, struggling into flannel trousers and a clean white shirt, and knotting his tie too tightly under the collar in his hurry.

Fortunately, in this building that seemed to sprawl as excessively as the Château de Versailles, the chapel was directly beneath Christopher's bedroom and he had only one flight of stairs to whiz down, taking care not to topple the statue of the Virgin that stood on the half-landing, before he arrived in the sacristy. Father Louis was already vesting when Christopher pushed open the door with a breathless apology for his punctuality. For he was not actually late. But Father Louis was clearly one of those people for whom *on time* means early. Father Louis, busy at the vesting table, had his back to Christopher and did not look round to acknowledge his arrival. He muttered, 'Cassocks and cottas in the cupboard on the left', and seamlessly continued his own vesting sequence – amice, alb, girdle, maniple, stole and chasuble, the last three all green silk today – while Christopher anxiously pulled down a selection of coat-hangers laden with black cassocks and pleated white cottas. He tried to judge by eye which one of this collection that was mainly intended for pre-teenagers might fit him and not look too ridiculously short. They all looked much of a muchness. He picked one at random and hoped for the best.

Christopher had not had time to notice whether Tom was up. Whether he had woken in time to get to Father Matthew's Mass at St Ursula's, wherever that might be. He did know where Tom's bedroom was, though. They had discovered on their return from the pub that their sleeping quarters were two doors apart on the same otherwise unoccupied corridor, and that they shared a bathroom just a little further down.

Christopher was still fastening the fourteen buttons of his cassock when Father Louis, now fully robed and holding the chalice ... topped with patten and bourse and swathed in the brocaded corporal ... turned towards him to indicate that he was ready. Abandoning the last few buttons of his cassock to fate, Christopher flung the cotta over his head and arms and let it find its own level as it went down, while Father Louis indicated with a jerk of the head that Christopher should precede him through the doorway into the chapel. 'The bell,' Father Louis muttered as Christopher was about to walk past it without pulling the brass chain – though there would be no-one in the chapel who needed alerting to their entrance, no-one needing this aural cue to stand up. Christopher was just in time to make a grab for the bell chain and to give it a startled jangle as he passed.

After today the chapel would be filled at this time with the hundred and thirteen boys who boarded. Now it was left to Christopher's imagination to supply them as his eyes briefly took in the empty space around him, and to his mind they seemed rather more than a hundred and thirteen, as well as sullen and aggressive, as in one of Ronald Searle's more disturbing cartoons. But it was only for a second. Priest and server turned their backs on the empty space and genuflected towards the altar. *'Introibo ad altare Dei,'* Father Louis intoned.

'*Ad Deum qui laetificat juventutem meam,*' responded Christopher.

'*...et te, pater, orare pro me ad Dominum Deum nostrum.*' To think that he might have spent an evening in here by himself, getting more apprehensive by the minute, instead of... Well, he had Tom to thank for that. Accepting Tom's suggestion that they go to the pub had changed everything. Tom had changed everything. Christopher had the feeling that something had departed. He tried to pin that something down, tried to name what it was. He thought it was ... emptiness. It was emptiness that had suddenly gone away ... if such an idea made sense. The emptiness of the five or so months since he'd stopped being a schoolboy. Working behind the trade counter of his father's builders' merchant store. Tom's recent path in life, Christopher had discovered, had been the same as the one that Christopher was about to set out on. Tom had come down from Oxford just last year; Christopher would be going up after the summer. Tom had read history, just as Christopher was going to. Tom was filling in a year doing a bit of teaching while deciding what he really wanted to do. Oops. '*Et plebs tua laetabitur in te.*' Nearly missed that one.

Tom had already taught two terms at the well-known Catholic public school called Bellhurst. '*Et salutare tuum da nobis.*' He'd explained his recent move here as the result of a personality clash, a phrase that Christopher had not yet learned might be a euphemism for a sacking. '*Et clamor meus ad te veniat.*' But it wasn't just the fact that they had things in common. Meeting Tom had been like bumping into an old friend. Really. It had been as comfortable and as reassuring as that. Tom had made him feel brave about what was going to happen to him tomorrow, in the classroom for the first ever time. '*Et cum spiritu tuo.*'

There was one thing, though, that worried him. A little dark thought that niggled. Tom, with his fair, almost ruddy complexion, laughing blue eyes and blond hair a little darker than Christopher's own, was undeniably good-looking. And Christopher had caught himself looking at Tom, in the pub last night, in a way that... Well, once you'd left school and put childish infatuations behind you, you were supposed, it was universally understood, to look only at girls. *'Amen.'* Christopher had never found himself looking at girls like that. Even when there were any to be seen. But this was an idle thought. Christopher shooed it away.

When it came to the Communion Christopher had a split-second decision to make. He doubted very much that he could be considered to be in a state of Grace. Teenage boys – or young men, whichever of those categories he put himself in – seldom were. On the other hand there was the saving Jesuitical counsel that if there existed a risk of giving scandal by refusing Communion when you would have been expected to take it, then you should take it anyway. And since in this instance Father Louis was not just the celebrant at Mass but also Christopher's new boss, Christopher reckoned there was nothing to be gained and much to be lost from scandalising *him*. He decided quickly that he would take the Host and signalled his decision by raising the silver and gold Communion plate and placing it under his chin. At that moment he heard the door at the back of the chapel open, then click shut, and the sound of someone padding up the aisle. He couldn't turn round. Instead he closed his eyes while Father Louis placed the Host reverently on his tongue. When he opened them again he was startled to see, kneeling next to him, one of the two female teachers he had met at supper, Miss O'Deere. She was clad in a long blue dressing-gown over fawn pyjamas and with crimson bedroom slippers on her feet.

Her hair was scooped up inside a hair-net. Christopher stumbled to his feet, remembering the drill, and held the plate close beneath her chin, while Father Louis, who was clearly used to this sudden *ex machina* entrance of Miss O'Deere, gave her the Host. *'...custodiat animam tuam in vitam aeternam.'* Then Miss O'Deere rose, turned, and could be heard flip-flopping softly back down the aisle, presumably to go and get dressed for breakfast. Christopher heard the chapel door open and then shut behind her.

At mid-day Father Louis, clad now in a black suit and carrying a rolled-up umbrella, left in a taxi for the station. Arrived in London he would meet some sixty or so of the boarders and escort them back on the school train.

Then, from lunchtime onwards individual boys began to arrive: rarities at first, like early swallows, but then homing in with greater frequency, either with their parents in cars or else by taxi from the station under their own steam. Utterly unlike the nightmare vision of aggressive truculence that Christopher had conjured in his mind in the chapel earlier, these boys seemed almost abnormally sober and well-behaved. Each one buttoned up and moving stiffly in the unaccustomed strait-jacket of his uniform, with school tie and hard lace-up shoes – a sensation forgotten for the best part of a month – and subdued by re-encounter with the cold marble and tiles of the cloisters and the lofty echoing spaces of dormitories and halls. Voices were for the moment quiet and respectful, youthful high spirits temporarily repressed. All that would change, as they acclimatised and re-established their places in the pecking order over the coming hours and days. Indeed this was already beginning to happen by the time the two coaches that had been chartered to meet the school train arrived and decanted their cargoes like bucketfuls of small, energetically hopping frogs.

Christopher and Tom did not have much opportunity for private conversation during this day of meetings, timetables, books and lists and lesson prep; though they'd managed to ask each other quietly at breakfast if they'd woken up in time to serve their respective Masses and were glad to get an affirmative answer each. But during supper Tom found a moment when no-one was looking at his lips to mouth to Christopher, 'Pub after?'

Christopher's face registered doubt and his lips began to frame the word '*but…*' only to be stopped by Tom's lips repeating the shape of '*after*' across the table. Tom turned to Father Matthew – he had quickly established which of the two priests would be the more likely to give a favourable answer to any enquiry – and said, smiling, 'You don't need me for anything else after supper, do you, Father? Or Mr McGing?'

'No. Sister will see the babies are tucked up. You two can consider yourselves free till about a quarter to nine in the morning. Provided your lessons are well prepared.' Father Matthew gave them a mock-stern stare through his thick glasses, but it quickly metamorphosed into a twinkle.

As soon as they were out of the staff dining room and everybody else's earshot Tom said to Christopher, 'We don't have to march out of the front gate in sight of all the dormitories and Father Louis's bedroom window. There's a gate into the road by the oil tanks behind the chapel. It's overlooked only by your window and mine.' He grinned. 'And we won't be there to watch ourselves go out.'

'And the gate's left unlocked? All night?'

Tom's grin broadened. He fished in a pocket and with a mini-flourish produced a shining silver Yale key.

'How did you get that?' Christopher was surprised, and impressed.

'I ran into the old gardener. Groundsman. Whatever he's called. Mr Barker. I remembered him from when I was here as a kid. Of course he didn't remember me. Probably just as well. Barker by name, Barker by nature. Always shouting at us, catching us out of bounds and so on. Of course I didn't remind him about that, but we had a chat. And he told me about the gate. If I wanted to go in and out any time without it being the talk of the school – all our predecessors did, apparently – he'd let me have a spare key. Took me down to his cottage by the vegetable plot and gave it to me. 'Give it back before you leave,' he said.'

'Before you leave?'

'He meant at the end of my contract,' said Tom. 'Whenever that might be.'

They made their way out by means of a door near the chapel, at the foot of the stairs that led to their rooms above. Then, with the help of Tom's newly acquired silver key, they entered the outside world of streets and houses. 'Funny, isn't it?' Tom said as the gate in the wall clunked shut behind them. 'All those years ago Mr Barker was something like a policeman – or a warder. Now here he is conniving at our escape. It's as if we're suddenly on the same side.'

'That's not odd at all,' said Christopher. 'It's you who's changed sides, from pupil to teacher. Child to grownup. The odd thing is that here are you and me, still sneaking out of school all cloak and dagger, just as if we were schoolboys ourselves, in fear of getting the cane if we're caught.'

Tom gave a snort of surprised laughter. 'You're funny,' he said. He meant it nicely. When they came to the corner of the road, the street on the left led straight downhill to the Admiral Digby. At this point a broad crescent of sea appeared above the rooftops in front of them. And, startling them both for a moment, for the previous evening it had not been visible, there on the horizon, serenely floating, was the long thin line of the coast of France. The setting sun – shining from the north-west at this time of year – was lighting the three hills behind Cap Blanc Nez a translucent green and the chalk cliffs, though they appeared no bigger than a row of nail clippings, a brilliant white. Cap Gris Nez, flatter and darker, stretched away to the right like a long tail. 'Is that what I think it is?' Christopher asked. 'Or am I seeing a mirage?'

'It is what you think it is,' Tom answered. 'I'd almost forgotten you could see it from here. It doesn't appear all that often: it's nearly thirty miles. And I've never seen it that clear before, all in Technicolor like that. Must be the time of day. Time of year…'

'Or time of the month,' suggested Christopher with a crude facetiousness that was so unexpected that it made Tom guffaw. Without thinking, he placed a hand on Christopher's shoulder, but then drew it back as smartly as if he had touched something hot. Christopher was also conscious that he didn't often make jokes like that. He'd surprised himself as well as Tom. It must be something to do with Tom's company, he thought vaguely, and with the surprising and delicious novelty of his feeling so comfortable in it.

Tom asked, a thought striking him, 'Are you always Christopher? Or do people call you Chris?'

Christopher looked at him. 'Always Christopher. Even my mother. No-one calls me Chris.'

Tom smiled. 'Then I won't presume to,' he said.

Inside the pub they were served, not by the woman who had pulled their pints the evening before, but by a man of about forty with high eyebrows above eyes that were strikingly large and shining, and dark brown hair that was slightly longer and thicker than the norm for 1962. 'Not seen you in here before, lads,' he said to them as he drew their pints of Tankard.

'We were in last night, actually,' Tom answered for both of them. 'But we didn't see you. Though, yes, we are new to the area.'

'Monday night, always a bit quiet. I left last night to Jenny.' He stopped pumping and held out his hand. 'I'm Roger, by the way.' His eyes seemed to flash, first at Tom and then at Christopher. Tom found himself oddly reminded of a lighthouse, glimpsed unexpectedly on a drive near the coast. 'And you'd better have these on me if you're new to the neighbourhood, and have already seen fit to pay a return visit after last night.' Tom decided that Roger was quite a handsome fellow – for someone of his years.

They shook hands and introduced themselves. Christopher, who saw no need for discretion, told Roger that they were teachers and where they worked. 'Replacing Richard Appleton then, are you?' Roger enquired.

'Yes,' said Tom, who had heard his predecessor's name but knew nothing else about him. 'I suppose one of us is replacing him, though I don't know which.' He grinned towards Christopher. 'But then they've had a big increase in numbers this term. That's why there are two of us. Before you ask why it's taking two people to replace Mr Appleton.'

'I wouldn't have been so impolite to new customers,' said Roger. 'Old customers, maybe, but not new ones. Young Richard was quite a regular here. Shame he's gone. He used to make us laugh.'

The table in the window was already taken: other people too had been struck by the exceptional view across the water. Tom and Christopher took their drinks outside instead, and sat on the low wall at the end of the garden, looking out to sea, in the last of the evening light.

'Well, what do you think so far?' Tom asked.

'Of the school?' Christopher queried. Tom nodded.

'Bit soon to say. Father Matthew seems friendly enough. But Father Louis's a bit of a stick, don't you think? And the women…'

'Miss Coyle and Miss O'Deere, and the matron – Sister, as we're supposed to call her. "When shall we three meet again?"'

Christopher laughed. He told Tom about Miss O'Deere's surprise entry into the chapel to take Communion in dressing-gown and slippers. 'It nearly threw me. I hadn't served Mass for years. I wasn't sure I'd remember the moves. Though I got through it somehow.'

'Ditto,' said Tom, relieved to hear that Christopher had had trouble remembering the moves. Since he'd expressed the intention yesterday of spending the evening at prayer in the chapel – though it had proved easy enough to dissuade him – Tom had been a little afraid that Christopher might be the kind of deeply devout boy who, at home, served Mass every morning. He added, 'Father Matthew did give me a few helpful prompts.'

'Which, as you can probably imagine, Father Louis did not. Where was this place you went to, anyway?'

'St Ursula's. It's actually in the grounds; it's a convent of Carmelite nuns; you get there down a lane through the trees behind the old tennis courts.' Christopher nodded, remembering that he'd seen the buildings on his first walk of exploration the previous afternoon. Then Tom suddenly pointed. 'Look at that.' The southern sky was turning to night while a glassy blue lingered briefly in the north and west. Far across the bay the lights of Deal and Dover began to twinkle and, further still, tiny moving pinpricks of light were the headlights of cars that drove, on the right-hand side presumably, along the lonely coastal roads of northern France.

'Can they see our lights too?' Christopher asked.

Tom turned and looked at him closely. At that moment he looked astonishingly young, even for his eighteen years. Fragile and vulnerable. And insubstantial as the dream vision across the water. Tom was shaken, startled, by the strength of the urge he felt just then to draw Christopher towards him in a protecting embrace. It was an urge that could not be given in to without bringing the roof beams of his world crashing about his head. Christopher's too, of course. He said, 'Better be heading back, perhaps. Big day tomorrow.'

***

From John Moyse's diary: Tuesday May 8th 1962

Back to the old prison camp. Sister says there are two new masters, both very serious. (Groan.) Why do we never get any who are fun or funny? Digger and Fordyce not back yet. Spam and chips for supper.

Later, an Armstrong-Whitworth Argosy sitting on the airport runway gunning its engines for about fifteen minutes then disappearing. Why do they do that?

THREE

It was raining next morning. That was only to be expected when France had been so clearly visible at thirty miles distance the night before. But the May downpour that made a Niagara Falls of the view from Tom's window seemed only too fitting a backdrop for the *rentrée*. The sounds of morning Mass drifted up from the chapel below as Tom was dressing: the sanctuary bell, the occasional Amen chorused by a hundred or more treble voices. Tom even made out the sound of Miss O'Deere opening and closing the chapel door as she made her precision-timed journey to Communion, while he was heading along the corridor to the bathroom. He almost bumped into Christopher, clad in loose-hanging red and silver striped pyjamas, coming out. 'You OK about everything?' Tom asked. 'Not too nervous?'

'I'll be all right,' Christopher said, neither sounding nor feeling as though he would be. Tom's supportive company over the last two evenings had done much to steady his nerve but there were limits even to that: Tom wouldn't actually be with him in the classroom when the moment came.

'Anything you need or want to know: here I am,' Tom said. 'And I'll be in the room next to yours all day. Don't forget the gym-shoe. Oh –' he remembered something, 'and don't forget the Angelus at twelve o'clock.'

'Oh Lord,' said Christopher, 'I can't remember how that goes.'

'Relax. All you do is stop the class, say, 'Now we'll stand up for the Angelus', and when they have, declaim loudly, 'The Angel of the Lord declared unto Mary,' then shut your mouth resolutely, glare at them and they'll do the rest. Couldn't be simpler.' Christopher gulped his thank you and they went on their different ways.

They were spared the baleful company of Father Louis at breakfast. He supervised breakfast in the refectory, sitting in solitary state at a small table on the edge of a sea of boys, like King Canute. But the others were all there. Miss O'Deere had clearly decided, on thirty-six hours' reflection, that she liked the two new young teachers and now engaged them in conversation about the boys they were going to meet, offering tips on how to deal with the one or two more difficult ones. But if Miss O'Deere had made up her mind that Tom and Christopher could be admitted to the fold, Miss Coyle seemed to have reached no such decision. She kept up a high-pitched, high-velocity monologue in an Irish brogue, directed at, rather than addressed to, Father Matthew, who had the opportunity to interject only polite nods and monosyllables. Perhaps everyone was nervous about the morning ahead and simply dealt with it in different ways.

'What's a lore-and?' Shuffling of feet and a palpable atmosphere of perplexity greeted the question that Father Louis, standing high on the stage, addressed to the boys at the end of the final hymn of morning assembly. He repeated it. 'What's a lore-and?' Again silence. With steely patience Father Louis offered a context. 'Obey thy lore-and I will be / Thine for all eternity… *Law and…* Remember that for the future. Because I shall.' He glared stonily at his audience for a moment, then turned his attention to a small card table that stood in front of him. 'One letter only today.' He picked it up and waved it. 'Lemarc.' There was a restive susurration from the boys that might have developed into a pantomime groan had the reins of discipline been in the less unyielding hands of Father Matthew. This happened every start of term. Lemarc's parents must have to write that first letter while the holidays were still on and secretly post it before their son left home on the Tuesday. Now Father Matthew crossed the floor and lifted the little table down from the stage while, unabashed, Lemarc made his way forward through the crowd to collect his unique missive. Father Louis nodded his head then, starting with Form One, the class teachers called their charges together and filed them out in a more or less orderly fashion.

Tom caught only glimpses of Christopher during the fast-moving hours which followed. He was tight-lipped at coffee time, frantically swotting up text-books at lunch break, but seemed vastly more relaxed – almost pleased with himself – on the games field for the last hour of the afternoon as the juniors were divided into three groups of very approximately twenty-two for games of cricket. Mr Charteris, one of the non-resident teachers, took the top game, Tom had the intermediately able, while Christopher got to umpire the rabbits. Tom was able to make a shrewd guess as to why Christopher seemed suddenly more at ease.

During the first lesson of the afternoon sounds of unruly laughter and noise had penetrated the wall of Tom's classroom – 2A – coming from the direction of Christopher's – 2B – next door. There had followed an ominous pause which in its turn had been broken by two very loud cracks. They were so extremely startling that you could imagine you'd heard the discharge of both barrels of a twelve-bore. There came with them two piercing yelps of pain which merged into a drawn-out sobbing wail, and then that diminuendo-ed into silence.

This reduced Tom's class to frozen silence too. They gazed up at him, ashen-faced. 'Let that be a lesson to you,' he warned them stonily. Then he permitted himself a complicit half smile which the boys were only too pleased to be able to return en masse with a tension-relieving group snigger. From that moment, Tom knew that he had won over his new charges and that, provided he took care, he would have no trouble with them. But he was worried for young Christopher. Until, that is, he saw him on the cricket field and realised that for him too everything was going to be OK.

'It seemed to do the trick,' Christopher said when Tom asked him about it as they embarked on a winding-down pint of Tankard later, in the pub garden. 'Though I wouldn't have hit the boy so hard if I'd known. Having never done it before, I didn't really know my own strength. I was terrified of not hitting hard enough. I felt rather bad about it at first.'

'Yes, but it only hurts for half a minute.'

'I know. And I only felt bad about it for half a minute. After that I considered the effect it had had and found I wanted to do it to all of them.'

'Well, make sure you don't give into that temptation,' Tom warned him. 'That way madness lies. Or something.'

'I know. I was only joking, really. I'll go more gently next time.'

'If there is a next time. After a debut performance like that I can imagine you'll never have to resort to the gym-shoe again. At least, not with those kids.'

'What I can't get used to,' said Christopher, swallowing a little beer and changing the subject, 'is being called *sir* all the time. It does seem a bit odd when you're still only eighteen. Like it's a joke or something.' But Tom knew he wasn't really worried about that, that he was simply talking because he was feeling high, following the successful conclusion of his first day's teaching. He had done a gamut of things – they both had – that included long multiplication, drift and trawl fishing, and round-the-class reading of a chapter from Alice in Wonderland, in each case picking up from the page that their predecessor, the unknown Richard Appleton, had marked as being the place where he'd stopped. Christopher now had the feeling that there was nothing he could not do – in contrast to the feeling he'd had when he woke up that morning that there was nothing that he could.

'Once the week is started,' Tom told him, 'it's as good as finished. Roll on the weekend. Not that it's going to be a very long one. Classes on Saturday morning, cricket in the afternoon – plus obligatory voluntary attendance at Mass on Sunday morning.'

'I see what you mean,' said Christopher. 'That does seem to reduce it to Sunday afternoon. I was thinking I might take off on a bit of a hike in the countryside.'

Tom hesitated before replying. He said, 'I was thinking something along the same lines myself.' That closed the subject. Neither of them wanted just yet to be the one who would make the simple suggestion that logically would come next.

On Friday morning Tom had his first sighting of Christopher in his gym kit. Christopher was marching his class of eight-year-olds along the main cloister towards the assembly hall / gymnasium. In white singlet and shorts he looked much like any other blond eighteen-year-old who was reasonably fit and athletic. Yet the unexpected sight of him, two heads taller than most of his charges, made Tom's heart stop – before it began suddenly to race so fast that he imagined that everyone in the vicinity, Christopher included, must be aware of it. Tom thought he had never before seen quite such a vision of cornflower-eyed beauty. It was probably the shock of that chance moment that emboldened him, or made him reckless enough, later in the day to say to a more soberly attired Christopher, 'Are you still thinking of going for a ramble on Sunday?' An almost imperceptible nod from Christopher was just enough to give him the courage to continue – 'Because I still am. What do you say to joining forces?' And Christopher nodded again and with a very solemn face, as if he'd been a young woman hearing for the first time a proposal of marriage, said, 'Yes. I think I'd like that.'

'I'll find out what's expected from us on Sunday and what's not,' Tom said.

'Perhaps better check with Father Matthew rather than Father Louis,' suggested Christopher. 'We'd be in with a better chance.'

'Ah, so you've worked that one out too,' Tom said, and Christopher gave a little snicker of a laugh.

Father Matthew was more than accommodating. 'Yes, yes, take the whole day if you want to. And if you don't fancy lunching with all of us old fogies you can ask Cathy to prepare you a picnic. She's quite used to that in the summer. Unless you feel flush enough after half a week's work to lunch at a hotel.'

'Not that flush,' said Tom, grinning. 'I think we'll take up the offer of a picnic. Thank you. That's really good of you.'

Tom wondered what Miss Coyle and Miss O'Deere would think if they'd heard themselves described as old fogies. He had estimated their ages at something under thirty in the case of Miss Coyle, with Miss O'Deere probably having a further ten on top. Father Matthew, he guessed, would be approaching sixty, while Father Louis must be in his early seventies. Father Louis was very quick and sprightly in his movements, yet in some ways he seemed much older even than that.

***

From John Moyse's diary: Friday May 11th 1962

One of the juniors, Tyler mi., got whacked so hard by one of the new teachers, Mr McGing, on Wed. that he's showing the bruise on his bum around the babies' dorms and charging a penny a look. It was quite something aparrantly. The noise was heard 3 classrooms away.

Spaggetti and chips for lunch. The spag in its usual weird pink sauce. Extra piano lesson.

FOUR

Sunday dawned, and was already bright with sunshine before six o'clock. As a concession to the holiday nature of the day, Mass was celebrated at eight o'clock rather than at the weekday time of seven thirty. The pews were filled with the one hundred and thirteen boarders in their best Sunday trousers, ties and blazers, while the resident teachers and Sister, also all in their Sunday best, formed a row of their own at the back. Father Louis was the celebrant, dressed in the snow-white vestments of the Third Sunday after Easter. Two of the senior boys, in smart black cassocks and freshly starched white cottas, served on the altar. Tom did not have much to do with the senior boys, but he knew the names of these two. One was called Dexter, the house captain of Fisher, and the other was the vice-captain of the rival house, More – named after the sainted Sir Thomas. His name was Moyse.

Sunday Mass was longer than its weekday counterpart. This was due to the singing of two hymns and the inclusion of a sermon. There was no pulpit or lectern in the chapel. To deliver his homily Father Louis simply walked down to the altar rail and stood on the low step in the centre, facing his diminutive congregation. He folded his arms inside the wide loose sleeves of his alb, so that his hands disappeared entirely, then, immobile and unsmiling as a rock, waited for silence. The silence was pretty complete already, but not until the smallest shuffle or creak or rustle of inattentiveness had been stilled and a sepulchral hush prevailed was he prepared to begin. Then at last he removed his right hand from his left sleeve just long enough to make the sign of the cross, before returning it there again. 'In the Name of the Father and of the Son and of the Holy Ghost.' A wave of motion blurred through the chapel as the hundred and eighteen other people present copied his gesture. 'Good morning.'

A subdued chorus of, 'Good morning, Father.'

'This year,' began Father Louis – he carried no notes – 'is the third year of the seventh decade of the twentieth century. We are a little way in from the start of the nineteen-sixties. In this decade we are seeing, and we are going to see – we hope and we pray that we are going to see – a most extraordinary and a most wonderful thing. Something glorious: maybe we can even use the word miraculous. We are standing on the threshold of one of the great transformations in the history of the world. For what we are seeing, what we are experiencing, is the apotheosis – the triumph, if you'd like a simpler word – of God's holy Church on Earth.

'Some of you are very young still, and you may not have a clear idea yet of what this means. You may not have a very clear idea of what the Church is. For you the Church is, perhaps, a building: a building that you know and are learning to love, in the town or village where you live. And also, of course, it is this chapel, here in our own school.' Father Louis withdrew his arms from the sleeves of his alb just long enough to gesture solemnly about him. 'It may also include the sight of a grand cathedral visited on holiday. But as you grow in your spiritual life, and as you proceed along the special and individual path towards God that He in his infinite understanding of you has mapped out, you will come to see that the Church is very much more than that. Now I want to plant one or two new ideas – pictures, if you like – in your minds.

'About nine hundred years ago there was a great expansion of the Church in the known world – throughout Europe and even the Near East. A writer of the time, a monk whose name was Raoul Glaber, wrote memorably that in the year 1003, especially in Italy and

Gaul, 'men began to restore and renew churches,' and 'all Christian peoples seemed to contend with each other which should raise the most superb houses of God.' So many were the new churches and cathedrals, and so quickly did the work advance, all done in clean white new stone, that it was as if, so Glaber tells us, the whole world were being covered in a white robe: a white robe of churches. Now I want you, all of you, to think about that idea and to think how beautiful it is. Remember that our Holy Mother the Church is the Bride of Christ and then you can picture that white robe as a bridal gown, or veil, if you like, of white lace. Consider that. Consider that beauty.

'Have you sometimes walked out of doors early on a fine morning, like this, like today's beautiful morning in May, or perhaps in late summer, and seen the silk webs of the spiders covered with countless number of sparkling drops of dew? I'm sure you have. Countless is the dew, and yet each droplet is possessed of the most radiant beauty as it mirrors the newly risen sun. Together those radiant drops, like jewels, seem to cover everything in sight: the grass, the flowers, the bushes and the trees. In just the same way is the Church now spreading her magnificent jewels across the land, across the world. In Africa, in America, North and South, in Asia and in Australasia too, the luminous jewels of the Church's institutions spread and grow, to sparkle in the reflected glory of our Maker, who is risen for us like this morning's sun. Conversions even in this country, England, traditionally called Our Lady's Dower, are rising at an unprecedented rate. I hesitate to say … no, I dare to say … that nothing can now stop this profoundly wonderful process, this new flourishing, the stitching together of this new white robe of 1962.'

A long pause. Not a rustle, not a cough. A hundred and eighteen pairs of spellbound eyes and ears awaited in silence absolute whatever might come next. 'And yet, and yet,' Father Louis resumed, his voice now almost whisper low, yet audible in every corner of the chapel, 'the great and wonderful web is vulnerable. It can be broken. As you know yourselves, when you all too easily destroy a garden web with a poking stick. So who, you might ask, is to protect this fragile, beautiful thing? Who are the guardians of the miraculous process? Into whose hands has it been placed in trust?' He paused for just a second. 'Allow me to tell you.

'The guardians of the white robe are the new generation of young Catholic men and women. The ones who are growing up in the 1960s. I am talking – as I see it dawning on you now, I see it in all your eyes – about yourselves. On each and every one of you depends the whole of this. No bigger trust will ever be placed in your hands as long as you may live. Live up to this gift of trust which God is placing in you and you shall share the glory of it, the glory of the garden – His garden – that is to come. Live up to this gift of trust by keeping the Faith. But fail – fail to honour that trust that has been given to you, each and every one – fail by abandoning your Faith, fail by neglecting to keep the Commandments, not the least of these being the so-called difficult Commandment – and the older boys among you will know already the one I mean – fail in these ways to help bring the process to completion, fail to participate in the process that is part of His Divine Plan – abandon wilfully the task that you know is yours to fulfil, and a terrible perishing awaits you. It is the shrivelling of the soul in this life, and death eternal in the next. Eternal death indeed, but nevertheless – nevertheless – undying pain.' Father Louis gazed piercingly at his very sobered audience for a second, then crossed himself. 'In the Name of the Father and of the Son and of the Holy Ghost. Amen.' He turned smartly back towards the altar while the boys leapt to their feet with jack-in-the-box alacrity for the Credo.

'That was a pretty ferocious sermon, don't you think?' Christopher said quietly to Tom as they made their way out of the chapel cloister towards the staff dining room, their path diverging at this point from that of the boys and Father Louis, who headed downstairs towards the refectory in the basement. 'I mean, even for the thirteen-year-olds, but some of them are only seven.'

'I think he always had a reputation for pulling no punches,' said Tom. 'And that went for his sermons as much as his approach to discipline. But yes, it came as a bit of a shock to me too.'

At breakfast Christopher brought the subject up again. There were only five of them at the table: Tom and Christopher and the three resident women. Father Louis was supervising the boys in the refectory while Father Matthew was having his breakfast cooked for him by the nuns at St Ursula's. 'Are his sermons always as hard-hitting as that one?' Christopher addressed his question to Miss O'Deere, with whom he now felt on comfortable terms. He was surprised to notice that the question flustered her, as well as eliciting an exchange of glances between Sister and Miss Coyle. And the answer that he got, no less than the reaction to his question, left him more curious than he'd been before. For Miss O'Deere simply grimaced and said, 'Well, yes and no.'

Miss Coyle at that point jumped in and announced brightly that she was going to spend the morning writing letters to her apparently multitudinous family back in Ireland. Then Miss O'Deere, who was not only the form mistress of Middle Three but also the school art teacher, told them all that she intended to spend the morning painting. 'While you two are off on a walk, I gather,' she added, turning to the two young men, and wished them an enjoyable day with unfeigned warmth, a wish which was perhaps more surprisingly echoed by the other two.

They had agreed that they would leave the grounds by what they now thought of as their private gate in the wall so as not to draw attention to themselves. Neither had articulated any particular reason why they might not want to draw attention to themselves. But Tom was surprised, after retiring to his room after breakfast and then emerging again, now in jeans and an open-necked shirt, to find that Christopher's idea of casual dress for a May Sunday morning had involved donning his cricket whites – cream shirt, cream trousers and white boots. Tom thought he looked stunning, and couldn't possibly say so, but was glad they'd decided against leaving by the front door.

Anyone emerging from any of the school's gates and walking around the outside of its walled enclosure – an entire street block which comprised the school buildings, grounds, sports fields and kitchen gardens, plus the whole of St Ursula's grounds and buildings – might have supposed that they were in the middle of deepest suburbia. Yet the appearance was misleading. On the landward side one row only of 1930s villas separated the school from a real countryside of green meadows and orchards of apple and cherry. And once they had discovered it they found the sunlit land, in this second week of May, was covered with a white robe, not of churches but of flowers. Hawthorn trees wore creamy white mantillas and from the roadside verges craned the heads of cow parsley, which Christopher remembered his mother calling Queen Anne's lace, to meet and join the overhanging drapes of may above. Here and there the robe was threaded with gold as early buttercups sprang through the netted white. As Tom and Christopher made their way into this Sunday-peaceful landscape thrushes and blackcaps sang and distantly, from opposite directions, two cuckoos called.

They walked in silence for five minutes or so, then Christopher said, 'You know all that Father Louis was saying this morning: about the triumph of the Church in the 1960s. Do you think he can possibly be right about that? I mean, is it remotely believable?'

Tom hesitated before trying to answer. An unbeliever in a believing world – with Catholic parents, Catholic family, Catholic school, Catholic friends and now his second Catholic job – he had been careful to keep the germs of his apostasy as sealed up and hidden from those near him as if they had been anthrax spores. But now, for the first time ever, he found himself wanting to give an answer that was not motivated solely by self-preservation but by concern for someone else. And his concern was not a simple one but involved a dilemma. His feelings about Christopher were complex, could not all be boiled down to simple lust, and involved a genuine desire not to deceive him in any way. In this important matter he wanted to give Christopher the truth. To say to him simply, 'I don't believe.' At the same time he knew that Christopher, young and rather unworldly as he seemed, might easily be shocked or scandalised or in some other way hurt by such a revelation. For a second or two he argued the toss with himself, then truthfulness won. It was not as if he were going to give Christopher his shocking news and then abandon him alone with it, after all. He said, 'I'm afraid I don't believe a word of it. Not the eventual victory of the Church Triumphant, not the Infallibility of the Pope, nor the Divinity of Christ, not the existence, in the end, of God.' He had turned quite red while reciting this, and was conscious of Christopher turning astonished, or perhaps uncomprehending, eyes upon him. 'There now, I've said it,' he finished.

'I see,' said Christopher. 'I need a moment to think how to reply.'

'And I needed a moment to think before I spoke just now. As you saw. It doesn't matter. You don't owe me a reply at all.'

'But I do,' said Christopher, and also began to blush, but to Tom's surprise underlined the blush with a shy smile. 'You see, I'm not surprised to hear you say what you just did. I think a lot more people would say the same if they were honest with each other or themselves.'

'I'm not honest with people,' Tom said. It came out rather gruffly. 'Not about that, I mean. You happen to be the first.'

'I'm honoured then. But seriously, what you said is much more intellectually honest than my position. You believe none of it, you say. Well, I suppose I could say I half believe all of it. What kind of a faith is that? And how's that for intellectual rigour? I'm like Sebastian in Brideshead Revisited. He liked to believe the Catholic dogma because it was all so pretty. Like wanting to become a priest when you were a child because you liked the beautiful vestments and the ritual of it all. Well, I was guilty of that too once.'

'You don't still want to become a priest now, do you?' Tom asked carefully. 'Or even half want to?'

'Not even half want to, you'll be relieved to hear.'

And Tom was. 'Well, to go back to your original question, if half the Catholic youth of today half believes like you do, and the other half totally disbelieves, like me – then I can't see Father Louis's dream coming true in this particular decade – or this particular generation.'

'And will we all be damned on that account?' Christopher asked.

Tom wasn't quite sure how seriously Christopher intended this. 'Maybe,' he said after a moment's thought. 'Maybe.'

After a while their path through the narrow lanes intersected that of the main railway line at a level crossing, then led them through deep cherry orchards on both sides of the road. The cherry blossom was already gone and the cherries were beginning to fatten up out of the dead flower stalks. Blackbirds hopped and chuckled like children among the branches as if unable to contain their glee at the thought of the feast that would be theirs in a few more weeks. Then, in a clearing among the orchards, a house appeared. It was a solid 'gentleman's' farmhouse, in glowing old pink brick, unmistakeably dating from Queen Anne's reign, with five first-floor sash windows symmetrically spaced, and with four more identical windows and central front door directly beneath. What kind of pediment or hood ornamented the front door could not be made out, as jasmine had been allowed to grow round it, trimly clipped and angled till it had itself become a green portico and hooded pediment. Under the eaves the white-painted rafter-ends formed a decorative beading between front wall and overhanging roof tiles.

At the sight of it Christopher stopped. 'Isn't that beautiful, now?'

Tom thought it was. A procession of thoughts ran through his head. Prosperous farm. Family. Contentment. 'That would do nicely,' he said.

'Yes, it would,' Christopher said. Then they looked at each other. Christopher began to blush faintly, and Tom smiled at him. He had asked himself a number of questions on discovering that Christopher was setting forth on their walk in his cricket whites. In respect of one in particular he felt, registering Christopher's blush, that he was getting nearer to an answer.

And Christopher, who had been trying not to ask himself the same question in regard to Tom now also found that, unasked though the question might be, the glimmer of an answer was appearing to him too.

They stopped for their picnic lunch a couple of miles further on, where an old stone cross was surrounded by a plot of mown grass just beside the road, but partially screened from it by poplar trees whose leaves shushed and scintillated extravagantly at every stir of breeze. Cathy had provided them with sardine and cucumber sandwiches, a pork pie each, a tomato and a hard-boiled egg plus a paper screw of salt. There were bananas, Rose's Lime Cordial in a Thermos flask to keep it cold, and a small bottle apiece of Carlsberg Pilsner – with an opener. 'Where did she lay her hands on that, I wonder?' Tom said, genuinely impressed at the discovery of the beer.

'She's done us proud all round, I reckon,' said Christopher.

After they'd eaten, and drunk both the cordial and the beer, they both pulled their shirts off – Tom first and Christopher copying him after a moment's indecision – and lay on their backs in the heat-fragrant grass in the sun. 'I can't do this for too long,' Christopher said. 'I burn.'

'I can imagine,' said Tom, trying to keep his tone neutral as he scrutinised Christopher's torso, and trying not to make that too obvious either. Tom's heart was knocking like a car climbing a hill in a too-high gear.

'You're lucky,' said Christopher, openly peering at Tom's slightly broader chest and more muscular arms. 'You're fair skinned too, but the sort that tans more easily.' Had Christopher's voice also struggled for evenness? Tom wondered.

Christopher had indeed been having trouble with his voice, fearing it would betray him. He didn't try to say any more, but found himself unable to shift his gaze, and his imagination, away from a line of bronze hairs that had caught his eye: they began to form just above Tom's navel, then regrouped more purposefully below it and finally arrowed down to disappear most provocatively inside his jeans. The sight, combined with the sunshine and the beer, made him feel dizzy. He tried to kid himself that he was not already in precipitous fall, rather as someone on the brink of being sick tries to tell himself – or will himself – not to be.

Tom picked up a dry grass stalk, checked that it was open at both ends and that no leaf node blocked its lumen, then he sat up and leaned towards Christopher, leaned right over him, and blew down the straw onto the fair skin of his taut stomach. Christopher giggled involuntarily and squirmed. 'Don't!' he protested. At one level, the instinctive reaction of a child to being tickled. But to the parts of Christopher that functioned as an adult something dreadful was happening. It was happening in his mind and he didn't want it to. Then it was happening inside his body too and there was nothing he could do to stop it or control it. When it at last erupted he heard himself whisper – or gasp – 'Oh no, oh no.' He started to sit up. And then in utter mortification he lay back down again and closed his eyes.

Tom could see what had happened. Even without the glimpse from the corner of his eye of the small round spot that had instantaneously blotted his cricket trousers. Tom didn't move away from Christopher or towards him. He wanted desperately to touch him, to make a gesture of understanding or comfort, but knew that it would not be accepted. Instead he whispered gently, 'It's OK, it's OK.' There was no reaction from Christopher. Tom repeated, 'It's OK. And it's happened to me before now.'

Christopher suddenly opened his eyes. Very wide. They were full of fear and doubt: two troubled, retreating figures – Adam and Eve expelled from Eden perhaps. 'I don't want to talk about it,' he said. He was blushing an unhealthily dark red.

'Then we won't,' said Tom. 'But don't worry about it.' Then he took a gamble. 'It's all right. You're with me.' He paused, awaiting the explosion, of whatever kind, that might very likely have been Christopher's response to that remark, but none came. Instead, Christopher lay back and closed his eyes again and the black blush began to drain from his cheeks. Tom lay back down again too. He was massively excited now himself, and his body ached for him to do something about it, but this was hardly the moment or the place.

When, as was inevitable after such a lunch, they needed to urinate before continuing on their way they did so at some distance apart and facing away from each other. This was in marked contrast to earlier that morning when they'd needed a pee-stop and had stood companionably side by side, each stealing the occasional sideways glance at the other and trying not to let it be noticed. But as they continued through the warm afternoon, making an approximate circle through the countryside on their way back to the school, and taking care to talk only of anodyne things that could embarrass neither of them, Christopher began to be more relaxed again in Tom's company and Tom, conscious of this, was glad. And by the time they stopped at a village ice-cream shop to buy two nine-penny cornets they were sufficiently at ease to be able to stage a laughing mock argument about who should pay for them. Then they experienced together the stomach-sinking moment of catching sight of Star of the Sea, their place of work and residence, as it reared over the rooftops of the suburban semis: its long roof ridges with their cross-crowned gable ends, the low tower over the chapel, and their two bedroom windows, though those were difficult to pick out precisely in that long wing of empty rooms above the chapel's stained glass lancets. They exchanged a glance and didn't need to put into words a shared feeling that their brief moment of freedom, whatever it might come to stand for, was over.

They both needed to spend some time preparing lessons for the next day but Tom did suggest, albeit a bit diffidently this time, that they might meet again at eight thirty and stroll down to the Admiral Digby for a beer before bed. He would not have been at all surprised if Christopher had said no, but in fact Christopher said yes, although in a tone of voice so neutral that Tom failed to read Christopher's feelings in it. Still, the 'yes' was a start.

Tom gave a knock on Christopher's door when the time came. 'We'll make a detour on the way out,' he said. 'There's something you ought to see.' Just opposite the chapel door another flight of stairs led upwards, above the craft workshop, to the classroom used by Form One, and to the art room. Here, not yet hidden away from curious eyes, stood Miss O'Deere's work of the afternoon – and probably other afternoons also: a sizeable canvas on which a still life was approaching completion. It was no pallid spinsterish watercolour but a bold and colourful work in oils which radiated energy and technical pizazz.

'That's a surprise,' said Christopher. 'I'd never have believed it of her. It just shows how you misjudge people at first meeting.'

'It surprised me too,' said Tom. 'I must try to think of her with more respect in future.'

'Funny thing about names,' Christopher said as they were walking towards the pub a minute later. 'Names like O'Deere. They sound comical when you first hear them, but after a little while you think nothing of them. We had a fishmonger called Mr Salmon at one time and nobody ever thought it worth commenting on.'

They were still talking about people with funny names, dredging up memories and family stories with a bit of an effort, when they arrived in the bar and had to break off to order their drinks. Roger served them, greeting them warmly (after all, they were beginning to be quite regular customers now) and exchanging bits of news and chat. But with him behind the bar was another, rather younger, man; he was tall and slim but wirily muscular, with intelligent brown eyes and thick copper curls. His face was freckly and his nose stubby, the bone structure finely sculpted. He wore a cheery look that might have been a fixture: like that of a cat that, while never running to fat, is sure of always getting a good dinner. When this young man had finished serving his own customer, Roger introduced him. 'Tom, Christopher, I'd like you to meet my friend Malcolm.' They all shook hands then, involuntarily, Tom and Christopher exchanged glances. It had been a small thing – it would be a few more years before Round the Horne would become a landmark BBC Radio show and *I'm Julian and this is my friend Sandy* a catchphrase – but Roger's meaning was somehow unmissable, and in exchanging their looks Christopher and Tom managed to convey more than they had said in all their small talk since lunchtime, and to unlock again whatever it was that Christopher's spectacular loss of control had temporarily shut down.

Later, when they got back to their bedroom corridor, they paused outside Christopher's door, which was the first one they came to. 'Better say goodnight then,' Tom said a bit hesitantly. Then Christopher said, even more uncertainly,

'Do you want to come in for a minute?'

'Yes,' said Tom, and they stepped together through the doorway into Christopher's dowdy bedroom. They stood facing each other for a few seconds in the narrow space available. Christopher said,

'I'm sorry I was so stupid, so childish, this afternoon. Not very grownup. I was a bit embarrassed. Still am.' He said this without emphasis or anything very readable by way of facial expression. 'You were so good about it.'

They were standing stock still, very close, still facing each other and now silent. Tom felt the heat that Christopher had absorbed from the sun during the day now radiating back from his body. It was as if he were standing in front of a small electric fire. He said, 'Last night when I … you know… I thought about you.'

Christopher's blue eyes widened: they made Tom think of thrushes' eggs. And his mouth opened as if to speak but no words came. But he didn't move away either. Instead Tom heard his own voice speaking, now hoarse and sounding as though it belonged to another. 'You looked great with your shirt off this afternoon.' Then, with neither of them quite able to believe this was really happening, Christopher began slowly to unbutton that shirt again, then discarded it on the bed beside him. And equally slowly, Tom began to do the same.

***

From John Moyse's diary: Sunday May 13th 1962

Served mass with Angelo. Fr Louis' sermon one of the bizzarrer ones ever. He says the triumph of the church militant is about to happen now, but could all be postponed if we broke the sixth commandment. At least I think that's what he was saying.

FIVE

Christopher mistimed his breakfast-time descent of the chapel stairs. Intending to land in the cloister half a minute after the boys had exited the chapel after Mass and made their way along the cloister and downstairs to the refectory, with Father Louis bringing up the rear like a venerable and silver-haired sheepdog, Christopher instead ran right into the old man as he emerged, a few seconds later than usual, from the sacristy. That was enough to make him jump nearly out of his skin, but when Father Louis addressed him, in tones of gravel, with, 'McGing, I'd like a word with you,' he had to make an effort not to wet himself. Clearly all was discovered, and all was lost.

'I didn't mean to startle you,' Father Louis said, with a momentary flicker of forbearing. He'd seen the effect he'd had on the young man. 'I'd like you to join me for breakfast in the refectory.' A grim and frightening prospect. But which was worse: a *tête à tête* with Father Louis at the lonely little table at the end of a room full of breakfasting kids, or trying to make small talk with Tom in the staff dining room alongside Father Matthew and the three hawk-eyed women? As if nothing had happened. As if everything were not now totally and irrevocably changed. Anyway, Christopher had no choice in the matter. If Father Louis wanted to have a word with him about last night, whether in private or in the presence of the whole school, there was nothing to be done. Christopher felt sick and dizzy at the thought of it. *A word*, Father Louis had said. What word could Father Louis possibly choose? He couldn't find one in his vocabulary that would be strong enough to express what Father Louis's reaction would certainly be to what Christopher had done with Tom last night... If he'd found out.

They were descending the polished wooden stairs in ominous silence, catching up on the last stragglers of the double file of boys. Could Father Louis know? Tom had prudently, and very silently, returned to his own bedroom just before dawn. But before that, while they slept, could it be that the headmaster prowled the quiet corridors in the dead of night, not just peering into open dormitories but turning the handles of private bedroom doors? Arriving in the teeming refectory, Christopher drew a wisp of relief from the discovery that a second place had already been laid at Father Louis's table. Some advance planning had gone into this breakfast-time interview. Father Louis was unlikely to have put out the second chair and place-setting himself in the middle of the night. But perhaps Sister... As a newcomer, Christopher still had very little idea how things actually worked here. Who did what, for example, on the headmaster's behalf? There might be spies among the boys even. He tried to put the idea from his mind.

The boys now stood behind their chairs in relative silence. Positioning himself behind his own chair, and with a gesture inviting Christopher to do the same, Father Louis waited until the silence had sharpened itself to pin-drop definition and then said Grace. Then he rang the small brass bell on the table in front of him and everyone sat down. The hundred and thirteen boys tumbled into their seats with the urgency of people playing musical chairs, while a bubbling of high-pitched chatter foamed up as if water were gushing from a suddenly opened sluice.

'I think you should be considering your future,' said Father Louis without preamble, and causing Christopher a second agony of vertigo and fright. He had been in the act of passing the toast rack politely to the headmaster. It dropped down hard on the table top, spilling one of six neat triangles of toast. 'As a priest,' Father Louis went on, without special emphasis and taking no notice of the heavy landing of his breakfast. 'The Church is in sore need of young dynamic priests. Of young men such as you. Young men who are ready to commit. You have an uncle in the priesthood, have you not?'

'I didn't know you knew that,' Christopher stammered. The word *commit* in particular had flustered him. He sounded as though he were responding to the announcement that a grievous sin of his had come to light.

'Canon James McGing of Blindley Heath in Surrey,' Father Louis went on in the quiet, unemphatic but inexorable way of those for whom the experience of being interrupted is a dim memory. 'He has strong hopes of your following in his distinguished footsteps.' Then Father Louis did break off while he picked up the crash-landed toast. A ghostly smile hovered briefly over his face. 'The choice of the word distinguished was, I need hardly say, mine, not his. He has written and asked me to do what I can – if indeed I can do anything – to nudge your ideas in that direction too. I have written back to him and assured him that I would at least bring the matter up.' He helped himself to butter and marmalade while Christopher removed with trembling fingers a slice of toast from the rack and laid it on his own plate. Father Louis pushed the butter towards him rather absently. 'Look at all these boys,' he said. Christopher looked. 'Do they look unhappy to you? Do they look disturbed?' Animated as the boys were by breakfast-time chatter and the urgency of feeding, Christopher could not say they did.

'People criticise us – criticise me in particular – for making regular, frequent, use of the cane. But you only have to look around you to see a happy, well-adjusted community of boys. Caning is not about causing pain, it's about discipline pure and simple. Like an electric fence for cattle, it shows where the boundaries are. The shock is momentary and the pain trivial; only the memory of it provides the deterrent effect – for a time. A rather short time in the case of cattle, a somewhat variable time in the case of boys. It depends very much upon the individual. Some will need it only once or twice a term; others, I'm afraid, almost every other day.' He stopped, bit off a mouthful of toast and marmalade and then chased it down with a swallow of tea. Then he resumed.

'My advice to you, McGing, would be: don't stint in the use of corporal punishment, but go gently with it. A little, applied lightly, but reasonably often. Never hit hard enough to break the skin, and flowing tears is usually a sign you've done more than enough. Father Matthew uses the cane more sparingly than I do, yet I feel sometimes he hits a bit too hard. Not his fault, of course: he is a bigger man. But that's a detail. Just as the cattle need their fences, so boys need boundaries to tell them where they are. And they need to know a little fear. A world in which adults fail to inspire fear in children would be a world in which children inspired fear in adults.' Father Louis looked directly into Christopher's eyes as he said this, and gave one of his death's head grins. 'Were that ever to come about it would be a very frightening world, would it not?'

Christopher admitted, with a startled nod that, indeed it would. He reached for another piece of toast with a tentative hand, as if expecting to have his knuckles rapped.

'You know,' Father Louis went on, as though the new thought led naturally from the last one, 'football is a good deal easier, and more enjoyable naturally, when you're not wearing stilts.'

'I beg your pardon?'

'In the seminaries these days they let the young men change into football togs just like anyone else. In my day, far from it.'

'You played football on stilts?'

'Had to. It was the rule. Since we had to wear our soutanes the whole time, and we weren't supposed to get them muddy, we wore stilts.'

Christopher tried to imagine Father Louis, half a century younger but still in full-length black habit, dribbling a football while teetering on stilts. He found it difficult to picture.

'That was in France of course, and back in the nineteen tens. Before the First World War. Things were very strict back then. A different world.'

'It must have been very difficult when it came to a throw-in,' suggested Christopher.

'Oh, we couldn't do those at all. One just had to give a jolly good shove with the foot of one of your stilts. As for Rugby, well unfortunately that was out of the question.' Father Louis's head shook almost imperceptibly with this expression of regret. 'I wonder if you'd mind passing me that last piece of toast.'

Tom had seen Christopher disappearing downstairs with Father Louis as he made his own way to breakfast. The sight gave him a sudden pang of anxiety and caused a momentary emanation of sweat beneath his arms. His reason told him that Father Louis could have no possible idea of what had taken place between the two of them last night in Christopher's bed. Nevertheless, as he entered the staff dining room he found himself trying to suppress reactions of panic. Father Louis might of course have found out about their all too regular evening visits to the pub and wanted to express his displeasure concerning those. It would be a minor matter if so but, if that were the case, why had Father Louis not chosen to confront both of them? Tom told himself to put his anxieties aside until breakfast was over and he could seek an explanation from Christopher himself. So, when Father Matthew had said Grace and the resident staff had sat down to their cereal and toast, Tom turned to Miss O'Deere and said cheerily, 'I saw your work in the art room yesterday. I was quite knocked out by it. By its vitaliy and boldness, as well as your technique. I had no idea you were so good.'

Miss O'Deere gave him a look of such pleasure and gratitude as to make anyone think she had never been paid a compliment in her life. 'Did you really think so, Tom?' she asked him. It was the first time she had used his first name. 'That's most sweet of you to say so.' Tom decided that her large grey-blue eyes, in their circlets of long black lashes that were like lace – what his mother would have called 'starry eyes' – must have been a feature of some beauty in her youth.

'Oh, Miss O'Deere's quite a star of the brush and easel,' Father Matthew said, and Sister surprised Tom by adding, 'She's a way too modest. She is, by a very long chalk. Would you know, she once exhibited in Cork?'

'To be sure, she did,' confirmed Miss Coyle, nodding her head in a sawing motion, and Miss O'Deere blushed and smiled with pleasure. When she'd recovered from the sudden onslaught of praise she turned back to Tom with a question. 'Do you paint at all yourself?'

'Not since I left school,' Tom admitted, 'and not terribly well then.'

'It's just a matter of practice,' Miss O'Deere assured him. 'If you have an interest in a thing it's good to keep it up.' She lowered her eyes, as well as her spoon, towards her bowl of Weetabix, and for the moment the conversation was finished. A few minutes later, though, she addressed Tom again. 'You know, I'd been thinking, though I felt a bit bashful about mentioning it – but now your kind praise gives me the courage to – I'd been thinking of asking you and Mr McGing – Christopher – if you would agree to let me paint the pair of you. A double portrait, if you like. I'd even thought of a subject. A biblical one, but with a modern touch. I was thinking of David and…' For a crazy moment Tom imagined she was going to say David and Goliath. '…And Jonathan.' But this was hardly any less crazy now. After last night.

'We'd be honoured,' Tom heard himself say, through a fog of unreality. 'I mean, I would be. I'm sure Christopher would be too. I'd have to… I mean, you'd have to ask him.' And Tom felt himself blushing to the roots of his chestnut-blond hair.

'He wants me to become a priest,' Christopher explained. Tom had caught up with him in their shared bedroom corridor during that short, tooth-brushing, interval between breakfast and the start of the school day. 'That and a certain amount about the benefits of corporal punishment.' Christopher was almost euphoric with relief at the fact that Father Louis's chat had not been what he was fearing, and also because he had something weird and wonderful to be saying to Tom during their first encounter since Tom's early morning departure from his bed. 'And about playing football while on stilts.'

'Playing football on stilts?' Tom was grinning madly, similarly reassured by Christopher's tale of nonsense, and glad that this potentially difficult meeting was turning out the way it was.

'That's what he said they had to do when he was studying for the priesthood in France. Of course it was a long time ago. Before the First War, he said.'

'That I can believe. But stilts…'

Christopher's brow furrowed faintly – so faintly that only the new Tom, Tom since last night, would have noticed. 'Do you think he might be ... ever so slightly ... going ... you know?'

'It's a possibility, I suppose,' said Tom. 'I have thought, once or twice... Anyway, it's a relief. When I saw him whisking you off downstairs I did wonder for an awful moment...'

Christopher's answer was a deep blush and an involuntary casting down of his eyes, which he managed to turn into a glance at his watch. 'Got to get into the bathroom,' he said. 'Before class.'

Christopher felt the sensations of one who crosses a heavy sea in a small and fragile craft. He would rise dizzyingly towards sun-touched wave crests. For whole minutes at a time, as the morning progressed from maths to history by way of French, he could feel certain that everything had come exactly right, and with the right person: Tom, the wonderful new creature who had miraculously entered his world. What they had done together last night was the right and natural next step on their happily converged paths – now path – through life. Then, in a sickening downward stagger towards the wave trough, all would turn to dark and shadow as his perception reversed itself. His acquiescence to Tom, won by Tom without the smallest show of resistance on Christopher's part, now placed him in a miserable and disadvantaged position: effectively trapped by the colleague whose bedroom was next-door but one to his own; his emotions and his present job – to say nothing of his future – held hostage by him. Foggily he was aware of himself managing his classroom by a kind of remote control while he wrestled with the idea that it was not even Tom who had taken him prisoner but his own folly and weakness. Sin was a word whose stranglehold on his moral vocabulary he'd been trying to loosen, but during those harrowing descents into the troughs it clutched at his thought processes with reawakened vigour.

Tom came into contact with Christopher at all the usual times that day, coffee and tea breaks and staff-dining-room lunch. He could see from his face – from his shoulders too, and even from the back of his neck and legs, so heightened now was his awareness of the fellow – that Christopher had no further wish just then to talk: that anything more than a 'Pass the salt, can you?' would have caused Christopher's sensitive soul to flinch and might even have been met with a rebuff. The gates which had been briefly opened to him after breakfast were now firmly, if only temporarily, closed. Tom didn't try to push against them.

Tom's feelings were pretty mixed too, though being a few years older than Christopher – and he was also a little more experienced in matters of sex and of the heart – he found it easier to hold them together, a manageable suspension of his emotions, like the oil and water in a vinaigrette. He too experienced the sunny feeling that everything had worked out better than he would have dared to hope, his barely conscious wooing of Christopher having resulted unexpectedly soon in a night of exuberant and boyish sex. Only in his case the shadows were provided by his knowledge of what had gone before, and what he was still a long way from being able to reveal to Christopher, the story of what had happened in the case of himself and David.

It was not until after supper that Tom judged that Christopher might be prepared to deal with him to the extent of having a conversation, though he sensibly did not propose having that conversation in the public space of the pub. Instead he said, 'I was thinking of taking a stroll by the sea. Feel like joining me?' He could hear an unaccustomed diffidence in his own voice, and then was conscious of a sudden surge in his heart rate when

Christopher, after an agonising second of hesitation, answered, 'Yes. All right.'

They walked in the opposite direction from the pub, along a track that slanted gently down the cliff-side to the sea. There was still an hour before the sun would set, but the sea was already beginning to adopt its glassy evening look. The coast of France, absent since they had first seen it nearly a week ago, was back in place again, today a thick dark crayon stroke on a sharp horizon, the sea below it now a hard and shiny floor of turquoise tile. Christopher began to chatter, to Tom's initial surprise, drawing his attention to sea-pinks and tiny yellow poppies that grew from hairline fractures in the wall of chalk. And then wild spinach and asparagus and white-flowering kale. Then Tom understood that these were easier things to name and point to than the baffling swells and surges that Christopher was feeling in his heart. So he made no attempt for the moment to steer the conversation anywhere else. Nor even, once they were out of sight of all save seagulls as they descended towards the rocky beach, did he try to kiss Christopher or take him in his arms. To be here was enough, he thought. He could not wish himself in a better place or time; his only desire the simple but unattainable one that this moment and this state of being should not end.

From the beach they watched the slipping sun briefly make brilliant the chalk cliffs and the green swards of the country across the water, and then a newly stirring evening breeze began to energise the lazy lap-lap rhythm of the near flat sea. At last Tom remembered something that he had to say. 'Miss O'Deere wants to paint the two of us.'

Christopher turned and stared at him. Then his face crumpled with a laugh. 'You're joking, aren't you?'

'Perfectly serious,' said Tom. 'And so is she. A double portrait. She's already chosen the subject. Biblical one.'

'What?'

'Try to guess,' suggested Tom.

'Don't tease me. It'll be the Moneylenders in the Temple or something dire.'

'Depends on your idea of dire,' said Tom, looking away from Christopher and back out to sea. 'She wants us to be David and Jonathan.'

'Good God,' said Christopher. There was a silence. Both were thinking, *love ...passing the love of women,* but neither was yet ready to go near the words. Instead, Christopher broke the silence with, 'Do you think we could call in the pub on the way back? I'm thinking I could probably do with a small beer.' So they turned and began to labour up the cliff path, leaving the sun to set in glory unwatched behind them, and the cliffs of France to blaze gold for an instant before they too sank back among the dark exhalations of the sea.

***

From John Moyse's diary: Monday May 14th 1962

Piano lesson with Fr Claude. He's letting me do the Moonlight Sonata at last but only on condition I do the last movement first. Says its too discourageing to learn the movements in rt order because they increase in difficulty. One way to look at it I suppose. Strange man but brill at keyboard. Knows just how to teach a piece of music the way I want to be taught it. Kind of instinct.

Vicker's Vanguard flying round in circles all day, skimming the runway each time. Every couple of weeks they do this.

SIX

A few days later occurred what the boys would later refer to as The Curious Incident of the Dog in the Chapel. Tom and Christopher, having spent most of the night together as they had done every night since Sunday, were dressing for breakfast in the prudent privacy of their own bedrooms. As usual the early morning quiet was only broken by the occasional muted chorus of Amens, and the ringing of the sanctuary bell, wafting up from the chapel. But then, unprecedentedly, a woman's cry of surprise was heard, followed by an audible buzz of schoolboy voices. The bang of the chapel door, twice, and then an outbreak of loud and anguished sobs. The time pretty exactly matched that of Miss O'Deere's habitual entry into the chapel to take Communion, in slippers and dressing-gown.

Christopher stopped still in the middle of fastening his tie, unsure whether to rush downstairs or to leave well alone. But he heard Tom's door open and close and then the unmistakeable sound of Tom running along the corridor towards the stairs. A few seconds later, tie roughly knotted and hair quickly brushed, Christopher followed.

A small wooden chair lived in the corner of the cloister, just outside the chapel door. Now Miss O'Deere sat enthroned on it, in a confusion of tears, handkerchiefs and dressing-gown. The chapel door repeatedly half opened then half shut as one by one inquisitive seniors popped their heads round it only to be shooed back inside by the two house captains, Dexter and Rickman, who, together with Tom, stood close around Miss O'Deere in attitudes of hesitant support and puzzled consolation. Miss O'Deere kept repeating, with only minimal variation – 'A dog! Of all things, why a dog? It's so awful! After everything. A dog!'

After about a minute Miss O'Deere managed to compose herself sufficiently to rise to her feet and say to the little group, 'Thank you, everyone, for your concern. I think I'd like to go back to my room now. By myself. I'll be fine.' Turning to Tom, the senior person present after herself, she added, 'I'll be at assembly as usual at nine o'clock. No-one need worry.' Then, with more dignity than might have been expected, she turned away and rustled off along the chapel cloister, her slippers slapping slightly on the polished tiles as she went.

Through the door of the chapel, still half opening and closing at intervals in response to the demands of human curiosity, it could be seen that Mass was continuing as normal, Father Louis on the altar steps giving Communion to the tail end of what had been a long queue of boys and giving no sign that he knew anything out of the ordinary had occurred. Tom spoke to the two prefects. 'You'd better go back inside now. I may want to talk to you about this later.' His tone of calm authority had the intended effect and the two senior boys disappeared into the chapel without a word.

'What...?' began Christopher when the door had shut behind the prefects.

'I don't know much more than you do,' Tom cut him off. 'As far as I can make out, Father Louis seems to have called Miss O'Deere a dog and ordered her out of the chapel.'

'How dreadful,' said Christopher and found himself reflecting that when we are truly amazed by something, our store cupboard of apt and powerful adjectives usually turns out to be empty.

Miss O'Deere's unexplained absence from staff breakfast created an atmosphere of unease. Neither Tom nor Christopher volunteered to tell a story they hadn't yet heard properly themselves, and nobody asked them to. They of all people would not be expected to know why Miss O'Deere was not at breakfast, and no other staff members' bedrooms were near enough to the chapel for them to have heard the rumpus. Yet there was an unspoken shared feeling that *something had happened*, even if nobody yet knew what, or whom to ask. Father Louis, breakfasting with the boys in the refectory as usual, was not available for comment – even supposing any of his staff would have been bold enough to question him on the subject. It was clear to everyone that the only way to find anything out was going to be to ask one or more of the boys, and equally clear that this could on no account be admitted to anyone else present. Tom was on the firmest ground here: he had at least attended the incident in a more or less official capacity and had actually let Dexter and Rickman know that he might want to question them later.

He found his opportunity at mid-morning break. He happened to bump into Angelo Dexter in the boys' locker room. This was just inside the door that the boys used to get in and out of the building. Dexter was just emerging from the boys' lavatory, while Tom was on his way out to check that the white lines of the cricket field had been freshly limed in readiness for the afternoon's games. 'Ah, Dexter,' he said. 'A quick word, if you can spare me a minute.' Checking covertly that no other staff members were in the vicinity he led the boy out into the relative privacy of the open air. 'Would you like to tell me exactly what happened in the chapel this morning?' He was a little afraid that the house captain – a mere eight years younger than he was, and only five years younger than Christopher – might tell him that it was no business of his: that what passed between the headmaster and one of his most senior employees was not the affair of one of the newest and youngest members of staff.

Fortunately Dexter was too used to accepting authority – his prefect status gave him a vested interest – to refuse.

Dexter looked Tom directly in the eyes with his own very large brown ones – Tom had not been fully aware of them before – and said, 'Of course, sir. But it was all really very odd. Miss O'Deere appeared at the back of chapel right on cue for Communion. (I don't know how she times it, sir: she must listen at the door.) Anyway, no sooner had she come in and closed the door behind her than Father Louis, who was coming down the altar steps with the ciborium to give out the Host, stopped dead in his tracks and said in a very icy voice – and I mean even icier than usual, if you know what I mean, like about a thousand degrees below zero, and that in centigrade – "Someone has brought a dog into the chapel. Will whoever has done this remove it immediately." Or forthwith. Or something like that. You know how he speaks.'

Tom was startled by the boy's very passable imitation of Father Louis's way of speaking. He hadn't known that was one of Dexter's talents. He wondered if he also entertained his mates by mimicking himself, or Christopher.

Dexter went on. 'People started looking round. Quite puzzled, actually, because nobody could actually see a dog. Then Father Louis began to sound… I've heard the expression, *He was beside himself*. Well, Father Louis sounded *beside himself* then. He pointed at Miss O'Deere and said,' again an impressive take-off of the headmaster's voice '"The dog standing there, on two feet, in the middle of the aisle at the back." Actually, he didn't say, "on two feet." I'm afraid I just put that in. Sorry. But it was at that moment that Miss O'Deere realised he was talking about her. And she screamed and ran out of the chapel. Simon and I … Rickman and I looked at each other and decided we'd better go after her. We did, but then a second later you arrived and of course you know the rest.' Dexter put his head slightly on one side. He had quite thick black curls, Tom noticed, and he wondered how they had survived massacre by the school barber. That shiny hair, brown eyes and olive skin... Angelo as a first name. He probably has an Italian mother, Tom thought. The boy only needed to look up a little way to meet Tom's eyes. In a year, Tom thought, they'd be of equal height. 'Do you think Father Louis's losing it, sir?'

'Losing what, Dexter?'

'Losing his marbles, sir.'

'Of course not,' said Tom. 'Whatever makes you say that?'

'Well, sir...'

'Listen, Dexter. Sometimes people who work very hard – and Father Louis is someone who works very hard indeed, as we all know – sometimes just for an instant something happens to their perceptions. Just for a moment. These things are called hallucinations. I'm sure that's a word you already know. Well, I think we can safely say that Father Louis suffered a momentary – if rather amusing – change of perception of that nature. And if anyone asks either of us anything about it – or asks Simon ... I mean Rickman, and do please pass this on to him, I think this is what we should tell them, don't you?'

Dexter was clearly delighted to be taken into Tom's confidence in this way – the words *either of us* had worked their magic spell – and Tom was pleased to see that the boy could be relied upon to play his part in what might have to be some sort of cover-up. 'A momentary change of perception brought on by over-work.' Angelo repeated the official line back to Tom, to check that he'd got it right.

Tom nodded gravely and said, 'Thank you. I knew I could rely on you to be sensible about this.' He treated Angelo Dexter to a very friendly smile and was almost ashamed of the pleasure it gave him to see it returned in equal if not greater measure.

The boys were supervised by Father Matthew at lunchtime, while Father Louis presided in the staff dining-room. He took no notice of the conspicuous absence of Miss O'Deere but chatted blithely about Common Entrance results, which had improved this year for the third time in a row. And nobody else wanted to draw attention to her absence or mention her earlier humiliation. It was generally known, though, because of the porous nature of the fabric of boarding-school life, that she had carried out her morning's teaching with impeccable professionalism and sang-froid.

At tea time Miss O'Deere did make a brief appearance in the staff room, nodding rather nervous greetings all round, including to Father Louis, who responded with a faint but unaffected smile. When she excused herself and left, again rather nervously, Tom was on the point of going after her but he was outmanoeuvred by Miss Coyle, who quickly left the room in Miss O'Deere's slipstream, presumably in order to offer her own woman-to-woman support, rendering any masculine ministrations redundant. Miss Coyle was a small, neat-featured woman with the large, lustrous eyes of the highly strung. Tom found himself thinking that she'd be considered pretty if she weren't a teacher – applying a label he never thought of attaching to Christopher or himself. Neither of the two women appeared at supper, and Sister gamely did enough talking for three, as if that would enable the absence of the other two to pass unnoticed.

A little later, when they had completed their preparations for the next day's classes, Tom and Christopher walked down, for the first time in several days, to the Admiral Digby.

Roger served them. 'Thought we'd lost you,' he said. 'Not seeing you for a while.'

'I don't know how much you think they pay junior masters,' Tom said with a laugh. 'But it doesn't run to propping up pub bars every night of the week.'

'Ah,' said Roger. 'Yes, I do know that. I was once a junior master myself. But a long time ago. And in a different place. Another world, almost.' He handed over their foam-capped tankards of Tankard, dealt with their money and handed back change. Then he treated them each to a big smile that looked like the prelude to something. And it was. He cleared his throat and said, 'This place has quite a history, you know. I mean the Admiral Digby. Admiral Robert Digby, to give his full rank, name and number. If you've a minute to spare I'll show you something. Down the stairs.' Tom and Christopher looked at each other and, in a reflex gesture, at their full glasses. 'You can bring your drinks if you like.'

Roger raised the flap that formed part of the mahogany bar counter and, with a flick of his head, beckoned them through it. 'Jenny, you'll be all right for a minute, will you?' he called into the public bar. Then he led them through a door into a rather grubby back hallway. Beneath the kitchen stairs was another door, marked with a warning notice. Roger opened it. A flight of wooden steps almost as steep as a ladder led the way down into the beer cellar. Roger switched on the bare bulb of an electric light as he led them down. They passed between standing casks of ale, tall stacks of crates – bottled beers and ciders, soft drinks, and soda-water siphons with silver triggers and necks. Then Roger opened another door, a door which didn't look like a door, but simply a panel of the wall, and led them into the dark.

Roger had pulled a powerful-looking torch from a bracket just outside the door and now he shone it ahead of them. They were looking into a tunnel that was hewn through chalk. White walls threw the torch's beam brightly back in their faces. Beyond the beam's reach the tunnel funnelled into a black hole. 'Are you brave enough?' Roger queried facetiously.

'I should hope so,' Christopher answered for both of them. They followed Roger on down.

The tunnel quickly began to descend more steeply, though it remained more or less straight. After a while a line of flints appeared, embedded in the walls on either side just above floor level, like the writing in a stick of rock. But as they descended, this horizontal stratum rose to waist height, then drifted up above their heads till it disappeared finally through the chalk ceiling overhead.

The descent of the tunnel lasted only a minute or two but the strange novelty of the experience lengthened it in the minds of Christopher and Tom. At last the torch's beam came up against something solid. A big metal door, fastened with heavy-duty bolts. Roger drew them back and pulled the door inward. They hadn't been aware of any mustiness or stuffiness in the tunnel, yet now the contrast was extreme as air rushed in laden with the freshness of salt and bladder-wrack and iodine and the ever-restless sounds of the sea.

They should not have been surprised. Where else would a tunnel beneath the cellars of a cliff-top house lead to, after all? But surprised they were. They pressed forward until they stood upon a rocky shore. Waves broke softly just a few yards in front of them, while a clear twilit sky spread like a canopy from the enfolding cliff-tops high over their heads.

'Wow,' said Christopher, 'this is amazing.' Tom echoed, 'Wonderful,' more quietly. A small rowing boat with a pair of oars manacled to it was itself fastened to an iron ring cemented into the cliff wall beside them, pulled up above the reach of the highest storm surge tides. Tom looked up and then back at Roger. 'I never guessed this was here. Can we be seen from up above?'

'You'd have to be pretty adventurous to try,' Roger said. 'In all my life I've never seen anyone peering over. A cat or two maybe.'

Tom remembered the view from the front garden of the pub. Across the cliff-top lane the land fell steeply and roughly away to where the unseen precipice must lie hidden among the tall clumps of ragwort and fennel. Roger was right. You'd have to be pretty sure of yourself to go looking for it. 'So what was it built for?' Tom asked. 'The tunnel, I mean.'

'A bit of low-key smuggling, we've always reckoned,' Roger said. 'A century ago and more. It was blocked up at the start of the First World War, I believe, then opened up but closed again in 'thirty-nine. After the war my dad had it re-opened. When I was a kid I used to swim off those rocks there with friends.' Roger looked at the other two for a second to gauge how his next remark would go down. 'Starkers.'

Christopher sniggered. Tom thought he could begin to see where this might be leading. He said, 'Nice,' non-commitally but overlapping with Roger's confessional: 'And Malcolm and I still do.' He continued smoothly, 'Taking a boat out on calm nights in summer. Do a bit of mackerel fishing. With just a very select few friends.'

'It sounds brilliant,' Tom said encouragingly.

'Well,' said Roger, picking up the signal, 'if you two ever wanted to come on such an expedition – with Malcolm and me – you'd be most welcome.'

'I think we'd like that very much, wouldn't we, Christopher?'

'Mmm – yes,' said Christopher, thinking that he had probably guessed the sub-text of all this correctly but that he would have to ask Tom about it later in order to be quite sure. Only Tom gave him the confirmation he was seeking right there and then by putting an arm around his shoulder and giving him a quick peck on the cheek.

Encouraged by this, Roger went one further. 'And if the two of you ever wanted to use the beach by yourselves any time, just the two of you, on a Sunday afternoon say, you'd be more than welcome to that too. Anyway, we'd better be off upstairs again.' He gave them a naughty grin. 'People might start to talk.'

***

From John Moyse's diary: Thursday May 17th 1962

Weirder and weirder. Father Louis went berserk in chapel and ordered Miss O'Deere out (oh dear) and called her a dog! (Oh dear oh dear.) Angelo and Simon went out to talk to her, and Mr Sanders and Christopher (sorry, Mr McGing) got involved. They seem to have sworn Angelo Dexter and Simon Rickman to secrecy about whatever was said, because neither of them wd tell a soul (mainly me) about it. Shame. It spoils a good story not to know the end.

After that the day continued in the normalest way which was somewhat boring. Supper was beans on toast. I suspect that Mr Sanders and Christopher go out to the pub in the evenings sometimes via the side gate.

SEVEN

The excitement created by the dog in the chapel incident died down over the next two days, mainly because both Father Louis and Miss O'Deere behaved as if nothing had taken place. Miss O'Deere resumed her habit of taking morning Communion in dressing-gown and slippers, and Father Louis continued to give her the Host without comment or any manifestations of erratic behaviour. In the case of Father Louis it was as though he had no memory of the incident, while Miss O'Deere was presumably acting on the principle of least said, soonest mended. Tom and Christopher both felt that the moment for bringing the subject up with her was now past, if indeed there had ever been one; any consolation that might have been necessary had presumably been supplied by Miss Coyle. In any case, they had more interesting things to occupy them.

A pressing concern of Tom and Christopher's was the matter of who and what they were. Not as two separate individuals but as the thing conjoined by sex that they had become. They hadn't yet talked about what they did in bed – had been doing now for the best part of a week – they simply got in and did it. But not discussing it did not mean not thinking about it, each in the privacy of his own deliberations. In Christopher's case rapture continued to be blasted from time to time by lightning bolts of guilt. He might be only half a believer, but the guilt that the Catholic religion fosters in its adherents is often the last thing left in place as belief ebbs away. Tom's source of private disquiet was a different one. He knew from experience how things could turn out. That this boy, blond and trusting, was on the brink of falling for him heavily. Just as David had done, so short a time ago.

But now, tonight, Christopher had found a peg to which he might attach his private thoughts as he hauled them haltingly into the open, between himself and Tom. Tom undressed in his own bedroom, as was now his custom, before knocking upon Christopher's door, pyjama-clad. Tonight he had hardly closed the door before Christopher, already in bed, sheet pulled down so as to expose him from the waist up began. 'You know, Malcolm, who we've only met once, do you think ... I mean, are he and Roger...?' He couldn't find a word he liked enough to use, especially because of what he wanted to say next. 'I mean, what about you and me? Are we...? I mean what are we? What do you think we are?'

Tom was not surprised by this, had been half expecting it even, and had waited for Christopher's trademark deep blush to accompany the questions when they came. But it didn't, and Tom found himself surprised instead by Christopher's steady, unflustered gaze into his eyes. He said, 'It's not the first time for you, is it? I mean what you and I do.'

'No,' said Christopher, and now he did drop his eyes.

'And nor is it for me, as I'm sure you would have guessed. One day we may want to talk about those other people, those other times. But probably not tonight. So you already know something about what we are. It doesn't need a label, does it? We're friends who ... whose friendship's something special, something extra. And we mustn't hurt each other, right?' Tom sat down on the edge of the bed and gently fingered Christopher's jaw and cheek. 'I promise, Christopher, I'll never do anything that might possibly, ever, hurt you.' And he felt the choking up of his throat, and knew Christopher could hear it in his voice, and he felt the sting of nearly shed tears behind his eyes, all at the same time as he realised that, when it came to hurting Christopher, yes, he almost certainly would. 'Move over,' he said, stripping off his pyjama top, and then allowing the bottom half to fall to the floor; the sudden appearance of his cheerful erection making Christopher forget his seriousness in a grin. 'Let a chap get in.'

Tom and Christopher met on their way out of their classrooms at lunchtime on Saturday and walked towards the staff dining room together. They must have both been a minute or two early as there was no-one else about. But there was no silence. Beyond the dining room the cloister led on to the assembly hall / gymnasium, and from behind the closed, light-varnished door of that room came the sound of the school's only grand piano being played ... well, not being played in the way that any of the pupils here could manage to play a piano. It sounded like an adult, and a professional musician at that. Tom and Christopher looked at each other.

'Moyse?' hazarded Christopher, though he didn't really think so. 'He's supposed to be the best in the school.'

Tom shook his head almost imperceptibly and pursed his lips – though only Christopher would have noticed. 'I don't think so. That's not a schoolboy playing. But what's the piece? It sounds amazingly difficult. Liszt or something?'

Christopher made the obvious suggestion. 'Why don't we go in and find out?'

They walked on as far as the door to the assembly hall, softly turned its polished brass handle, and then slid inside in the reverent way that latecomers to a concert do. But their entry had a galvanic effect on the pianist. Who was Father Claude.

Father Claude was grey-haired and had a face that seemed to be all caverns and hollows. Every day he cycled the four miles from the abbey and back. Father

Claude taught Latin and music as well as being the form master of Upper Three. The door hadn't even closed behind Christopher and Tom before the priest sprang to his feet, slammed shut the keyboard lid and marched towards the only door. Since that was exactly where his young colleagues were standing, it meant a march on them. Perhaps subconsciously remembering what everyone said you were supposed to do in the event of being charged by a rhinoceros, Christopher and Tom swiftly stepped aside from the doorway, allowing Father Claude a clear exit.

Father Claude was by no means built in the manner of a rhinoceros. Though quite tall, he was slight and trim for a man in his late fifties, but his normally sallow, caverned-out face had turned an untypical purple. 'How dare people listen at doors!' he muttered, though without turning his head towards either of them as he passed.

Peering through the doorway after his disappearing back view, Tom was not too taken aback to call out, 'Was it Liszt, Father?'

'Chopin,' called back Father Claude. 'Scherzo in…' But which key the piece was in they were unable to catch as Father Claude, not marching as far as the staff dining room, opened the door to the polish-smelling lobby that led to the front door and then slammed it behind him. A few seconds later they heard the muffled slam of the front door also as he let himself out of the building.

They looked at each other, too astonished for a moment to laugh. Then Christopher said, 'He is a funny chap, isn't he?'

'A rum cove indeed,' said Tom, borrowing the slang of his parents' generation. Then Miss Coyle and Sister appeared from round another corner and everyone went in to lunch.

The first sitting for their portrait took place that afternoon. Miss O'Deere had repeated the request she had made to Tom, though this time to him and Christopher together, that they would oblige her by being models for her new work in oils. 'It seemed an opportunity too good to pass up,' she had told them. 'With two such very young and – dare I say – handsome men on the premises, and this idea I'd had at the back of my mind for oh such a long time of doing a painting of David and Jonathan.'

When they arrived in the art room a little while after lunch Miss O'Deere was already there and most of her equipment – a stretched canvas, easel, palette, brushes and well-squeezed tubes of oil paint – already set up. They were both wearing cricket whites, a little self-consciously, but that was what Miss O'Deere had asked them ('Would you mind terribly?') to turn up in. She explained now, though they had already understood, that this was not to be a portrait in classical, or imagined biblical, robes but a picture of the two young men in an approximately modern setting. The background would be a cricket field with, in the far distance, a cricket game in progress on it. And since exactly such a scene could be observed right now through the art room window, the First Eleven attempting to win back the reputation it had lost to the junior department of Dover College the previous year, the choice of background seemed a perfectly sensible, practical one.

'I'd like to capture the two of you from, roughly speaking, the waist up. I wonder if we could try a few possible poses first, as I haven't quite made up my mind.' First they tried standing exactly side by side and staring squarely forward. Miss O'Deere laughed. 'No, I didn't think that would really do. It makes me think of that American picture of the farmer and his wife staring out of the canvas through old-fashioned spectacles. All you'd need would be the pitchfork.' Tom and Christopher laughed too, while from outside came the bark of Mr Charteris, who was one of the umpires, calling, 'Wide!'

Other positions were tried out, one or two so suggestive to the minds of Christopher and Tom that they had to be careful not to catch each other's eye lest an uncontrollable giggle betray them. At last one was found that seemed to tally with Miss O'Deere's concept as well as to meet the demands of the more general artistic goal of unity. Tom, the taller of the two by an inch or so, was to stand facing front, but with his right foot a little bit back, and out-turned, so that his shoulders angled slightly in towards the centre of the picture and towards Christopher, who would stand on his right – that is, on the left side of the picture as viewed from the front. Christopher would be at a forty-five degree angle, half-turned towards Tom but their shoulders would not touch: a gap of about six inches would separate them. However, Christopher's left arm, slightly bent at the elbow, would fall lightly across Tom's shoulders, allowing his fingers to be just visible from the front as they lay over his left collar bone. As if in response to this touch of the hand, Tom's face would be turned slightly further back towards Christopher than the line of his shoulders would suggest, in order to invest the composition with movement and the hint of a conversation just about to start.

Once this was all agreed on and the pose adopted by the two young men Miss O'Deere got rapidly to work on the outline of the tableau with a confidently deployed charcoal stick, while a youthful cry of 'Howzat?!' and simultaneous applause erupted in the hot distance outside.

'I wonder,' Miss O'Deere spoke her thoughts aloud a few minutes later, 'if it might not add something if you were both bare-chested, at least in part.' This time Tom and Christopher did look at each other, and couldn't suppress a laugh, though to their relief Miss O'Deere laughed too and said, 'Oh come now, don't be coy; some models have to do this nude, remember,' so they both took their shirts off and resumed their pose. 'No,' Miss O'Deere said almost at once. 'That's too much. A little more subtlety required.' Again various halfway solutions were tried and at last one was found that Miss O'Deere was confident would work. Tom would keep his shirt on, though unbuttoned to the waist – a central wedge of chest and his navel thus exposed – very loose at the neck, and with rolled-up sleeves. Christopher, with his less full-face attitude, would however have his torso entirely bare, his unbuttoned shirt thrown off from arms and shoulders, though still tucked into trousers and hanging inverted down the back and sides of his legs. Tom thought, though he had no mirror in which to check his theory, that the scene now looked not only artistic but a little bit sexy too. He didn't dare to voice this thought to Miss O'Deere.

The outline was soon done and Miss O'Deere began to squeeze paint out of tubes. 'You know,' she said, her tone of voice indicating that she now wanted to talk of something other than the job in hand. 'That business in the chapel the other morning. It was silly of me to get so upset at the time. I must apologise to you both for the scene I made. But these things take you by surprise and you react in a way that you always thought you wouldn't.'

'I don't think you made a scene,' said Tom robustly. 'I think you reacted perfectly normally to something so unexpected.' He added, 'I'm pretty sure I'd have done the same,' which made both Miss O'Deere and Christopher laugh.

'Well, thank you for your cheering words, Tom,' Miss O'Deere said, still smiling. 'But you say unexpected. Well, unexpected in the event I suppose it was. But in another way not really unexpected in the light of … well, the general tendency of things.' She paused, her face assumed a more serious expression and she jabbed a little streak of flesh-coloured paint onto the canvas. 'You see, I do know – while you're perhaps just beginning to hazard guesses – what is happening to Father Louis.'

'And what is happening to him?' Tom asked, though by now he was pretty sure he knew.

'He's beginning to show signs of … well, what are we supposed to call it these days? Premature senility perhaps. He hides it as much as he can, of course, and Angela Coyle and I do our bit to help as much as possible.'

'What sort of help do you mean?' This time it was Christopher who asked.

'Well, I just mean little things. Little practical things. But things which might become bigger things if not dealt with. A stitch in time, you know. An instance: he did the Common Entrance application twice over. It would have looked decidedly odd if two identical sets of forms had arrived from the same school, now. As charmed luck would have it he gave both sets to me to post, so I was able simply to not send the second one.'

'Yes I see,' said Tom.

'There've been other things.' ('Over,' came shouted from beyond the window.) 'Bills. It got as far as someone arriving in the middle of last term to physically cut off the electricity supply. There would have been major questions asked, by the abbot and by the parents, if that had come to pass. But fortunately Angela was there, ran the cheque-book to earth, put it under Father Louis's nose and he signed it in the presence of the engineer, who phoned back to the electricity board there and then. Disaster thus averted.'

'I see,' said Tom again. 'Yes, we had made our guesses about Father Louis, but we hadn't realised all that had been going on. It sounds as though you and Miss Coyle have been doing a wonderful job. But aren't these illnesses called – so-called – progressive? Isn't it just going to get worse, and it won't be possible to go on covering up for him for ever?'

'Can you hold your chin up a fraction higher, Christopher? Yes, that's perfect. Thank you. Yes, you're quite right, of course. We can't go on like this for ever. Angela and I had a little talk about it just the other day. We felt we ought to try and keep things going on as they are till the end of term and then let Father Matthew have a word about it with the abbot.'

'Does Father Matthew know all of this?' Christopher asked in a strangulated voice, as he carefully tried not to drop his chin.

'In general, yes. But we've tried not to give him cause for alarm. Hiding some things from him when it was possible to. That doesn't sound very good when put like that, but we've tried to act for the best all along. Tried to handle it ourselves as far as possible.'

Evidently the loyalty of the female members of staff to Father Louis went back a long way, and must run deep, if even the deputy headmaster was being kept in the dark about what was going on. Tom wondered, given that Father Louis had now reached the stage of mistaking one of his most senior and trusted staff members for a dog, what might still be in store between now and the end of term: a term which still had ten and a half weeks left to run.

It was Christopher who brought up the subject of Father Claude's extraordinary behaviour before lunch. 'It did seem a bit out of proportion,' he concluded. 'But then he hardly knows us. He's hardly ever at lunch or coffee break, and when he is he never talks to us beyond a hurried good morning.'

'A very shy man,' Miss O'Deere said firmly. 'He's not one who's comfortable in the adult world. But give him time and you'll find he'll unbend a bit. He needs to trust people. He plays superbly. You should hear him on the organ in the abbey church at a Sunday High Mass. A real artist of the keyboard. I'm sure he'd let you hear him play if he knew you a bit better. I'll try and have a word with him. Though, as you've noticed,' Miss O'Deere gave them a cosy little smile, 'he's not the easiest person in the world to have a word with.'

Miss O'Deere had promised she would keep them no more than an hour at this, or any, sitting and she was punctilious in letting them go immediately the hour was up. She continued to work at her easel, though, doing, as she said, 'the bits I can work on without wasting your time.' It had been an hour of surprises for both Tom and Christopher. Then it was as much as either of them could do to prevent themselves from actually running as they left the art room, crossed the table games room and headed up what they now looked upon as their own private staircase outside the chapel.

Little by little, Tom was relieved to notice, Christopher seemed to be overcoming the feelings of guilt that he obviously had about having sex with a man: having sex with him. Not that Christopher had expressed those feelings in words. But they'd been intermittently evident since Sunday, in Christopher's blushes and hesitations, his distance on Monday, and his later groping towards the subject by bringing up the question of Roger and Malcolm. Tom understood Christopher's scruples only too well, though. Both of them were Catholics and, as teachers in a Catholic school, were expected to be upholders of everything that church stood for as well as exemplars and role models for the boys in their care. The Catholic Church was strict to the point of tyranny in matters of sexual conduct. Young men such as Tom and Christopher were expected to contain themselves until such time as they married a Catholic female virgin. Even then, they had both been taught, the sole valid object of sexual congress was to procreate children. That a degree of pleasure might attend the process was a mere biological curiosity, and one to be glossed over, certainly not to be held out as one of the possible reasons for having sex in the first place.

There was no question of having sex before marriage. Sex with a woman outside marriage was one of the gravest of grave sins. Masturbation, practised alone, was not quite as bad – though nonetheless mortal, and punishable by eternal torment in Hell – but worse by far, by very very far, was to have relations with a fellow member of your own sex. Mutual masturbation was almost infinitely serious, as were other possibilities, which went un-named and un-described, as though even to speak of such things might conjure them into existence, corrupting the mouths and minds of those who named them or even imagined them, and – dare one even think such a thing – put ideas into the heads of such misguided young people as might perversely decide that such activities were worth trying. But the ultimate evil, the sin for which no eternal punishment could be sufficiently severe, did have a name-check in the familiar little red Three-penny Catechism. It was to be found among the quintet of offences that were listed in answer to the question: *What are the five sins that cry to Heaven for vengeance?* Nobody today remembers the names of the first four, but the fifth – its rearguard position in the list highlighting its status as the most heinous of the most heinous – was referred to as the Sin of Sodom.

The only known antidote to any of this was the Sacrament of Confession – though even the efficacy of that relied upon genuine Contrition on the part of the sinner, together with a willingness to Atone in whatever way might be appropriate, as also a Firm Purpose of Amendment.

Confessions were heard every Friday evening at Star of the Sea, by an elderly priest who came over from the abbey specially and who had no other contact with the prep school or its pupils. There was a very sensible rule that forbade the hearing of the boys' Confessions by any priest who was in a position of authority over them within the school. The event was enormously popular, especially among the younger boys, as it took place during prep. Each form was summoned out of the prep room in turn – strictly speaking it was not a summons, only an opportunity for those who wanted to confess, but in practice everybody always did – and all would hare down the cloister towards the chapel in the attempt to be first in the queue when they got there. Ten minutes in the chapel, queuing to confess your sins and then doing so, were felt to pass far more entertainingly than in an uninterrupted prep session of maths or Latin.

Christopher had not been tempted to join the queue. The kids might willingly confess their faults weekly, and he himself had been doing so monthly up till now. Yet meeting Tom and becoming his lover rather precluded the continuance of this routine since Christopher – though wracked with the old inescapable Catholic guilt – did not feel in the least Contrite, nor ready to Amend his ways; still less did he fancy the idea of Atonement. Fortunately the Church only actually bound you to a minimum of one Confession per year, for all her encouragement of greater frequency, and that mandatory

Confession was supposed to take place around the time of Easter. This year's Easter having already come and gone, and Christopher having carried out his annual obligation then, he decided it wisest to wait until the next one before queuing up for the confessional again. He would see how things stood between Tom and himself next springtime.

They had not, up to now, attempted to sodomise each other. Christopher had not given Tom any indication that this was an interest, or an ambition, of his. In fact he had no experience of it and was too timid, especially in view of his three years' juniority to Tom, to make any move in this direction. Tom, although slightly more experienced in this particular field, had not made any move either, for fear of shocking Christopher and perhaps frightening him off. They were quite happy for now – in fact extremely happy – courting eternal damnation by carrying on as they were.

'I know I'm not your first.' Tom was startled to hear Christopher come out with this, out of the blue, even though he knew it was only a matter of time before Christopher would want to know those things about him. He wanted to know those things about Christopher too, a degree of prurience inextricably entwined, of course, with the desire to get to know his new lover better. But that could wait. Christopher had got round to the question first, and he was entitled to his answer. In any case, telling Christopher about his first sexual experiences would be easy. It was his most recent history that would be difficult, even though that had not involved actual sex.

Christopher mistook the second's pause while all this spun through Tom's head for hesitation. 'I mean, you don't have to tell me about the others if you don't want to.' He plunged a hand awkwardly into the sand beside him and pulled it up piled high. The grains poured down on all sides and between his fingers as if from a broken hourglass. They were lying on Roger's hidden beach in the little cove, outside the door of the tunnel, naked except for their gym shorts, and alone beneath a sky as bright and flecked as a jay's wing. It was Friday afternoon, but a half holiday in honour of St Augustine.

'My first one?' Tom smiled into Christopher's set face – it seemed on the borderline of scowling – just six inches from his own. 'His name was Jeremy.' It was a relief to be able to say that, not to have to talk about David. 'Someone I used to play with in the holidays. We were both fourteen. We were often in each other's bedrooms because we both had train-sets.' It crossed Tom's mind that the eighteen-year-old Christopher perhaps still did. 'When we got bored with the trains we used to have mock fights on the beds. Sometimes we'd grab each other's knob by accident through the trousers.' Christopher's face had lost any inclination to scowl and was showing unmistakeable signs of an interest that went beyond mere concern for biographical completeness. 'Then we started doing it on purpose. One day doing that made me come – which I'd never done before. He could see the shock in my face, and feel it through my body, I suppose. He asked, "Has that never happened to you before?" and I shook my head.' Tom looked carefully at Christopher to make sure it was all right to proceed, and decided it was. 'He said, "Look, I'll show you something." And he stood up off the bed, pulled his shorts down a little way and - well, did it in front of me. I was shocked to see what happened, but I could guess from what I felt in my pants that I'd just done exactly the same.'

Christopher said nothing to all of this but now looked expectantly at Tom, who took his cue to wind up the story. 'We continued to play together for a few more months after that, though we'd rather lost interest in the trains. Then we rather lost interest in each other. To be honest, I suppose it was he that lost interest in me. He began to sniff after girls and was a bit puzzled when I didn't seem to want to. Of course, I was puzzled that he did. There was no-one to tell me, then, that I was a different kettle of fish from him. I didn't discover that till years later, when I went to university.'

'But it was just sex, wasn't it?' Christopher suddenly wanted to know, and at the same moment the rusty old door in the cliff-side banged open and Roger, closely followed by Malcolm, came walking towards them. They wore swimming trunks and carried towels, Malcolm's in his hands and Roger's around his shoulder.

'Coming to ask you if you'd like to join us on a mackerel-fishing trip tomorrow night,' Roger called to them before he'd quite reached the spot where they lay, and only giving Tom just enough time to say, aside, to Christopher,

'It was only sex. Nothing beyond that.'

Although they had not been officially on duty their absence had been conspicuous. There had been a 'development', Miss Coyle lost no time in telling them when they ran into her in the main cloister on their way in. Father Matthew had been looking for them and now awaited their return.

'What's it about?' Christopher asked, flustered. People are always flustered on being told that people have had to go looking for them when they've been elsewhere, having sex.

'I don't think you ought to hear it from me,' Miss Coyle said, and briefly frowned so deeply that her whole head of dark hair bobbed forward stiffly as if making a reluctant curtsy. 'I think it would be better man to man.' The curtsy over, she spun away from them and clicked off down the cloister in the high heels she always wore: she was a very petite woman.

They found Father Matthew in his office – which doubled as the stationery store – halfway along the chapel cloister. The door stood open. To their relief he was in relaxed mode, sitting behind his desk with a pipe in his mouth and the Daily Telegraph open in front of him.

Feeling no need to knock on the open door, Tom and Christopher walked straight in. Father Matthew looked up with a smile. He gestured to something in the paper. 'They've invented a new kind of polythene bag that you can't suffocate children with. Personally, I can't see the point of a polythene bag that you can't suffocate children with.' He chuckled at his joke.

'We heard something had happened,' said Tom. 'Miss Coyle wouldn't tell us what it was, only that you wanted a word. Is that right?'

'More or less. It's Father Louis. He's had a blackout. It seems he was giving one of the boys a wigging for running in the cloister, when he suddenly fell to his knees. Someone came running for me immediately and someone else obviously went to fetch Sister. We got him to his feet and managed to help him up to his bedroom. Sister called Doctor Wilson and he came at once. Did all the tests for stroke, of course, but there were no indications of that. But Wilson's told him to rest over the weekend and Sister to keep an eye on him. Wilson doesn't think there's much to worry about. Just a momentary loss of consciousness caused by a change in blood pressure. The only thing was, he didn't seem to remember having had lunch. He kept asking for it.' Father Matthew smiled a mischievous smile. 'Sister reassured him it would soon be teatime.' He put his hand beneath his scapular and fished in the breast pocket of his tunic to pull out a large watch. 'Which it very soon will. The only thing is, we're all going to have to muck in a bit over the weekend... If you're going to be around, that is?'

It was not the moment for saying no, or for mentioning an invitation to go mackerel fishing, though perhaps their weekend plans appeared written on their faces for Father Matthew continued, 'I'm not going to spoil your weekend, chaps. Not if I can possibly help it. It's a holiday weekend anyway. It's just that there are a couple of things to be covered. Letter copy for Lower Four tomorrow morning and letter writing on Sunday. Maybe a morning dormitory inspection or two, and a dormitory round at bedtime. But that's all. Will that be OK?'

Pleased to have got off so lightly, both young men nodded their heads with almost imbecile eagerness. 'Good. We can sort out the details later. I'll be saying school Mass for the next couple of days at least. St Ursula's will have to requisition someone else from the abbey. It isn't as though they don't have spare capacity.'

Tom said, 'Why did Miss Coyle say it was a man-to-man thing and we needed to talk to you about it?'

Father Matthew raised his iron-filing eyebrows above the steel rims of his spectacles. 'Miss Coyle is so *con delicatezza* sometimes I wonder the wind doesn't lift her up by the petticoat and waft her out of the window... Probably because when Father Louis collapsed he wet himself slightly. None of the boys noticed and they wouldn't have been shocked or embarrassed if they had. These things happen. Only the Miss Coyles of this world are offended by them.' Father Matthew stopped smiling suddenly and peered gimlet-eyed at the young men. 'While we're on the subject of Father Louis, perhaps I could ask you what you know about the dog in the chapel incident? I know only what some of the boys have chosen to tell me, and I stress the word *chosen*. Miss O'Deere has not made a point of mentioning it to me – I might almost say she has made a point of *not* mentioning it to me – which I can entirely understand. And at the time when it happened I was saying my own Mass over at St Ursula's, of course. But I gather you two were pretty near at hand. Is that right?'

Tom gave Father Matthew an account of what he'd seen and been told, as well as a summary of his conversation with Dexter. He was too discreet to draw on the conversation they'd had with Miss O'Deere in the art room while they were being painted, and was a bit taken aback to hear Christopher, who had been almost silent till now, abruptly launch into a full report of it.

Father Matthew listened with interest, and also with a degree of surprise that he tried, not entirely successfully, to conceal. 'Well, well, well,' he said when Christopher had finished. 'Nothing I hadn't guessed, I suppose. Though you've told me a few things I didn't know for absolute certain. The electric bill story's quite a corker.' He shook his head.

'I can't see why she and Miss Coyle would want to keep everything hidden from the abbot till the end of term,' Christopher went on innocently. 'I'd have thought it was the easiest thing in the world to announce Father Louis's retirement due to ill health and for you to take over smoothly.'

Father Matthew gave a quiet chuckle and exchanged a man-of-the-world look with the slightly older Tom. 'Nothing's ever quite so simple in the monastery. You know the word Byzantine, I suppose?'

'It's a kind of architecture, isn't it?' Christopher tried. 'You know, like Westminster Cathedral.'

'It means something else as well,' said Father Matthew.

Tom came in. 'I think Father Matthew means that the decision-making process of the monastery chapter is as tortuous as that of the Byzantine emperors' court.'

'Something like that,' said Father Matthew.

'I suppose it was naïve of me to think that anything in life might be simple,' said Christopher, and the three of them laughed.

***

From John Moyse's diary: Friday May 25th 1962

This was a half holiday. St Augustine's is tomorrow. Should be a whole holiday but tomorrow is Saturday, so a half holiday anyway. Father Louis announced this at assembly – to applause. The other half of the holiday is tomorrow morning, which wd be fine but we still have to do letter-copy which rather knocks a hole in it. Still, beggars can't be choosers. Anyway, Father L is now hors de combat for a bit. Fell over in the cloister after lunch. Concussion I think, but I wasn't there to see.

A Boeing 707 flew over the school and landed at the airport. First one I've seen, except for Airfix kits which the juniors are making like crazy and covering selves wth glue. Must have been on diversion. Fish and chips for lunch.

EIGHT

Letter copy was a forty-minute Saturday activity at the end of the morning classes. The actual weekly letter home would be written after Mass on Sunday morning, but on Saturdays the boys were expected to prepare a draft version in a special exercise book with a cream coloured cover. This was then checked on the spot by the form teacher, who truffled out errors of spelling, grammar and punctuation. It was widely assumed by the boys that this was a smokescreen for the real reason the draft letters were read – censorship. In fact it was not. Although the boys might feel cautious about expressing negative thoughts concerning the school in the Saturday draft, it would have been perfectly possible to change things in Sunday's fair copy, which went to the post unread by any member of staff. And, oddly enough, for all the suspicious grumbling that went on, it was rare for anyone to resort to this simplest of strategies.

Christopher normally monitored his own class during letter copy. But this Saturday things were slightly different. Not only did letter copy take place immediately after breakfast because the day was a whole holiday (thank you, Saint Augustine), but there was a necessary reshuffle: Father Louis was still under Doctor Wilson's orders to rest in bed, so Tom took Christopher's class in addition to his own and Christopher found himself monitoring Form Lower Four – Father Louis's form – instead.

Lower Four was the highest class in the school. The theory was that, following success in the Common Entrance exam its members would move seamlessly into the Upper Fourth forms at their respective public schools when they were transplanted in September. Christopher had not encountered Lower Four in the classroom before, although he knew all their names by now – they included all the prefects: the two house captains, Dexter and Rickman, and their respective deputies, Abelard and Moyse – and he had occasionally umpired some of them on the cricket field. Now, as the letter-copy session progressed and Christopher began to examine the developing scripts, he was made very aware of how advanced the writing skills of these thirteen-year-olds were in comparison to those of his usual charges in Lower Two with their average age of eight. But even in this exalted company one stood out from all the others. It was the vice-captain of Thomas More house, Moyse. Though it wasn't till he reached the end of the letter – *With Lots of Love From* – that he discovered that the boy's first name was John.

Christopher found himself on the brink of calling him John by accident, but caught himself just in time. In front of all his classmates that would never do. The poor kid would have been ribbed by them till the end of time – or the end of term, whichever arrived sooner – and would have been called Mr McGing's pet. And that wouldn't have done much for Christopher's standing either. 'Well, Moyse,' he said correctly, 'I'm impressed by the way you write.' The boy had managed to describe very effectively his own surprise and elation at bowling Dexter out during a recent cricket game. Dexter was unchallenged as the school's best bat and was a far better cricketer all round than Moyse. Christopher had umpired that game, as it happened, and so had witnessed the event and shared the general surprise at Moyse's coup. Now Moyse had concluded the brief paragraph: 'There was a general shout of triumph from my team, everybody seemed to stand tall like at the end of a concert. Only the sea in the distance beyond them stayed horizontle, shining towards me like a blue smile.'

After he had dealt with *horizontle* Christopher asked, 'Do you write other things than letters, or class-work?

Do you ever write just for the fun of it? Because you want to?'

'I keep a diary, sir,' the boy responded brightly.

'Every day?' Christopher asked, at the same time warning himself not to pry. But he was genuinely interested, and when Moyse answered with a nod and a smile, added, 'How much do you write?'

'Oh, just five or six lines a day. That's all there's room for.'

'I see. Maybe next year you should get yourself a bigger diary and write a bit more.'

'I could do that this year,' said Moyse. 'This term, I mean. If I had a spare exercise book.'

'Hmm,' said Christopher in the most schoolmasterly tone he was able to manage. 'I wonder if that could be arranged.'

'It would be awfully nice, sir.' Moyse's smile broadened. He was a run-of-the-mill kid when it came to looks, Christopher had always thought, but that smile did something for him.

'I'll see what I can do,' Christopher said, then turned away abruptly to the boy who sat next to Moyse and who had managed to spell the word *biscuit,* Christopher could not help noticing at once, without the help of the letter U.

You weren't supposed to notice the good looks or otherwise of the boys you taught. Nobody had ever told Christopher that; it was something he instinctively knew: a survival instinct perhaps, that was essential in young schoolmasters. Nevertheless, it was impossible not to be aware that the two house captains, Dexter and Rickman, already showed the makings of two very handsome young men. Moyse and Abelard, their seconds in command, could not but appear rather nondescript in comparison. Unfair, really, but you always ended up being compared to somebody, and life was life. Of course, beauty in the early teens was no guarantee of beauty at twenty or twenty-five, and those who were gifted with good looks as young adults often had not been favoured in that way when they were teenagers. That was life too.

Those boys of Upper Four were only two years younger than Christopher had been when he'd fallen for a boy called Peter – and done a bit more than simply fall for him. They'd both been nearly sixteen. Christopher had been ready to tell Tom this little bit of history on the beach that day, but they'd been interrupted by the arrival of Roger and Malcolm, all ready for a bathe, and since then the opportunity hadn't really presented itself. Although he and Tom spent every night, and a good part of every evening together, and talked about everything under the sun, the moment had to be right to bring up a subject like that and, even though it had already been obliquely referred to, Christopher hadn't found that moment.

The other thing that still hadn't been discussed between them, but again only referred to obliquely, was the relationship between Roger and Malcolm. Were they actually a pair of …? But Christopher still couldn't find an appropriate word to use to Tom. He suspected that Tom couldn't either, and that that was what kept the subject locked up and away from them. That in turn locked up the bigger mystery of what it was that Christopher and Tom were, or were becoming. What kind of an item was Tom-and-Christopher? Or was even the word *item* too freighted with dangerous meaning?

Perhaps one of those questions, at least, might be opened up just a little tonight, Christopher thought as he wrote his own letter home to his parents that morning after the boys had finished letter copy. Tonight was to be the mackerel-fishing expedition with Roger and

Malcolm – Malcolm who did not actually live with Roger but who shared a house with his parents a few miles away, in Sandwich. Christopher did at least know that.

When Roger and Malcolm had appeared on the beach the previous day and invited them to join their fishing trip, both Tom and Christopher had imagined for a second that it would be in the little coracle of a boat that was manacled to the cliff beside the tunnel door. But Roger had at once explained that Malcolm was the owner of a vintage sailing boat, a Whitstable oyster smack named Orca, which he kept at moorings in the estuary of the Great Stour at Richborough, near the power station, midway between Sandwich itself and the river mouth. They might have stayed on the beach with Roger and Malcolm then and learned more, but it had been time to return to school and they simply said thank you for the invitation and arranged a time of rendezvous. Then they left Roger and Malcolm to their own peaceful afternoon among the waves.

Even their own sunbathing session had come about quite casually. They'd gone to the Admiral Digby for an early afternoon, half-holiday, drink and been invited to stay on when the pub closed its doors, then sent down the tunnel to enjoy themselves in whatever way they chose. Roger, not yet a friend exactly, had been a model of tact and not come down to join them, but – even more diplomatically – had let them know that he'd be arriving soon after five with Malcolm in tow. As he had.

Now, this Saturday evening, they drank a beer together as the pub closed and the last customers drifted slowly away, and then Roger led them through the backstage areas of the pub and down the cellar stairs, while the long-suffering Jenny did the last of the washing-up.

'It can't be a total secret, this tunnel, can it?' Tom put this to Roger as they made their way down it. 'I mean, Jenny must know. Other customers must know where you – we – disappear to sometimes.'

'Well, of course Jenny knows.' The beam of Roger's torch alighted on the row of glistening flints. 'And of course the older regular customers know. All right, I was probably exaggerating when I first told you it was a great secret, but I didn't know you two very well then, did I? Just – I suppose – kind of guessed we'd hit it off all together. I still didn't want you to think you could tell all and sundry about it. Hoped you'd understand. How old were you in the war?'

'Not quite five on VE day,' said Tom. 'And not *quite* thought of when it began.'

'June baby?' Roger asked.

Christopher answered. 'Yes, and me too, but only two when the war ended.' He didn't bother Roger with the extraordinary fact that they had the same birthday.

'Well,' said Roger, 'for those of us who're ten or so years older ... oh all right, twenty or so years older – what I mean is, we're quite in the habit of keeping our neighbours' secrets. Careless talk costs lives and all that. Unlike our neighbours on the Continent, of course. Rather the opposite from what I've heard. 'Course that may just have been wartime propaganda, but I suspect there's a grain of truth in it. Anyway,' he sounded as if a new thought had struck him, 'you may find that to your advantage one way or another, some time or other: I mean about the discretion of the older generation.' He paused for a second. 'Malcolm and I have often found ourselves thankful for that.' And that left neither of them in any doubt about what he was referring to.

Christopher began to wonder whether this might be the moment to ask Roger about himself and Malcolm, but quickly realised it wasn't, since they were now arriving at the heavy door at the tunnel's end. Roger quickly checked his wristwatch – causing the torch beam to dance around the chalk walls like Tinkerbell – and said, 'Well, he told me he'd be there and waiting for us at eleven thirty. Let's see if he's kept his schedule.' He drew back the bolts on the door to the beach.

As Tom and Christopher had been walking towards the Admiral Digby earlier, they had been conscious of the stillness of the evening and the clearness of the sky, with a nearly full moon just clearing the rooftops to the east. France had been clearly visible across the darkening water from cliff-top height. But on exchanging the stuffy air of the tunnel for the iodine freshness of the beach they found the foreign coast had disappeared from sight, hidden, down at beach level, beyond the brow of the sea. Their attention was caught almost entirely by what occupied the foreground and the centre of the scene: tied up at the long jetty, her red and green navigation lights dim in the silver brilliance of the moon, loomed the elegant outline of the smack. It would have looked even more elegant, not to say romantic – something out of Treasure Island – had it been set with sail, but, as Roger had told them in advance, in view of the almost total absence of wind they were going to rely on its diesel engine tonight instead, and the dark sails were tightly furled.

'Took your time, didn't you?' called Malcolm, a neat dark silhouette, leaning over the side towards them, shining a torch.

'Didn't expect to find you on time for once,' Roger answered back. They were walking along the jetty now; then climbing aboard, clutching at, then ducking under, the shrouds and backstay; Malcolm's hand was half extended, prepared to steady uncertain movements among unfamiliar obstacles on board: storage chests, coils of rope, a Primus stove... The boat acknowledged their arrival by rocking, just once, and then returning to its point of rest as each of them stepped aboard. Roger indicated a narrow thwart plank fixed near the stern on which Christopher and Tom could park themselves, then nonchalantly cast off fore and aft while Malcolm started the engine. It gargled into life immediately, leaving a small malodorous cloud of smoke to hang among them for a second, then disappear.

And then they were under way, nosing out across the dark water. No lights were visible on shore at first, but as they gained some distance the hidden streetlamps of the cliff-top lane began to wink at them, and then the lights of houses beyond – the Admiral Digby's included, no doubt. After a couple of minutes, as they left the shelter of the cliff-hemmed cove the lights of farther-off roads and habitations came into view. Some clusters of light sat proudly at cliff-top height, others straggled in ragged lines down gullies towards the sea where river courses had given easy access to the shore. A little more time elapsed and then the bright conurbations of Deal and Dover – the one with summer-lit pier, the other with its arc-lit busy docks – edged their curious muzzles round the headlands.

The sea was treacle smooth, the light of the moon ricocheting off its flat-domed swells as off something nearly solid. You felt you could walk upon it, as the boat itself seemed to, its rhythmic rise and fall a matter of inches only, slow and steady as a sleeper's breath. Malcolm gave them a short history of the Orca. 'Built in Whitstable in 1891 and used for oyster fishing. Carvel build (means the hull planks don't overlap but are butted up) and with gaff cutter rig.' He pointed out the furled sails one by one. 'Mainsail, foresail, topsail (which we're not wearing tonight) and jib. One day you'll see them hoist and that's a good sight. She's about as small as a smack can be without being classified as something else. Twenty-four feet long on deck and drawing four and a half. But at that size the two of us can handle her under sail, and with the engine I can drive her by myself. She was at Dunkirk.' There was a note of pride in his voice as he said this, so Christopher, forgetting that Malcolm was only about ten years older than he was, asked,

'Did you go?'

Malcolm laughed. 'No. The Orca wasn't in my family then and I was only a nipper.' There was a pause. Then he said, 'Roger went.'

Roger, whom the others had turned to look at, said, 'That's right. I was nineteen. I went with my father and a friend in a bigger boat than this. A whole lot of us went in convoy, escorted by a destroyer named Sappho. We brought back thirty-six men. We looked like a slave ship by the time we got home.' Then he looked as if he didn't want to say more on the subject and Malcolm gave him an odd little look. Tom guessed there was something of envy in it – of an experience that had been Roger's but could never now be Malcolm's.

Tom thought this as good a moment as any to ask the question that had been on his mind – and Christopher's. 'So,' he changed the subject, 'how did you two meet?'

Malcolm looked at Roger, and Roger at Malcolm, but there was no doubt as to who was going to answer. 'Malcolm came to work at the Admiral Digby. In my parents' day – when he was barely old enough to hold a pint mug in his hand.' Malcolm chuckled at this. 'I worked there too, on and off. It was when I was working as a teacher, away from home mostly, but back here in the school holidays. We – how shall I say this? – got to know each other little by little. Unlike some people one's heard of who seem to take life a bit on the faster side.' Roger grinned as he said this and Malcolm came in with,

'Wasn't me that was the slow one. But Roger, careful schoolmaster he was, and working in his parents' pub ... Mister Cautious back in those days.'

'Someone had to be, Skipper,' Roger said. 'And has to still.'

'Why did you stop teaching?' Christopher asked Roger. Only as the words left his mouth did he realise what a gaffe he might be making. Reddening rapidly, though fortunately almost invisibly in the subdued lighting of boat and moonbeam, he quickly went on, 'I'm sorry; that was rude of me; forget I asked.'

But Malcolm and Roger both laughed at his embarrassment and Roger said, 'There was nothing fishy about it at all. No scandal attaches to the ending of my schoolmaster days. My parents wanted to retire (they've got a bungalow at Kingsdown now) and me to take over the pub. Simple as that. And I'd had enough of kids by then, I reckoned.'

And found Malcolm still working there, waiting for you after years? Tom wondered. He put it more diplomatically than that. 'And Malcolm...?'

Malcolm spoke up for himself. 'I was back in Sandwich, working with my own father in his boat repair yard. Otherwise I wouldn't have been able to afford this thing. She came to us in settlement of a bankrupt customer's bills.' Malcolm smiled broadly. 'It's an ill wind that blows nobody no good.'

'Any,' corrected Roger, who clearly hadn't forgotten his teacherly reflexes entirely, and Tom pondered on the complications that must bedevil Malcolm's life, living with his parents still at – what? thirty-one or thirty-two? – and spending time with Roger on the pretext of fishing trips or whatever else could be dreamt up. At least Roger's own parents were out of the way at Kingsdown. But a pub... A public house was what it meant, and what it was. Hardly the most hidden away of venues for a long-lived liaison.

Tom would not interrogate them further, and Christopher, who had now more or less got the information he wanted and could chew on it in private like a dog with a rather special bone, did not want to ask any more questions just yet either.

The other two sensed this also. Malcolm said, after a moment's silence, 'Nearly there.'

'Nearly where?' Tom asked. They were riding over a featureless no-man's-water, just a little way from England, but a long, long way from France.

'Nearly where the mackerel are,' Roger answered.

'How does he...?' Tom turned to Malcolm. 'I mean how do you...'

Malcolm's answer was a grunt, delivered through a self-confident smile, but Roger answered, 'I don't know how he knows. I don't believe he knows himself, but somehow he always does.'

'Look.' Malcolm recovered articulacy, and pointed a little way ahead. The smooth giant saucer shapes of the swell were being disturbed by something, and shone with pinpricks of reflected light, as uncountable as the stars above. Meanwhile Roger stood up and, to the amazement of his two guests, began to fuss with the lighting of the Primus stove, then reached into a firmly deck-screwed box for utensils and a battered frying-pan. A moment later he'd also rummaged out a half-pound pack of Anchor butter and dropped about half of that into the pan with a dodgy-looking fish slice. 'Now let's go fishing,' he said.

Malcolm was already handing out alarming-looking, hedgehog-sized, spools of line that bristled with silver hooks. Following Malcolm's example, and paying attention to his warning to be wary of the hooks, they began to unwind them, dropping the lines over the side. 'No bait?' queried Tom.

'Why waste money on bait when they'll come to a bare hook on a bright night?' answered Malcolm, while Roger admonished them all to get stuck in before the butter burned.

The biting began at once, almost before they'd realised the lines had touched the water. 'Pull 'em in now,' said Roger.

'I've only paid out about five hooks,' Christopher protested.

'Doesn't matter.'

Christopher obeyed. They all did. Astonishingly, every hook returned with a glistening, threshing mackerel impaled upon it; the colours of moon-silver, luminous blue, and shiny green and black somehow flashing alike from fish bodies and the sharp scattering surface of the sea. The fish thrashed so energetically as they were hauled in that Tom and Christopher several times just missed slashing their thumbs to ribbons on the hooks as they detached them. Christopher lost one of his mackerel as it threw itself desperately out of his squeezing hands and back into the sea. He thought of pictures he had seen of the miraculous draught of fishes. The strangeness of the moment borrowed the character of a dream. As each wriggling captive came loose it was killed by banging the back of its head smartly on the gunwale, then dropped into a bucket. The first four didn't even get that far. Roger slit their bellies, scooped their guts out and overboard in one deft move and tossed them, dead but still thrashing, into the foaming butter in the pan. It had all taken just a minute and a half.

There was a lull. The sea ceased to churn, the mackerel in the pan began to give off a miraculous fresh sea and butter smell, and the others squirmed quietly in the bucket. The four men sat, for a moment idle and silent, while the boat, drifting just now without either power or sail, turned half round on itself and back again, causing the lights of Deal to swing far to port then back to starboard again.

They ate their trophies in their fingers, burning their lips. No lemon wedges or pepper enhanced their flavour, and they needed none. Christopher couldn't remember fish tasting as good as this. Short of consuming it raw and alive, still swimming in the sea, you couldn't have eaten it fresher.

The Primus was turned out, the pan rinsed in the sea and they cast their lines again. More sedately this time, and more sedately did the fish approach the hooks. The ritual eating of the first of the catch would not be repeated. If they wanted another snack later on it could be prepared at a more leisurely pace. Now they fished steadily, every ten minutes increasing their joint tally by another thirty fish. As the bucket filled so it was emptied now into a series of polystyrene boxes. They would be sold from the beach before breakfast.

At last, at getting on for three a.m., the engine was started again and Malcolm pulled on the tiller to make a course for the Kent shore. The turn coincided with the arrival of a wave – a wavelet, really, but the only one that had materialised till then, and a surprise on this night of calm. The combination of wave and turn caused the boat to roll suddenly to port, tilting the deck about fifteen degrees. It was only for a moment though. The wave passed, the turn was completed and the boat rocked back to its normal plane. But that brief lurch downwards had overbalanced Christopher so that he fell against Malcolm as he stood at the helm. 'Sorry,' Christopher said, his mouth almost in Malcolm's ear, and Malcolm turned and grazed Christopher's cheek with a kiss, simply because the cheek was there. Then they disentangled themselves.

'Do we call you Christopher or Chris?' Malcolm asked.

Tom, who had observed the kiss, answered before Christopher could. 'Always Christopher, this one. Not even his own mother's allowed to call him Chris.'

Shortly after that, light began to creep into the eastern sky and then a little breeze came. Malcolm looked at Roger and said, 'Perhaps a little sail on the way back?' and Roger said, 'Why not?'

Malcolm turned the boat's head into the wind and began to show the novice sailors how to hoist the sails, but quickly spotted that Tom had already identified the halyards and looked as though he knew what to do with them. 'You've sailed before,' he said. Tom said, a bit bashfully, that he'd done a bit of dinghy sailing at Poole Harbour on holiday as a teenager. Malcolm obviously approved. 'Best way to start. And Christopher?' But Christopher had never sailed before. Malcolm said, 'Then let's begin.'

As the mainsail, then foresail and jib, were hauled aloft they could see that they were a dull rust red. But later, as the breeze began to power them towards the land and the eastern sky turned bright pink, the sails began to glow like red flames in its reflection. Christopher found the effect astonishing, the moment one of beauty.

'How's the painting going?' Roger asked as, all seated facing one another, they let the boat carry them inshore. He had offered them the use of the beach that afternoon but they had declined, explaining they were due to sit a second time for Miss O'Deere.

'She'd made great advances on it since we last sat,' Tom said. 'The cricket field's nearly all done, though the distant figures haven't materialised quite yet. She's very good, you know.'

'And the subject of this painting?' Malcolm asked, though Tom was pretty sure he'd already have been told this, since they had told Roger some time ago, and especially with the subject being what it was.

'David and Jonathan,' said Christopher, trying not to overload the announcement with meaning.

'Ah yes, I remember,' said Malcolm. 'First mate here did tell me. *My brother Jonathan. Thy love to me was wonderful, passing the love of women.* Has this Miss O'Deirdre told you yet which one of you she thinks is which?'

The sun was climbing the sky over the North Foreland as they drew near to the home beach and cliffs. It was impossible at first for Tom and Christopher to guess which point on the shore was their little cove: the coast viewed from here was a new found land. But Malcolm and Roger knew of course, and were steering directly for it. Still it remained obstinately hidden from them until they were almost upon it and only a minute or two from the jetty. Like many things in life, Christopher found himself reflecting, as he stood up, ready to lend a hand with tying up.

***

From John Moyse's Diary: Saturday May 26th 1962

Christopher McGing says he'll get me a new book to keep this diary in. Brilliant if he remembers. People often don't – then you fall back on 'It was the thought wot counted'. Father Louis still out for the count.

NINE

Mackerel were served in place of the usual bacon and eggs to all who breakfasted in the staff dining room. Bread-crumbed and grilled, and garnished with wedges of lemon. One was delivered to Father Matthew, who was deputising for Father Louis downstairs in the boys' refectory, and one was sent up to Father Louis himself, still confined to his room on doctor's orders. Everyone praised their meaty freshness; even Miss Coyle showed enthusiasm and said how the taste took her back to when she was a little girl and had gone fishing with older cousins in Dingle Bay on the coast of County Kerry.

Christopher was a little fuddled after a night's sleep of only two hours, between the return from the fishing trip and Sunday morning Mass – at which Father Matthew won everyone's gratitude for preaching the shortest sermon anyone could remember sitting through. Though reminding himself that he had agreed to supervise the letter-writing session for the senior boys he remembered also a promise that he had made, but in the adventures of the previous night all but forgotten. After breakfast he went to the stationery cupboard in Father Matthew's office, which was unoccupied at that time, and removed a fresh cream-covered exercise book from the stacked stock – an action which would have been punished by four strokes of the cane had it been carried out by one of the boys. Sensibly he waited till the end of letter writing, waited till the boys were filing out into the school cloister, before calling back the one he wanted to speak to. 'Moyse.'

'Yes sir.' The boy stopped in his tracks and did a smart about-turn. He didn't actually salute but came pretty close to it.

'Something for you.' Christopher held out the exercise book. They were alone in the cloister at that moment:

Moyse's contemporaries had all disappeared in the direction of the sunny outdoors.

The boy's face lit up with a radiant smile. 'Oh, wow, sir. You remembered, sir. Thank you, sir.'

'My pleasure,' said Christopher. He really meant it. It had been the easiest of things to do, the cheapest of gifts, but it had given Moyse a measure of delight that would have seemed disproportionate and absurd had it not been so touching. In his turn Christopher now found himself unexpectedly moved by the moment. But it was not a moment to be prolonged further. 'You're very welcome. Make good use of it.' Christopher nodded his head curtly to signify the end of the interview and after one final, 'Thank you very much indeed, sir,' the boy sped off down the cloister at a pace that was the maximum consistent with not actually running – which, even for prefects such as Moyse, was against the rules.

Tom and Christopher might have been called upon to do dormitory duty that night. It would have meant monitoring the boys as they got ready for bed, curbing unruly behaviour between then and lights-out, and enforcing the rule of silence for the brief period after that before everyone was asleep and silence maintained itself. But in the end they didn't have to, due to the unexpected resurrection of Father Louis at supper time. With a steely smile that admitted no counter-arguments he made it clear that it would be back to business as usual from now on. Father Matthew would revert to his usual evening dormitory duty, and Father Louis would return to his morning routine, waking everybody up at five minutes to seven with the school bell – a duty which had fallen to Father Matthew for the last two mornings – and then saying morning Mass and supervising breakfast. It was Father Matthew who made the facetious aside to Tom, as they chanced to walk out into the cloister together when supper was done, that the rapid recovery of the headmaster had been due to the healing properties of his breakfast-time fish.

Tom replied that he was glad the threat of dormitory rounds had been lifted: there was something on TV that he wanted to watch. Actually it was something he and Christopher wanted to watch together, but he didn't spell that out. And as it was nothing very elevated in tone, but actually The Benny Hill Show, he didn't spell that out either. Instead he added jokingly, 'I'm surprised Father Claude didn't get roped in for the extra weekend duties.' Then he was surprised to see from the sudden frown on Father Matthew's face that the remark had been understood as a serious one. And he was further surprised to hear the deputy headmaster say,

'No, Tom. Father Claude in the dormitories would not be a good idea. You know, avoiding the occasion of sin is not only something we must do in regard to ourselves. Sometimes we find ourselves in positions where we have a duty to help others avoid it.'

Tom was speechless for a moment, standing alone with the priest in the otherwise empty cloister, and he felt his skin tingle with the shock of dismay. If Father Matthew meant what Tom thought he did it was either a monumental indiscretion on his part or else such a major sign of readiness to take Tom into his confidence concerning high matters of policy that he ought to feel flattered. Unsure, he began, 'Do you mean…?' but was then rather relieved when Father Matthew's hand, raised in a gesture of warning, cut him off in mid-sentence. His relief was partly due to the fact that he had no idea how he could possibly have completed the question.

'No, no, no,' Father Matthew said with some force. 'Nothing has ever happened. But it's a question of taking the right precautions with people. Different ones for different individuals. We all of us have our different weaknesses – which are not blameworthy in themselves. It's only in how we manage them that there can be any question of blame. Which is why I used that heavy phrase, the occasion of sin. Perhaps it was too heavy for this conversation.' Father Matthew smiled again and his eyes regained their usual twinkle. 'Allow me to withdraw it. All I wanted to do was to set your mind at rest. To let you know that Father Louis and I are very careful as to whom we trust, and with what they are entrusted.' Then he looked stern again for a moment. 'That goes for everybody. All the staff who are employed here.'

Trying to get away from the unwelcome suspicion that the last comment was aimed directly at himself, and that maybe Father Matthew was taking advantage of his facetious question to fire a warning shot across his and Christopher's shared bows, Tom said, 'But in that case, should he be working with children at all? I mean…'

'Perhaps you'll think I'm contradicting myself, Tom. Having talked of protecting people from the occasions of sin … but there are limits to how far this can be taken. We can't live in a world without other people – and the temptations that some of them may pose for some of us; we can't very easily live in a world without children.' His smile reasserted itself, but wanly. 'Nobody has ever supposed that fully clothed children or adolescents present any kind of temptation in this particular case.'

'Well, as you can imagine, I had no answer to that,' Tom told Christopher when he'd repeated the gist of his conversation with Father Matthew to an astonished Christopher, lying on his bed with him a few minutes later. Christopher's minute transistor radio was on, playing a Tchaikovsky symphony to which they were paying much less than half attention. 'I wish I knew how it is that he and Father Louis know that fully clothed boys present no temptation to Father Claude but that naked ones – presumably – do. But there was no way I could ask him!'

Christopher said, 'I've always thought there was something a bit odd about him. Father Claude, I mean. A bit ... different. Remember that time we tried to listen to him playing the piano?'

This didn't go down too well with Tom. 'Odd and different? Would you say there was something odd and different about us too? Or about Roger and Malcolm? Something that other people would notice?'

'I didn't mean that,' Christopher said awkwardly. 'Having an interest in kids who are forty years younger than you is a million miles from ... from us. Or from Roger and Malcolm.'

'OK,' said Tom, deflating. 'You're probably right after all. I mean, that what you thought you didn't mean is probably true after all. We probably do appear odd and different. Because of ... you know. Our colleagues may suspect it. We can't even be sure the older boys don't gossip among themselves. You know, I think perhaps Father Matthew was trying to warn me.'

'Warn you? Of what? About not molesting the boys? Or against me?'

'I don't know,' said Tom. 'I just got a feeling for a second or two when he was talking to me that he knew about us. I put it out of my mind, thinking I was just being over-anxious, but now, listening to you... He talked about taking the right precautions with the right people and that everyone was different: everyone had different occasions of sin. And he made it clear he was talking about different members of staff. So ... including me.'

'And me,' said Christopher.

'Still,' Tom said. 'Remember what Roger said to us about being grateful for the discretion of the older generation? Well, what Father Matthew said may well have been a shot across our bows. But perhaps he also meant to let me know that, although he knows what's going on between us, he'll turn a blind eye if he can.'

There was a thoughtful silence after that, during which they became aware of the Tchaikovsky symphony playing tinnily on the top of the nearby chest of drawers. They shared a love of classical music – and a passion for Mozart in particular. They had other common interests too. Wildlife and the countryside. Cricket. Tennis. The Goon Show on the radio. The history of the building of the railway network and the industrial revolution in general. The novels of Hemingway and Greene. Roger Moore as The Saint on TV. Guinness. The poetry of Yeats and Ogden Nash. Turner's paintings. Hoffnung's cartoons. They even enjoyed each other's feeble jokes, which was just as well. 'On a more pleasant subject,' Tom said, 'we've had an interesting adventure on a small boat. What do you say to trying a bigger one?'

'What do you mean?' Christopher asked. He freed an arm and rumpled Tom's hair. 'Are you thinking of buying a floating gin palace?'

'Bigger than that, actually. But less expensive. It's half term in another week. What do you say to taking the ferry over to France for a couple of days?'

'Wow,' said Christopher. 'I'd sort of said I'd see my parents. But I could do that another weekend, I suppose.'

'In other words, yes,' said Tom. 'You'd like it as much as I would. We'd be able to do just as we please. Not having to look over our shoulders all the time.'

'Yes, you're right,' said Christopher. 'I'd like it very much.' He grinned and snuggled against Tom like a cat. 'I wish I'd thought of it myself.' It appealed more and more as he thought about it. To spend time alone with Tom, without having to be wary of judgemental eyes and ears around them, in a country where you couldn't get sent to prison for doing what they routinely did in bed together. It was the nearest thing he could imagine to heaven.

The same went for Tom too.

When something surprising happens a second time we are no longer surprised by it. And so Tom was less alarmed than Christopher had been a couple of weeks earlier, on being accosted by Father Louis on his way to breakfast and invited to share his private table in the boys' refectory.

'Look around you.' Father Louis gestured with energetic nods of the head as they both began to spread their toast triangles with butter and marmalade. 'Do these boys look unhappy to you?'

'No, Father,' said Tom. 'When you consider that they'll have their noses pressed hard to the grindstone in their various classrooms in just one hour's time, they look rather happier than you might expect.'

'Good. Good man, Sanders. I'm glad to hear you say that.' Father Louis gave Tom a smile that was, for once, not a death's head grin, but something that conveyed real warmth and was accompanied – this was without precedent, in Tom's experience at least – by a chuckle. 'Perhaps I could call you Tom, at least for the duration of this little *tête-à-tête*.'

'Yes, of course, Father.'

'It's due to discipline, Tom. It really is. There are those who would urge us to break the rod and spare the child.' He permitted himself another, though this time more ghostly, chuckle when he'd said this. Then he looked earnestly into Tom's eyes. 'They would be wrong, Tom. They would be very, very wrong. None of this...' He gestured around him with his right hand – Tom was alarmed to notice that he had his teacup in it – 'None of this, this atmosphere of ordered calm and well-being,

107

would be possible without the firmest discipline. Do not,' Father Louis now glared fiercely at Tom, 'misunderstand me – as some do wilfully – and interpret my words as meaning, be heavy with the cane. On the contrary, be light with the cane. Apply it without causing any but the most momentary pain. But do not shrink from using it. Not over-often, but regularly. Let the boys see that you carry it with you when you do the dormitory rounds.' As Father Louis and Father Matthew always did. They each wore a slender bamboo switch, some two foot six inches long, tucked through their belts, invisible beneath their scapulars, but with the tell-tale outline of the top end of it visible through the fabric against their chests. 'It is the deterrent effect that is the most beneficial. They must learn to fear the cane, and to fear you. That is the way to give them the freedom that they – that all boys – need. Freedom within strict bounds that they can understand. Do the opposite, Tom: give in to them when they test the bounds, try to get their loyalty and affection by being soft and the opposite will happen. They will take advantage, stab you in the back.' Father Louis's teacup came to rest on the edge of his saucer, to Tom's only partial relief. 'Dear me, I've seen this all too often. So many times. Dear me, indeed.'

Tom wondered if that was what had happened to Richard Appleton. Had he been too soft on the boys? Had he been stabbed in the back before he got sacked? Tom wanted to ask about his predecessor. The opportunity had never arisen before. 'I did wonder…' he began. But the opportunity was still not to be granted him.

'Tom, what was it brought you here? I hardly remember now. Weren't you transferred from Bellhurst for some reason? Not that it matters for one moment. Tell me about young McGing. Is he going to make a go of it, do you think?'

Tom was now on the edge of his seat with tension. Father Louis had raised his teacup again, but only one side of it, so that it was beginning to heel over like a beached boat when the tide goes out. Already a few warning splashes were slopping into the saucer, and it would be only a matter of seconds before it capsized completely and emptied its entire cargo over the white tablecloth. In front of a hundred and thirteen pairs of impressionable eyes. Tom was too far away to reach out easily and grab the cup without standing up to do so, but to sit and do nothing while the teacup tempest turned to outright inundation didn't seem to be an option either.

'I think he's doing splendidly,' Tom said, almost booming the words, and then, to the waitress who was most fortunately hovering almost at Father Louis's elbow as she refilled the boys' cups from a huge green enamel jug, 'Flossie, could Father Louis have a drop more tea?'

Flossie grasped the situation at once, to Tom's surprise as well as relief. With her free hand she picked up their small tea-for-two-pot and said, 'Steady your cup, Father,' which he promptly did, too surprised, perhaps, to object that it was still more than half full. Flossie now filled the wayward cup almost to the brim, thus averting the immediate disaster but – as so often – making a near certainty of another one in the longer term.

'I'm glad to hear it.' Father Louis's attention had quickly returned to Tom. 'I think he's a good boy and will do well. His uncle's a parish priest, you know. Recently made a canon. I pride myself on being a good judge of character, and choosing well. Take the house captains, now. Dexter and Rickman. Perfect choices for the job. Dexter a bright young man, full of energy and talent. Almost too much energy, I used sometimes to think. Harness it, I told myself. Channel it into constructive outlets before he goes to the bad, I told myself. And lo and behold – a model of what a good house captain can be. Now Rickman. Sensitive boy. Head in the clouds, artistic. Nose always in a book. Give him something practical to do – bring him down to earth a bit. I made him captain of More, and there we are. Another splendid prefect.

'Moyse and Abelard now. Not natural leaders, those two. Moyse the artistic one, Abelard the plodder. Yet I made them vice-captains this year and it's done them a power of good. Excellent seconds-in-command, heads firmly screwed on, and improving at Rugby in leaps and bounds all last winter. Now at cricket too, I hear. Didn't Moyse bowl Dexter out last week?'

Tom nodded his assent, and felt a wave of relief as Father Louis at last let go of his teacup at the same time as embarking on another slightly new topic. 'There will come a time,' he said, now in a low confiding tone and leaning in across the table towards Tom, 'a few years from now, when the abbey will expect me to retire as headmaster here.' Years? thought Tom. Months, surely, or even weeks. 'And there will be the question of my successor.'

'Father Matthew, I suppose,' said Tom smoothly, despite having heard Father Matthew express his doubts as to the likelihood of that.

'Maybe, maybe,' Father Louis answered, sounding a little impatient. 'But I'm not sure that Father Abbot may not have other ideas. It may just be the case that he's thinking of putting a lay teacher in at the top here instead of a monk.'

'A lay teacher?' Tom was genuinely surprised. 'Someone from the existing pool of staff? I mean, either from here or from the senior school. Or someone from outside?'

'I imagine the abbot would consider both possibilities. But I was thinking about you.'

'About me, Father? In what connection?'

Father Louis answered in an even tone that conveyed neither impatience nor its opposite. 'As a potential candidate to be my successor in a few years' time.'

Tom felt light-headed with astonishment. Father Louis really was losing his marbles. But, as always happens when someone we believe to be barking mad suddenly says something that is enormously flattering to us, Tom immediately wanted to find Father Louis as sane and sapient as Solomon, and to believe that the compliment he'd just been paid was born out of a deep instinctive knowledge of his capabilities and character. 'Good heavens,' was what he said.

'Sometimes there is a curious, almost paradoxical advantage to be gained by placing a very young man in a very senior post. I plan to make my view known to the abbot at the meeting of the deans later this week. I thought it would be only fair to let you know my line of thinking beforehand.'

'Well, that's very...' But Tom really had run out of words. Fortunately they would not be needed. Father Louis interrupted his fractured interjection to ask if Tom would kindly pass him another piece of toast, and then, when Tom had done so, seamlessly moved on to tell him about an article he had read in The Times about new possibilities for rearing chickens intensively in cages that would reduce the price of chicken meat, 'so dramatically that even the poorest of households will soon be able to afford a roast fowl for their Sunday table.' Father Louis smacked his thin lips.

**

From John Moyse's Diary: Sunday May 27th 1962

The resurrection of Father Louis occurred around teatime today. He was back on full form by evening. Some talking in dorm one after lights out, and he had them all downstairs in their pyjamas and gave all twelve of them three strokes. Nothing wrong with his rt arm at least.

Also, Christopher did remember the book he promised me for writing in. So he really is OK. Question now is: what to fill those pristine white pages with? And what to call it: a commonplace book, a journal?

(Nota Bene: experimenting with colons.)

***

From John Moyse's Diary: Monday May 28th 1962

Father Louis had Tom Sanders down in the refectory at breakfast. Whatever they talked about it must have been something momentous. Flossie had to be called in to stop Fr L spilling his tea.

Still can't decide what to call the new journal. Meatballs for lunch.

TEN

The Saturday morning that was the start of half term presented a jewel-bright sky and a sparkling sea. For once the boys were eager to get out of bed. Many were already dressed and packing weekend bags by the time Father Louis came gliding through the dormitories, swinging the morning bell. Tom and Christopher breakfasted hurriedly and made their way to the station on foot, a good half hour ahead of the two bus-loads of boys who would be heading for the London-bound school train. They didn't want to be engulfed on the platform by a swarm of youngsters all curious to know where they were off to together. Father Matthew and Miss O'Deere knew of their plans, and probably other staff did also, and they felt that was already quite enough.

They caught the Folkestone Harbour train, headed by a Battle of Britain class Pacific. In a chalk cutting above Folkestone town the last few coaches were uncoupled from the rest of the train which then steamed off towards Folkestone's main station. Their tail-end section was picked up by a sturdy black tank engine, which led them down the steepest slope either of them could recall descending in a train. Over the brown house-tops, dropping rapidly to the sea; crossing by a steeply inclined bridge Folkestone's miniature inner harbour, full of sailing boats and fishing smacks on both sides of them, and pretty as a picture in a Ladybird book. Braking sharply they entered the harbour station, which curved neatly along the outreaching breakwater, where their ferry waited. She flew the French ensign and was called the Compiègne.

They spent most of the crossing out on deck. The massive white walls of Kent grew smaller, while reaching like outspreading arms further and further across the sea behind them. Meanwhile the thin white line of France ever so gradually re-configured itself as the towering, thrusting capes of Blanc and Gris Nez. Black-backed gulls glided alongside them, sometimes only a yard or two away. There was no England for them and no France, just two chalky rims to their world of sky and water. The big birds travelled insouciantly between them, hitching rides as and when it suited them, on the slipstreams of conveniently headed ships.

The proud heights of Blanc Nez withdrew surprisingly rapidly behind the newly prominent cliffs and lighthouse of Cap Gris Nez, and then they were steaming southward alongside rolling hills, vividly green in the midday sun. Ahead of them the cathedral at Boulogne already showed, crowning its hilltop site, but from this distance the size of a barnacle atop a shard of stone.

They had made no plans, had no particular ideas about where they might stay, and had brought nothing with them beyond passports, sponge-bags and a change of socks and pants. When the ship docked, burrowing its way up-river into the heart of the town, they were wonderfully unencumbered in comparison with the other disembarking foot passengers, most of whom were trailing suitcases onto the platform of the maritime railway terminus, and they felt somehow superior – in a very odd sort of way – to those other voyagers who had felt it necessary to bring their cars.

Both had been to France before. Tom, when a teenager, had spent a summer's scout camp on a hillside near Dieppe; Christopher had been taken to Paris by his parents two years before over an Easter weekend. They both knew that the first things you did on arrival were: have a coffee, eat something, drink some wine. They'd already had a coffee on the boat – which counted, since the boat was French – and now, as they adjusted their watches, they realised it was already after one. This surprised them a little; the day still had the feel of fresh early morning: a little trick this, perhaps, played by the sea. With the last rump of foot passengers – those who hadn't headed straight for the connecting train – they crossed the harbour bridge that led away from the car ferry quays and into town.

Compared to any town either of them had seen in England, this one had an astonishing number of cafés and restaurants in proportion to other businesses, ranged along its streets. Each one had a board outside, propped on the pavement, advertising *croque-monsieur*, *hot-dog* and *moules et frites*, as well as a few small tables and chairs lined up outside the window under an awning. They were hesitating as to which of these identical if enticing establishments they should have lunch at, when a very young man popped out of a doorway and said, giggling at his own cheek, *'Messieurs, par ici,'* and waved with his serving cloth towards a vacant table beside him.

They would probably have moved away and gone somewhere else – anywhere else – as a matter of principle: taking offence, in the British manner they'd been brought up in, at his directness. Only he struck them both – Christopher guessed him to be aged eighteen like himself – as quite outrageously attractive. He wore the traditional waiter's white apron over his threadbare black trousers and white open-neck shirt. The apron was fastened around a waist that was even slenderer than Christopher's. His whole frame was so slight that you felt a strong south-westerly ripping up the Channel could have picked him up and blown him over the house tops. A mop of shining black hair framed a triangular face in which nostrils and mouth were prominent, well sculpted and large. Thick black lashes shielded deep blue eyes which were also large, and smiled. Tom and Christopher had not reached the stage of admitting to each other that they found other men attractive – except each other – and so no glance was exchanged between them. Each kept his frisson of delight for himself alone, but each knew at once that this would be the café at which they would lunch.

A couple of paces brought them to the empty table, They sat down, and their waiter made a great performance of wiping it cleaner than it already was with the cloth that, along with his apron, was his badge of office. Tom, although having limited experience of French waiters, knew a little more about the ways of the homosexual world than Christopher did, and was pretty sure that this boy was behaving towards them not just as a waiter reeling in a catch of new clients but as someone who recognised two fellow members of his own sect.

The waiter went away for only a few seconds before returning with a rather soiled menu card. 'Are you new to Boulogne?' he asked them, speaking in French but slowly and carefully to make sure they would understand him, and looking very intimately into first Tom's and then Christopher's eyes.

They told him that they were – in French, which was easily done. But they were conscious that the gap between teaching *je suis, tu es, il est,* to seven-year-olds and possessing real fluency would become painfully exposed were the conversation to develop further. For the moment it didn't. The waiter trotted out a few conventional phrases about the attractions of Boulogne and its beaches while they examined the menu and glanced quickly at neighbouring tables to see what other people were having. Those who weren't simply nursing a coffee while chatting to friends were mostly dealing with hot bowlfuls of mussels in their steam-opened shells, accompanied by heaps of crisp French fries, as golden as the soggy offerings they were used to at Star of the Sea were grey. Taking their cue from the mussel-eaters, Tom and Christopher ordered the same and, because those people were sipping tall glasses of blond beer rather than wine, it was beer that they chose by way of drink. Folklore might insist that the French sipped wine all day long at café tables, but here no-one was doing it. Perhaps that would come in the evening.

After he had taken the order indoors the waiter returned with napkins, knives and forks, and a basket of baguette chunks. How long were they staying in Boulogne? he asked them. Had they found a place to stay?

Answering those two questions they made the pleasant discovery that it is easier to get by in a foreign language when you are speaking to someone you find charming and sexually attractive and who clearly feels the same about you, and who, in addition, listens patiently to what you have to say and kindly pretends not to notice your many mistakes.

'There is a small hotel just up the street from here, which I can recommend. It's cheap but clean and it's run by two friends of mine. Two male friends.' The waiter paused just long enough to see how this last bit went down; then, seeing cautious smiles appearing on the faces of Christopher and Tom, he went on, 'I can phone them now, if you like, and get an exact price; then I can book you a room if you decide you want that.' He held up both hands, palms outward. 'But no sales pressure, I promise.'

The offer seemed genuine enough and they accepted it. When the waiter had gone back indoors Christopher, who had not twigged as quickly as Tom but had now caught up, said, 'Are we that obvious?'

'It looks like it. At least to him and his kind. To our kind, if you like. But with any luck, not to everyone.'

'Although,' said Christopher, 'on this side of the Channel it shouldn't matter if we were. – Were obvious,

I mean. We're not breaking any laws just by being who we are.' He looked pleased with himself, as if a lucky penny had just dropped.

'It's true,' said Tom. 'Good, isn't it?'

The waiter returned a minute later with steaming bowls of mussels and another one full of chips, with mayonnaise and lemon quarters and finger bowls, and with the news that a double room was being held for them if they wanted it. The price, once they'd done the conversion into pounds from francs, seemed absurdly cheap. They said they'd take it. 'My friends are called Thierry and Robert. I couldn't give them yours because I forgot to ask. So just tell them you're the friends I phoned about. I'm called Armand.'

Tom and Christopher gave their names, which Armand repeated once to make sure he'd heard them right, and then the three of them shook hands. Armand left them to eat their meal in peace – and he had other customers to serve – but later, when they were paying their bill, he told them about a late night bar which, 'perhaps you might like.' Following their still rather guarded expressions of interest, he gave them an address and directions to it. It wasn't very far either from here or from their hotel, he said – here and the hotel both being in the Rue Faidherbe. He threw in the information that he would be going there himself after he finished work.

The hotel was simple, its entrance hall cosily furnished with worn armchairs, and presided over by a glossy black mynah bird in a big cage: it greeted their entrance with a dreadfully lifelike impression of a racking smoker's cough. Thierry and Robert, alerted to the new arrivals by the lung-dredging noises of the bird, both came forward from behind the reception desk and shook their hands. They were much younger than Tom and Christopher had expected, their expectation being based on what they knew of hotel owners and managers rather than on reckoning how young any friends of Armand would probably be. They both looked no more than thirty.

Thierry was a shortish, stocky man with close-cut hair and a neat moustache. His manner suggested army captain or sports coach; perhaps he'd been both. Robert tended towards his physical opposite, being slender and willowy, having lank dark hair that fell in curtains into his ears and eyes, and with just a hint of femininity about his movements that grew slightly more pronounced after a couple of minutes' conversation with the two new arrivals. He took a key from the board behind the reception desk and led them up a narrow, twisting staircase, pressing time-switch buttons to light their way as he went, then unlocked a room and showed them into it. Unblushingly he gestured towards the double bed. *'Ça va?'* he queried. Will that do? It was Christopher who then blushed deeply enough for all three of them, though he managed to hide this to some extent by feigning great interest in the view down into the street from the net-curtained French window. Which left it to Tom to assure Robert that the price was fine, the room likewise, and that they would take it for three nights.

Robert left them, backing out of the room while grinning broadly beneath his Niagara Falls of a fringe, so that after he had gone they were left with a memory of that sudden grin: it survived his departure like the Cheshire Cat's. Then they threw themselves down on the bed and briefly tussled each other in the way young lovers have always done since the invention of hotels.

They went out and nosed their way to the beach, zigzagging through the side streets around the Place des Victoires towards Boulevard Sainte-Beuve, which took them there directly. Edged by a line of cafés and fishing-tackle shops across the sand-blown little roadway, the beach was a broad crescent of yellow sand bounded at its nearer end by the long breakwater of the inner harbour, alongside which their ferry had glided – giving them an inviting glimpse of this very beach – on their inbound journey. Now family groups were sprinkled lightly over the vast expanse. Waves rolled gently at its edge, their force tamed by the massive outer harbour walls a mile or two off shore. In the gap between those walls could be seen the bright crescent moons of the Kent cliffs.

'Thierry and Robert, you know,' Christopher said, once they were stripped to the waist and sitting down on the sand, 'are they … you know … like Roger and Malcolm. I mean, a couple.' He stared fixedly at the distant cliffs as he said this, as if trying to discern the figures of Roger and Malcolm, out fishing in the Orca perhaps, on the other side.

'I'd be surprised if they weren't,' said Tom. 'Yes, I think they're like Roger and Malcolm. They're like us.'

Christopher turned towards Tom. 'It's bloody amazing, isn't it? Running a business together, quite openly, and nobody saying a dicky-bird.'

'Sometimes the French just do seem to get things right,' said Tom, and smiled at his lover.

They hadn't thought to bring swimming-trunks or towels. But one or two teenage boys and young men were sunbathing or walking down to the water in their underpants without raising eyebrows among the matriarchs nearby, and Tom and Christopher followed their example. Trustingly they left their watches and wallets among their clothes while they waded out for a short swim among the – shockingly – cold waves. Their trust was not misplaced; the family atmosphere of the beach appeared to be its own safeguard, and all was found intact on their return.

Ships and boats came and went, oddly near at hand beyond the jetty, and the wakes of the larger ones, the Folkestone ferries, walloped the shore with a succession of rumbling rollers. Imperceptibly yet implacably the sun shifted its position in the sky until it was no longer afternoon but early evening and time to move inland.

'Remember when you were a kid,' said Christopher as they threaded their way back, 'and had been at the beach all day: how there was a very special feeling about when you got home. The house felt different, and time seemed to have got out of kilter, and what with the wind and the sun on you, you still felt naked under your clothes, and you couldn't quite adjust to playing normally before supper time. Remember that?'

Tom didn't answer at once. Christopher, he thought, was not far removed from still being that kid. Tom had been afraid that Christopher would fall for him, was falling for him already, indeed had already done so. He was surer than ever of that now, even though the disciplined Christopher took great care not to let it show. It was not 'just sex' for Christopher. But Tom had failed to beware himself. He knew now, though – self-deception lit up and exposed by a quick harsh sunbeam of self-knowledge – that he had fallen for Christopher head over heels: that he was falling in love with an eighteen-year-old for the second time in one year. 'Oh yes,' he said eventually, his voice a little thin. 'I remember.'

Thierry was not to be seen at their hotel when they got back, but Robert chatted tail-waggingly to them as he gave them their key. No doubt, he said, Armand had given them all the gen they needed to spend a Saturday evening in Boulogne.

'He mentioned a bar called Le Chat qui Pêche in the Rue Inkerman,' Tom said. He didn't think Robert would be fazed by this.

Robert was not. 'I imagined he would. It's very near. Just after the Place des Victoires and turn right. I might pop in there later myself if it's quiet here. I'd better give you a key to the front door, though. We may have gone to bed by the time you come back.' He found a key in a drawer and handed it to them, directing a smile towards Christopher and then, at Tom, a wink. Behind them the mynah bird gave a discreet cough.

They treated themselves to a proper dinner in the Place Dalton, at a restaurant that was tucked away behind a bank of sea-food: trays of oysters and crustaceans of all kinds, ranged on a long zinc counter at the side of the street. The restaurant beyond looked very expensive and they wouldn't have dreamed of going in if Armand, who had recommended the place, had not also told them that, provided they stuck to the set menus and avoided the Carte, it would not break the bank.

The oysters looked exciting but they had not eaten them before and neither wanted to make a fool of himself in front of the other by trying them now. Instead they chose a colourful terrine of fish and vegetables, then *lotte à la Dieppoise*, which was monkfish with mussels, prawns, cream and white wine, a selection of Normandy cheeses, and then an Ile Flottante by way of a dessert for which they didn't really have room, but ate anyway.

When they'd finished eating it was still too early for a late-night bar so they walked back to the beach. The reddening sun was sliding towards the sea, preparing to set. It caused a ferry that was just sliding between the harbour's jaws to become a tower of brilliant white which seemed to rise, as if by a momentary touch of magic, from a point a couple of metres above the surface of the water. They watched the sun sink, just as they'd often done from the cliffs of Kent. Only this time it was the lights of England, not France, that glimmered into life beyond the sea as darkness fell.

'Turn again, Whittington,' Tom said, and steered Christopher across the beach-front road and into the nearest of the brightly lit bars. It was full of locals, mostly young men, beginning to be Saturday-night boisterous, some smoking and playing table-football or pinball. But as they sipped their way through a time-passing glass of lager they began to take particular notice of one couple, seated at a table, who were very different indeed. The man, aged perhaps sixty, wore a fisherman's sweater and baggy cord trousers. He had a mane of grey hair and an untrimmed beard of great length; he could have sat as a model for Moses or some other Old Testament prophet. He wouldn't have done for Father Christmas, though; there was no twinkle in his eyes; those were dark and recessed in deep caverns on either side of the crag that was his nose; they burned with something that might have been sexual hunger, or madness, or rage. He was speaking, holding forth, in an interminable monologue whose words they could not hear through the din of the bar and the table games, though they sounded like English words, while the woman who sat opposite him listened with apparently devoted attention, gazing at him with an expression that might have been rapt – or else totally vacant, her mind somewhere else.

She was round-faced and big-eyed, her hair only beginning to go seriously grey; she was perhaps ten years younger than the loquacious man. She was dressed, despite its being a warm June evening that hung on the coat-tails of a positively hot June day, in a black mackintosh, buttoned high up to the neck and all the way down to where it finished, below her knees, and a pair of black wellingtons took over the task of covering her legs and feet.

'Do you suppose those are the only clothes she's got?' Christopher said quietly to Tom. 'And that she's got nothing at all on underneath?'

'You could be right,' Tom answered. 'But I've just realised something else.'

'Don't say you know her.'

'No. But I think I know him. When I was at school – not where I taught before, but where I went from eleven to eighteen – there was a monk who got the sack, or left – I can't remember which, it happened in the holidays and it's a long time ago – well, I'm pretty sure it's him. Well disguised by hair and beard of course, but those eyes…'

'What was he sacked for?' Christopher wanted to know. 'Was it … you know … with boys?'

'No, I don't think so. I don't think his interests lay that way. I think he may have been a bit of a boozer, actually.'

Christopher looked across to where the man was refilling his glass with dark red wine from a decanter that had held nearly a litre when they first came in but which now held less than half of that. 'Yes,' he said. 'That I could imagine. A drunk monk.'

'The rumour went round after he'd gone that he'd fallen in love with a nun from a nearby convent and eloped with her.'

'Oh my God!' said Christopher, unsuccessfully trying to stifle a loud guffaw. 'And d'you suppose that's her?'

Tom gave a quick look. 'Eight years down the line? On the run with a nun? It's possible, I suppose. But the nun thing was only a rumour, and those do have a habit of not being true.'

'So if he's the drunk monk, then what's she? Oh I know!' Christopher's eyes lit up. 'She's the undone nun. The drunk monk and the undone nun. Are you going to introduce yourself?'

'I don't think I dare.' Tom laughed. 'And he's not going to recognise me. I was about fifteen when he last saw me, and he didn't know me terribly well even then. Leave well alone, I think. Drink up. We'll find The Fishing Cat.'

There it was, just off the Place des Victoires, exactly where Robert had said it would be. The sign outside, they couldn't help noticing, had been crudely altered by hand so that it read, not Le Chat qui Pêche – the cat who fishes – but Le Chat qui Péche ... which they were both fairly sure meant, the cat who sins. The door was shut but it opened to a tentative push, which caused a young man who had been sitting inside to rise up and block their way. *'Bonsoir,'* he said without a smile. *'Et qui êtes vous?'*

'Deux amis d'Armand,' Christopher answered immediately, which made Tom smile, because that sounded as though it might be a euphemism for something else. The man on the door caught the smile and returned it – probably the same thought had struck him – while Christopher added, rather unnecessarily for someone with his accent, *'d'Angleterre.'* The doorman said something which neither of them could catch, then stood aside to let them in.

They found themselves in a room that at first appeared so dark as to resemble a cave. As their eyes adjusted they realised that the walls were painted black, while the ceiling was veiled with purple silk fabric – probably a couple of bedspreads – that had been pinned to it and which now bellied downwards like the sails of a ship. There were wall-bracket lights, whose radiance was subdued and diffused by pierced-metal shades, while on and behind the bar the servers and their wares were illuminated by banks of red and purple candles in jam jars. Although it was hardly novel décor for a night spot in 1962, Christopher had never seen anything like it in his life and his eyes wandered the room in wonder, his mouth ever so slightly agape. While Tom, who had once been to a night-club in London, took the place more easily in his stride. There were tables and chairs around the walls and in between them vast cushions lying louchely on the floor. It was barely ten o'clock and there were few customers yet. But two, sitting on stools at the bar caught their attention. Both were male, aged about thirty, as far as they could make out in the dim light; one had an arm around the neck of the other, and from time to time they unselfconsciously put their faces together and kissed.

Christopher turned towards Tom. He wanted to make some banal comment, only he didn't want to, and Tom forestalled him anyway by seizing him and giving him a lively kiss, which nicely startled Christopher with its energy and eagerness. When, half a minute later, they pulled apart, Christopher finally did come out with a banal comment, couldn't help himself, 'Now I know why it's called French kissing,' and immediately wished he hadn't, though Tom seemed not to mind.

They were at the bar now. The nearest barman greeted them with as broad a smile of welcome as if they'd just passed an initiation test. Perhaps they had. Neither of them knew what might be considered cool by way of a drink in here at this time of evening. Looking around through the gloom, it was not easy to see what other people had in their glasses. They went for the safest, least exciting, most easily pronounced option, and a moment later were sitting with two glasses of draught blond beer in front of them.

The place began to fill up. If Tom or Christopher had thought they might simply blend into the background here, they were wrong. Young men, singly and in pairs, made it a priority to approach them and question them, either in French or in diffident English. Newcomers did not turn up at The Fishing Cat every weekend: in particular, few of the thousands of British travellers who passed through the port of Boulogne found their way here: not even those whose temperament and inclinations it would have suited.

A young man called Michel took them over. He was about Tom's age, ruddy-complexioned and with thick, curly, dark brown hair. His eyes, dark and lustrous as damson plums, were even more beautiful than Armand's. His style of dress struck them as impressive: he wore a one-piece workman's overall of blue denim, nothing unusual in that, except that as far as one could see – and one could see quite a long way – he had nothing on underneath it. No shirt or vest, certainly, and since the dungarees were cut so low at the sides that his naked hips were visible, it could be assumed there were no underpants either. His feet were clad, though: in sandals and bright mauve socks. But the assurance with which Michel carried this ensemble off made Tom and Christopher feel it was they who were oddly dressed. The jeans, open-necked Aertex shirts and plimsolls that elsewhere enabled them to blend in with any casually dressed crowd of their own age seemed almost square here. Anomalous. Dull. Altogether too normal. What was the word that people had begun to bandy about, perhaps quoting someone like Freud? Heterosexual.

But Michel didn't seem bothered. He was interested when they told him how they earned their living. 'All those teenagers! *Quelle tentation!*' Tom put him right. The kids at Star of the Sea were barely into their teens when they left the school, while the ones they themselves taught were aged between seven and nine. Real children. And – he felt it important to assure Michel of this – neither of them was remotely interested sexually in those.

Michel was a painter. *('Moi, 'suis peintre.')* A smile of pride appeared on his face as he announced this, which was the more charming for the fact he didn't know it was there. 'Canvasses, that is: not other people's houses.' He had to admit he hadn't sold any of his work yet, but then look at Van Gogh. Michel earned his daily bread by working in his parents' shop. *'Quincaillerie.'* Between them all they managed to work out that this was an ironmonger's, or hardware store. 'Go on, say it,' Michel challenged them. *'Kang-kye-ye-ree.'* They did their best. His father had died, so his mother ran the shop by herself now. Luckily he was on hand to help out. He had no brothers or sisters. He looked at them silently for a second after saying that, allowing them to work out for themselves what he didn't want plonkingly to spell out: that one day the business would be all his. It had done no harm to Vermeer that he had inherited his father's businesses, after all. *'Mais qu'est-ce que vous buvez?'* Beer was hardly the thing. He was going to have a white rum with Coke, which was all the rage now. Would they like to…? They would, and did.

Christopher wanted to know more about Michel's painting. Water colours? Oils? After two sittings for Miss O'Deere and rather more than two drinks already tonight he was a real expert now. Michel would be interested to know that they were the models for a painting in oils that was probably being completed this very weekend. He told the whole story.

Michel's laughter threatened to capsize his rum and Coke. 'David and Jonathan – two young *pédés* painted semi-nude by an English *vielle fille*.' He went on laughing as if he would have found it difficult to imagine anything funnier.

Again Tom found himself dispelling Michel's preconceptions. First, Miss O'Deere wasn't English but Irish. And she wasn't such an old spinster as that. Nor should Michel imagine that she painted like the typical primary school, primary colours, art mistress. Then he relented and laughed. Why should Michel take his word, though, after all? He'd need to see the finished painting and make up his own mind.

Michel apologised with a smile. Of course Tom was right. And of course they only had *his* word for the quality of his own work until they saw it for themselves. Which they must do tomorrow. Would they honour him by visiting his studio? He laid his drink down on the bar counter and placed one arm around Tom's shoulder and the other round Christopher's. Then he drew their heads towards him, first Tom's, then Christopher's, and gave them each a kiss on the cheek. As he did so, Armand appeared at their side. Michel introduced him – 'Though I think you know him already. This is Armand. *Mon ami, mon amant et ma vie.*' My friend, my lover and my life.

***

From John Moyse's New Journal

I'm calling it a journal after all. The New Journal. And call me John, by the way. Though it doesn't quite have the ring of Call me Ishmael, that can't be helped. Nobody can choose their own first name.

Halfterm began today. (Though that's a bit of a misnomer this term, as we're only 1/3 through. But the long second half is being split by an extra weekend which will include prize giving, sports day and the Old Boys' cricket match.) I went on the school train as far as Tonbridge, then got the other train to take me home. Parents at the station, which was good. When I started boarding school they'd drive me all the way, then they took to driving me as far as Tonbridge only, now just to the station. Perhaps when I'm older I'll have to walk home from there. (Only joking.)

The puppies are so big now. One's going to the Arbuthnotts and one to Auntie Ginny. We're keeping one of the girl puppies (I know you're supposed to say bitch, but it seems horrible to say that about a dog) to be company for Martha. She's very sweet and lively. Called – which I knew already of course – Teal.

Weather's great. I did some sketches in the afternoon of the tractors making hay. They're earlier than last year. Bet someone's written a proverb about that.

What can you say about being at home? Only that it's so totally different from school. And that unlike school where things happen as fast as fireworks all the time, home is where nothing ever changes.

ELEVEN

Architecturally speaking the cathedral was surprisingly good. Surprisingly because it had been designed, not by a professional architect but by a local priest, more or less on the back of an envelope, in the early nineteenth century. It was a longish climb up the Grande Rue, but an impressive sight once you got there, its hundred-metre-high dome, which acknowledged the influence of Rome's St Peter's and London's St Paul's, hogging the skyline. Inside it was light, white-painted, classical, Italianate. Somewhat elongated vertically, pulled up into the sky, as if painted by El Greco. The slender, tapering Corinthian pillars that strode elegantly down the nave were as finely proportioned and delicate as racehorses' legs.

Tom was not sure why he, a firm non-believer, and Christopher, a steadfast waverer in the matters of belief and piety, should have made the effort, on such a sunny morning, on the one Sunday of the summer term on which it was no part of their school-masterly duties, and when they had such skull-shattering hangovers, to get up and breakfast in time to climb up to the walled citadel of the town for eleven o'clock Mass. But it was Whit-Sunday, the feast of Pentecost, and they had done it anyway, almost without it having to be discussed. Now here they were.

The cathedral was full, the congregation smartly clad for the most part, the men in suits and ties, the women in bright summer dresses and floral hats. Tom and Christopher began to feel self-conscious in their own casual jeans and open-necked shirts, the same ones they had worn the day before. At least there was no-one here who knew them. As foreigners and strangers they enjoyed the same unaccustomed freedom in their anonymity that they'd enjoyed in Le Chat qui Pêche – or

Péche – the night before, even if they couldn't behave with quite the same abandon, kissing and fondling each other publicly, here in church.

The priest's vestments and the altar cloths and tabernacle curtains were red: the colour of fire. To commemorate the day that God had shown himself in the form of parted tongues of flame to the apostles as they cowered, barricaded in the upper room, in fear of the angry mob below in the street. That day their faith had been strengthened and they had gone bravely out into the crowd, speaking in tongues, and converting three thousand souls to the cause of Jesus Christ. So went the reading, first in Latin and then in French, from the Acts of the Apostles, and was then developed in a rather ponderous sermon by the celebrant priest.

It occurred to Christopher, as his mind inevitably began to wander away from the French priest's words, that he too had experienced a moment of strengthening: in his own understanding of who and what he was, of what he and Tom were beginning to be. It had come in the bolstering experience of meeting first Armand and then Michel: a couple whose respective ages, they guessed, pretty closely matched their own. And then there was the slightly older pair, Thierry and Robert. Robert had joined them all in the bar last night, as he'd said he might, and then all five had returned to the hotel, to have a final Cognac with the reception-desk-bound Thierry. After that, Armand and Michel had woven their way a bit unsteadily towards the door, leaving Tom and Christopher to climb the stairs, equally unsteadily, and Thierry and Robert to lock up and put lights out. It was no surprise that they should have such cracking hangovers now.

Eventually Mass came to an end. *Ite, Missa est. Deo gratias*. The congregation began to pour out of the wide open west doors, a slow congested lava flow of floral hats, and the sunshine streamed in. Then Christopher was startled, though rather more than startled, to recognise, and be recognised by, a face he knew. In suit and tie, and in the company of three other people, presumably his parents and an elder sister – was Angelo Dexter, house captain and prefect, a world away from any context they had ever shared.

'We've heard so much about you both.' Despite years of marriage to Mr Stephen Dexter, his wife Artemia had not lost her grip on her original Italian nationality, which was displayed proudly in her accent, looks and bearing. They all stood on the cathedral steps, talking. At least, Artemia talked. How much Angelo had benefited from his time at the prep school, now sadly drawing to a close, but what promising hopes for the next stage of his life, moving on to Downside. His cricketing prowess much improved, thanks no doubt to the efforts of Tom in these last few weeks. And what a charming surprise to all meet up across the Channel like this. What a beautiful day. But the Dexter family must not keep Tom and Christopher – all first names now – from whatever they were planning to do. Artemia was not an insensitive woman, and could see that the young men were slightly embarrassed at being 'discovered' under-dressed for Sunday Mass during what should have been a holiday from school and school's boys. So she reined in her natural instinct to eulogise everyone and everything and gave them a brief outline of her family's plans for their remaining twenty-four hours in Boulogne, probably with the deliberate and kind intention of enabling her son's teachers to not bump into them again if they didn't want to.

'It could have been worse,' said Tom afterwards. 'Better to run into Dexter and family at High Mass than in a late-night dive full of French poofs.'

'Even if we were dressed more for the bar than the cathedral,' said Christopher, forced to agree that Tom was right. But he thought, *poofs – is that what we are?* It was the first time either of them had used a word, any word, that might have to define them.

It was everything that a struggling young artist's studio should be. A half-made bed in one corner, gas-ring and sink in an alcove. A couple of small chairs, just as in Van Gogh's painting of his own studio, plates overflowing with cigarette-butts, an easel set up under the north-facing skylight, canvasses on stretchers, in frames, or simply rolled and tied, lying or standing or leaning against every wall. Above all it was in France.

There was no doubting Michel's skill as a painter. Although Tom and Christopher had to take the quality of his two or three abstract daubs on trust since they lacked the critical wherewithal to assess them, it was easy to gauge the technical expertise and assurance of his representational canvasses. There was Boulogne harbour, the Saturday morning market in the Place Dalton, and a view of the town's rooftops cascading downhill from the citadel to the sea beyond, which could only have been painted from the gallery that ran round the cathedral's craning dome, every detail picked out lovingly with fastidious brushstrokes. And if these were not enough to demonstrate their creator's painterly worth, the clincher was a portrait of Armand – life, character and likeness – in the clothes and attitude of a young Renaissance nobleman. Once they'd demonstrated their enthusiasm for that one, Michel felt confident enough to unroll another canvas, half-hidden among a pile of others, that depicted Armand again, full-length and full-face, but this time with no clothes on at all.

'You're invited to supper,' Michel said. Involuntarily they glanced around the cluttered space, wondering how this could be managed. Michel clarified. 'Not here. At my mother's. Armand will be there. You'd like to come?'

They were touched by the diffident tone of his last query – unlike anything else about him up to now – and said yes, they'd very much like to, but wouldn't it be imposing on his mother to expect her to cook for two people she'd never met?

'Au contraire.' Michel silenced their polite noises. His mother loved to meet his friends and cook for them. Armand she positively adored. Tom and Christopher exchanged glances at this. Parents happy in the company of their offspring's same-sex partners was far removed from anything in their own experience or imagining. The address was given. Boulevard Auguste Marlette at the top of the town, just outside the citadel walls. The time, seven thirty for eight o'clock.

It was a solid and imposing house, about a century old, occupying what must be one of the prime sites in Boulogne, on a broad tree-lined road, a stone's throw from the cathedral but without being cramped by the admittedly picturesque narrow streets that formed the Old Town proper and which lay behind the rampart wall opposite. The big dining-room-cum-salon into which they were shown was furnished opulently, with much gilt in evidence on picture frames and Second Empire furniture, and wall-lights and chandeliers with glass-bead cascades and swags. They might have expected Michel's mother, occupying such a setting, to be a grand and chilly presence, but she was nothing of the kind. She at once invited them to call her Sabine rather than Madame, poured them all (Tom and Christopher had coincided with Armand on the doorstep) an aperitif of

Framboise, a raspberry liqueur lightened with white wine, and managed somehow to join them, between occasional sorties to the kitchen – alternating these with her son – in small talk so relaxed as to make it seem she might have known them for years.

It was a Sunday supper, so not presumed to be the main meal of the day. Nevertheless, it began with a green salad, continued with a whole roast leg of lamb with a garlic purée and green beans, and rolled on unstoppably through a platter of cheeses and a strawberry and blackcurrant tart, two bottles of Fleurie, a small glass of Sauternes to accompany the tart, until groaning to a halt with a small black coffee, a large amber Armagnac and a Belgian chocolate apiece. Christopher and Tom had already eaten quite well at Armand's café at lunchtime.

Michel had changed, for dinner with his mother, into fawn slacks and the navy and white transverse-striped top that was the uniform of the stage Frenchman the world over. The openness of his relationship with his mother presumably didn't extend quite as far as to permit him to turn up at her table in just dungarees with nothing underneath. The meal itself was the occasion, and the friendly ambience a part of that. So it hardly mattered that the conversation for the most part rose to no great heights of originality or sophistication, or that none of it would remain in their memories afterwards … except for one pronouncement, almost a little homily, which Michel's mother made to the four young men over the coffee and Armagnac.

It didn't arise from anything that had been discussed before. 'You must take every advantage,' Sabine suddenly said, leaning forward on her sofa, 'of what you have now. I've said this before to Armand and my son, and I apologise for repeating it once again. But you, Tommy, and you, Christophe, should hear it too. My husband, Michel's father, and I planned so many things that we would do when we retired. We put away the good times for a rainy day, if you wish, at least we put away some of them. And before he was sixty Victor died. What was the use, then, of an idea we'd had to see Africa together, and *Amérique du Sud*? You must make use of the time you have together, you young men, all of you, because you can never have the least idea of when that time will end.'

Christopher had never been spoken to by someone else's mother in such a way before, in an intimate way that addressed both Tom and himself, not as two separate friends of Michel's – and they'd known even Michel for barely twenty-four hours – but as a single entity. For that was clearly how she saw them, even if they themselves had not quite got there yet.

Furthermore, she brushed aside all offers of help with the washing-up. She had a woman who would come in the morning, whose job it was to do all that.

They were back at Le Chat qui Pêche, Michel re-inhabiting his more usual minimalist outfit of dungarees. Christopher, noticeably drunk by now, was standing close to him. 'It was wonderful, what your mother said to us. It made me feel … well, you know, back in England I sometimes felt worried by all this. Felt bad about it, I mean. Sex with men. Guilt. But now, here, meeting all of you – you especially – it's made such a difference. A new way to see life, and myself…' Christopher was saying all this in English, his French wouldn't have been up to it even if he'd been sober, and Michel wasn't understanding every word of it – he was hardly sober himself – but he easily got the general drift. He put his arms around Christopher and hugged him close.

So close that Christopher could feel the twin ridges of their cocks pushing together through their clothes. He hadn't realised that he was hard, but of course he was. Mustn't touch that, he told himself. Michel belongs to Armand, as I do to Tom. But his arms were round Michel's back, returning his embrace, and Michel's back was naked except for the webbing of his dungarees. Christopher felt his own hand slipping behind the webbing and down, till it was caressing the smooth hot dome of one bare buttock. It was a lovely sensation, and nothing wrong in that, he thought. It's just his cock I'm not allowed to touch.

Tom had his back to this scene, in conversation with Armand and, tonight, Thierry, whose turn it was to go out, leaving Robert at their hotel's reception desk. It was Thierry's sudden glance over Tom's shoulder to where Christopher and Michel stood that alerted him. He turned and took the situation in at once. He took the single stride that was the distance between them, roughly pulled Christopher away from Michel and said to him, 'Cut that out.' It was an expression he'd heard in American films and TV series but never used himself. He was surprised to hear himself saying it now. Turning to Michel he said, 'Leave the boy alone. He's mine. I didn't bring him here for sharing.' Wisely he resisted the urge to give Michel a hefty shove, and only half heard the overlapping protests of the others behind him. Armand, optimistically: 'We're all good friends here, Tom. Don't spoil it. *Laisse tomber.*'

Christopher knew exactly what Tom's next words would be when he turned back to him. He'd heard these too on TV and in film. 'Come on. We're going.' He didn't protest but with a shrug and an apologetic grimace back at the others allowed himself to be half pushed, half followed, to the door.

Neither of them spoke on the short walk back to the hotel, and when they collected their key from Robert with no more than a gruff few syllables, Robert understood well enough that no cheery good-night conversation was called for, let alone a convivial Cognac nightcap, but only a polite flick of the hand as they turned towards the stairs. The mynah bird was conscious of no such constraints however. It gave a gut-wrenching cough and said in French, 'See you in the morning.'

Upstairs Tom undressed, still without speaking. Christopher could see him trembling with held-in anger; he wasn't surprised by what happened next. Tom turned Christopher round and pushed him face-down onto the bed, roughly pulled down his jeans and pants, undid his own and, uninvited, thrust himself inside. Though out of self-interest as well as concern for Christopher he did anoint himself with spittle first.

Afterwards Christopher dissolved in a flood of noisy tears. It was not any pain that made him cry; that had been slight and felt only briefly by someone as drunk as Christopher was; it was shock and dismay at the whole situation – which seemed to be a collapse of everything at once: relationship with Tom, his own poise and self-esteem, that new experience of meeting people like themselves here in Boulogne that had stiffened his spine and given him a new sense of his own identity and worth. I know nothing about myself, he thought. Less even than I imagined I did before I came here. I am a child and a fool. Then he realised that Tom had subsided on top of him, was frantically starting to caress his hair, his shoulders and even his ears – everything, in fact, that was within his reach. And Tom was crying too. Between great heaves of breath and spasms of tears that could not be identified by either of them as coming from the other or himself, Christopher heard Tom say, 'I'm sorry, I'm sorry. My Christopher. I love you so much.'

Christopher found himself unexpectedly trying to comfort Tom, twisting round to touch the man whose last few words had propelled him like rockets from an abyss of despair into a stratospheric happiness he'd never even guessed before. He said, 'It was my fault. I was an idiot. I love you. With all my soul.'

'Do you? Can you? After … after that? I promise you I've never behaved like that before. Done that with a boy, yes – a man rather – at Oxford twice, but not hard like that, not in anger…'

'Sometimes we behave out of character.' For a moment Christopher became the adult of the two. 'I did in the bar just now. Too many new sensations, new ideas. All got me confused.' With an effort he twisted himself right round underneath Tom. He was feeling almost his normal self again when he said, 'I'm going to be OK, though. OK with you, I mean.'

'I'll have to go and find Michel and apologise,' Tom said in the morning, before they were even out of bed. Christopher didn't try to persuade him otherwise. Though he didn't say this out loud either, he too thought it would be a good idea. They steadied their heads and stomachs with croissants and bowls of coffee and chicory which steamed. The mynah bird, for once in tune with the prevailing mood, said, *'Ça fait du bien, et ben oui, ça fait du bien.'* Does you good, oh yes it does. Does you good.

Tom found Michel at his studio on the corner the Rue Faidherbe made with Rue Hamy. He came down to the door in dressing-gown and bare feet. When he saw Tom he gave a shy grin – perhaps he felt apprehensive and wanted to disarm him – which made things suddenly easier. 'I'm really sorry about last night,' Tom said gently. 'Shouting, making a scene. It wasn't necessary. We'd had a bit too much to drink.'

'We all had. I have to say sorry too. Your friend Christopher's extraordinarily beautiful. I shouldn't have started flirting with him. Let myself get carried away.' His face took on an anxious look. 'Things are OK between you, I hope? You didn't let it become a drama?'

A smile that he had no control of appeared like magic on Tom's face. It was one of the broadest that had ever been there. 'Far from it. We were friends again by the time we got home,' which was not exactly true, 'and after that, well, that was the best thing ever.' Which was.

'Sometimes it's like that,' said Michel, though he was neither older than Tom nor better versed in the ways of love. 'You have a row, you make up, and you're the better for it.'

'But it was better than that even. You know that moment when for the first time you both say, *Je t'aime*? Well…'

Michel did know, but he didn't need to say so. Spontaneously they fell into an embrace, out on the pavement, with Michel in nothing but his dressing-gown, and now it was Tom's turn to feel the full sexual radiance of Michel beamed towards him. Felt something else too, in the more tactile meaning of the verb, just as Christopher had done just hours earlier. In their surprise they stayed clinched together for perhaps a minute, though both were morning-careful not to let their hands wander. It was Tom who broke the embrace at last, gently and a bit reluctantly. *'Soyons sage,'* he said. Let's be sensible. 'I came to put things right, not have them all go wrong again.'

'You're right, of course,' said Michel, and laughed. 'But you're a handsome boy too, you know. *Un vrai beaugosse.*'

Tom batted back the compliment to Michel. It was impossible not to, and it had the extra force of being true. They made their polite noises of departure, or rather said, see you later, with a last rendezvous in Le Chat qui Pêche fixed for the evening. Then Michel said, 'Somebody waved to me just now. Or waved to you, to your back. A kid or young teenager in the back of a car. A British car heading down to the port. Do you know anyone like that here?'

'*Merde,*' said Tom. '*Merde, merde, merde!*'

Tom found himself in a quandary. Christopher would need to know exactly what Dexter had seen in order to be ready for anything he might say or do once they were all back at school together. But after the fuss he'd made with Christopher and Michel the previous night he was loth to divulge the details of the scene. Described to Christopher it would appear much less innocent than if Christopher had witnessed it in person. He turned this over as he walked back to the hotel, finally making up his mind to say nothing to Christopher for the moment but to bring the subject up lightly, almost as a joke, when the four of them were together again that evening. In company together the situation could be seen in an unthreatening light – Tom counted particularly on Armand here, remembering how relaxed he'd been about the little episode last night. So Christopher would understand that nothing incorrect had happened but still have time to prepare himself should Dexter have the bad taste to bring up the subject with either of them or – at this thought a cold trickle of fear ran down Tom's spine like a melting icicle – spread it around the school.

The sky was a transparent blue and the sun hot as they lazed on the beach that morning. They heard the siren of the eleven o'clock ferry announcing its departure and a little later saw it, half hidden by the struts and walkway of the long jetty, making its serene progress between the port and the open sea, taking the Dexter family with it. Christopher said nothing to suggest that he remembered they were on board the ship while Tom, who remembered few things more clearly right now, did not see any good reason to remind him just yet.

At midday they made their way back to the Rue Faidherbe and the café where they had first met Armand and had lunch the last two days. They were startled and dismayed – taking it almost as a personal affront – to find the premises shuttered with an iron grille and padlocked. Then they saw a folded piece of paper Scotch-taped to the grille on which was written both their names. Mollified, they read the note.

Forgot to say you Monday is closed all day. We dine together? Chez Alfred, Place Dalton coin Rue des Pipots. After at the Cat who Sins. Meet first in bar next Chez Alfred. Seven a-clock is good? Bisous, Armand et Michel

As they turned around themselves, eyes scanning the street for an alternative lunch spot, one that *was* open on a Monday, they heard a male voice calling Tom's name: 'Sanders, Sanders.' Their eyes focused on a bearded man facing them across the road. 'Oh Lord,' said Tom, 'It's the drunk monk.'

The man crossed the street towards them. 'Saw you at Mass yesterday in the basilica. People say cathedral, but it isn't one, you know. Hasn't had a consecrated bishop since before the revolution. No *cathedra* in it, you may have noticed. No bishop's chair.' Rapidly he looked Christopher up and down then turned back to Tom. 'This your young lad, is he? Very brave of you, I must say, flaunting him round the Continent like that. Very Paul Verlaine and Arthur Rimbaud. When I saw you at Mass

I couldn't quite place your face, though I remembered it well. Then it all came back.'

'Hang on, hang on,' said Tom. 'All what came back?'

'I'm sorry. You must forgive me. I shouldn't be nosey. But gossip is at a premium here. I have only the old Benedictine grapevine to fall back on. I'd heard you went to teach at Bellhurst but left under a ... well, you know what I mean. And I may have jumped to conclusions but I presumed this,' he gestured towards Christopher, 'was the boy, though perhaps I should say young man.'

'I think you've jumped to very much the wrong conclusion,' said Tom, with a cold brittleness in his voice that Christopher hadn't heard before. 'Yes, I did teach at Bellhurst for a time, but now I'm at Our Lady, Star of the Sea, the prep school for St Aidan's Abbey. Meet my fellow-teacher Christopher McGing. And you can call me Tom.'

The drunk monk looked wildly into both their faces for a second, then a calmer look came into his eyes. 'I'm very sorry, gentlemen. It appears I've made a dreadful gaffe. I think the best thing I could do is offer to stand you both a drink.' He looked up the street. 'I found one open just up there. Please call me Martin, by the way.' A little stiffly they all shook hands.

You could manage to see people in a different light, find them less threatening, Tom decided, when you'd drunk a glass of wine with them, especially one that they'd paid for. Nevertheless he thought it prudent to drag Christopher away from their new drinking companion when the second set of wine-glasses had been drained and Martin was offering them a third in what looked like becoming, for him at any rate, a long afternoon's journey into oblivion.

'It can't be much of a life,' Christopher said after they'd left the bar and were looking around for something solid to put into their stomachs, a sandwich perhaps, or a bowl of chips. 'I mean it sounds dead romantic on the face of it, roaming the Continent with the woman you love, rootless, teaching a bit of English for a bit of cash when the bar bills are called in, but it wouldn't be really, would it?'

'No,' Tom said. He was impressed at how neatly, and how promptly, Christopher had summed up Martin's situation. Even though Martin had referred to the woman they'd seen him with as his sister, it was clear that they weren't expected to believe him. They were expected to see through it, in fact. None of them had mentioned the fact that they'd been in the same bar a couple of nights before, it was easier not to.

Christopher said, 'The so-called sister. Do you suppose that's sister as in religious sister – nun?'

'I suppose she could be both. I mean, blood relation as well as a nun – some monks and priests do have sisters who're nuns, religion seems to run in families – but I reckon she's his common-law wife, ex-nun or not.'

'I agree.'

Christopher had managed to see everything else about Martin so clearly, that Tom wondered what he had made of his mangled version of the story of himself and David at Bellhurst. Tom did mean to tell Christopher about that one day, but he wasn't sure when that day would be. Fortunately Martin, despite his drink-sodden condition, had understood the magnitude of his original gaffe and not returned to the subject over their two glasses of wine. Whether that understanding would have survived many more glasses Tom wasn't sure, and that was the main reason he'd dragged Christopher away. Even so, Christopher might very well tackle Tom at some point about Martin's odd misunderstanding of their situation and of who he thought Christopher was, and throughout the afternoon Tom half expected him to, though he didn't. And he was also all the time conscious that there was something else he needed to explain.

Christopher and Tom, Armand and Michel had an early evening beer, as arranged, outside one of the grand, chrome and plate-glass *brasserie* bars in the Place Dalton, looking across at the church of St Nicolas in the centre of the square. When it was time to eat they had only thirty steps to take to reach the restaurant Chez Alfred on the corner. Christopher and Armand walked three or four paces in front, but it was not quite far enough to prevent Christopher hearing Michel say *sotto voce* to Tom, 'Is that going to be awkward for you, that kid this morning?' And to hear Tom reply equally quietly, 'Not if we play it right. But go carefully, I haven't told Christopher yet.'

Christopher very naturally spun round and asked, 'Told me about what? What kid?' Tom explained, more or less. Christopher said he thought no possible harm could come from Dexter's having seen Tom in conversation with a young Frenchman in the street.

Tom looked uncomfortable. After shooting a glance at Michel, he said, 'It was a bit … well, Dexter might have thought he saw something he didn't. And I was going to tell you this anyway. Michel and I made up our argument with a hug on the pavement. Just a friendly hug. Young Dexter, not knowing the situation, might have made something else out of it altogether. That's all. But we need to be ready for Dexter when we get back to England.' Beside him, Michel nodded his support.

Christopher felt dizzy. Wine at lunchtime, now the first beer of the evening. Perhaps that was it. Dizzy, but angry too. 'You're the limit, Tom! You make a big scene last night because I give Michel a friendly kiss, but then, when you're apologising to Michel for over-reacting you do exactly the same thing, only not in the privacy of a bar full of … like-minded people but in the street, where you were spotted by a boy, a prefect, from the school where we both teach!'

'Go easy,' Tom told him and tried to reach out to touch him, but Christopher flinched away. Michel had the unhappy look of someone who would like to smooth things out but knows that if he tries he will only iron the creases in. It was Armand who said, 'I'll talk to Christopher. See you in the restaurant.' He put an arm lightly round Christopher's shoulder and when that was not shrugged off, dismissed the older two with a nod of his head, turned Christopher round and walked him into the nearest alley.

With a hand on each shoulder Armand turned Christopher to face him. *'Mon vieux, qu'est-ce que tu as?'*

'I'm sorry, Armand. *Pardonne-moi.* I'm behaving like an idiot.'

'No, really, you do not.'

'He's three years older. To the day. I feel so young sometimes. And stupid.' Involuntarily Christopher screwed up his face.

'Moi aussi. Il a quel âge, Tom?' Armand asked.

'Vingt-et-un.'

'And you ?'

'Eighteen.' In his agitation Christopher couldn't remember it in French.

'Comme Michel et moi. C'est exactement pareil. Just the same. I have eighteen, Michel twenty-two. So I feel young and stupid sometimes with Michel. You, me, we're the same. *On est dans le même bain.* And sometimes they like us because that. It is not all bad news.' Armand smiled encouragingly.

'There's something else. It's not just that he hugged – embraced – Michel in the street and the wrong person saw him.' (Armand, whose hands had been grasping

Christopher's shoulders up till now, at this point let them fall to his sides.) 'Today I learned – discovered – there was someone else before. Another boy.'

'Always there is someone before if you have *un amant plus âgé que toi. Ne t'en fais pas.* Michel had many before me.'

'Tom too. Even me. I had two affairs with boys at school. But I think this last one of Tom's was different. It was a boy in the school where he worked as a teacher before this term. Tom had to leave the school because of him.'

'Et ça, tu l'as découvert aujourd'hui? Comment?'

'We met someone in a bar by chance – *par hasard* – who knew Tom at school. It doesn't matter. He said something by accident, then realised he'd made a gaffe. Oh, what's French for gaffe?'

'Gaffe. You love Tom?'

'Yes.'

'Et lui? He love you?'

'Last night he said for the first time, I love you. I wanted to say it weeks before but stopped myself.'

'Then Tom also want to say it weeks before. *Tu t'inquiètes* – you are worry – for nothing. Tom love you, then the past, it finish.'

'But it's such a recent past. Just months ago. Just weeks ago, perhaps.'

'One day he tell you the *histoire*, when he want to. But you are worry for nothing. You are sad … no, not sad…'

'Upset?'

'Peut-être – but only because you fall in love. But he with you too. Every people can see. *Allons-y.* We go *rejoindre* Tom and Michel. All will be happy. All will be good.'

Christopher doubted this. But Armand, who must have been a month, or a week or two, ahead of Christopher on his journey into first love, was right. When they pushed open the door of the restaurant Chez Alfred, there facing them across the busy, suddenly bright little room were Tom and Michel, sitting at a table for four which was already set with a carafe of red wine and an optimistic four glasses. Michel looked happy to see them arrive, but the expression that appeared on Tom's face on seeing a tentatively smiling Christopher was in the nature of a transfiguration – lit up by a radiance that Christopher had nowhere before seen.

***

From John Moyse's New Journal

Whitsun is special somehow. I never noticed this before. Because it's so short, I suppose. Not like Easter and Christmas which go on for weeks. When you get home the garden's unrecogniseable, all green and everything grown sky-high. And the weather is very warm but still fresh. Meals outdoors, and things that never tasted good before, like gooseberry tart are suddenly magically good. Especially with double thick cream and not custard. The birds begin to stop singing, though they still do. But the cuckoo goes on, and on, and on, just like in the rhyme.

I played the last movement of the Moonlight Sonata and it seemed to go quite well. Of course my father wanted to know why I didn't play the first movement – like everyone else does. I said that's why: because everyone else does.

Watched the Dam Busters on TV. It's a cracking film.

TWELVE

The weather for their return trip was exceptionally fine and clear. So that the magical point at which both sides of the Channel, both sets of white cliffs, are equally near at hand seemed for Tom and Christopher to extend in a time-bending manner. This was only partly a consequence of the slow nature of Channel ferry crossings in general. Though it seemed too obvious to mention, both of them were conscious of the symbolic nature of the moment, as they stood on deck, jackets and trousers flapping, the midday, midsummer sun lighting Cap Blanc Nez and Shakespeare Cliff with fierce impartiality. They stood poised between two existences, in two quite different worlds.

They hadn't looked for such an epiphany. They had set off to France in the simple expectation of a cheap weekend somewhere new, somewhere they could be themselves and go unrecognised. Well, in that last detail they had been wrong: they'd been recognised by more than one person, and on one of those occasions in embarrassing circumstances. But things had turned out surprisingly on a broader front too. They were returning with new knowledge. They were two homosexual men. They were in love. Now they would always compare the life they were returning to – a life spent concealing their true natures and their relationship against the drab background of a religious boarding school – with a completely different existence: one in which men could kiss in the street, could make friends with, and be supported by, other male couples; and where a small and unpretentious coastal town could have a bar catering very largely for people like themselves. All this was just thirty miles away – and the two sides could see each other's lighted windows at night.

Neither of them wanted the crossing to end. The walls of England and France appeared to rise and fall slightly as the resistance of the calm water regularly lifted the ship's bows, in the comfortable slow rhythm of someone breathing in their sleep.

Both were happy. They might regret their destination and compare it unfavourably with the place they had just left. But they knew they would share its deprivations together. Just as they would share a narrow bed that night. And the next night. And, as far as they knew, for ever after that. There remained the gnawing anxiety caused by the need to deal with Dexter. But together they would find a way to overcome even that.

'How was France?' Roger asked as he pulled their pints of Tankard. It was oddly different being back in an English bar after seeing the inside of so many French ones. You saw everything through eyes that had been somehow re-focused, heard the pub's bustle with differently adjusted ears.

'We had a good time,' said Tom, cautiously understating things.

'I can imagine you did,' said Roger, casting a shrewd eye over the two of them and filling out Tom's brief answer quite correctly in his own head.

'Everything's so different.' Christopher couldn't stop himself; unlike Tom, couldn't be circumspect. 'We found a bar … well, a special kind of bar… Do you know Boulogne?'

'Been over a couple of times.' Roger's eyes twinkled his amusement. 'What kind of bar were you telling me about?'

'Don't tease him,' said Tom. 'You know exactly what he means.'

Roger laughed. 'I suppose I do. I'm only a bit disappointed we've never found it when we've been to

Boulogne.' Roger had to break off to serve someone else, while Tom laid coins on the counter in payment for the two pints. That was another odd thing about coming back. You had to pay for each drink in advance, before you even took a sip out of it.

Later Roger found a moment to join them as they sat in the garden, nursing their drinks. 'Never a very busy evening, the Tuesday after a bank holiday. You should have seen it last night.' He cast his eyes up. 'The Whit-Monday hordes. But you were telling me about Boulogne.'

Tom, a bit more relaxed out here in the garden and after half a pint of beer, told Roger they'd stayed in a hotel run by two young men and mentioned that they'd made friends with 'another pair of young lads,' one a waiter, the other a painter who had the lucky backstop of being the heir to an ironmongery business.

Roger took a sip from his own pint mug, which he'd had the forethought to bring out with him, and said, 'I sometimes imagine Malcolm and me running this place together. It'd be OK in London perhaps, or one of the other big cities. But here… You can't tell how people would react. You could lose customers, see the business go under, be hounded out…'

'Do you suppose that'll ever change?' Christopher asked.

'There was this thing called the Wolfenden Report a few years ago. Have you heard about that?' Although Tom nodded, Christopher shook his head. 'Well, it was pretty sympathetic. Some people say it might help to get the law changed here. But that'd take years and even changing the law would only be the first thing. Changing people's attitudes… Well, I don't know. That might take a generation.' He gave them each a mock serious stare. 'To say nothing of the organisation you two work for. I mean the Holy Roman Church. The Roman Empire of the mind. Look, got to go.' Roger stood up. 'Glasses to collect, customers to serve. Malcolm'll be about on Friday night if you want to drop by and say hallo.'

In recounting the story of their weekend to Roger they had been careful – even Christopher had been – not to include the stories of the two surprise encounters that had played a major part in it. Both had good reason not to drag up memories of what the drunk monk had accidentally let out of the bag, and as for the Dexter problem, that had been dealt with, quickly and masterfully, by Tom, almost as soon as they were back in the building and before it could even become a problem.

Dexter was one of those boys whose parents brought him to school by car at the end of half-terms and holidays. Tom thought this was fortunate. Had he been one of the horde that arrived from London on the train no end of damage might have been done on the journey. For all the discretion and aloofness from common gossip that his prefect status demanded, Dexter was only thirteen after all – and only human. So Tom made a point of coincidentally appearing in the main cloister, ostensibly in a hurry to be importantly somewhere else, during the two-seconds' gap between the boy's farewells to his parents – Tom did *not* want to get into another round of hand-shaking and small talk with Mr Stephen and Mrs Artemia Dexter just two days after the last one – and his sprinting away to join his friends and perhaps imparting his astonishing news about Tom and Christopher being together in Boulogne, to say nothing of Tom embracing a young male stranger in the street.

'Dexter,' Tom said, in his cricket-umpire voice.

'Sir.' Dexter turned towards Tom and stood to attention, though without actually saluting.

'My cousin spotted you in Boulogne yesterday, Dexter.'

'Your cousin, sir?'

'I have a cousin who teaches English in Boulogne. He spotted you waving from your parents' car window. My back was turned or I would have returned your greeting. And talking of greetings, you might have been surprised to know that men kiss their male cousins in France, even when both of them happen to be English. Or did you know that already, Dexter?'

'I knew that already, sir. It's the same in Italy, sir. He doesn't wear many clothes, your cousin.'

'Unlike you and me, Dexter, who observe school hours and get up early, my cousin teaches in the afternoons and evenings, to business people mainly, after they finish work. For him ten o'clock in the morning is rather early to be up and dressed.'

'I see, sir. Did you and Mr McGing have a good weekend in Boulogne, sir?'

'Very good, thank you. You seem to have enjoyed yours as well. Your face is two shades browner with the sun.'

'Thank you very much, sir.' Dexter knew when a conversation had been wound up. He didn't skid away round the corner as the younger boys did, but nodded fractionally and walked away with the dignity expected of a member of Lower Four who was also a prefect and a house captain, as though he too had to be, importantly, somewhere else.

Tom had never told an outright lie to a child before – though whether Dexter still counted as a child was debatable. Well, he'd never woven such an elaborate tapestry of falsehoods for anyone. He felt a sense of shame at having done so. But he told himself that, bearing in mind his responsibility towards Christopher as well as the need to safeguard his own interests, he'd had no alternative. And the sense of relief from anxiety and doubt that this satisfactory encounter gave him was transformed, once he'd told the story to Christopher and seen his lovely face irradiated by the good news, to elation.

Christopher, calmly confident in his classroom the next morning, the strict though just master, omniscient, impartial, yet sufficiently sure of his authority to remain friendly, found himself marvelling at the fact that he was the same person who, in France, had groped a near stranger in a louche bar, had shed lover's tears, tears of shame, of rage and of reconciliation, and that he had let himself be penetrated by Tom, himself in a lather of anger at the time, in an undignified heap on a hotel bed. 'Collinson,' he said, in a voice that was firm and which threatened to turn severe at the mere thought on Collinson's part of backchat, 'the answer is not to be found outside the window. Apply yourself to the problem in hand. It's long multiplication you need, not long stares into the middle distance.' He'd learned this manner of speaking from Tom. It always went down well. He'd even learned from Tom how to end the unproductive little dialogue – 'Lloyd-Williams, what are you laughing at?' 'Nothing, sir,' – with the line that Tom had learned from one of his own teachers when he'd been a pupil here. 'There's a place near Canterbury for people who laugh at nothing.' The place, as the boys knew full well, was Chartham, the local lunatic asylum.

The weekend just past now seemed most improbable, France weird and a million miles away. Yet only last night, a few hours after their return from the continent, and immediately on their return from the Admiral Digby, Tom had submitted to being fucked, face down on his narrow bed, his legs spread helpfully and his rump ever so slightly raised, offering the initiate a guiding hand at the beginning, as Christopher went through this particular – and in the end most enjoyable – rite of passage into homosexual manhood. That had been real enough, the real Christopher in love with the man he was fucking... The class tittered softly at the coded reference to Chartham, like a sauce gently bubbling on just the right application of heat, and Collinson, with a grin but no backchat, got back to his arithmetic.

Tom and Christopher were on their way to the television room, after staff supper, to watch Doctor Kildare. Even before they got there they could hear the sound of the piano in the assembly hall beyond being played rather well. 'Father Claude?' Christopher said, with a puzzled look at Tom. Father Claude had usually cycled back to the abbey by five o'clock. It was unlikely that today was an exception, since he hadn't been at supper.

The piece, whatever it was, came to an end. Tom opened the door a couple of inches and peered through. The pianist was not Father Claude but John Moyse. Something made Tom look round into the back of the hall. Moyse was not alone but had an audience: an audience of one, who was Angelo Dexter.

'Good, isn't he, sir?' said Dexter, not at all put out by the intrusion, and his calmness seemed to spread to Moyse, who had startled slightly on seeing the door opening but now sat blithely on the piano stool with a look on his face that suggested that further compliments would not be rebuffed.

'Yes he certainly is,' Tom said, and Christopher, walking further into the room, asked, 'What was that? It sounded familiar but...'

Moyse answered from his temporary throne. 'It's the middle movement of the Moonlight Sonata. – Beethoven,' he added helpfully.

Dexter said, 'He's learning it backwards. Like a Black Mass. Very perverse, I call it. Still, it was Father Claude's idea, not his. He's saving the easy first movement till last. You can't help some people, can you?' Dexter rolled his large eyes. 'Some people like to do everything the wrong way round. Or do I mean, simply the other way?'

'If you don't know what you mean, young man, don't ask me to try and help,' said Tom, and smiled to show that this was a joke. 'I think we'll leave you in peace now.' He turned back to John Moyse. 'Seriously, I'd no idea you were so good.'

Christopher added, 'Not just a writer with a future but a pianist as well.'

Moyse grinned rather extravagantly and said, 'Thank you, sir,' while Dexter added, 'Rachmaninoff and P.G. Wodehouse rolled into one. Can't do much better than that.' Tom and Christopher withdrew behind the door and shut it after them. Almost immediately they heard the piano start up again. Not, this time the gentle canter of The Moonlight's central *allegretto* but the furious gallop of its *presto* finale, as Moyse spurred it up and onward with great brio and only a dusting of wrong notes.

It was Christopher and Tom's turn to be startled as they turned back into the television room to find themselves nose to nose and eyeball to eyeball with Father Louis, who had also been drawn by the music to the assembly hall door. 'Who's that in there?' Father Louis demanded. 'Playing the grand piano, and after Night Prayers too.'

'It's John Moyse,' Christopher told him. He could hardly have withheld the information, as Father Louis had only to reach out and open the door again to see for himself, though he hadn't intended the boy's Christian name to pop out the way it had.

Father Louis hesitated a moment, on the brink of opening the door, but listening to the music at the same time. He began to frown, but then his eyebrows went up and his eyes opened quite wide. 'He's awfully good, don't you think?' He paused another second. 'Did you tell him he really shouldn't be in there at this time of evening, and certainly not using the assembly hall piano for his practice?'

'No,' said Tom, without elaboration.

'I think perhaps that was as well.' Father Louis nodded his head, minimally and in slow motion. 'Sometimes one has to make exceptions to rules. I'd heard Moyse was talented; I'd no idea he was as good as that. Perhaps we should all tiptoe away and let him finish his practice in peace, eh?'

'I don't think it's practice, exactly,' Christopher said, jumping in, only seeing Tom's warning glance a split second too late. 'I think it's more in the way of a performance.'

Father Louis might have reflected that whereas music practice tends to be a solitary activity, the idea of performance usually involves the existence of an audience, and then have wondered who, in this instance, the audience might be. If he did, he chose not to pursue the line of thought. Instead, he said to Christopher, 'I mentioned you at the decanal meeting earlier this week. I told the abbot and the other deans that I had a potential candidate for the priesthood under my roof, and about the wishes of your uncle, Canon McGing.' Father Louis treated Christopher to a truly terrifying smile. 'They wished me luck in encouraging you along what is – as they all well know – a more than arduous path.' He grunted. 'I tell you this for what it's worth, anyway.' Then he turned to Tom. 'I haven't yet shared with them my feeling that you would be a potential headmaster here in years to come: a possible successor to me when the time is right. I feel that, when it comes to bringing you to their attention the time also needs to be right. Slowly, slowly... But I am impressed, so far, with both of you. I'm neither as deaf as a post nor as blind as a bat, and I hear good reports from all sides. I've sampled homework from both your classes and found it well executed and fairly and accurately marked.' He grinned suddenly, in a way that threatened to tear his head in two. 'Anyway, I'll leave you in peace now. You'll be missing Doctor Kildare.' On the other side of the door the Moonlight Sonata's *presto agitato* galloped to its breakneck halt, punctuated with its two final, peremptory, hoof-stamps.

The David and Jonathan picture was finished. Tom and Christopher had sat for Miss O'Deere a total of five times in the weeks before half-term, and been mesmerised by the picture's progress. Miss O'Deere had painstakingly applied layer upon layer of paint, lighter flesh tones each time, until their two bodies, burnished and high-lit, positively sprang out of the canvas towards the viewer, while behind them the background of cricket field, pavilion, distant match in progress and surrounding trees grew ever more three-dimensional as Miss O'Deere's brushes worked their magic and made the distances recede. Completed in their absence over the half-term weekend and unveiled shyly for them on their return by its creator, the portrait looked stunning. They told her so. She had nothing to be shy about, they said. Quite the reverse.

Miss O'Deere was relieved and delighted. 'I like to think it captures the spirit of friendship, a friendship which is pure and good, one that has nothing in it of ... oh how I hate to use the word but these days everyone does ... of a sexual nature. If there is anything that is good in this picture, then it is that: a portrait of fine feelings. And now I sound pretentious and silly.' She laughed.

Tom assured her she did not sound pretentious and silly at all, but neither he nor Christopher was able to pick up the baton of her previous remark. They found themselves struggling not to exchange glances. Because what was most apparent to them, even more than the fact that the portrait made them both look very beautiful indeed, was that, despite Miss O'Deere's stated intentions, her canvas seemed vibrant with sex and charged with erotic power. You felt that if you reached out and placed one hand on David and the other on Jonathan the electric current that came surging through your heart would be too much for it to bear.

They talked about this afterwards. They agreed that it looked like a portrait of two very young men in love. Even if Miss O'Deere could not, or would not see it that way, it was obvious to them. They were secretly delighted by that. It would be their very private secret, unsuspected by anyone else who might see the painting. 'Like the picture of Dorian Gray in the book,' Tom said.

Christopher didn't like the analogy. 'But that got old and horrible as Dorian pursued his life of debauchery. I don't want our story to end like his.'

'Well, all right,' Tom conceded. 'It's not really like the Dorian Gray thing. I just meant that it's a picture concealing a secret. Ours.' Christopher accepted that.

The following day Miss O'Deere waylaid Tom in a quiet bit of cloister and told him, her voice coloured equally by excitement and nervous dread, that the picture had been sent off to be assessed as a possible entry in the summer exhibition of the East Kent Arts Society. If accepted it would hang on public view in the chapter house of Canterbury Cathedral. It might actually attract a buyer – not that Miss O'Deere was looking that far ahead, or thinking in such mercenary terms. 'I didn't tell you all this yesterday,' she added. 'I hadn't quite made up my mind to submit it. I wanted to see your reaction, and Christopher's, to the finished work. But you were both so positive about it, and that gave me the heart to go ahead. I hope you'll think I did the right thing.'

'Of course you did, of course you did,' Tom told her. He could hardly have said anything else. But privately he was less sure. And when he passed this news on to Christopher, his lover shared his apprehension. Memories of the perilously close encounter with Dexter in Boulogne were still fresh and raw, and if the explosive charge of Dexter's own memories had been to some extent defused by Tom's quick thinking, the memories themselves had not been brainwashed away. The two young men began to feel less secure in their conviction that the secret of the painting was safe: that the hidden code of the David and Jonathan portrait could not be cracked.

Thousands of people would pass through the exhibition in Canterbury Cathedral. Might Dexter's parents be among them? They might not be interested in art at all, but they lived at Headcorn, which was not a million miles from Canterbury. More like twenty. And what about Angelo himself? If the picture did get accepted, Miss O'Deere, for all her modesty, would be unlikely to say nothing about her achievement to the pupils she taught. She wouldn't hide her light under a bushel measure. No-one would. She'd want to take a party of boys to see it: in all probability senior boys rather than juniors, and the two house captains would certainly be included.

Then what of those other thousands of visitors? Not everyone in the country led as sheltered a life as Miss O'Deere's or was as innocent (?!) as a schoolboy. Miss O'Deere had said, with a slight tremor, that not only would the local press be invited to criticise the exhibits but representatives from the national papers too. Professional art critics, Christopher and Tom knew, were not naïve. They saw through layers of meaning in works of art, stripping them bare as easily as other people pulled petals from artichokes, to find the bristling choke and the tender heart beneath. Tom and Christopher found themselves hoping, though regretting this as a piece of covert disloyalty to Miss O'Deere, that the picture would be found wanting by the Arts Society judges and so not find its way to public display in such a prominent place as the principal ecclesiastical building of the realm.

The physicality of Malcolm, seen close at hand, was something quite special, Christopher thought for the first time, sitting in the pub garden with him – and Tom of course – on Friday night. Perhaps it was because it was the first time that just the three of them had had a conversation together, without Roger, who right now was unavoidably detained indoors serving his customers alongside his other staff. Compared to the trim muscularity of Tom, or his own bantam build, Malcolm's frame was quite farmer-like in its robustness. Building boats was no doubt a physically demanding occupation. He wasn't conventionally handsome, but his perennially mischievous expression lent something extra to his snub-nosed, brown-eyed, freckled face. His red hair had recently been cut. It was no longer a thicket of copper curls but bristled like a scrubbing-brush, or the mane of a hedgehog. All this Christopher found himself taking in as Tom recounted the latest developments in the story of the David and Jonathan picture.

Malcolm thought it was very funny, promised to go and see the picture in Canterbury Cathedral if it made it that far, but was sure they had nothing to worry about. Tom and Christopher might see their relationship captured in the picture but nobody else would.

'You haven't seen the picture,' Tom told him. 'You might think differently if you had.'

'Well, even if,' Malcolm said. 'Suppose people thought the picture showed David and Jonathan as two homosexual men, that wouldn't mean that the same went for the two sitters. Be reasonable. It's not going to have your names written on it, is it?'

'No, it isn't,' said Tom. 'Although there are plenty of people who'd know who were are, if it came to it. Our current employers for a start. But I'm sure you're right. It's just that nothing seems to be quite reasonable at the moment.' Tom told Malcolm about the headmaster's *idées fixes* that Tom should succeed him as head of Star of the Sea while Christopher become a priest. 'I'm afraid he appears to be losing it. Please don't tell anyone else, though. It's supposed to be a well-kept secret.'

Malcolm promised not to pass on this parcel of news, while Christopher wondered whether falling headlong in love always, automatically, meant that you started fancying your other friends too. 'I still don't get,' Malcolm branched sideways, giving Christopher the earnest look of a seeker after important knowledge, 'what is the difference between a monk and a priest. In your church, I mean.'

'Easy.' Christopher was eager to answer. 'A monk is someone who lives in a monastery and devotes his whole life to God through prayer and work. Some monks are priests as well, usually the better-educated ones. And priests are simply Catholic vicars or parsons. At the abbey probably half the monks are priests and half are not; they're called lay brothers. All the ones who teach at Star of the Sea are priests.'

'OK then,' Malcolm pursued him with a smile. 'Monastery and abbey. Enlighten me.'

'It's kind of the same answer. All abbeys are monasteries, not all monasteries are abbeys. It depends on the title of the head of the house. If he's an abbot his monastery gets called an abbey, if he's a prior then it's a priory. Usually abbeys are bigger than priories but not always. Our one along the coast here has an abbot and a prior, apparently – neither of whom we've met. The prior in this case is simply the abbot's second-in-command.'

'So if you did become a priest,' Malcolm said slowly, leaning towards him, grinning, 'how long would it be before you became prior?'

Tom answered. 'About a hundred and twenty years, I imagine. But I think I can promise he's not going to go along that road.' He turned to Christopher. 'Hmm?'

'I should hope not,' Malcolm said to Tom. 'With looks like he's got. Aren't you the lucky one?' Before Tom could decide whether this was a charming remark or whether Malcolm needed to be told where he got off, Malcolm added, 'We're taking the boat out for a bit of a sail on Sunday. Want to come along?'

***

From John Moyse's New Journal

The second movement of the Moonlight is jolly good. In the middle section there's a beat that's just off the beat. It's like the pendulum of a clock that you're carrying. It sways about just a little unexpectedly, a sort of lolloping lurch, however carefully you're carrying it. You can hear a dog's heart doing that sometimes if you're playing with it and are up close. I suppose it'll be the same one day when I have a girlfriend.

I played the second and third movements to Angelo. He liked it. Funny how we seem to be becoming friends now. We've always been friendly, but that's not the same. It's funny in two ways, because it's really only been since that day I bowled him out in the cricket match that it's happened, and you'd expect the opposite really: viz: that he'd be furious with me. Also funny because everyone knows who his real best friend is.

He – I mean Angelo – told me he'd seen Tom and Christopher together in Bouloygne at halfterm, which is interesting. You forget sometimes that teachers need friends too. Like Mr Appleton did, but he made bad choices and look what happened to him. Still, we've got Christopher instead, so it's an ill wind that blows nobody any good. I was wrong about Christopher at the beginning of term, to think he was all dead serious and no fun. Actually he's great.

THIRTEEN

Father Louis said Mass on Sunday morning. His sermons were always rather grimmer than Father Matthew's but, on average, two minutes shorter. What you lost on the swings...

When the time for the sermon arrived Father Louis moved to his usual place at the gap in the middle of the altar rail, on the low step, and waited, face immobile, severe, his arms folded beneath his green chasuble, until the stillness in the chapel was so absolute that you could hear the dust fall. Then he removed his right hand from under the vestment and made the sign of the cross with it.

'In the name of the Father, and of the Son, and of the Holy Ghost,' he began. 'Today is the First Sunday after Pentecost.' He paused. Rather a long pause, and he stared rather strangely into the wall at the back of the chapel. Then he refocused his eyes on his congregation and said, 'The Four Last Things. Death, Judgement, Hell and Heaven. We name them every day of our lives without much thought. The words come to our lips without effort. But what do we really know of them? We talk of the Last Day, the Day of Judgement, the end of the world, the end of time. It seems to us a long, long time away, a very long way into the future. But...' His voice dropped a chilling tri-tone. 'It may be a lot sooner than we think. And what will happen on that day, that Day of Wrath? *Dies Irae, dies illa, solvet saeculum in favilla.* All earthly things dissolve in flame. All earthly things dissolve.

'We know more than this. Just a little. Thanks to the prophetic visions of St John the Divine. We learn from St John – to whom Christ appeared in a vision on the Island of Patmos, and dictated to him seven letters, one to each of the seven churches (we would probably call them dioceses today) that made up the early Christian Church. Christ appeared that time to John as Christ in Majesty, a sight to inspire awe, terror even, because he wanted John to know, and to pass the message on, that on the Last Day He would come not only as Saviour of the world but as a scourge of the wicked: a scourge of those who had turned from His holy way and set themselves on a different path, in opposition to His will. Christ appeared to John amidst seven golden candlesticks, the hair on his head snow white, like wool. His eyes like flaming fire, his feet like molten metal in a crucible. His voice came like the sound of water in deep flood. A sword emerged from his mouth, sharp on both its edges, and his face was like the noonday sun. And what Christ told John was this.'

Tom and Christopher looked at each other. Father Louis's voice, always full of chilly intensity during his sermons, seemed to have reached a new degree of vehemence. It had also risen steadily in pitch and was growing quite loud. Again his eyes seemed to disengage from his audience and to peer into a distance that none but he could see, above their heads at the back. A little uneasy shuffling could be heard among the younger boys at the front. Tom and Christopher shot quick glances sideways at their neighbours – Miss Coyle on Tom's left, Miss O'Deere and Sister on Christopher's right. They all could see apprehension in the others' eyes.

'"I will come like a thief in the night," he told John to write to the Church of Sardis. To Smyrna he was to write, "Do not be afraid of the suffering you are to undergo. The devil will imprison some of you for ten days and you will be sorely tested. But keep faith with me to the point of death and I will give you the crown of life."'

Father Louis drew breath. He drew the air in as though glass fragments laced it. His eyes grew wide, seeing things that his congregation could not. It seemed that he had urgent things to impart… 'To the Church at Ephesus Christ promised the fruit of the tree of life, which grows in Paradise. To the Church at Thayatira, "I know of your faith, your love, your endurance, yet here and there I have fault to find with you. You allow the woman Jezebel to mislead my servants with her teaching. They fall into fornication and eat the food that is sacrificed to false gods. If she will not mend her harlot's ways I have a bed ready to lay her in…"'

'This really isn't suitable,' said Miss O'Deere to Christopher. 'Not suitable at all.'

'"And those who commit adultery with her will be in sore straits if they do not repent their wrong-doing. And her children I will kill outright…"'

'Is there any way we can stop him?' Tom said to Miss Coyle. Several of the senior boys were looking back towards them with anxious faces, looking for guidance from the adults: what to think, what to do.

'If only Father Matthew could be here,' Miss Coyle whispered back to Tom. 'He'd know what to do.'

'Someone must walk up the aisle and stop him,' Tom said. 'Miss O'Deere?' She was the senior person present, but even as Tom spoke her name the question *Who will bell the cat?* went through his mind. And Miss O'Deere, presumably remembering the curious incident of the dog in the chapel, shook her head in a small, sharp movement. 'Sister?'

Tom was going to suggest to her that this was a medical emergency but he didn't have to. Sister was already rising from her seat. She walked across in front of the others and set off, after a quick genuflection in the aisle, towards where Father Louis faced her, his eyes now glazed and fixed on her, the words still tumbling out of his mouth. 'Who will bell the cat?' Tom was startled to hear his own thought spoken aloud, although quietly, by Christopher.

"'I know of thy doings,'" Father Louis was saying, apparently addressing the approaching matron, "'and find thee neither cold nor hot. Being what thou art, lukewarm, thou wilt make me vomit thee out of my mouth.'"

The two house captains and Edward Abelard were now following Sister supportively down the aisle. The juniors in the front rows sat frozen with shock. Sister broke into a run and was in time to catch Father Louis as he began to fall, and Angelo Dexter, who was nearest behind her, helped to take the headmaster's weight and to stop him dragging Sister over on top of him as he went down.

The reason John Moyse was not among the group of senior boys who joined Sister in rushing to Father Louis's aid was that he was serving Father Matthew's Mass at St Ursula's. Directly Mass was over one of the nuns entered the sacristy with the message that Miss Keegan was on the phone, urgently requiring to talk to Father Matthew. It took John Moyse a few seconds to remember that Sister did actually have a name and that Miss Keegan was it.

Father Matthew, still in all his green Mass vestments, was back a minute later. He explained to John that he had to return at once to the school, as Father Louis had been taken ill during the Mass there and was awaiting the arrival of an ambulance. John could either come with Father Matthew and have breakfast at school or stay where he was and enjoy the customary treat for whichever boy served the St Ursula's Sunday Mass: *viz,* (as John himself would have put it) breakfast cooked by the nuns.

John thought about this for a moment. He wasn't quite sure yet which of two kinds of writer he was going to be, the journalist, who deals with things as they happen, or the commentator, who writes after a period of reflection, and with posterity in mind. But he was already too late for a scoop: he was in fact the only one of the hundred and thirteen boys who had not been an eye-witness to whatever had happened in the school chapel. Furthermore, the school Sunday morning offering of greasy bacon, cooked en masse in a rather slow oven, and eggs, which had all been broken into a vast metal tray, then cooked in the same slow oven until they formed a solid mass which had to be cut into squares, each square with an overdone yolk at its centre, bore no comparison with the breakfast the nuns provided for their Sunday chaplain and his server of the day. At St Ursula's John could look forward to an individually fried egg, crisp bacon, with tomato and fried bread. Sometimes a slice of black pudding or a mushroom graced the plate as well. John's moment of uncertainty was a short one. He decided to stay where he was. He could catch up with the news at his leisure later, writing it up in a measured way when the time was right. Ambulance-chasing reportage was not going to be his thing. It was wonderful how a well-cooked breakfast, or even the prospect of one, could impinge upon the future direction of a writer's career.

Miss Coyle had phoned the doctor initially, but he had told her – perhaps because it was Sunday morning – to dial 999. The ambulance arrived at the same moment as Father Matthew returned from St Ursula's, a little breathless after a very fast walk across the grounds. As soon as he had seen the ambulance's doors close on Father Louis, who had been loaded aboard on a stretcher, he went downstairs to supervise the boys' breakfast, jokingly apologising for the fact that the eggs were a little more overdone than usual this morning but hoping that, in the circumstances, he could count on their understanding. As soon as the meal was over he went to the staff dining room and asked if everyone there would mind waiting for him a moment longer, while he telephoned the abbot with the news. From overhead came sounds that indicated that the bed-making and teeth-cleaning rituals which occupied the fifteen minutes between breakfast and dormitory inspection were degenerating into a pillow-fight in dorm five. Sister raised her eyes to the ceiling as she got up, telling Father Matthew that she too would be back in one minute. Thirty seconds after her exit the sudden cessation of sound from above signalled her abrupt arrival in dorm five and the equally abrupt restoration of the *status quo ante*.

The prospect for Tom and Christopher of an afternoon's sailing naturally receded. But not for very long. On his return from the telephone Father Matthew surprised them by remembering, despite the drama of the morning, that they had plans to be out most of the day with friends, and he insisted that they should not cancel their expedition. 'Arrangements with friends have to be respected when humanly possible,' he told them, smiling his understanding. 'Friends are a precious commodity, not to be messed about. Many a good friendship has been ruined by a missed appointment.' Letter writing would be supervised by himself, Miss Coyle and Miss O'Deere between them. There were no other duties to be undertaken today. Today they could stay out as long as they liked. 'But from tomorrow, if the two of you could muck in a bit with dormitory supervision in the evenings, well, that would be much appreciated, since I'll have to do Father Louis's morning rounds till further notice and I wouldn't mind a brief respite in the evenings. But I'll do a quick final round just before lights-out, junior and senior, just in case. If there's any caning to be done I'll do it then.' Clearly he did not want the two young men bestriding the dormitories armed with a gym-shoe apiece. And then he dismissed them all with a calm wave of both hands. Everything was under control, the briefing was over.

Roger drove them to the Orca's mooring at Richborough. They both realised that they hadn't been inside a car for weeks. Again the countryside was wearing a bridal veil of white. Not this time of hawthorn and Queen Anne's lace, but in hanging tangles, pink and white, of briar and eglantine: the wild roses of early summer, the dog roses that gave notice of hot dog days ahead; while the roadside verges overflowed into the roads themselves in waves of tall white flower-heads of cow parsnip, hemlock and wild carrot. The forecast had been good, and proved correct. Bright sun and warmth, a few stray frothy clouds, and just enough wind to make sailing possible.

The tide was exceptionally high. When they had hoist sail and eased their way into the current at the mouth of the Great Stour they could see the marsh grasses and samphire plants barely showing their tips above the inundation of the sea; it was like sailing a channel through a rice paddy. The real sea at last met them with the playful buffet of small waves.

'How much longer do we have the pleasure of your company?' Malcolm suddenly asked, so suddenly that Tom had to ask him what he meant. 'I mean the end of term. What happens then?'

Christopher answered the easy question. 'Twenty-seventh of July. Six or seven weeks away.'

Tom spoke next, before anyone else had a chance. 'Christopher has his place at Oxford waiting for him. I go there too and find a job. Any kind of job, teaching or not. It's only a year since I came down. I still know people there.'

Christopher looked at him, unable for the moment to respond. Neither had broached this subject before now, though thoughts about what would happen when term finished had been reverberating ominously in Christopher's mind like distant thunder. This was his first intimation that Tom had thought about it too. Christopher's face cracked into a smile. 'Yes,' he said bravely, 'we've got it all worked out. We find a way, just like you two've done. You're like our inspiration.' He'd never thought of that before. The words just came to him.

'You'll come back sometimes, I hope,' said Roger. 'Wouldn't like to lose touch.'

'Indeed not,' Tom answered for them both, and Christopher thought that especially he'd want to keep in touch with Malcolm, who was looking stunning today with tanned bare legs, very short shorts and a T-shirt that almost matched his brilliant hair.

A plane was flying in circles overhead, a four-engine passenger plane in BEA livery. Every fifteen minutes or so it overtook them, shortly to turn inland over the low cliffs and disappear. 'It's some sort of training flight they do, isn't it?' said Tom. That's what he'd told Christopher anyway, remembering from his first, schoolboy, time at Star of the Sea.

'Circuits and bumps, they call it,' Roger said. 'Pilot training. Got the longest runway here second only to Heathrow. Practice in landings and take-offs combined is what it is. Or so they tell me. They come into the pub sometimes, trainers and trainees.'

'After they go flying, I hope,' said Christopher facetiously, 'rather than before.'

'You'd be surprised,' said Roger with a straight face. Christopher wasn't always certain when Roger was joking. Next time the plane came over Christopher gave a friendly wave to the crew.

'In case we meet them in the bar some time,' he explained. 'I could say, did they see me waving?' Tom thought: he's still a child in so many ways, and all of them lovely. He leaned forward, enough to make the Orca roll a fraction, and further tousled Christopher's already wind-ruffled hair.

They turned back across the bay after a time and headed down towards Deal. Malcolm let Tom take the helm for a bit, and then Christopher – under his careful supervision. Roger acted as lookout all the while: mainsail and boom massively reduced the helmsman's view. Roger pointed to waves breaking further out to sea. 'The Goodwin Sands,' he said. 'Though you probably know that already. Mentioned in Shakespeare, no less.'

'The great ship-swallower,' Malcolm added cheerfully. 'But they shelter this area we're sailing in: the Downs.' A little further along the coast Roger pointed out the hamlet of Kingsdown, which seemed to be arrested in mid-tumble down the Cliffside, and they managed to pick out his parents' retirement bungalow. They all waved, just in case. They had sandwiches and flasks of coffee with them, which they ate and drank as they returned. It wasn't a fishing trip as such, but the mackerel were always there and so, with bare-hooked lines they bagged a few. It was a perfect afternoon, the kind on which, however late you leave it to turn about and sail for home, it always seems too soon.

They drove back to the Admiral Digby in two cars. Roger drove Tom while Christopher was the passenger in Malcolm's. 'Do your parents never suspect anything?' Christopher asked his chauffeur. 'I mean, all the time you spend with Roger and not having a girlfriend and so on.' He needed to know about this. If the thing he had with Tom was going to last any time at all there would be his own parents to deal with, his sister and two brothers as well. The more he could arm himself with the experience of others the better prepared he would be.

'Well,' said Malcolm thoughtfully, 'let's say they do and they don't. I work for my father in his boatyard. I'm his only son to hand the business on to after he retires. I don't suppose it's in his interests really, to go querying my friendship with Roger. Supposing he feels he oughtn't to have a son like I am and then feels obliged to turn me out, what good's that going to do him? Who'd help him run the business then? Who'd he leave it to?'

'I see,' said Christopher. He thought, like me and my father's builders' merchant business. Except my father could easily afford to lose me, with my two brothers both more keen on the business than I am. Lucky Michel over in Boulogne. Heir to his father's business and his father already dead, so unable to object to his choice of partner even if he wanted to … and his mother totally supportive of him and Armand…

'There's my mother, of course,' Malcolm went on as if he'd been following Christopher's thoughts. 'She probably does know, but will never say anything to dad – or anyone else – in case it upsets everybody's apple-carts. Anyway,' Malcolm gave a complacent laugh, 'doing the job I do and built the way I am, it's not as though most people would take me for a nancy-boy at first glance.'

Or even at second glance. Christopher was finding it difficult not to peer sideways at Malcolm as he drove. At his impish freckled face with its snub nose and crown of copper-wire-brush hair. At his muscular bare forearm, lying relaxed on the seat between them, ready to jump to the gear lever when necessary, at a second's notice, its corona of red hairs shimmering to gold as the sun ignited each one. At his bare bronzed legs, similarly clad in a shimmer of gold hair, muscularity accentuated by the upward pressure of the car seat below, his very short short trousers little more effective than a fig-leaf in concealing what lay beneath. Christopher's hand itched to stray down to those grand thighs and caress the nearer one, or else insert his fingers like a solid wedge between them where they met.

Suddenly Malcolm said – it was like a small explosion of inward thoughts that could no longer be contained – 'Jesus Christ but you're a little beauty and no mistake.' And it was Malcolm's hand that in the event found its way to Christopher's jeans-clad thighs; the jeans were still wet in patches, the normal result of an afternoon spent in a boat. Malcolm stroked Christopher's right thigh up and down just a couple of times, then let his hand lie where it was.

After a moment of hesitation and wonder Christopher put his own hand on Malcolm's thigh too, so that their arms crossed. He was exquisitely tempted now to worm his fingers up into Malcolm's tight shorts. But: mustn't grab his cock, he told himself, just as he'd told himself on another occasion only two weeks ago. The situation would be beyond mending, for all four of them, if he did.

Malcolm clearly had the identical thought. He too let his hand lie just where it was, making no further attempt to stroke the younger man. And so, their eyes resolutely peering ahead of them through the windscreen at a countryside lit magically by the midsummer evening sun, they completed their short journey in silence, neither of them either wanting or needing to speak, Malcolm only removing his hand from Christopher when they approached the T-junction before the Admiral Digby and he needed to change down into third. Meanwhile Roger and Tom, driving a few yards ahead of them, were light-heartedly crowing to each other that each had found the most perfect young man in the world, perfect for himself, that was: fair of face and form and beautiful within.

Neither Christopher nor Malcolm was so insensitive as to refer to what had taken place between them in the car, not even by so much as the exchange of a look, as the four of them sat over their pints of beer in the garden of the Admiral Digby. From time to time they were reduced to three, since Roger was called away at intervals to serve customers when his staff found themselves stretched. After one of these absences Roger returned with a customer in tow. Even before he arrived at their table to be introduced there was little doubt about who he was. He was in the uniform of a British European Airways pilot trainer captain.

When he had been introduced and had sat down with them, Captain Gradely – Jimmie when off duty, he told them – turned to Malcolm, whom he'd evidently met before, and said, 'That's a handsome boat you have. Seen it in the bay a few times over the years but never connected it with you – till Roger told me just now. And was that you gave us a wave as we went over earlier?'

'No, that was me,' said Christopher, and felt both ridiculous and childish as soon as the words were out of his mouth.

'Well, that was very nice of you,' Captain Jimmie told him, sounding quite sincere and not at all as if he thought Christopher's interpolation or his wave were ridiculous or childish at all. He was a round-faced man with smiling eyes and greying hair who gave the impression of someone happy in his skin. Tom thought he looked like a younger, fitter Father Matthew. 'It does get a bit monotonous flying round in circles all afternoon,' the pilot continued. 'Anything to liven things up. Trouble is, most of what livens things up are mistakes on the part of the trainee, and they're not moments you particularly enjoy, as you can imagine.'

He turned back to Malcolm. 'Your boat. Ramsgate smack, isn't she?'

Malcolm nodded. 'More or less. She's actually a miniature Whitstable oyster smack or yawl if you want to be very precise. But a smack, yes, you're right.' There followed quite a technical conversation about boats between Malcolm and the pilot, in which expressions like lugger and ketch, clinker-built, cutter-rigged and foresail kept surfacing like dolphins out of a murky sea. Jimmie was obviously something of a sailor himself and Malcolm was probably glad of someone to talk to who was neither the boy he'd called beautiful just an hour ago nor that boy's boyfriend.

When the boat conversation had run its course Tom asked why BEA used the neighbouring airfield for its training flights when it was so far from London. Jimmie was happy to answer. 'Two things, really. I'm sure you know it's mainly an RAF base. But they don't use its full capacity, so it's part-leased to Kentish Airways. But they don't make full use of it either: they're pretty small. Of course it's a diversion airfield for planes in trouble on the approach to London – Heathrow or Gatwick – but that doesn't happen every day. So we can rent training slots there quite cheaply. The second thing, of course, is that nowhere except Heathrow has a runway anything like as long – and we can hardly use Heathrow for whole afternoons at a time. Round here there's only Lympne and Lydd along the coast, and they're both too small for anything of any size. Lympne's even got grass runways still, and we'd hardly want to try unsticking a Vanguard from that.'

'I know,' said Christopher. 'I flew from Lympne to Beauvais the first time I went to France. In an old Dakota. The take-off did seem a bit hairy.'

Tom had never flown, but found he had no end of questions to ask that he'd never before thought he wanted the answers to. The others also found their boyish enthusiasms for all things to do with aeroplanes and the professionals who flew them re-kindled by this chance meeting with an avuncular man in a pilot's uniform. 'It's a pity I can't take you chaps up on one of my training circuits,' Jimmie eventually said. Perhaps he was thinking that that would take care of the answers to their many questions all in one go.

'It would be fun,' Christopher said, trying not to get his hopes up.

'I don't know,' the pilot mused. 'Could we pretend you're a pack of journalists or something? Or the BBC making a radio documentary?' He shook his head. 'No, I don't think they'd wear that in the guard room. You'd need letters of introduction or something.'

'And press cards,' Tom added. 'And the BBC would be carrying huge tape machines and mikes.'

'You're right, of course. Oh well. Pity,' said Jimmie. 'Nice idea though. But if I suddenly think of a way to wangle things I'll let you know. Promise.' He looked around the table. Everyone's glass was empty. There was an uncomfortable second, with everyone on the brink but not on the brink of putting a hand in a pocket and offering to buy the next round. Then the moment was saved by Roger, who appeared from indoors, a ground-floor *deus ex machina*, with the appropriate number of pint mugs on a tray.

***

From John Moyse's New Journal

The Vanguard flies over all day long. It's route must look like the outline of a paper-clip. It appears three times. First, without warning it comes over the trees, as if out of the trees, droning over the rooftops of the school, itself as big as the rooftops and so close that you can see the captain in silhouette inside the cockpit. It's a turbo-prop so has long slim engines. The propellers fill a flat circle of the air with shimmering quarters of different shades of silver and grey. Its landing gear hangs beneath it like giant fat car-tyres. It slides down through the sky towards the runway then, while it is still in the air, it disappears over the brow of the hill. Now it is silent.

Half a minute passes. There is a roar, carried on the wind towards us. Then appears the plane again in its second shape. This time so far off that it is like a miniature pencil shooting vertically from nowhere into the sky. We see it's white back, and because of the steep angle the tops of its broad dark wings. It's too far away – 5 miles? – to see its engines. As it levels out it disappears, becoming just a horizontal line too thin to see as it flies away, disappearing into its private haze of smoke and shaken air like a cuttlefish into its own cloud of ink.

Five minutes later it is born again. This time it is in the south, flying east across the bay, a cigar shape with tall upright tail fin, a distant silhouette against the sun, slipping occasionally behind a shred of cloud. It's too far away to hear it's engines, and it's wheels are tucked up and invisible, like the feet, hidden in feathers, of a flying bird. Then this shape too disapears behind trees. When next it comes into sight it will be school-size and noisy erupting again from out of the tree.

Three shapes for just one object. Not bad. I said this to Angelo who I was walking round the playing fields with. Is that what the Blessed Trinity is all about? Angelo thought perhaps I had a point. That maybe everything in life was like this if you thought about it hard enough. Then we wrestled a bit on the ground. Meanwhile, a most beautiful sailing boat in the bay, small but with a nice array of brown-red sails, gliding like a swan on the calm water. Too far away to see the crew. I did a sketch of it on a scrap of paper. Might make a painting of it later. Angelo said, why bother? Since I'd won the art prize last year. I said, why didn't <u>he</u> do a painting of it? Then he might stand a chance of getting the prize <u>this</u> year. He paints brilliantly when he can be bothered.

I missed the most amazing event this morning. Though Angelo told me every detail. While I was at St Ursula's with Father M, Father L began a sermon on the Apocalypse. Though he seemed to get overwhelmed by the subject and started to spout huge chunks of the Apocalypse, unrefined. He called Sister a Jezebel and said he would vomit her out of his mouth. Then he collapsed, and was saved from falling by Angelo, Simon and Edward. They thought he'd had a stroke, and I agree. I remember Grandpa after he'd had his. Anyway, Father L is in hospital now. We await developpments.

FOURTEEN

'I worry about his speech.' Miss Coyle voiced this anxiety at breakfast on Monday, then realised that what she'd said needed clarifying. 'I mean the Headmaster's Report. On Prize Day. It's only three weeks away. We'd already started work on it. But if I try and complete it for him he'll not be pleased. That's the long and the short of it. He'll not be wanting to stand up and read words that another person has put into his mouth.'

'That's assuming he actually can stand up and read words at all,' Christopher chipped in. Father Matthew turned to him with a gently reproving frown.

Cathy came into the room with the morning's post. Miss Coyle and Miss O'Deere traditionally sorted it between them. Letters for the boys went on one pile, to be put in alphabetical order later, those for the office on another, much smaller pile, while any for resident staff were simply handed to them across the cereal bowls and teacups.

Today there were two items for the breakfasting teachers: one white envelope for Miss O'Deere and one blue air-letter addressed jointly – which was a bit embarrassing – to Christopher and Tom. Tom took it quickly, saw that it had a French postmark, and rapidly stowed it into the inside pocket of his tweed jacket for later consumption. Miss O'Deere, more bravely, opened hers at once – although her fingers trembled: she too had looked at the postmark first, and knew who it was from.

'Oh my goodness!' she said, after skimming the letter in a couple of seconds. 'My goodness me! What a lovely surprise.'

'Good news?' Tom asked for the sake of form. He could see and hear that the news was good and had made a pretty easy guess as to what it was.

'Dear me, yes. Oh yes indeed. It's the East Kent Arts Society. Our picture – yours, Tom, and yours, Christopher, not just mine – is to be hung.'

'Congratulations,' everyone said, reaching across and round the table, standing up to shake her hand, the problem of Father Louis and his Prize Day address temporarily forgotten, along with the crisp blue air-letter that had arrived for the two youngest members of staff, puzzlingly addressed to them jointly from somewhere abroad.

'Of course it's hardly a new experience for you,' Tom said gallantly. 'We haven't forgotten that you've been hung before – in Cork.' Though hearing himself say this he couldn't help feeling there was something not quite right about the way he'd phrased it, and that that diminished the gallantry somewhat.

'Oh but this is a much bigger affair by all accounts. National press... Oh my goodness. What a way to start the week.'

'A very good way to start the week indeed, I should say,' said Sister calmly. 'If it ends as well as it's begun it'll be a week to remember and no mistake.'

'It's a pity it's quite so early in the morning,' said Christopher. 'Otherwise we could all celebrate with a drink.'

'Now, Christopher,' said Miss Coyle, her tone mock severe, but her smile betraying her. 'Now, now.' It was the first time in all the five weeks he'd been here that she had addressed him by his given name.

The letter from France was, unsurprisingly, written in French. Both Michel and Armand had signed it but the body of the letter had been written by Michel. His handwriting was of the kind that is as cryptic as it is elegant, but once they had made the effort to decipher it, working deductively from the pen-strokes that comprised the simplest, common words, like the de-coders of the Rosetta Stone, they found the business of translating it relatively simple. It said, approximately, this.

What a pleasure to meet the two of you last week. Boulogne is a quiet place, and even Le Chat Qui Pêche can be a bit same-ish, even if it's new to you. People in there still talk of you both. So does my mother, who has good memories of your visit to her house.

We also think of you very often. We would like to come across to England some time on the ferry, and it would be nice to see you again. I imagine it would not be convenient (!) if we were both to descend on you in the boarding school where you work. Your colleagues might draw interesting conclusions! Perhaps, after the end of the school term we could all meet in Dover or Folkestone and try some of your famous English beer – and your English gastronomy too (only kidding).

But more than that, we would like to welcome you back to Boulogne at any time you want, as our guests, to stay with us as long as you want. Maybe we could make some visits together into Deepest France. (Bring a compass, and garlic for the vampires.) But we are serious about this. Please write back and we will arrange our next meeting. Bien amicalemet et grosses bises.

'Well,' said Tom, 'we haven't dared to talk about plans for the summer yet. It's rather lovely to find that other people are doing our thinking for us.' And Christopher thought, we have friends who are couples, Roger and Malcolm, Michel and Armand, and who think of us as a couple too. It was a big new idea to be getting his head round. Although he loved Tom and was desperately in love with him, a little part of him was conscious that he was very young to be half of a happily-ever-after couple, especially when Oxford still lay ahead of him, a big un-fished sea. He had only ever met two other couples of the same sex, and was already a little bit in love with one half of each of those: with Armand, whose signature sprawled across the paper he held in his hand and, nearer home, the slightly older, flame-haired Malcolm, who had caressed his thigh, and been similarly caressed in return, in a car. The future might not be an easy thing to handle.

At supper time Sister was able to give the assembled staff news of Father Louis. She had been to the hospital in the afternoon and been admitted to his bedside. She would presumably have been a difficult woman to say no to in this situation, dressed as she was in her starched nursing sister's uniform with its flowing tent of a headdress, shiny pocket watch prominent on her bosom. She had found the abbot already sitting in the visitor's chair, dressed in his black suit and dog collar, his silver cross and chain of office round his neck. Evidently it was a piece of good sense, when on a hospital visit, to let people know who you were.

There had been a minor clash of perspectives between the abbot and the registrar on duty that Monday afternoon. The registrar had explained that it was not easy to say whether Father Louis had actually had a stroke or not. He was not even partially paralysed and his speech was unimpaired. You couldn't peer inside the brain very easily in those days: CT scanners in every hospital were still a distant dream. But what could be said for certain, the registrar told the abbot, was that there was some confusion in Father Louis's mind between what belonged to the real world and what did not. The registrar was not theologically trained but he did recognise the source of Father Louis's earnest proclamations about the Lamb and the seven seals, the beast with the ten horns and seven heads, and his warnings about the number 666.

The abbot had objected. To someone like Father Louis, for whom the Apocalypse and other biblical texts were the subject of daily scrutiny and meditation, the events and objects described by St John in detailing his vision on Patmos were as much a part of the real world as the hospital, built in the middle of the previous decade, in which Father Louis now lay. It was a common misapprehension, the abbot explained gently to the registrar, that the present had a dimension of reality about it that was greater than the realities of times past and times to come – including those events foretold by St John that had been revealed by God to him but to no-one else before or since. The registrar had taken this to mean that both the abbot and Father Louis believed St John's vision was to be interpreted literally, that it was a true and accurate account of what was in store for everyone, and had fled aghast. Sister had had to go and track him down in another part of the hospital.

She found him more at ease with someone in a nurse's uniform than he had been with the two priests, and he was happy to relay to her the consultant's opinion that Father Louis would be able to leave hospital after a few days, though probably not to return to work, at least for the time being. But, as Sister now told those at the supper table, it was difficult in the case of Father Louis, a monk and a headmaster, to separate work from life. The normal rules, going to work in the morning, returning to relax in the evening with wife and children, did not apply. Miss Coyle reminded the group of the Benedictine motto: *Laborare est orare*, to work is to pray. For Father Louis the two activities were one and the same, and inseparable from the business of living and breathing. Like the duties of a monarch, they could cease only with his death.

The normal rules didn't really apply to any of them. Working and living in a boarding school meant that you were seldom if ever totally off duty. You really had to leave the premises for that to be the case. Visits to the pub, for Tom and Christopher, plus their occasional journey through the tunnel to the secret beach, and sailing trips, were the only times they could be absolutely sure of private time and space. Especially now, with Father Louis away and them helping out with dormitory rounds in the evenings. Here was Tom now, coming into the room to eat his late, warmed-over supper, and it was Christopher's turn to go and replace him on duty upstairs.

The juniors were supposed to prepare for bed in silence, then read quietly till lights-out, although the rule of silence was fairly lightly enforced. Provided that silence fell reasonably swiftly at the approaching footfall of authority, and provided that breaches were not too raucous, Father Matthew and Sister – and now, this evening for the first time, Tom – were not heavy-handed in enforcing the rule during this winding-down of the school day.

With the seniors, the twelve- and thirteen-year-olds, things were slightly different. They were considered to have more discretion and so were allowed to talk quietly till their own, later, lights-out. Even so, the occasional outbreak of horseplay or fighting would be stamped on pretty quickly. Tom, on the earlier shift, had not only to maintain an approximation of silence among the juniors but also to make sure that everyone washed properly, including necks and behind the ears, and that all teeth were assiduously brushed. Christopher, taking the later shift this first evening, had the less demanding task. The seniors did not need their evening washing routines supervised: they could be relied on to carry this out correctly as a matter of course, as befitted their growing senses of personal hygiene and *amour propre*. It was really only necessary for Christopher, arriving to monitor dormitories five and six, to check that the bath rotas were being adhered to: the right boys in the right cubicles at the right time, on the right day, and nobody making unreasonable, selfish demands on the hot water. Other than that his task was a relaxed one: to maintain a low-key presence, visible but not oppressive, and also to offer an ear to those of the boys who were in the mood for a moment's end-of-bed banter or chat.

Christopher was not surprised to find that among those who were keen to engage him in conversation this evening was John Moyse. He was glad of that. You didn't, and mustn't, have favourites among the boys, but sometimes it just happened that you found that you did have. In Christopher's case it was, among the seniors at least, John Moyse. Well, so be it. The essential rule, after that, was that your enjoyment of one boy's company in preference to that of others must never become apparent to anyone, and especially not to the boy himself. But since he had already sat down impartially on some half a dozen beds and whiled away a pleasant minute in conversation with their six different occupants, he did not feel he was in any danger of breaking that rule tonight when John Moyse's, 'Sir, can I ask you something?' invited him to sit on the end of that particular bed.

'What do you think,' John's question began, 'will happen when Father Louis comes back from hospital? Will he be able to go on as usual or...?'

'We'll have to wait and see,' Christopher said. 'Every case is different. So we won't know exactly what's going to happen until it happens. That's how life is, sometimes.'

'It's a stroke, isn't it, sir?'

'Very possibly, but again it's not quite sure. There are some very common symptoms of stroke, losing power in one or more of your limbs for instance, or having problems with speech, and Father Louis doesn't seem to have those. Anyway, that's what Sister says. She went to the hospital and saw him and the doctors this afternoon.'

'My grandfather had a stroke,' John said. 'He had to spend all day in the kitchen, peeing into a saucepan.'

'What? All day?' Christopher queried, with mock incredulity and a poker face. 'Did the doctors tell him to?'

Moyse rewarded him with a grin and a peal of childish laughter that his teenage self wasn't quick enough to suppress. 'You know that's not what I meant, sir!'

'As a future literary giant, Moyse, and one who has been compared favourably with P.G.Wodehouse by no less an authority than Mister Angelo Dexter, it behoves you to be more careful with your syntax. Avoid ambiguity whenever you see it rear its ugly head.' He permitted himself to pinch the boy's big toe through the blanket for a moment, after he'd stood up and before moving off to continue his rounds. 'Goodnight, Moyse.'

'Goodnight, sir.' And John, who had no reason not to let Christopher know that he was rapidly becoming his favourite master, made him a present of a heart-melting smile.

A second later Christopher passed the open cubicle that was shared by the two house captains, Simon Rickman and Angelo Dexter. Rickman, a cherubic-looking boy with blond curls, was tucked up in bed and absorbedly reading a Dennis Wheatley, but of Dexter there was no sign. 'Where's your partner in crime?' Christopher asked the boy.

'Monday's his bath night,' Rickman explained laconically.

'Maybe,' said Christopher. 'But it's nearly lights-out. Everyone else came back from the bathroom ages ago.'

'I know, sir,' said Rickman. 'But he likes a good long soak. He's like a woman in that way. My sister's just as bad. I put it down to the Italian in him. (In Dexter, I mean: not my sister, obviously.) He has a love of creature comforts that doesn't quite go with our stiff-upper-lip and cold-shower traditions in England. You'd understand if you met his mother.'

'Actually, I have met her. Anyway, thank you for enlightening me. I think I'd better go and chivvy him along. Father Matthew will be up to do the lights in five minutes.'

Rickman was right. Dexter was still in the bathroom, in sole possession, occupying the only cubicle whose curtain was pulled shut. But the long soak that Rickman had talked of had clearly just come to an end, since, at the moment at which Christopher enquiringly tweaked open the plastic curtain, Dexter was getting to his feet, prior to stepping out of the bath, and startling Christopher with an exceedingly full erection. Christopher could find no words for a second, his full attention taken up with the sight of Dexter's appendage and its surprisingly luxuriant surrounding crop of hair.

Christopher's momentary loss of speech gave Dexter the advantage. He seemed quite unabashed by the situation. And unashamed of his erection. The reverse, if anything. Seizing the initiative he asked, 'Could you dry my back for me, sir?' Then, seeing the look of frozen horror on Christopher's face, his mouth open but still not functioning as an organ of speech, he added helpfully, 'Father Matthew always does.'

If this were true, Christopher thought, it shed a new and unexpected light on Father Matthew's ways of relating to his charges, or at least to one of them. But he also thought that more probably it wasn't true, and that Dexter needed putting kindly but firmly in his place for his cheek. But before Christopher could summon any form of words that would do this Dexter said, even more helpfully, 'My towel's just there. Can you reach it?' And before he knew it, Christopher found that he had done just that, and had started to rub it across the back and shoulders of the boy, who had now stepped out of the bath and was – rather more modestly, which was something –presenting Christopher with a view of his back.

Christopher began the drying process diffidently, like a domestic cleaner whose responsibilities include the dusting of a porcelain statue known to be priceless. Dexter said over his shoulder, 'It was funny seeing you in Boulogne. Actually I mean that nicely. And Mr Sanders having a cousin there too. It's funny seeing people in a different situation from the normal one. You know, out of school, I mean.'

'It was funny seeing you there too,' Christopher managed to say.

'They kissed very enthusiastically for two cousins,' Dexter went on. Christopher felt himself go hot and his face flush. He was glad the boy couldn't look directly at him. 'I mean, I've got Italian cousins and I kiss them, but not like that. Anyway, Mr Sanders says that's France for you.'

'Well, I wasn't there to see, so I wouldn't know.' Christopher hoped Dexter wouldn't detect the shake in his voice. He risked an outright lie. 'When I met the cousin, they exchanged a peck on the cheek. It didn't seem anything out of the ordinary.'

'What's his cousin's name?' Dexter asked.

'Michel,' Christopher answered promptly. He was not a practised liar but he did know that, in general, the more true facts you could weave into any tissue of deceit, the better. He hoped that Dexter had not asked Tom the same question and been given a different name. But Dexter seemed satisfied with Christopher's answer.

'All right.' Christopher was in command at last. 'Your back's done. You can do the front yourself.'

Dexter promptly turned to face him and started towelling his tummy and chest. 'Cover that thing up now,' Christopher admonished. 'It isn't decent.' He hoped the boy had not noticed the inevitable hardening of Christopher's own cock in his trousers. 'And then get off to bed before lights-out. Prefects are supposed to set good examples.' He gave the boy a quick smile that was meant to be schoolmasterly but which actually came over as conspiratorial. Then he turned away quickly before Dexter had a chance either to carry out his command or to challenge him by flouting it. Or to challenge him still further by flaunting *that*.

Christopher was in two minds as to whether to tell Tom about this incident. He was uncomfortably aware that Tom might be furious with him for the way he'd handled the encounter, especially in view of the dangerous situation that the two of them had been placed in by Dexter's two sightings of them in Boulogne. It would only need a third incident for Dexter to be able to triangulate the position of things and get an absolutely positive fix on what was going on between the two young teachers. Catching either of them out in a lie about the name of Tom's supposed cousin would provide exactly that. So it was important to find out whether Tom had given the cousin a name when he'd had his pre-emptive conversation with Dexter after half-term, and also to let him know that Christopher had already supplied the boy with the name Michel.

He took the coward's way out in the end. When they were in bed later that night he asked out of the blue, 'When you were telling Dexter about your so-called cousin in Boulogne, did you give him a name?'

'I don't think I did,' Tom answered after a moment's thought. 'Why?'

'Because I thought that, just in case he ever brought the subject up again, with either of us, we ought to be able to agree on details like that. I know you told Dexter your cousin was a teacher of English. Perhaps we should agree that his name's Michel, since that really is the case and easier to remember than something we just make up.'

'I don't think you need to worry. Dexter's not the police or the Spanish inquisition. He's hardly likely to start giving us the third degree over this. But if he did, then supplying the name Michel wouldn't go a long way to putting his suspicions to rest. As an Englishman of Irish extraction I'd be unlikely to have a cousin whose name was Michel, even if he did live in France.'

Christopher tried not to show any physical reaction to this bombshell. But that was difficult when he was lying in Tom's arms in a single bed, their two bodies touching all the way from cheek and chest to thigh and foot. Tom said, 'Are you OK? Sudden twitch?'

'Fine,' said Christopher gamely. 'Nothing at all.' And to add verisimiltude to his answer he gave Tom's cock a playful tweak.

***

From John Moyse's New Journal

I played the first movement of the Moonlight Sonata at my lesson today. Father Claude was absolutely right. It's incredibly easy if you come to it after doing the second and third movements first. I only spent two days practising it and I found I could play it almost at once as if I'd always known it. In a sense I had, because everyone knows it, or has some idea of how it goes at least. Father Claude said it was really good (he's not usually magnamonious with praise, so that was quite a thing) and except from making a few suggestions for making one or two details more – 'telling' was the word he used – said there was really nothing more I needed to do with it, just play it the way I was doing. He then added, because there's always something with him, that any further improvements would have to wait till after I was forty because you have to be forty to really be able to understand Beethoven. I've heard the same said about some of Shakespeare's tragedys. But why forty for God's sake? As if on the last day of your thirty-ninth year you still play the piano or read Shakespeare like an overgrown kid, then you wake up the next morning and everything is revealed to you… I don't think so.

There was time left over at the end of the lesson and we talked about Father Louis. Well, Father Claude said most, because he knew most. That he was born in Ireland (Father Louis I mean) but went to France to study for the priesthood in 1899. It seems an incredibley long time ago. That after he left the seminary he worked in a parish in Lille near the French Belgian border, then when the war – the first one that is – started he became an army chaplin with the British. That he drove ambulances and carried stretchers on the Somme and Passiondale and other places. Then after the war he did missionary work and teaching in the French West Indies. (This was news to me as I'd always thought the West Indies were British.) I've always wondered about the patch of whitish skin he has above one eye. Apparantly some oik of a teenager he was teaching smashed him over the head with a bottle. And not long after that he came to England and joined the Benedictines. Teaching French at St Aidans since before the second war, becoming master of discipline (which sounds a bit extreme) in 1939.

It all makes you think what an eventful life people have had if they get to a good old age. I started to ask Father Claude what he had done but he rather brushed me aside. The only thing I got out of him that was new was that he used to work in a bank.

Now with Father Louis in hospital Father Matthew is doing the morning wake-up. It seems odd hearing his voice and seeing him swinging the bell when you open your eyes in the morning but I suppose we'll get used to it. Even odder is to see Christopher in the dormitories in the evening. I suppose Father Matthew can't be on duty 24 hours a day! He (Christopher) came round last night and was very friendly. Sat and chatted for some time. It's funny the way he uses this schoolmaster way of speaking sometimes, like he's taking the Mickey out of himself, because actually he's only 4 or 5 years older than me, so underneath he's probably still a kid. I suppose the special way of speaking is for the young boys in his own class who don't know that it's not the real him. They say he even uses that old joke about people who say they're laughing at nothing. 'There's a place near Canterbury...' When he talks to me he sort of swings in and out of it like some kind of virtuoso trick. Tom Sanders does the same sort of thing. Then when you think about it, Tom is only about 3 years older than Christopher, so he's probably pretending to be two diff. people as well, like a role in a play. And he, like Christopher, still looks like a big teenager. He's probably also still very young inside.

Don't know what got into Angelo tonight. He decided to take his bath at the last possible minute and Christopher had to tell him to hurry into bed before lights-out. Angelo getting told what to do ... that's something that hasn't happened for a long time. I suppose he was just trying to see what would happen if he pushed Christopher a little, but it's not like him to do that normally. Have to ask him in the morning.

FIFTEEN

'I think what I perhaps might do,' said Miss Coyle at breakfast, 'is to take one of his old Prize Day speeches from perhaps three or four years ago and use it as a model, just updating the details here and there as necessary, then he might feel comfortable about reading it, recognising it as his own work and all.'

The others nodded their polite agreement, though all their faces hinted at serious doubts as to whether this would work. Christopher asked, 'But where would you find his old speeches?'

Tom supplied the answer. 'They're printed each year in the school magazine.' He turned to Miss Coyle. 'Presumably there's a stack of back numbers somewhere?'

'That's right,' she answered. 'They're kept in the big cupboard in Father Matthew's office.'

'That's interesting to know,' said Christopher. 'Perhaps I'll go and have a look at them sometime, when I'm at a loose end for five minutes.' He didn't say why he thought this would be interesting, and even Tom was slightly surprised.

'The devil finds work for idle hands,' said Sister, apparently on auto-pilot.

To Christopher's surprise the other two women rounded on her smartly. 'And since when would it be the devil's work for a young teacher to familiarise himself with the history of the school he's teaching at?' Miss Coyle said, though she sounded amused, not annoyed, as she said it.

'Indeed yes,' added Miss O'Deere, then laughed. 'Whatever's got into you this morning, Sister? The devil's work indeed!'

'Well, I don't know...' Sister began but at that moment Cathy reached round the door and deposited the

196

post on the table. Only one of those present received a letter this morning. It was Miss O'Deere. She opened it there and then and a number of white cards came spilling from the envelope. 'Oh look. It's invitations to the private view. Canterbury Cathedral chapter house. On the twentieth, at six o'clock. The twentieth, that's…'

'Wednesday of next week,' Tom got there more quickly than Miss O'Deere could. He had better reason to have the following week's days and dates already matched up in his head. As did Christopher. The private view would take place on the eve of their shared birthday.

Miss O'Deere was rounding up the stray invitation cards that had fallen onto the table. 'They've sent me … um … six tickets. Oh dear, now, who's going to be able to come, and who has to be left behind?'

'Well, somebody who runs a car would be a good start,' Tom suggested practically. 'Perhaps Mr Charteris.'

'The two boys must certainly go,' said Miss Coyle. 'After all, they feature prominently in the painting.' Coming from her, the generous spirit of this proposal surprised both of them.

'Well, no doubt it'll all sort itself out between now and then,' Miss O'Deere said, getting to her feet, breakfast being done and Assembly only twenty-five minutes away. 'But Angela's right, of course: the boys must come. Absolutely.' And now even Sister nodded and smiled her agreement. Nothing further on the subject of idle hands and devil's work would pass her lips this day.

Christopher asked Father Matthew if he might have a look at the old school magazines in his office. 'Any time you like,' Father Matthew told him. 'Just go in and if I'm not there help yourself.' Which Christopher did. He discovered that the magazine was a joint one, shared by the public school, St Aidan's, and the prep school. Inevitably the doings and achievements of the senior school weighed more heavily in the content of each issue than those of Star of the Sea. But even in the chronicles of St Aidan's there were things to catch his eye. Staring out of one grainy photograph in the most recent back number was the face of his predecessor, Mr Appleton, seated amidst the public school's First XV Rugby team, and billed in the photo's caption as the team's coach. Going back a few more years Christopher found a portrait photograph of Father Louis, and an article about him, on the occasion of his transfer from head of French at St Aidan's to the headmastership here at Star of the Sea. He was as surprised as John Moyse had been to learn of his life-saving work in the trenches of the First World War, and of his subsequent career in France and her colonies. Even more surprising was it to learn that he'd left Ireland to join a seminary in Brittany at the age of fifteen.

And then, going back to the issues between 1948 and 1951, Christopher found what he was really looking for. Tom, photo of, throwing the javelin at Star of the Sea Sports Day. An eleven-year-old Tom, very blond, very slender but not fishbone thin. A poem by Tom aged ten – it would do him no favours to quote it here – and a short essay, 'Why I Like Living by the Sea', which showed promise and an imaginative turn of phrase. Christopher read both this and the poem several times, almost committing them to memory.

Then there was another photo of him, in an unidentifiable bit of countryside, with other boys, on some field trip or outing. Tom was grinning, so were most of the other boys, but Tom alone stood arms around shoulders with the boy beside him. It gave Christopher an unexpected frisson which was not altogether pleasant. Because the frisson was one of jealousy. Christopher knew at once that to feel jealous over this was more than absurd. This dark haired child – whose name was D. Mower if the caption correctly followed the faces from left to right – could be nothing to Tom now; Tom might not even remember his name. Nothing was more pointless or ridiculous than retrospective jealousy, Christopher told himself. This was eleven years ago; he was looking at a photograph of two children, members of a group, who might not even have been friends. He laughed aloud in Father Matthew's otherwise empty office, which sounded strange, then clapped the magazine shut – though not without a last look at Tom's face, which in this photo too looked lovely – and exchanged the claustrophobic little room for the long vistas and chill polished tiles of the chapel cloister.

Christopher pondered on what he'd just seen as he walked along. If a photograph like that could have such an unexpected effect on him, he couldn't help thinking, what would happen when the David and Jonathan portrait was unveiled at Canterbury next week? How were other people going to react? And if he could be jealous of a child from eleven years back in Tom's past, how would Tom feel if he knew about what had taken place in Malcolm's car? Christopher told himself he would make sure never to be alone with Malcolm again.

The abbot stood alongside Father Matthew at Assembly next day. Both were tall men, the abbot with a fine head of silver hair to match his pectoral cross and chain of office, and they made an imposing pair on the raised platform of the school hall. Father Claude sat in his accustomed place at the keyboard of the grand piano, head slightly bowed, ready to accompany the next hymn.

'Father Louis will be returning from hospital at the beginning of next week,' the abbot informed the boys.

'He is recovering very well, but will need a little time to convalesce. For the rest of this term, therefore, Father Matthew will be taking charge of all routine matters concerning school administration and,' he paused just long enough to show a wry smile, 'dare I say it, discipline. Father Louis will, however, continue to be headmaster. But his stewardship of the school will be like the Queen's. You will have learnt that the Queen, while commanding our allegiance and respect, reigns over us but does not rule. Day-to-day decisions are taken on her behalf by her Prime Minister, Mister Harold MacMillan. So it shall be with Father Louis and Father Matthew – like monarch and first minister. I shall rely on you all to give them both your unqualified loyalty and support in difficult times.' The abbot made beady eye-contact with a representative selection of individuals in each row of standing youngsters. 'And now, I think Father Matthew would like to add a few words of his own.' There was some spontaneous applause. A number of the younger boys had not clapped eyes on an abbot before, let alone heard one speak. The novelty was as great as that of a dog on two legs and dancing.

'Will anyone be telling Father Louis that he isn't in charge any more?' Mr Charteris said to the staff room at large during coffee break.

'And what about next term?' Tom asked the supplementary question since no-one had volunteered to answer Mr Charteris. 'Are they planning a permanent replacement?'

Christopher said, 'If it's going to be someone from the abbey, shouldn't they be over here already, getting the feel of the place?' But he got a look from most of the others which hinted that it wasn't his place to be saying this.

'Perhaps they'll advertise,' said Father Claude, mildly enough, but causing people to take notice because he seldom took coffee with the other teachers, preferring his own company or that of the grand piano, and even when he did deign to visit the staff room seldom spoke.

'It ought to be Father Matthew, of course it ought,' said Miss Coyle. 'Everybody would agree with that.' Nods of the head from all those present – Father Matthew was not – indicated that this was so. Miss Coyle finished, 'The whole situation is most unsatisfactory. Most unsatisfactory.' Which caused Christopher to wonder if she had ever watched Thunderbirds.

'Listen,' said Miss O'Deere, perhaps feeling that a change of subject would lighten the atmosphere. 'Mr Charteris has kindly negotiated the use of the abbey's mini-bus for next Wednesday and will be driving me, Mr Sanders and Mr McGing into Canterbury for the private view. There are spare seats and two spare invitations, so… Well, I leave it to anyone who'd like to come with us to 'make themselves known' as Father Matthew would say, and if there are more than two, you'll have to argue it out between you.' This caused a ripple of laughter and a little chatter, which Tom and Christopher didn't listen to very carefully, as they were going to Canterbury anyway – just as those who have heard themselves announced as the winners of any contest seldom listen for the names of the runners-up.

It was Tom who brought up the subject of their impending joint birthday, the day after the private view. By coincidence it was also, this year, the feast of Corpus Christi: a moveable feast in the Church's calendar, hopping about, parallel to the date of Easter, always on the Thursday in the eighth week after that feast. It actually commemorated the Last Supper but, like the Queen's official birthday, was celebrated in better weather than you could expect on Maundy Thursday. And here it would be the occasion of a whole holiday. 'We ought to do something. Go to London? See a show? I don't know.'

'Won't we be expected to take part in the procession in the afternoon?' Christopher queried.

Tom groaned. 'I'd forgotten that. But we could have lunch out somewhere and be back in time for the bloody procession. Or else we could go out to dinner in the evening.'

Not usually the one to take the bolder initiative, Christopher trumped Tom on this occasion. 'We could do both.' He hoped that at least some part of the day's celebrations might include Malcolm, even though that would naturally mean Malcolm and Roger. He hadn't forgotten his resolution not to let himself be alone in Malcolm's company. He also wondered if Tom and he would be exchanging presents. That would pose a bit of a problem, with shops not very easy of access and the two of them spending as much of their free time together as any pair of young lovers could. Unlike Christmas, when an exchange of gifts with loved ones was the norm, birthdays were usually a one-way street of present giving. The situation between Tom and himself was a new one in his experience. (And probably in most people's. How many couples on the planet were born on the same day of the year?) It would be embarrassing if one of them bought a present and the other did not. This must be what it's like to have a twin, he thought. He'd have to buy a card from somewhere at least.

Tom came to the rescue of Christopher's floundering thought process. 'Why not? You can buy us a pub lunch and I'll do dinner in the evening. Then we won't have to go choosing the wrong present for each other. We'll exchange cards though, won't we?'

Bath time for the boys came round twice a week. There being an odd number of days in every week, this meant that each boy had a bath at alternating three- and four-day intervals. Tuesday and Friday, for instance or, as in the case of Angelo Dexter, Monday and Thursday. On the two days following Christopher's bath-time encounter with the boy Tom did the senior dormitory round and Christopher the junior. Tom was wary of encountering Dexter in the rather intimate context of his dormitory at bedtime but in the event found him no trouble at all on either night. Tom sat for a moment on Rickman's bed and exchanged a little banter with both him and Dexter. It was all very light-hearted and inconsequential. Nothing was said by Dexter about Boulogne or cousins in France and Tom began to feel relieved, reprieved almost. Their two encounters in Boulogne plus anything that Dexter might have deduced from them had gone to the back of the boy's mind, no longer featuring as important. School life had advanced an eventful couple of weeks and any thirteen-year-old would by now have more interesting fish to fry.

Back on Monday Tom had been on the point of asking Christopher, on his return from the senior dorms, if he'd had any trouble with Dexter, but as Christopher hadn't brought the subject up and all seemed well with him, had decided to let the matter lie. Which, he now thought, was just as well.

When Christopher next did the senior dormitory round it was Thursday. He was not able to forget the fact that it was Dexter's bath night again and, like Tom on the previous two nights, approached his encounter with him with some nervous apprehension. One of the boys in dorm five waylaid him with a string of questions about the American political system, of all things, which he was hard put to answer, and in dorm six John Moyse wanted to know if he'd ever been sailing: something his uncles were very keen on. Christopher was glad to be able to say that he'd been out in a sailing boat the previous Sunday. 'In the bay?' Moyse asked him. 'In a boat with reddish sails?' Christopher told him, yes, and that the correct description of the colour of the Orca's sails – Malcolm had told him this – was tan. 'I already knew that, sir. I just didn't expect that you did,' was Moyse's answer to that. But he added, 'You're lucky to have friends who own a boat like that. She's a real beauty.' And Christopher wondered what the boy would make of Malcolm if he were to meet him – and what he'd think if he knew what had happened between the two of them in the car.

When it was nearly time for lights-out and Christopher did his final round to check that all would be found in order when Father Matthew arrived to physically pull the switches, he again found that the sole absentee from his bed was Dexter. Rickman, now on the final pages of his Dennis Wheatley, broke off to grin up at him and say, 'Well, I think you can guess where to find him by now.'

'Thank you, Rickman. Yes I do. And I shall get along there now and do just that. And if I don't get there soon enough Father Matthew can tan his freshly-bathed posterior and good luck to him.' Rickman's snort of laughter followed Christopher out of the cubicle and down the corridor. Had there been more in his phrase, *you can guess where to find him by now,* than an innocent remark? Christopher wasn't sure. Having even the ghost of a guilty conscious turned you as paranoid as Hamlet's uncle.

He made his way along the corridor to the bathroom exactly as on the previous occasion. Only this time his feelings could not have been more different. This evening he knew what was going to happen when he got there and he was pretty sure the same went for Dexter too. As before the bathroom was empty except for one occupied bath cubicle, curtained shut and presumably containing Dexter. Christopher was just about to put his head round the curtain and deliver a schoolmasterly injunction to Dexter to get a move on when another figure came skating round the corner into the bathroom, his slippers aquaplaning on the linoleum. It was John Moyse.

'Sorry Christopher, I mean Mr McGing, sir. I forgot to clean my teeth.' He went to the row of washbasins, selected one at random, pulled brush and paste from the wash-bag he was carrying and embarked noisily and very rapidly on the cleaning process, like some small mammal that lives life at ten times' human speed and carries out every action at absurd velocity.

Christopher acknowledged Moyse's arrival with an abstracted nod and half smile and then returned his attention to the curtain-closed cubicle. Instead of pulling the curtain wide open immediately, for he was inhibited by the attentive presence of Moyse almost at his elbow, Christopher put his hand round it and rapped on the wood of the partition. 'Time to get out and into bed, Dexter.'

'Isn't that a contradiction in terms, sir? Out and into.'

Christopher heard Moyse's spluttering guffaw behind him. 'Yes it is, Dexter – and you, Mr Well-Known Author Moyse – but you knew what I meant. I'm serious. It's lights-out in five minutes.'

'There's always one, sir, isn't there?' came from behind him. Moyse had finished the teeth-cleaning process and was calmly stowing away his equipment. 'These Italian stallions think they can get away with anything.'

'So do famous authors, Moyse, especially when they're approaching the end of their last term at prep school. You won't have it so easy at Downside.'

From behind the curtain Dexter interrupted. 'Are you going to dry my back again, Mr McGing? I guess I'll have to do without that at Downside. Or wouldn't Mr Sanders approve?'

Christopher turned round to Moyse first. 'Get off to bed now. You heard what I said about lights-out.' He managed to keep his tone light: he didn't want Moyse to see that he was rattled.

''Twas ever thus, sir,' said Moyse, seeming to take the situation in his stride. 'One rule for the house captains, another for their deputies – or vice captains, whichever you like to call us.' He cast his eyes up, giggled, then skittered away along the lino, while Dexter called after him, 'Sleep well, captain of vice.'

Christopher turned back to finish dealing with Dexter. At the same moment the plastic curtain swished open and there was Dexter facing him in all his naked glory, but still standing up inside the bath-tub, from which the water was already draining away. Because of his position on the slightly raised bottom of the tub, Dexter was now as tall as Christopher and able to look him straight in the eye. Christopher's confusion could clearly be read from his face, and Dexter's own face folded into a sympathetic smile as he said, a cute question-mark in his voice, 'Pass the towel?'

'All right, then,' Christopher said. 'But you've got to behave yourself.' That was as near as he could get to saying, don't wave your dick in my face.

Dexter knew that. 'Sorry about that, sir. But, you know, these things happen.'

Christopher managed not to glance down too obviously. Though his peripheral vision informed him that Dexter's state of excitement was only partial this time, not as extravagant as on the last occasion. 'Hop out then and turn round. I'll give your back a quick wipe and then you must do the rest yourself.'

When the boy's back was turned Christopher obligingly started to rub the towel between his shoulder blades while, as before, Dexter chatted to him over his shoulder. 'You and Mr Sanders like each other a lot, don't you, sir?'

Christopher kept his head. 'We'd hardly have spent a weekend in Boulogne together if we didn't.'

Dexter went on, 'Miss O'Deere says she's exhibiting a picture of you both in Canterbury Cathedral next week. Or exposing a picture, as they say in French. *Elle vous expose.*'

'*Et toi, tu t'exposes tout le temps,*' Christopher had the presence of mind to riposte. 'You make an exhibition of yourself. With me.'

Dexter showed himself delighted with this bit of banter by giving an unselfconscious laugh. Christopher felt that he was riding a tiger's back, or surfing a wave's crest: it was exhilarating but dangerous; impossible to guess what would happen next, or how long he could stay in control, or when the crash would come. He now found (how had he allowed this to come about?) that he was towelling the boy's buttocks and thighs, despite the fact that Dexter could easily have reached these if he chose. Then Dexter turned round towards him suddenly. He gave a shrug and a disarming can't-help-it kind of smile. 'Sorry, but sometimes it just happens.'

It was happening to Christopher too. He hoped the boy wouldn't look down and take note. But he did take note. And commented. 'Happens to everyone.' Then he giggled, which surprised himself as well as Christopher. But before Christopher had time to react in any way the boy grabbed the towel from Christopher and, his composure now in ruins, bundled it around himself, anxious to hide what a moment before he had been only too happy to display. He turned away from Christopher, at the same time whimpering, 'Oh no. Oh fuck. No!'

Christopher turned away from even the back view of the boy, trying to reduce the measure of his humiliation. He was pretty shaken too. 'It's OK,' he managed to say. 'Don't worry about it. Get your pyjamas on and go to bed. There's still a minute before lights-out.'

'I'm really sorry, sir,' Dexter said, a child again. 'You won't…'

'Of course I won't. You don't have to ask. Get a good night's sleep. And … don't worry…' Christopher could hear Tom's voice saying almost the same words to him a few short, long? weeks ago. '…That also happens to pretty well everyone sometimes.' Then he hopped smartly out of the bathroom, just as Moyse had done two minutes earlier, before Dexter had a chance to say anything else.

***

From John Moyse's New Journal: Thursday June 14th 1962

Of course the reason for Angelo's new enthusiasm for his friendship with me is that we shall be together at Downside in Sept. and you-know-who won't be, because he's down for Ampleforth. It's going to be hard, everyone splitting up in this way, Edward off to St Aidan's along the road, and the others going to Bellhurst… It's going to be all change this year.

Angelo very odd about this bathtime business and Christopher. I asked him about it last time and he said that he was just trying it on with Christopher, pushing him a bit. I told him that was behaving like a twelve-year-old. (He's going to be 14 in October.) Then he changed the subject and said he liked Christopher and enjoyed talking to him. Well, so do I, but I don't roll my eyes at him and ask him to dry my bum after my bath.

Tonight I made a point of forgetting to clean my teeth and going in there while they were chatting. I thought the atmosphere rather strange to say the least. 'Highly charged' is a phrase I've read. Sounds about right. Spoke to Simon on my way back to bed. He thinks Angelo's going through some sort of crisis about changing schools and all that, which I can understand. Said his brother (Simon's not Angelo's) was just the same when <u>he</u> changed schools. Then Angelo came back sort of black in the face as if he'd turned into a thunder cloud and wouldn't speak to either of us but just climbed into bed very fast and pulled the blankets over himself. I said goodnight but he didn't answer. Simon and I said goodnight to each other and then I came back to bed.

The juniors have been watching a TV series based on the William books by Richmal Crompton. I saw a bit of one. The boy playing William is far too old and big. Sort of long and skinny, which looks odd in short trousers. He's called Dennis Waterman I think. Very lined face, but he knows how to act, which some of the other kid actors don't. Though the boy who did Corky the Circus Boy was pretty good. I suppose it's difficult to have it both ways. To be young and able to act at the same time. Mr Charteris said something like that about Romeo and Juliet. That by the time an actress was old enough to play Juliet she was too old to play it... Or something like that. It seemed to make sense at the time.

SIXTEEN

The question of who should be given the remaining two invitations to the private view of the East Kent Arts Society exhibition was solved at a stroke when Miss O'Deere and Father Matthew separately came up with the idea, during Friday morning's coffee break that the ideal candidates for joining the party might be the two most recent winners of the school's annual prize for art. Last year's winner had been John Moyse. The winner in the previous year, a French boy called Luc Scott-de-Martinville, had already left the school, but this year's winner, due to receive his accolade in five weeks' time and already aware of the impending honour, was none other than Angelo Dexter. A picture he had done of a fishing smack with all its red-brown sails set, and shining in the sun, had clinched it for him.

As Miss O'Deere and Father Matthew patted each other on the back, metaphorically speaking, for coming up with the same sensible idea, Tom's heart sank a little at the prospect of his two principal anxieties – public reaction to the David and Jonathan picture, and whatever Dexter knew or didn't know about himself and Christopher – coalescing in the chapter house of Canterbury Cathedral next Wednesday. And if Christopher's heart did not lurch even more precipitously downward at the news, given his own recent and private dealings with Dexter, that was only because he was not in the staff room at that precise moment. But Tom told him pretty soon afterwards, and then it did.

The events of the previous evening had imprinted themselves so powerfully on Christopher's sensual memory that he was having difficulty focusing on anything else. Every awful second of what had happened repeated itself in an interminable loop. He felt, every few seconds, the sensation of the towel in his hands and rubbing at the boy's shoulders: that came back again and again like the stabbing reminder of a day-old wasp's sting. It was the same with the sound of Dexter's voice whimpering – 'Oh no. Oh fuck. No.' The clean, soaped, scrubbed smell of him. To say nothing of the photographic images that had burnt their way onto his retina as if he'd been staring at the sun.

He hadn't been able to talk to Tom about his first encounter with Dexter in the bathroom. How immeasurably more difficult this would be now! All he could manage to do was to ask if Tom would do the senior dormitory round for the next few days, and to hope that he could engineer things so that Tom was on senior duty next Monday – Dexter's next bath night – without Tom noticing anything odd in that.

Tom did notice something odd in it. But he'd noticed a lot of oddness about Christopher in the last few days. He wasn't entirely sure about the cause or causes of this, though he had one or two ideas. He decided to say nothing for the moment, and agreed to the change of dormitory roster without question.

They spent Sunday afternoon lazily on the beach in the little cove that was accessible only by boat or through Roger's beer-cellar tunnel. They had taken to lying naked on the sand, at least for part of the time, and horsing around a bit, though more often than not they stopped short of actually making love, having an instinctive respect for the abrasive properties of sand. And they would usually be at least minimally fig-leafed in either swimming-trunks or shorts by the time Roger, or Roger and Malcolm, joined them later in the afternoon.

But on this occasion Malcolm surprised them by arriving through the tunnel door much earlier than usual and alone. If he was startled by their nakedness he gave no sign of it, greeting them with his usual cheerful grin, and though Tom and Christopher were startled by his sudden materialisation they took good care not to show it, but brazenly returned his smile, still lying on their backs in the sun.

'Hope you don't mind if I follow your example,' Malcolm said. 'Get my kit off and have a quick dip. Roger wants to go through some paperwork with me. It'll be late by the time we get down here, knowing him. Told him I'd get a quick swim in first.' He was already undressing as he spoke, neither shyly nor with any obvious suggestion of showing off, but quite unselfconsciously and not bothering, since he was speaking at the same time, to turn his back. Then Malcolm did exactly what he'd said he would. Strode away from them and, a little gingerly because of the rocks, entered the water, which was smooth and placid, as it had been now for some days.

'He's got a bloody good body on him, I must say.' Tom made the obvious comment, perhaps deliberately getting it in first, before Christopher would feel that he had to.

They watched Malcolm's head appear and disappear among the wavelets for a few minutes without speaking. They had had their own dip ten minutes before and were just beginning to feel dry, so they were not inclined to plunge in and join their older friend. And when those few minutes were up Malcolm rose up out of the water and came back towards them on the beach. He stood beside them dripping and Christopher, realising that Malcolm had brought no towel with him, on an impulse threw him his own, with which, in an action that reminded Christopher eerily and uncomfortably of Dexter three days earlier, he dried those parts of himself that necessarily had to be stuffed back inside his shorts.

Then he thanked Christopher as he threw the towel back to him, pulled the shorts on, said, 'See you later,' and, with his other clothes draped over a shoulder, turned and made his way up the little beach and disappeared through the iron door.

As soon as Malcolm was out of sight, Christopher said, 'I was looking through old school magazines a few days ago. There was a picture of Richard Appleton. He didn't only teach here, I discovered. He was also a rugby coach at St Aidan's. We still don't know why he left.'

Christopher stopped at that point and didn't seem to want to add anything, so Tom said, 'Well, you could have asked Malcolm just now. Since he knew the fellow. Missed your chance.'

'It would have been a bit out of the blue,' Christopher explained. 'Since he had no clothes on. Not quite the moment. Another time.' He paused again but this time picked up the thread again himself. 'There was an article by you. And a poem. I thought them both beautiful.'

'Oh no!' said Tom, wriggling in genuine embarrassment and covering his face with his hands. Christopher began to recite the poem, which he now had by heart, but Tom stopped him. Christopher said, 'There were pictures of you too. You were a lovely kid.'

Tom laughed. 'I looked just like any kid of my age, I think. No better, no worse.'

Christopher didn't press the point. Instead, he asked, 'Who was D. Mower?'

'Who?' Tom's surprise showed on his face.

'In one picture you had your arm around a boy called D. Mower. I just wondered who he was.'

'D. Mower? D. Mower... No, I don't remember. Oh hang on, now I do. You mean the photo of a group of us on an outing, on the way to see St Augustine's Cross or something. Mower. He was in the same class as me.

Daniel, I think his first name was. We weren't special friends or anything. I'd almost forgotten him.'

'So he wasn't anyone important to you?' Christopher seemed very much to need a repetition of Tom's disavowal.

'No,' Tom said, smiling. 'We weren't in love or anything, if that's what you're thinking. We were only about eleven when the picture was taken, for heaven's sake. I don't think we were even friends in any real sense of the word. We just happened to be standing next to each other when the picture was taken. A burst of high spirits.'

Christopher seemed satisfied with this. Tom thought he actually looked relieved.

Although Tom had guessed that Christopher's asking him to do the senior dormitory round for the next few nights had something to do with Dexter, he had not registered the fact that his previous stints with the seniors had never coincided with the boy's bath night. He was a teacher, not a detective, after all. But then came Monday. Like Christopher before him he was surprised to find, just before lights-out that Dexter's bed – on which he had sat briefly some twenty minutes before, exchanging a few civilised pleasantries with the boy and his cubicle-mate Rickman – was now empty. 'Where's he gone to?' he asked Rickman, who was now ploughing his way through the early chapters of Lorna Doone.

'Having a bath, sir,' Rickman replied, his voice hinting at a weariness engendered by repeatedly having to answer the same silly question. 'He always leaves it to the last possible moment. I blame the mother.'

Tom grunted in reply, then went off to the bathroom to chivvy the other house captain along.

'Dexter, what are you playing at?' he asked in a jovial tone as he walked into the bathroom. One cubicle alone was curtained shut and occupied; nobody else was there. 'You prefects are supposed to set an example of punctuality – has no-one told you that? – not be following the example of the halt and the lame. Get a move on now.' He said all this without pulling aside the curtain. He had no doubt that it was Dexter on the other side, and no wish to come face to face with the boy when he was naked. Things were awkward enough as it was.

But the curtain was twitched slightly open from within and Dexter's head of shiny black curls appeared round it, about two feet above the floor, grinning mischievously like Puck. Clearly he was still sitting in the bath tub. 'It's my Italian side, sir,' he said. 'Latin sensibilities and tardiness and all the rest.'

'Well, can you stop being Latin just for five minutes while you hop out of there and into bed? After lights-out you can be as Latin as you like.'

'Kiss my cousin if I had one, you mean? Or make do with whoever if not. Sorry. I'm talking nonsense. Because we're all leaving, we get like that. It's called de-mob happy. Will you help me dry my back, sir?'

'Certainly not,' said Tom. 'Get a move on and get to bed.' A new possibility struck him. 'Dexter, have you been drinking?'

'Christopher does. Dries my back for me, I mean. I didn't mean drinking, sir.'

'Christopher? Mr McGing to you, if you please. And I sincerely hope he doesn't dry your back. But if he does, then he should know better than to waste his time mollycoddling the house captains.' Now Tom did draw the curtain open, his surprise and anger showing in the gesture, though he was managing to keep them out of his voice still. At the same moment Dexter scrambled to his feet, though remaining inside the bath, to face him. Fortunately for Tom's state of mind he was not sporting an erection: his appendage was an unthreatening after-bath thirteen-year-old's. But, raised those crucial inches by the floor of the bath, he was disconcertingly almost the same height as Tom. For a second they eyeballed each other, shock on both their faces. For a moment both wondered whether Tom would lash out at Dexter, either physically or with words. But that moment passed. Then another moment passed as each wondered who would be the first to speak, and what he would say.

But the first person to speak was Father Matthew, just then entering the bathroom through the open door. 'Well, well. What's going on here? Dexter, get off to bed now and stop showing off to Mr Sanders.'

'I asked him to dry my back, Father, but he wouldn't,' said Dexter.

'I should hope not,' said Father Matthew briskly. 'It's much too late for all that. Just look at the time.' He took his pocket watch out and thrust it under Dexter's nose. 'Lights should have been out two minutes ago. You'll have to get into bed in the dark. You dry yourself down now – unassisted – and put out the bathroom lights before you leave. Goodnight now.' He turned Tom round with a friendly hand on the shoulder and walked with him out of the door, while Dexter's slightly subdued goodnight floated in the air behind them. 'Well, Tom?' Father Matthew said as they walked together along the corridor to turn the lights out in dorm six, 'Anything to report? Or can we leave everyone to rest in peace?' If he had heard anything of the conversation that preceded his arrival in the bathroom, or had picked up on the atmosphere that existed between its two occupants, he was choosing not to show it.

Tom found Christopher a few minutes later. Along with Sister and Miss Coyle he was watching the television news. Tom was unable to make a scene with Christopher there and then, nor did he want to arouse the women's curiosity by hauling Christopher out of the room and tackling him in the cloister. And then, when the news was finished, Christopher was unusually adamant about wanting to watch the programme that followed it. So Tom had to exercise the virtue of patience until bedtime. Usually, if they were both in the television room at this time, one would leave first and the other, to avoid suspicion, delay his departure until a few minutes later. Tom went first on this occasion. But when Christopher, some twenty minutes later and now in his pyjamas, pushed open Tom's bedroom door, he found him still fully clothed and sitting upright on the end of his bed.

'We need to talk,' Tom said.

Christopher, who had expected to find Tom inside the bed and waiting for him naked, was aware at once that something was seriously wrong and, since he'd spent the whole evening acutely conscious that this was Dexter's bath night, felt glumly sure that he knew what it was. The sudden blush that pinked his face told Tom that no further preamble was required.

'Angelo Dexter. What have you been doing with him?'

'Doing with him?' Christopher managed to sound more aggrieved than he had the right to be. 'I've done nothing with him? Why? What's he said?'

'He says you dried his back for him after his bath. Is that true?'

'Oh that.' Christopher wanted to make light of it but this time his voice betrayed him.

'Yes, that. Did you dry his back for him? And what about the rest of him?'

'I dried his back for him, yes,' Christopher said, his words slow and careful as footsteps into a minefield. 'But only because he said Father Matthew always did.'

'Father Matthew?! And you believed him? And thought nothing of it? You touched a naked child – who was in your charge – and had your hands all over him!'

'It wasn't like that, I promise.' He tried not to think – *no, it was worse than that.* 'You make it sound like something dirty.' But the memory of Angelo Dexter and his towel flooded back into his mind and destabilised his conviction.

'That's how other people would see it – will see it – if ever it came out. Dexter's already a loose enough cannon as it is. There's no end of possible trouble in store for us because of him. Didn't you give a thought to that? And to top it all off, now it turns out he's coming to Canterbury with us to see us posing as David and Jonathan.'

'He isn't a child,' Christopher came back. 'He's a teenager, same as me. We're only five years apart in age, Dexter and me. Look at you and me, three years apart. It's not so very different.'

'It's totally different. Or do you equate yourself and Dexter with yourself and me?' Tom's voice was raised now. It was fortunate that theirs was an otherwise uninhabited corridor. 'It is totally different. You and I are in the adult world together, responsible for ourselves. Dexter's a schoolboy, entrusted to us by his parents. And quite apart from that, you and I are lovers. We say, "I love you," to each other twenty times a day. Or had you forgotten that? You don't say that to Dexter, I suppose? Or he to you?'

'Of course I fucking don't. Of course I don't. And nor does he. Don't be sarcastic now.'

Tom calmed a little. 'OK. I'm sorry. I'm sorry I spoke to you that way. But you need to tell me exactly what happened. Every detail. I need to know, because tomorrow or sometime soon I have to look Dexter in the face again, and at the moment I don't know how I'm going to manage it. So please, my darling… The whole story, please.'

Christopher had sat down on the bed beside Tom halfway through the previous exchange. Only now did Tom reach out and take his hand.

Haltingly, Christopher coughed up the details. He told Tom everything that had been said and had taken place. Then, as he reached the end of his story, he saw that tears were quietly flowing down Tom's cheeks, and that Tom was doing nothing about them but just letting them flow and fall.

Tentatively Christopher put his arms around Tom. He was relieved when Tom responded to the gesture and turned it into an embrace. 'Tom, I'm sorry,' Christopher said, almost in a whisper, in Tom's ear. Then neither of them spoke for a few minutes but simply sat on Tom's bed rocking each other gently.

At last Tom pulled his head just far enough away to be able to speak to Christopher while looking him in the face. But he still kept one arm round him, and held one of Christopher's hands with his spare one as if he feared Christopher might fly away from him like a bird. 'There's something I have to tell you,' he said. 'And I'm sorry, because I should have told you this before. Should have told you on day one. And certainly after we met that mad monk in Boulogne. I knew you'd guessed something, but that day we had other fish to fry. Then you started questioning me about that boy at school, Mower or whatever his name was.'

Christopher didn't say anything. He just looked into Tom's eyes like a seal waiting to be clubbed.

This is the moment I really hurt you, Tom was thinking. *As I always knew I would.* It would hurt Tom too. As much or maybe more: that depended on how Christopher would react. He took a breath that Christopher could hear, and feel through his clothes, and began. 'You've wondered why I came to work here when I did. Of course you have. Middle of the school year. Just two terms after starting my first teaching job at Bellhurst. It must have puzzled you. You've never asked. Too polite, I suppose. Too sensitive. Too good. Too good for me, anyway.' He looked ready to start crying again, but Christopher calmed him by stroking his hand. 'I had a love affair there, with a boy. That's the truth of it. A sixth former. Almost exactly the same age as you. He'll be nineteen in July.'

'You keep in touch?' Christopher's voice a whisper of panic.

'No. I'll come to that.'

A part of Christopher didn't want to know any more: the part of him that had forborne to question Tom about his recent past did not want to be hearing this. But another part of him even more desperately needed to know it all, however awful it was going to be, and wanted no detail to be spared. 'Tell me what happened, Tom,' he said in as neutral a tone as he could manage.

'His name was – is – David. David Matthews. Blond, like you. A fraction smaller, maybe. The resemblance ended there though. Don't worry: he wasn't your look-alike; apart from being very nice he wasn't much like you in other ways.'

Christopher didn't say anything but he didn't stop stroking Tom's hand either, so Tom continued. 'When I started at Bellhurst I hadn't been exposed to the company of eighteen-year-olds since I'd been one myself. At university your friends are your own age: you move up the years with them and don't have a lot to do with people who're three years younger. But back at a public school, I was surrounded by them. Well…

'I was far the youngest teacher on the staff. Some of the boys in the Upper Sixth made me welcome almost as if I was one of them. Actually it was flattering. I wouldn't have expected it to be, but it was. I learnt, sort of by osmosis, that there were affairs going on. Two or three pairs of boys who roomed together were actually couples. I kept that to myself: never passed it on to other staff – though some of them might also have known and kept it to themselves; I'd no way of knowing. Anyway, the boys seemed to assume I did know, and knowing that secrets were safe with me increased their trust. David wasn't one of the couples – I mean he wasn't one half of a couple – but he knew all about them. His own roommate was a big hulking bloke who I didn't think was very good-looking (nor did David, I discovered) but who boasted of his female conquests in the holidays, and around the Bellhurst area at weekends. (Another piece of privileged information I turned a blind eye to.)

'The ones who were eighteen – including David – were allowed to go to pubs at weekends, provided they had their parents' permission. There was an unspoken tradition they didn't use the same pubs as the teachers – and we didn't muscle in on theirs. I never tried to push things by joining them in their pubs.

'But the day before half-term of that first term – I know, I know, it's only seven months ago – I went after supper to a pub I hadn't used before. And there (surprise, surprise) was David on his own. I'd never thought I liked him more than I did the others, or that he'd taken a bigger shine to me than the others. But at that moment … this is difficult to explain … I suddenly did. And he realised it. You see things in people's eyes or feel it somehow in the air…' Tom was on the point of saying, *just like with us,* but he stopped himself in time.

'I offered him a refill and he accepted. We sat and talked, about nothing much – boring things about school, I suppose: I don't remember. The thing I did know, and he knew too, was that we'd kiss at some point on our way back through the dark. And we did.'

'David,' said Christopher coldly. 'David and Jonathan.' He'd stopped stroking Tom's hand. 'Did you have sex with him?'

Tom breathed out slowly, and just loudly enough for Christopher to hear. 'Oddly enough, no. Not then. Not at any time. That might surprise you, seeing I don't suffer from religious scruples, and I didn't even back then, and I soon discovered David didn't either. But I was scared for my job. Petrified. If anything happened and we got caught … I'd go to prison. David knew that. He was as ready for sex as I was, but he was afraid too. For himself, and also for me. But that's running ahead. You asked me to tell you the whole thing. Without spinning it out I'll try to.

'After that first evening and that kiss I dreaded meeting him next day but I needn't have. He said, "Have a good half-term, sir," with a smile, in front of the other boys, and then disappeared into the coach heading for the school train. But when half-term was over, there he was in the same pub again. Did I go there on purpose? You bet I did. Did he? Of course. And then it all took off. We fell in love. We found time to be together when we could. It couldn't be very often: other boys would have noticed. We met once in the Christmas holidays. It was stupid and dangerous but we did. At a cinema. We might have decided to be hung for sheep as lambs, but we were still too scared to do anything, both of us. By the beginning of the next term it was on the tip of my tongue to tell him I loved him, but I managed to bite it back. If I had done, I know he'd have said the same to me, and then God knows…

'Anyway, it was bad enough. However careful we were, people couldn't help noticing – weeks passing – that we were together more than most boys and masters. Someone would walk into a room and find us talking, or catch us walking back from the pub. After a few times, people put two and two together. Of course they talked.'

'And it all came out?'

'I was hauled up in front of the headmaster. He kept it very general. Said I'd got too close to the boys. Perhaps I was too young for the job I had, and ought to be somewhere with a different age group. He didn't mention any boys by name, didn't mention David, which was sporting. He got in touch with our old man – Father Louis sends him quite a few boys each year – and leant on him, I suppose, to give me the job here. So here I am. Of course he told me never to contact any of the boys again. If I did, or even tried to, there'd be all hell to pay. I believed him.

'I had to leave there and then, not even go to my room to get my things. They were sent on to me at home.'

'Hell,' said Christopher. 'What did your parents say?' Though that was hardly his main concern.

'The school concocted a story, which I had to go along with, that I couldn't rub along with two of the senior teachers and they'd said I had to leave or else they would. My parents must've seen through it at once, it was pretty flimsy. But it had to do. They wouldn't have wanted to … they didn't dare to unpick it and discover something worse. So there we've left it, as far as the folks are concerned.'

'And you haven't tried to see him again?' Christopher found his feelings pulled dismayingly this way and that. 'You were deeply in love with him, but you just dropped him when you were told to? Then you fell in love with me instead? A few weeks later? On the rebound?'

'If you want to put it like that, I suppose, yes,' said Tom wretchedly. 'I don't know. I can't know. But I knew I couldn't pursue him. And I can't ever. It couldn't do him any good, and he'll know that by now, or very soon. It was something that had no future – it's obvious now – a teacher and a pupil. Whatever was I thinking? you must be asking. It was wrong and it should never have begun. I let it begin because I wasn't clever enough, or experienced enough, to keep my distance, not to fall in love.'

'So how is it different with us?' Christopher asked, still chilly. 'I'm hardly any older than David, so you say.'

Tom said desperately, 'You're not a schoolboy. The position's all different. When you move to Oxford I can come there too, find work. I'll get onto Gabbitas and Thring. We've talked about it. We can have a future.' He didn't sound altogether convinced. He needed Christopher to be convinced first. 'I know,' he said. 'What can you make of someone so … inconstant … that he falls in love twice in half a year?' He realised that Christopher had not actually let go of his hand. He wasn't stroking it but he hadn't withdrawn his own – yet. He took a risk, because he couldn't not do. 'Or could you say that the past is the past and everything became different once I met you? Could you bring yourself to say that, Christopher? To realise that it's true? I don't know if you can.'

There was a silence while Christopher thought about this, and Tom went back over what he'd told Christopher and wondered if he could have put any of it differently and whether things would be any better now if he had.

You could fall in love more often than was convenient, Christopher found himself thinking. Especially when you were very young. Or be infatuated at the very least. Tom had been very honest with him, he was sure. The thing between him and David had been sexual, of course it had, yet they hadn't actually had sex… Christopher was a bit surprised about that. But Tom had had no need to lie to Christopher about that detail, since they'd both been honest about having had sex with other people in the past. The more he thought about it the more he realised that Tom's confession could easily have been much worse. Tom had fallen in love in the wrong place at the wrong time. No-one had died. Tom hadn't even had sex with the boy. Was it really so different from … well, from himself and Malcolm in the car? Christopher hadn't felt any pressing need to confess to that.

'I think it's OK, Tom,' Christopher said, after the longest pause in any conversation that Tom could remember. 'I mean, I think we are. OK, I mean. I think we're OK.'

'I'm sorry I had to tell you that,' Tom said. 'But I told myself I'd be honest with you one day. And it looked as though today was going to have to be that day. You need to be careful with Dexter, that's all. That's what I also needed to show you. It's not really a question of what you do or don't do. That's what I discovered over the David business. It's about how people see things. Which actually is probably the only reality that exists – unless I'm quite wrong and there really is a God after all. It's not what you do, it's what you're seen to do that counts in life.'

Christopher said, 'That's cynical.'

'I don't want to be cynical. I'm not. I just want to be realistic. I want you to see how things are. I needed to warn you. To be careful with Dexter. With all of them.'

There was another silence. Then Christopher said, 'I understand. I do. I'll be much more careful with Dexter from now on. Not just for me. For both of us.'

Tom hugged him, and rolled him backwards onto the bed. The Dexter problem seemed smaller now. The threatening images that had filled both their minds, multiple pictures of a handsome yet dangerous boy, framed again and again in the curtains of a bath cubicle, receded like a series of portraits along a dark corridor from which you tiptoe away to go in search of light.

***

John Moyse's New Journal: June 18th 1962

Father Louis came out of hospital today. However, he's not back here yet. He's gone to the abbey to convalesce for a few days. He's supposed to be coming back on Thursday in time for the Corpus Christi procession.

It's strange to think of him reduced like that. Not being a proper headmaster any more. When I remember him mostly as so forceful and fierce. The evening I first came here as a new boy, and nobody knew what to do or where to go, he caught hold of me in the prep room after roll call and put his two forefingers in my mouth and pulled them apart to stop me running away. Then he asked me in his most gravely voice what my name was. Of course he had to take his fingers out of my mouth to hear me answer. And when I had he didn't say anything. No welcome or 'I hope you'll be happy here'. Just walked away to do the same thing to someone else whose name he couldn't put to the face. I suppose that was what teaching methods were like when he was taught them, back in the nineteenth century. And those fierce RI lessons he used to give. 'From cover to cover,' waving the little red catechism. 'We had to learn it from cover to cover. By heart. Or we'd be caned.' Then he thought he'd let us off lightly when he only gave us massive chunks to remember, and caned us if we couldn't remember those.

Father Matthew so different. Strict but friendly. Though never too friendly. Always dignified. Taking the roll call that first night, people learning to say the word 'Adsum' for the first time. One boy's name was Clough (he's left now) and we all thought it was Fluff and everyone giggled. Father Matthew saying patiently, 'Settle down now, settle down.' And he's been exactly the same ever since. Even though you see things differently when you're thirteen to when you were eight, and Father Louis's fierceness doesn't seem quite so scary as it used to (though perhaps he won't be even the least bit scary when he comes back) Father Matthew just seems exactly unchanged. A calm and resuring presence.

Father Claude another kettle of fish altogether. In his own world at the assembly hall piano on the first morning. But singing the morning hymn brought lumps to my throat and made me cry, and afterwards walking along the cloister Father Claude saw that and stopped me and asked what the trouble was. He sat me on a seat and I told him it was my first day and hearing the music and trying to sing had made me homesick. And he said something to make me smile – I don't remember what. I didn't speak to him again for days but then he came to my second piano lesson with Miss Coyle and listened quietly to whatever I was playing and went out again without saying a word. And after that Miss Coyle came to me and said I was to have lessons from Father Claude himself from then on, which was an honour because he normally only taught the seniors. It sounded as if he was Artur Rubinstein or something, which of course he isn't, even though he is very good. I played the Mozart Fantasy in D minor at my first lesson with Father C. And the lesson was terrific. As they've all been ever since.

Tom did the dormitory round again tonight. Like Christopher he's very friendly and likes to chat. Angelo did that silly thing again about having a late bath and winding Tom up. Which makes no sense because he likes Tom – and Christopher – as much as I do. But he got hoist by his own whatsit as Father Matthew came to put the lights out and did so and Angelo had to get himself to bed in the dark. Not that he'd find that difficult.

Astonishment all round. Angelo and I are invited to a private view on Weds evening of a picture exhib. in Canterbury. Miss O'Deere had the invitations as her picture is one of the entrys. It's a picture of Tom and Christopher on a cricket field apparantly, though we haven't seen it yet. Angelo and I are going because of winning the art prize, but it seems a bit unfair on Simon and Edward. But I asked them and they said it didn't matter. They're not that keen on paintings, either of them. There'd only be orange juice for the kids, Edward said, they won't give us a real drink, and anyway, we'd all seen Tom and Christopher on a cricket field about twice a week for yonks and hardly needed to see a painting of them. But I think any escape from the building for a few hours must be worth it. And Canterbury's OK.

SEVENTEEN

Tom and Christopher knew that when Mr Charteris arrived with the minibus Dexter and Moyse would make a dash for either the front seats or the back ones, the only question was which. When the moment came the youngsters also seemed undecided for a nanosecond but then made for the front of the vehicle with the speed of bullets and installed themselves alongside Mr Charteris, who was dapper in a bow-tie for the occasion. Tom, Christopher and Miss O'Deere shared the roomy rear section. Miss O'Deere leaned towards her two younger colleagues as they were setting off. 'I should have said this ages ago, but do please call me Molly.' This was unlikely to be overheard by the boys in front, who were talking quite loudly about makes of car to Mr Charteris.

In those days there was no such thing as Park and Ride, or pedestrian zones, in historic cities like Canterbury. Mr Charteris simply drove the minibus into the High Street and parked near the cathedral – something difficult to imagine now. There was a way to enter the exhibition, clearly signed, which didn't involve going through the cathedral nave, but Mr Charteris said – and the others agreed with him – that it would be a waste of a visit to Canterbury if they didn't look inside the main body of the building, and so they went in by the usual entrance of the south porch. Mr Charteris, whose main subject was history, and church architecture one of his special interests, directed them to look at the medieval stained glass, jewel-like in its cobalt blues and ruby reds, in the north aisle as they walked through, while telling the story of William of Sens, architect of the early Gothic east end of the building and of his unfortunate death tumble from the scaffolding while on a tour of inspection. Then they turned left into the cloisters.

All four cloisters were hung with paintings. Only those
which had been judged to be of the highest quality were
given space inside the chapter house, which leads off the
eastern side of the cloister court. Inside the chapter
house trestle tables, respectably swathed in floor length
white linen cloths, were reassuringly heavily laden with
schooners of sherry. There was orange juice for those
who wanted it, but Miss O'Deere surprised her
colleagues – and pleased John and Angelo no end – by
saying that they, dressed up so nicely for the evening in
their long trousers, blazers and ties, could join the adults
in a glass of sherry if they wanted one. She had reason to
be in a good mood. There in the most prominent of
positions, on a screen in front of the east wall, below the
vast stained glass window and directly facing the
entrance door, was Molly O'Deere's double portrait of
Tom and Christopher as the cricket-playing David and
Jonathan. They had all seen it – and so had everybody
else – even before their attention had wandered to the
table and its cargo of glasses. Flanking it were two other
large oil paintings: one of the sun setting behind the
three stark cooling towers and single chimney of the
Richborough power station, the other an exterior view of
the east end of Canterbury Cathedral itself in driving
rain.

'She's really good, isn't she, sir?' Tom looked down to
find Dexter, a small-scale young man with a glass of
amontillado sherry in his hand, eager to seek his
agreement and approval.

'Yes, she is, Dexter. You're quite right. She has a real
talent.' This was the first time Tom and Angelo had
spoken to each other since the bathroom exchange two
nights ago. Tom was as eager to declare a truce as
Angelo seemed to be.

'And she catches your likeness very well, sir. And
Christo... I mean, Mr McGing's too, of course. You

look a very handsome pair.' A flicker of anxiety crossed the boy's face. 'I didn't mean any disrespect by that, sir.'

'I know you didn't. And, since we're not at school right now but simply two young men drinking sherry together, you needn't 'sir' me all the time. At least, not this evening.'

'Thank you.' Angelo took a small sip of sherry to prevent the *sir* slipping out of his mouth automatically. The truce was sealed.

'It really looks good in this big space,' Christopher said, and John Moyse who was standing beside him added cheerfully, 'It's just brilliant.' It began to be apparent that their good opinions were shared by other people present who had no reason to be biased in the picture's favour, as the little party from Star of the Sea naturally were. Its summery greens and whites, and the vibrant flesh tones that Miss O'Deere had conjured up for the young men's faces, arms and torsos, were shining like beacons across the room and drawing a growing crowd towards it.

Favourable comments were made on Miss O'Deere's technique. Towards the end of the sittings she had made the inspired decision to place a cricket ball in Tom's right hand. This brought a wonderful splash of ripe cherry colour close to the very centre of the canvas: the additional touch was now quite rightly eliciting praise. Also, in the distance, where dark trees marked the far edge of the field, gaps in the foliage gave glimpses of a field of buttercups beyond, brilliant in the sun. But most of all, the words of praise were targeted on the artist's capture of youthful male beauty, of character and atmosphere and the something special that existed between David and Jonathan, with the frisson that gave the beholder.

It was a wonderful experience, Tom and Christopher both discovered, to stand, incognito because fully clothed, shoulder to shoulder with admiring strangers. Then, occasionally, someone did spot them in the crowd and realise who they were, and talk to them; also to the charming teenagers who were with them – and were now happy to enjoy a little reflected glory – and even to Mr Charteris. And whenever this happened one of the party would go and haul Miss O'Deere out of whatever patch of self-chosen obscurity she happened to be standing in and bring her into the circle of admiration too. It was she to whom the praise was due, after all.

It was quite difficult to tear yourself away and go and circulate, to view the other pictures on display, but in the end good manners required you to, if nothing else. Tom found the problem with sherry was that no sooner had you started one than it was gone. He chose a moment when neither John nor Angelo was looking in his direction – he didn't want to set a bad example – to equip himself with a second glass for his journey round the room and the cloister garth beyond.

None of them wanted to leave, but at last it was time to. Mr Charteris, no less than Christopher or Tom, would have liked to instigate a visit to the nearest pub, but the presence of the two youngsters unfortunately forced the proposal to remain unvoiced. Still, there was an ebullient atmosphere in the minibus as they drove back to school, while John Moyse recounted a long and highly improbable anecdote about a cat belonging to a cousin, which had fallen downstairs in the dark one night and broken its hip. When they ate the late supper of cold chicken and salad that Cathy had prepared for them, the two boys were allowed to join the adults, for the first time ever, in the staff dining room.

Tom and Christopher were spared dormitory duty on the evening of the private view. Father Matthew and Sister shared it between them. Father Matthew had very decently said that he would do it again the next night, the whole holiday of Corpus Christi. 'A little birdie tells me that you both have a birthday to celebrate tomorrow,' he told them. 'You might appreciate a free evening in the circumstances. Though it would be nice to see you at the procession in the afternoon if you can make it. It'll be Louis's first engagement, and I'm sure he'll appreciate the support of as many staff as can get there.' They promised to be on parade at three o'clock.

'How did you know we both have a birthday tomorrow?' Tom asked, a little surprised. They hadn't announced the rather strange coincidence to any of their colleagues.

'The information is spelled out very clearly in your *curricula vitarum*,' he said with a curious smile, unhesitatingly inserting a correct Latin plural into the English sentence.

Tom said, 'Of course,' equally smoothly, though he did wonder, with a momentary chill, why Father Matthew might have been re-reading his CV and Christopher's two months after their appointment to their current jobs. Perhaps he simply had a very good memory, Tom told himself. Anyway, he'd been saved from actually having to ask for a free evening.

The morning dawned fair and blue-skied, as had all the mornings of the past two weeks. Father Matthew said the Corpus Christi Mass in the white vestments that were appropriate for the day, and three of the youngest boys in the school, in white shirts for the occasion, made their First Communions during the course of it. They were given a special breakfast afterwards, at which Sister presided, and at which chocolate cakes, jellies and lemonade made special guest appearances.

In the staff dining room it proved impossible for Tom and Christopher to keep the fact of their two birthdays secret. A near dozen birthday cards arriving for each of them told their own story: six months away from Christmas it is hard to mistake two handfuls of birthday cards for anything else. Happy Birthdays were said, and some surprise expressed at the coincidence of their both having been born on the same date.

Father Louis arrived without ceremony or fuss in the middle of the morning, driven by the prior in the monastery car. Father Matthew and the women were there to welcome him but Christopher and Tom were not. They had gone back to Canterbury by the train.

It hadn't been a part of their plan originally, but, having seen the picture of themselves the previous evening, they found themselves unable to resist an unexpected urge to go and see it again. It was as if they had been hypnotised by seeing it in the public domain, and by the very positive reaction to it at the private view. Before then, seeing it unwrapped from time to time from the old curtain that had protected it in the art room, they had been only dimly aware of the painting's power. They had seen it 'as through a glass, darkly'. Last night they had come before it, and before its reflected image of themselves, face to face.

And now here it was again, at half past eleven this fine morning. Small groups of people filed round the cloisters and the chapter house, looking at the bright canvasses on display, some pointing out a detail, some admiring, some commenting critically. The chapter house seemed bigger. It lacked the previous night's crowd and party atmosphere and no longer had sherry-laden tables in the middle of it. A voice hailed them, entering the chapter house a minute or two behind them. They turned in surprise, recognising the voice. It was Roger. Beside him was Malcolm, padding along like a big ginger tomcat, an amused expression on his face.

'Well, so there it is,' said Roger. 'And here you are. We had to come. Too curious not to, after all we'd heard about it. Malc's taken the morning off work. You too by the look of it.'

Christopher explained about it being Corpus Christi and a whole holiday, added a bit unnecessarily that they'd already been here the previous night and then, because their rather rapid return seemed to call for an explanation other than sheer narcissism and vanity, went on to say that it was both of their birthdays and they were in Canterbury to celebrate the fact.

'Both your birthdays?' Roger queried. 'Pretty bloody unusual, that,' he commented in reply to Tom's nod. 'We'd better celebrate that with a drink somewhere in a minute.'

Malcolm, who had been staring fixedly at the picture all this time, said, 'Bloody amazing. The picture, I mean. You were right, Tom, and I didn't believe you. It's a picture of two young men in love. You couldn't possibly see it and not realise that. It's also beautifully done. Some birthday present you two've got.'

One or two visitors, perhaps catching the end of this conversation, turned to look at the quartet of young men and realised that two of them were the models for the double portrait. A little knot of people was soon gathered around them, talking and asking questions, and the group was joined, half a minute later, by someone else they knew, Artemia Dexter, Angelo's mother, who was with a woman friend.

'What a surprise,' said Mrs Dexter. 'But actually two surprises. First the beautiful picture by talented Miss O'Deere. We had little idea she could produce a work like this. And now, here are her two sitters in person, as handsome in life as in art. You must be feeling very proud.'

'We're very proud of Miss O'Deere,' Tom said loyally. 'We can't take any credit for the picture. But it is an honour to be associated with such a fine work.'

235

Christopher tried to memorise Tom's sentences in case he needed them in the future, while Malcolm's broad grin nearly erupted in a laugh.

Mrs Dexter's friend, a busty woman in a floral dress who had not yet spoken or been introduced, said, 'The piece has an incredible energy about it – like an electric charge – like the creation of Adam on the Sistine ceiling.'

Malcolm hid his grin in a smirk, Roger looked at the floor, Tom and Christopher wished that floor might swallow them, and suddenly realised their folly in coming here today. Mrs Dexter said, 'Patricia, you go too far. You're embarrassing my young friends. The Sistine Chapel ceiling indeed. But I haven't presented them. Tom Sanders, I think it is, and Christopher Mc…'

'McGing.'

'I'd like you both to meet Mrs Jamieson. Patricia Jamieson. She writes for the Kent Messenger.' The implications of this last bit of news sank in slowly as, in their turn, Roger and Malcolm were introduced to the two ladies.

'I was here yesterday evening,' Patricia Jamieson said to Christopher and Tom. 'I believe I saw you at a distance but our paths didn't actually cross. And I didn't want to embarrass a certain young man who was enjoying what might have been his first glass of sherry.' She smiled mischievously. Of course, as a friend of his mother's, she must have recognised Angelo. 'My review of the exhibition will be in tomorrow's issue. At least it should be. Sometimes they hold things over for a week. You know what they're like.'

When they had extricated themselves from the company of the art critic and Angelo's mother, as well as those other exhibition-goers who were keen to talk to them about the David and Jonathan, the four men made their way across the close to the City Arms, where they bought pints of beer. Tom and Christopher, at least, felt they needed them. As an afterthought they ordered rounds of ham, and cheese and pickle, sandwiches.

'Do you think she'll put all that into her review?' Christopher asked the others. 'About the Sistine ceiling.'

'I doubt it,' Tom said, though he didn't sound very confident in his doubting. 'She was probably just trying to impress us, trying to find something to say on the spot.'

'If she was trying to impress us,' Roger pointed out, 'she'll probably be trying even harder to impress her readers in the Kent Messenger.'

'The Sistine ceiling,' Malcolm said. 'You have to admit, she had a point. I think your Miss O'Dreary's got an amazing talent. What's she doing wasting it on a school full of kids? And by the way, you both look terrific.'

'This birthday of yours,' Roger said, probably thinking a change of subject might be welcome. 'What are you going to do to celebrate it?'

'We're supposed to be spending the afternoon at a procession, like they do in Spain and Italy,' said Tom. 'But then we thought we'd go into town later. Probably have dinner at Marchesis'.'

'And how old have you just become, if you're not too old to be asked that?' queried Malcolm. Christopher said that he had turned nineteen at about ten o'clock that morning, and Tom, admitting to twenty-two, said he thought he'd been born at about two in the afternoon. 'In which case,' said Malcolm, 'you're still only twenty-one. Enjoy it while it lasts.' It was on the tip of Tom's tongue to ask Malcolm how old he was, but as it wasn't Malcolm's birthday and as the answer would have to be within a year or two either side of thirty, he left the question un-put.

'Well, if you fancy a nightcap after you've had your dinner out, then come on down to the Digby and have one on me,' Roger volunteered. And when they had finished their lunchtime beers and sandwiches, he drove them back to school, dropping them off a little way up the road, at their own request, to avoid arousing the interest of inquisitive staff or kids.

Everyone filed into the chapel when the bell went, on the dot of three. Father Louis officiated, making his first public appearance since his return that morning, resplendent in an ornate golden cope, with Father Matthew at his side, dressed in a not much less elaborate blue and white one. Father Claude sat at the harmonium, dressed in the bat-winged black cowl that was appropriate for his role as master of ceremonies, and accompanied the singing of the traditional opening hymn, O Salutaris Hostia. Then Father Matthew read the introductory prayer, and the procession moved off.

First to move down the aisle were the four altar servers in their cassocks and cottas: they were the two house captains, Dexter and Rickman, plus their two deputies, Edward Abelard and John Moyse. Someone had dug out four red cassocks for them to wear which, as a change from the usual black ones, gave them a decidedly festive appearance. Abelard took mighty swipes at the air with the incense-filled thurible as they began to walk, which created billows of smoke and caused an outbreak of violent coughing among the juniors on his side of the chapel. Immediately behind them walked Father Louis, now holding the gold and silver monstrance before him like a radiant sun, with Father Matthew looking very solemn in his wake. Behind them, filing out of the front rows first, came the junior boys in their best shorts and blazers. The seniors followed and then, last of all, came the resident teachers plus Mr Charteris and another non-resident master, who both lived so near at hand that it would have been difficult for them not to turn up, with Sister bringing up the rear.

Out of the chapel they moved in stately flow, along the chapel cloister, left into the main cloister and then out into the hot sunshine via the front door, which had been opened for them in advance. Father Claude had left the harmonium as the chapel emptied and now bustled back and forth along the line of the procession, keeping the boys in time and in tune with the aid of a pitch-pipe and his own cracked baritone as they sang Praise to the Holiest from specially Roneo-ed sheets.

Across the gravelled parking area the procession moved, then round the corner of the building, to the rear of the school, among the cricket pitches and between the tennis courts, coming to a stop at last under the far trees under which an improvised altar had been set up and decked with flowers by the nuns of St Ursula's. Here the nuns joined them for more prayers and a blessing, before they set off once again, this time through the gate and into the secluded, wooded gardens of St Ursula's, finding time to sing all the verses of Sweet Sacrament Divine before they reached the convent itself.

Ark from the ocean's roar… As Christopher sang the familiar words they struck him forcefully for once. This place, this afternoon's activity, really was a haven from the world outside. The morning had disconcerted him. Last night the picture of David and Jonathan had sent his spirits soaring. It was beautiful, and he and Tom were beautiful, their secret safely encoded in the brushstrokes. But this morning the code had been broken by one person at the very least. By going back to Canterbury today they had caught themselves out. It had only been vanity after all. Tom had been right to compare the picture with the portrait of Dorian Gray. The picture had drawn them with its power and ensnared them with its beauty. It was only a matter of time before it did them harm. *Sweet Sacrament of Peace. Sweet Sacrament of Peace...* This present moment, this quiet afternoon spent in meditative procession through the secluded gardens of a convent, might be the end of peace for Tom and him. *Sweet Sacrament of Rest...* The end of peace, the end of rest. He would ask Tom what he thought later.

By the time the procession entered the nuns' chapel Father Claude was already seated at the console of the organ there, and producing warbling sounds from it, ready to launch into the opening chords of Tantum ergo Sacramentum as soon as the whole procession was inside.

Father Matthew, not Father Louis, led the final prayers. It seemed that Father Louis was going to be a figurehead pure and simple now, as the abbot had told everyone. He would walk in glory, bearing the Body of Christ aloft in the gilded monstrance, but when it came to speaking, that would be Father Matthew's prerogative from now on.

After the final Benediction and the singing of Sweet Saviour, bless us ere we go – *Through life's long day and death's dark night, O gentle Jesus, be our light* – the boys and everyone else filed out onto the nuns' lawn for buns and lemonade. In the minds of the younger boys at least, these were the principal objectives of the whole exercise, and since the nuns were as pleasingly generous with the food on this occasion as they had been in previous years, there was a general feeling that this sunny afternoon was far from being a wasted one. On the contrary it had been a great success.

The birthday boys took the bus into town later, and dined at Marchesi Bros' on rump steaks, with Stilton cheese to follow, which they washed down with a bottle of Beaujolais. Christopher hadn't needed to bring up the subject of his anxieties about the picture. Tom had got there first, while they were in Tom's bedroom, changing to go out. 'Are you still worried about what that art critic's going to write?' he asked.

'Yes,' said Christopher baldly, pulling on a clean pair of blue jeans. Some of his clothes now lived in Tom's room. It was not always easy to keep track of them.

Tom tried to reassure. 'She's the only one who's said what she did. Even Mrs Dexter thought she was being silly.'

'But you and I know she wasn't being silly. She got it right.'

'The boys didn't spot anything. They just saw it as a beautiful painting and complimented Molly, as we're now allowed to call her.' Tom rummaged in a drawer for a shirt.

'You're being disingenuous,' said Christopher, 'if I've got the right word. The same thoughts may well have gone through John and Angelo's minds. Only they could never have said what that woman did. Not to a group of their teachers. Two thirteen-year-old boys. Put yourself in their shoes.'

Christopher had a point. At least, that is what Tom said to Christopher. Because he wanted to reassure his lover and comfort him, he did not voice his real thoughts: that Christopher was absolutely right and that Tom was just as alarmed as he was. But they had let the matter drop after that, had finished dressing, and by unspoken agreement refused to let their worries spoil their dinner.

On their return from town they took up Roger's invitation to a nightcap at the Admiral Digby. They found Malcolm in the bar, on the customers' side, and slightly – and charmingly – tipsy. When they had drinks in their hands they all moved out into the garden. The shortest night of the year was still only at the twilight stage. 'Don't worry, I'm not driving home,' Malcolm told them. 'I'm staying the night. Throw caution to the

241

winds for once. The way you two seem to. Time Roger and I took a leaf or two out of your book, I reckon.'

'Don't get too carried away,' Tom warned him. 'We're not as brave as all that. Only foolhardy sometimes, like this morning in Canterbury. Exposing ourselves as a couple to the public gaze. We won't be doing that again in a hurry.'

France was on the horizon this evening. Fading now to a grey streak, but its lights just beginning to shine out as the daylight went. Tom raised his glass to 'friends over the water' and Christopher and Malcolm followed suit, while Tom and Christopher both remembered that they owed those friends in France a letter...

At that point Roger joined them at their table in the half dark. 'We're going mackerel fishing on Saturday night,' Malcolm said. Looking out across the calm water had reminded him. 'Conditions should be perfect, if the forecast doesn't change. Fancy coming along again? Have a bit of a sail. Your predecessor came with us once, I remember. Sick over the side, he was. Not such a good sailor as you two are.'

'Perhaps he wasn't so lucky with the weather,' Tom said, in a spirit of easy generosity towards someone he'd never met and probably never would.

'Been meaning to ask you,' Christopher said, more than a little tipsy himself now, and ready to start a conversational hare that he hadn't been bold enough to approach a few days before, when he was lying naked on the beach. 'What actually did happen to Richard Appleton?'

Malcolm answered without hesitation. 'Ran off with a fourteen-year-old boy from your school. That got him sacked.'

A cold chill ran down the spines of Christopher and Tom and they caught each other's eye in a mutual glance of horror. 'Jesus Christ,' said Christopher.

'Eloped to Gretna Green together,' said Roger, poker-faced. 'And lived happily ever after.'

There was a thunderstruck silence, then all four burst out laughing. 'Oh, go to hell, man!' said Tom. 'You had me there, you really did.' He picked up his beer mug and made a pretend lunge at Malcolm, as if to throw its contents over him. It was quite clever of him not actually to spill it.

'Well,' said Roger when everyone had recovered, 'the truth wasn't all that different, when I think about it. It involved sex, as these matters usually do. You know – do you know? – that he also taught at the big school – St Aidan's, isn't it? Coached the Rugby team. Well, he got friendly with one of the boys in particular: too friendly, some would say, but this one was eighteen, not fourteen, and a day-boy, not a boarder. Not many years younger than him, really. He used to go to this boy's house at weekends and ... now that you've both jumped to the obvious conclusion, I can tell you that you're both wrong. The main reason for his visits, the main object of his interest, was this boy's elder sister. Well, cutting a long story short, the two of them, Richard Appleton and the sister, were found in bed together. There was no end of a row, of which we only heard the distant reverberations, and inevitably that was the end of Richard as far as your two schools were concerned. He said a breathless goodbye and left. It must have been shortly before the end of last term, if I think about it. And then you two came along. End of story.'

'Yeah,' said Malcolm, 'that's how it is when sex and religion get mixed up. At least, when sex and religious institutions get tangled. Sex is a real old spanner in the works sometimes.'

'It's the dog in the chapel,' said Christopher, thinking this a very inspired metaphor, and himself very clever for coming out with it so spontaneously. But the others didn't seem to catch it. Malcolm then made the point that, as no-one had to drive, and it was still a double birthday, a second nightcap seemed about due.

They stayed at the Admiral Digby till closing time, though moving indoors from the garden a little before that. They reconfirmed their arrangement to go fishing on Saturday night. Then they had another couple of drinks, whiskies by this time, before they left, with friendly kisses all round on the doorstep – though circumspectly on the inside of the door before it was opened, not out on the pavement where any Dick or Harry might see. They weren't as drunk as all that, and they weren't in France ... though even there Tom had managed to get into trouble doing just such a thing. And even now, the kiss that was exchanged between Christopher and Malcolm lasted long enough to cause Tom and Roger to give each other a look that indicated that their forbearance was being ever so slightly stretched. It was after midnight when they got back to school. They went directly to bed, crossing nobody's path on the way, which they reckoned fortunate, and just managing not to overturn the statue of the Virgin on the landing of their stairs as they floundered up. Which was also fortunate. For these reasons (the preservation of the statue excepted) they remained in ignorance of the domestic earthquake that had taken place in their absence until breakfast the following day.

***

From John Moyse's New Journal: Thursday June 21st 1962

The longest day of the year and first day of summer, also called midsummer's day which doesn't make too much sense.

Nothing got written yesterday, so this is really the account of 2 days in one.

Yesterday evening Mr Charteris drove Angelo and me, Miss O'Deere and Christopher and Tom (I can't really call them anything else these days) to Canterbury Cathedral. So beautiful, and even if it goes crooked where the nave got tacked on to the choir, well that's part of the charm. (The crookedness may even be a symbol of something mysterious for all I know. They did odd things in the middle ages.) Mr Charteris made us look at the mediaeval stained glass. Effect spoiled somewhat because not all of it there.

Angelo and I did chin-ups on the bars in the glassless cloister windows, seeing who could do the most. Ended in a draw cos some official saw us and stopped us. Luckily none of our party saw.

Reason for visit: this famous painting by Miss O'Deere. What can I say? Are Angelo and I the only people who can see this? Like in The Emperor's New Clothes?

Miss O'Deere has painted D and J (or do I mean T and C?) as the sexiest pair of male lovers in the history of art. Either she doesn't realise this or does a fab job of pretending she doesn't. And obviously A and I couldn't say this to her or to T and C – let alone Mr C. Supposing everyone else had the same thought but daredn't say anything? Then it really is like the Emp's new clothes.

The other thing is: it really is a beautiful picture. You'd say it was painted with authority. We'll never laugh at our old art teacher again. She's totally brilliant. She got T and C to the life. And once you've seen the picture you realise that T and C really do look at each other the way D and J do in the picture. They've been doing it all the time and nobody noticed. It took the picture to show me that. Maybe that's the point of painting?

Enough philossophy. A and I got given sherry as a token of respect for our increasing maturity (in all ways I suppose) and it was quite good. Made me feel a bit hazy on the way back. Angelo saw this awful woman friend of his mother's at the exhib. But luckily she didn't see us. She writes for the Messenger.

Chicken and salad in staff dining room. Another 1st. Everyone seemed very high after seeing the picture – which really was the star attraction at the exhibition by the way – or maybe it was the sherry or maybe just me. After that Angelo and I talked for a long time in the chapel cloister and some things got said that shouldn't have done. But nothing actually happened.

Today Father Louis came back. He led the procession in the afternoon (whole hol: Corpus Christi) but didn't actually speak. He stands and walks OK but looks like a waxwork with hollow eyes. You have to say it's sad to see him like that.

My last procession at S of the S. It felt so safe and comforting, never thought this before, and everything will be so diff next year. Me walking second behind Angelo and You-know-who, alongside Edward who swung the thurible about so violently I thought he'd take someone's head off with it, and looking at the curls at the back of A's neck – which I'd never done before! And thinking about last night. And the whole thing somehow moved me. And I never realised before that that's the whole object of processions – and maybe the whole religious ceremonial bit, the dressing up and the ritual, is simply exactly that. Maybe even the theology and the doctrine too. Oh dear. More philossophy!

Father Claude had me start to learn a new piece last week. It's the Arabesque by Schumann. It's not very difficult, but Fr. C. thinks it'll be a good thing to show off with when I start at Downside, as it shows the maturity (he says) in my playing. It has a very slow and sad coda, which he says is Schumann lamenting the loss of childhood. It sounds quite an adult sort of grief to me.

Time to stop. T and C not on duty tonight. Fr M says they've gone out to dinner cos it's their birthday. Who's he kidding? Or who's been kidding him? Friends (or whatever) don't have their birthdays on the same day! I draw my own conclusions – as does A!

EIGHTEEN

Tom and Christopher blundered into the staff dining room together, forgetting, under the pressure of blinding hangovers, their usual rule of entering a few minutes apart. Father Louis was taking breakfast in his own room so Father Matthew was downstairs with the boys in the refectory; Sister and Miss O'Deere were also, for some reason, somewhere else. The only person who was there to look up from her Cornflakes as they entered was an ashen-faced Miss Coyle.

'Ah, there you are,' she said to them, staring at them with eyes that were wide and wild. It was clear that she had been crying. 'There you are. There you are at last.'

'Good morning, Miss Coyle,' Tom said and then, because of her evident agitation, had to add, 'Are you all right? I mean, is everything all right?'

'You obviously don't know,' she said, almost biting her lips as if the words were stinging them. 'But then, how would you? Out pleasuring yourselves till all hours. And no-one at all to set a good example to the boys. It's a scandal. It is, it is. A very scandal.' Her whole face quivered.

'Miss Coyle,' Christopher broke in, 'whatever's the matter?'

She waved her hands in the air. They seemed to writhe above the breakfast things. Her head shook. 'Too awful. Too awful to talk about. Even to mention. At breakfast. The Sin of Sodom.'

'The Sin of Sodom? At breakfast?' Tom said, astonished. He might easily have laughed, but Miss Coyle's anguish was too real a thing, and that, coupled with the anxieties that Christopher and he already shared, left him a very long way from laughter.

'Our two house captains. Rickman and Dexter. Of all the boys... Our two loveliest boys. Or so we thought.

Only thought they were lovely. The shame, the shame.'
Miss Coyle's hands dropped down from the air like birds
alighting, and she used one to mask her face above the
Cornflakes. Tom and Christopher could hear her begin
quietly to sob. They looked at each other, too astonished
to speak. Then Sister came into the room.

'Now, Angela,' the matron said, 'You'll need to pull
yourself together before nine o'clock. We can't all go
around crying now, not in front of the young boys.'

For a startled moment Tom thought that Sister was
referring to Christopher and himself as the young boys,
but it was only for a moment. Miss Coyle was form
mistress of Form One. Sister turned towards the hung-
over young men. 'I suppose you know by now,' she said.

'Only in the vaguest terms,' answered Christopher.

'Which is probably quite as much as you ever need to,'
she said in her starched, dispensary, voice. 'They've
spent the night in separate rooms and they're to have
breakfast after nine o'clock, after school's started, one in
here, the other in the refectory. Father Matthew spoke to
them a second time before he said Mass. Father Odilo is
coming over from the abbey specially to hear their
confessions, and their parents are coming to collect them
later in the morning.'

'Good God,' Tom said, his head thundering. 'But isn't
all that a bit extreme?'

Sister seemed to grow two inches taller. She tightened
her lips, but then had to release them to say, 'If you'd
been there last night and seen what I saw... Well, that
was extreme. Extreme in the extreme.'

'You mean they were actually...?'

'I'll spare you the details, if you really don't mind.
Suffice it to say I caught them, just an hour after lights-
out, *in flagrante delicto*, if you please, in Rickman's
bed.'

In spite of the millrace of thoughts and fears that was rushing through his mind, Tom found space to notice that he really did want to know exactly what had taken place – who was doing what to whom – and to wonder how, in the face of Sister's understandable disinclination to tell him, he could find out. Quite obviously, by the time Sister had alerted Father Matthew and brought him to the scene (or had she sent the boys in their dressing-gowns to knock on his bedroom door at ten at night?) whatever activity they might have been involved in would have ceased.

'Does Father Louis know?' Christopher asked.

'We thought it better not to excite him,' Sister said, in genuine innocence of any ambiguity in her words.

Christopher pursued this, sounding almost angry, and causing Tom to look at him in surprise. 'Has anybody thought to tell him he's no longer headmaster? Or not de facto headmaster at any rate.' Except for Miss Coyle, now staring stonily at her unfinished Cornflakes, they were all still standing, between the door and the breakfast table, while the tea and toast slowly cooled.

'We'll have to tell him, of course,' said Sister. 'Later today. About the boys, I mean. He chose them very carefully for house captains. They were the apples of his eye. He'll notice very quickly if they're not around, whatever else might escape him in his present state. The other question...' She paused, tightening her lips again and putting her head very slightly on one side. 'It's a grey area, as they say these days. I think we'll have to wait and see the course that things take. All sorts of different things. I'm sure you understand what I mean.' With a set expression on her face she pulled the nearest chair back from the table and sat down, and the two men, as if playing musical chairs, immediately followed her example. As they all began reaching for tea and cereal – the tea most desperately needed by the two hung-over young men – Miss O'Deere entered the room. Her face told them as eloquently as if she'd spoken that she knew at least as much as they did about this morning's – or rather last night's – news.

Christopher took advantage of the general confusion at the end of breakfast, of which no-one had been able to eat very much, to slip away upstairs and find Angelo Dexter. Sister had said he'd been put in one of the spare rooms above the chapel cloister which were usually used for visiting priests, while Simon Rickman had been placed, at what was presumably supposed to be a fire-break distance, at the opposite end of the building, in the sick bay. Did schools have contingency plans for this particular eventuality, Christopher wondered, in the way that governments had plans for nuclear attack and which were put smoothly into operation – one hoped, in the government case – as soon as the alarm was raised?

It was not difficult to find the door behind which Dexter had been bundled away. Sounds of suppressed weeping were coming from behind it. Christopher knocked and, without waiting for an answer, went in. Angelo was sitting on the narrow bed, fully dressed except for blazer and tie; his suitcase lay open on the floor at his feet, with piles of books and clothes beside it. Gone were his poise and his nearly adult assurance. Gone was the young man who had stood in the chapter house at Canterbury, sipping sherry and talking about art. Here was just a child again: a very hurt and frightened child. His face looked as though he had been crying for hours, perhaps for the whole of the night that was past, and the tears that were streaming down his cheeks didn't look as though they would be stopping any time soon.

Christopher didn't pause for even a second before he did what came spontaneously from his heart. He sat down on the bed, right next to Angelo, put an arm around his shoulders and pulled him towards him. Almost to Christopher's surprise, Angelo not only did not resist the intimacy but leaned in towards Christopher and rested his head on his shoulder. For the best part of a minute neither of them spoke. Christopher felt Angelo trying to take hold of his free hand, which was resting in his lap. Christopher let him hold it, and after a few seconds, clasped Angelo's hand in return.

'It's OK, old chap,' Christopher said at last, and heard himself sounding like someone who was thirty years older than Angelo rather than just five. 'This is a horrid moment, I know, but it will pass. All horrid moments do. When today's over, and when you go to bed tonight, you'll already feel better about things than you do now. And as the days pass, so the hurt will go too. It's like breaking a leg, or having an operation in hospital: the pain at the beginning seems unbearable, but it begins to lessen from the first moment on, even though you don't realise it to begin with. One day you'll look back on this morning, and last night too perhaps, as something as distant and unreal as a dream.'

Angelo didn't reply but his whole body shook, and he nestled for comfort even closer to Christopher, as if he wished he could climb into Christopher's pocket and stay there, safe from the world for ever.

Christopher said, 'There's no blame attached to this. No wrong. No fault. No sin. Adults – people in authority – get things very muddled up sometimes. There's nothing that you did that I haven't done myself. That I did with other boys at school. I was just lucky enough not to get caught, that's all. And other things ... which I think you know about. Things concerning Tom and me. And talking of Tom, he, like you, once got kicked out of a school because of a boy. It does happen to people, you see, and they survive it.'

'What about Simon?' Angelo asked. 'Will he be all right?'

'I haven't seen him. I'll try to. And if I get the chance, I'll tell him what I've told you. He'll be OK, though, I promise you. Time will make it OK for both of you.'

Angelo shook himself out of his abject sprawl over Christopher, like a cat that has had enough cosseting for the moment. 'It was only like a game, you know. Like play-fighting, really. It's not that we were in love or anything.'

'That's probably a good thing, then,' said Christopher, though he felt sorry in a way that love hadn't come into it. However, they were only thirteen. 'Look, I can't stay more than a minute or two, I'm afraid. There's morning assembly and then I have to teach.'

Dexter said quietly but in a firm voice, 'Don't go.'

'I have to. I'll talk to Simon if I can. You'll be OK. I promise.' He paused for a second, then said, 'I won't forget you, Angelo, and after this morning you won't forget me either. But you're a big strong chap now. In three months' time you'll be at public school and all this nightmare will be forgotten.'

'Downside. They won't take me, will they? After this?'

'If the public schools refused entry to everyone in your situation, they'd be half empty, Angelo. And now I really must...'

Angelo felt Christopher's muscles tense as he prepared to stand up, but before Christopher could carry out the action the door opened, un-knocked upon, and Sister entered. At least they were no longer in the tight embrace of a minute before.

'Mr McGing,' Sister said, 'I am surprised to find you here.' Then she turned away from him to address Angelo. 'Finish your packing now, and be down in the staff room for breakfast at five past nine on the dot.

Cathy will serve it to you, though for sure you don't deserve it, for sure you don't.' She turned back to Christopher and said, 'Come now, Mr McGing. Let's leave Master Dexter to himself now. It's nearly nine.'

Christopher's last sight of Angelo, as he half turned back at the door through which Sister practically shoved him, was of the boy's mask-like, swollen face and his hollow, desperate stare.

In the corridor outside Christopher was startled to find himself face to face with John Moyse, who jumped when he saw him, and looked almost as small and frightened as Angelo had done. Christopher didn't give the boy a chance to speak. 'If you're looking for Angelo, he's in here.' He gestured to the door he'd come out of. 'Sister's there with him right now, so check she comes out before you go in. And if you talk to him, just tell him he's done nothing wrong. Then he'll be OK. That's what I tried to do.'

'I've just been to see Simon, at the other end of the building,' John said. 'That's more or less what I tried to tell him.' His voice sounded as fragile as the rest of him looked.

'You did the right thing, John. Look, I must go. If you miss assembly, say I sent you for some French exercise books from the stationery cupboard.'

Christopher was late for assembly himself. Tom hissed in his ear, 'Where have you been?' but there was no time to explain, and after assembly they both had to begin their respective classes, teaching extempore, dragging half-remembered facts from heads that still banged from last night's alcoholic intake and rocked from the morning's news.

At mid-morning break Father Matthew paid a visit to both of their classrooms in turn as the lessons ended. He wanted to speak to them in his office in two minutes' time. He had to visit another classroom with some other important message in the meantime, so they were spared a tight-lipped march down the long cloisters as a trio.

'It's more than unfortunate,' said Father Matthew. 'The timing could hardly have been worse.' They were sitting in his office now. Father Matthew's eye had lost its usual friendly twinkle. He too had had a bruising morning. He had taken morning assembly manfully, introducing the hymns and reading the prayers, then making the day's announcements, which included the seismic one – which he delivered poker-faced – that Dexter and Rickman had withdrawn from the school and that Abelard and Moyse replaced them as house captains with immediate effect. (Edward Abelard and John Moyse had been apprised of their sudden promotion even before breakfast, but this was news to everyone else. All had looked round to see the faces of the two new house captains, but only Edward Abelard could be spotted, standing in his usual place, wearing his usual expression of phlegmatic calm. John Moyse was, for once, unaccountably absent.) Lastly, Father Matthew had imperturbably read out the names of those who had received letters and laid the boys' post on the little table, which Father Claude then lifted down from the stage.

All that had been before the arrival of the newspapers. Now Father Matthew thrust two of them across his desk towards Tom and Christopher. One was, predictably, the Kent Messenger. The other caused the young men more of a shock. It was The Times. Both were open at the arts page. In the Messenger, Patricia Jamieson had written the following. 'Star of the exhibition is, without question, Molly O'Deere's *David and Jonathan*. Young male beauty at its most virile is here celebrated with unrestrained passion and delight. Passion and delight also illuminate the faces and inform the figures of the two young men, their mutual enchantment plain to see.

A courageous painting in every sense, O'Deere's eye-catching, and eye-opening work deserves...'

Stricken with horror and red-cheeked, Tom and Christopher shifted their gaze towards The Times. A small, somewhat tucked-away, review had been headed: Libido in the Cathedral. It began: 'What a garden of forbidden delights is hinted at in Molly O'Deere's audacious and technically assured treatment of David and Jonathan. Two young men in the full flush of their youth and beauty contemplate each other with the most rapt attention. As they stand on the nearer edge of a cricket field, ignored by and ignoring the distant players, they have eyes only for each other. O'Deere leaves us in no doubt...'

'Were you expecting this?' Father Matthew's question cut sharply in upon their thoughts as they read.

'No, Father. Absolutely not,' said Tom, with that assurance of tone (which Christopher had yet to master) that sometimes must be called upon to bolster a half truth. Or a less-than-half truth. 'What a shock.'

'I'm at a disadvantage,' said Father Matthew wearily. 'I haven't seen the painting. If I had... Oh, whatever was Molly O'Deere thinking of? This will upset her most dreadfully, of course. Innocence is one of God's great shields against the swords and arrows of the world, of course; but I still wish sometimes that Molly was a bit more... But you two gentlemen – men of the world to some extent, I would have supposed – should have seen ... shouldn't have gone along with all this. You must have had an inkling at least of what would happen. And it needn't have happened. You two, if you'd had your bally heads screwed on, could have made sure it didn't.'

'We're dreadfully sorry,' said Christopher, trying to keep his voice from trembling.

'We'd no idea she was going to enter it for an exhibition,' said Tom, 'let alone that it would attract the attention it did. We just thought she was an amateur painter who wanted to do something a bit big for a change.'

'Well, she's certainly succeeded in that,' said Father Matthew, without smiling.

'Does she know about the reviews?' Tom asked.

'Not yet,' said Father Matthew. 'Nor does Father Louis. I'll need to talk to Miss O'Deere later. I think I'll leave Louis out of it for the time being. He'll have enough to think about with the Dexter and Rickman business. But Molly, yes. She'll be looking in the papers herself, no doubt, without needing prompting from anyone else. I really wanted to talk to you two before I spoke to her. Find out what you knew – or, apparently, didn't.' He gave a grim look to each of them in turn. 'I'd prefer you not to discuss this with anyone until I've spoken to Miss O'Deere.' He pulled his pocket watch from under his scapular. 'Great heavens, quarter past eleven. I've got Dexter's parents to deal with at twelve, and Rickman's at twelve thirty. Let's hope they haven't seen the papers.'

'Dexter's mother was with the Messenger reviewer yesterday morning,' said Christopher uncomfortably. 'They're best friends, apparently. We met them in the chapter house.'

'Dear Lord... Well, thank you for telling me that, anyway. Forewarned and all that, I suppose.' A new thought caused a frown to appear. 'By the way, you don't happen to know where Moyse was during assembly, either of you?'

'It was my fault,' volunteered Christopher, speaking a little too rapidly to inspire confidence. 'I sent him to get some French books I'd forgotten.' Tom shot him a look of surprise.

'During assembly?' Father Matthew also sounded surprised. Perhaps more than surprised. 'When he was just being announced as house captain?'

'I know, Father. It was bad timing. I'm sorry, I should have thought. It's been a bit of a morning.'

'Hmmm,' said Father Matthew. He quickly looked at his watch again. 'Look, get to your classes now, or we'll all be late. Sorry I've made you miss your coffee.'

Of all the days to have to forego mid-morning coffee, Tom thought. His head pounded.

It wasn't until lunchtime that Tom had a chance to speak to Christopher alone. They coincided in the cloister just outside the door to the staff dining room. Nobody else had arrived. 'Where did you get to after breakfast?' Tom dived straight in. 'I needed to speak to you.'

'I had to go and find Dexter. I couldn't let him go without saying goodbye.'

'If you value your skin you could've.' Tom wasn't in the giving vein.

'He was in a bad state,' Christopher defended himself. 'Couldn't stop crying. Somebody had to put him straight.'

'Put him straight? What do you mean?'

'I told him there was nothing wrong in what he'd done. That every teenager did it, and that in a short time it would all be water under the bridge.' He stopped short of saying, *I told him that we did it.* He stopped short of saying, *I told him you'd been sacked from your last school because of a boy.*

'Well, that was brave of you,' Tom conceded. 'I hope nobody saw you go there.'

Christopher felt like groaning aloud. But there was no point withholding the next bit. Unlike his private confidences to Dexter, this would certainly come out at some point. 'Sister saw me. She came into the room while I was talking to him.'

Tom actually did groan aloud. 'You fool. You bloody fool. What did she hear? What did she see?'

'Nothing. Nothing at all. There was nothing to hear, nothing to see.'

'So you were just standing – what – across the room from him?'

'If you must know, I was sitting on the bed beside him.'

'Oh don't tell me! With your arm around him? I can see it so easily. Him in tears on your shoulder? Trying to hold your hand?'

'Not when she actually came in. We were just sitting.' Christopher was nearly in tears himself.

'OK,' Tom said. 'I didn't mean to shout at you. I'm sorry. Only I'm not in a very good state myself. But what about Moyse? Where does he come into this? You told Father Matthew you'd sent him to get some books... During morning assembly, for God's sake! You could see Father Matthew didn't believe you.'

'I met him looking for Angelo as I was coming out. He knew where I'd been just as I knew where he was going. I told him I'd cover for him if he was late for assembly. I didn't know he'd miss it altogether. Or that his name would be called out, announcing his promotion. Sorry, it's just all been going horribly wrong.' At that point Christopher might well have broken down in tears, but he was forced to pull himself together by the arrival of Miss O'Deere, coming along the cloister from the direction of Father Matthew's office. Miss O'Deere was dabbing at her cheeks with a handkerchief as she walked.

'Oh dear, Molly,' Tom said, once she'd arrived beside them, suddenly feeling a great and unexpected tenderness towards her. 'Let's just all go in and sit down.' He opened the dining room door and let her precede him through it. A moment later she, Tom, and Christopher were seated at the otherwise empty table while Cathy, who had just arrived, hovered uncertainly with plates of fish pie.

'Father Matthew showed you the reviews, I suppose,' said Tom glumly. 'It's a bit ghastly, I know. But we'll all live through it.'

'What do you know?' Miss O'Deere rounded on him sharply, her grey eyes wide open and angry in their oval frames of dark lashes. 'To think what people saw in that painting! It's too horrible. Sex, sex, sex. It's all some people can think of. I think I'm wishing I'd never been born – which we're not supposed to wish, ever, and I've never, ever caught myself thinking before. It's no wonder Angela was so upset.'

'Miss Coyle?' queried Christopher. He had forgotten the storm over the breakfast teacups. Too much else had happened.

'She's distraught,' said Miss O'Deere. 'She won't be down to lunch. And she doesn't even know about the papers yet.'

'Oh, right,' said Tom, trying to make sense of all this. 'But wasn't she getting it a bit out of proportion? Two teenagers caught in bed together. I mean, I know they shouldn't have been. But it isn't the first time it's ever happened. And I'm sure it won't be the last.' He plucked desperately at Shakespeare's sleeve in search of support. 'I mean, we've all read Romeo and Juliet.'

'But not Romeo and Romeo That's what makes it all so much worse.'

Cathy gave up at this point, placed the tray of fish-pie plates on the sideboard and left the room.

'And those two, of all the boys. She doted on them. Both the same age as her son: Dexter to the month, and

Simon Rickman to the day. A coincidence. Now a dreadful one.'

'Miss Coyle has a son?' Christopher asked, floundering.

'Born the same day as Simon Rickman, as it happens. Like a sort of twin, she could never help remembering. Her own son taken from her at birth, when she was little more than a child herself. That's how things were in County Kerry in those days, and it's not so long ago.'

'Taken from her at birth?' said Tom, barely understanding.

'Placed in the care of the Redemption Sisters in Killorglin and raised by them till this day. She never allowed to see the boy, never to meet him when he grows up, never allowed to know his name. A terrible, terrible thing is sex. Especially when forced upon you in your teens.'

'And sex gets all the blame for everything?' Tom asked very gently. 'And there's none left over for the way people react to it?'

'You do very well to take a soft line on it, Tom,' Miss O'Deere addressed him – in sorrow, not anger, Tom thought. 'I think I begin to guess why, perhaps, and the guess gives me no pleasure at all, but only pain and more pain.'

'I don't think our company's doing you a lot of good right now,' Tom said to her. 'Perhaps Christopher and I should leave you in peace.' He got up from the table and Christopher followed. Rather shaken, they went down to the kitchen and asked Cathy to make them a sandwich. It looked as though the staff fish pie was destined to remain untouched.

That afternoon Christopher supervised junior athletics – the boys were honing their timings and capabilities in advance of Sports Day in three weeks' time. Tom meanwhile umpired junior cricket, half conscious of the runners doing circuits of the track which ringed the cricket pitches. Tom thought it a good idea to have a word with the two newly promoted house captains. When the game was finished he caught up with John Moyse, after stumps had been drawn following the end of his own, senior, game and the shin-padded, bat-carrying boy was walking back towards the school building. 'So you're captain of More now,' Tom said. 'Congratulations.'

'Thank you,' said John, turning to face him. It struck Tom that he looked quite different today. Smaller and thinner, and his usually sunny face had an odd pinched look, as though crushed between millstones. 'But getting the job in these circumstances... I mean, I feel I don't really deserve it.'

Tom had gone looking for the boy because he wanted to have the prefects on his and Christopher's side before their situation became even more precarious than it was already. But he put that aside now: it was John, evidently, who needed comfort from him. He spoke more gently. 'You mustn't feel like that. Very few people in high places are there because they deserve to be. These things are much more often a matter of chance than we realise. The only thing that matters is that you do your best in the job once you've got it.'

'It's only going to be for a few weeks,' John said, a bit sourly.

'Then make them a good few weeks. It's a feather in your cap, whatever the circumstances. Something that'll stand you in good stead when you get to Downside. We're here to support you, anyway: the resident teachers. Just wanted you to know that.'

'Thank you.' Then, 'Sir, will Angelo be going to Downside? Or will all that be scrapped?'

'He's your best friend, isn't he?' Tom said, understanding for the first time and wondering why he hadn't worked it out ages ago. 'I'm sure he'll be going to Downside. Things will go on as if nothing had happened, just with a few weeks' longer gap than usual, that's all.'

John's face almost kindled to a smile, but didn't quite make it. Next time, Tom thought. And then, here I am doing exactly what I blasted Christopher for doing earlier. Conspiring with boys. Getting down to their level. Making matters endlessly worse. With an effort he got back to his original purpose. 'Just one more thing – er – John. Father Matthew's got an awful lot on his plate right now. So if you ever think you need to talk about anything – or want advice about anything, though I'm sure you won't – just come and talk to me or Christopher. Ask us anything. Any time. Understood?'

Tom suspected that John saw through this as easily as through a glass of water, but it couldn't be helped. He didn't expect the boy to take him up on his invitation right there and then, but he did, and the question that John put to him nearly made him jump out of his skin. 'Tom, was Christopher in love with Angelo?' The sudden use of the three Christian names, like three cymbal clashes, startled him almost as much as the question itself.

Dear God, Tom thought. It really was all over. The boy knew everything, just as Angelo had done. But luckily the question was one that could be answered easily and truthfully – almost the only question that could be. 'No, John. He wasn't. He liked Angelo, yes, just as he likes you. But you mustn't go looking for anything beyond that. It doesn't help anything to feel jealous afterwards.' He moved on to risky ground. 'Not of Christopher. Not of Simon Rickman.'

'Oh, the Simon Rickman thing.' The boy shrugged. 'That had been going on for ages.'

'For ages? And people like you knew about it?'

'We knew and we didn't know, if you see what I mean. They had a cubicle to themselves, after all, with a curtain. But they weren't always as quiet as they thought they were being, and that sort of drew people's attention. Angelo and I never discussed it, though.'

'Thank you for being candid, John,' said Tom. He looked around to see if Edward Abelard was about but he wasn't. 'And thank you for talking to me. I'd like you to tell Abelard what I've told you – I mean about us being here to support you if you need us. And about talking to us if you think there's anything we need to know. But the other part of our conversation – the private bit – I think that should stay just between ourselves, don't you agree? Do you know the expression 'off the record'?'

And then John's face really did light up with the long delayed smile, although it was a bleak and wintry one. 'Of course I do, Tom. A journalist like me has to know these things.'

Tom laughed, from relief – and from another feeling he couldn't quite put a name to. 'Get along now. Get changed for tea.'

'Thank you, Tom,' the boy dismissed himself, and then headed off round the corner of the building in his whites and shin-pads at a brisk trot.

If John Moyse had been prompt in taking up Tom's invitation to talk freely to him, then Edward Abelard was not going to be outdone. Less than half an hour after his conversation with the former, Tom was accosted by the new captain of Fisher in the school cloister.

'Excuse me, sir,' the boy began. 'Do you think I could have a word with you?' He wore his usual expression of imperturbability. Abelard had a flattish, round, almost saucer-like face and large round eyes, but the look in them – ever since Tom had known the boy – always suggested that any feelings he possessed were permanently disengaged, their motors idling in neutral. 'Moyse has just told me that you said we were to come to you if we thought there was anything needed saying – I mean especially in connection with recent events – I mean the Angelo and Simon thing. And there is something.' Abelard looked around the cloister, where a number of boys were walking, or standing in groups that talked, gesticulated and laughed. 'Do you think we could be somewhere a bit more private, sir? It's about Father Claude.'

Tom felt a new wave of shock wash over him, but managed not to show it. He said, 'The great outdoors shall be our conference chamber, Abelard. Nobody's found a way of bugging that – yet. So let's take a walk round the cricket field. Lead on.'

Rather to Tom's surprise, Abelard led the way out by the main door next to the headmaster's office, a door the boys were not supposed to use. But it was the quickest way and, after all, Abelard was now a house captain.

They skirted the crowd of boys who were roller-skating on the paved play area and headed across the grass among the cricket pitches and the running track, where people were scarce and eavesdropping difficult. 'I don't know if people know this, sir,' Abelard said in a junior officer kind of voice. 'People in authority, I mean. Like Father Louis and Father Matthew. But it's about Father Claude and corporal punishment.'

'Father Claude and corporal punishment?' They sounded like two characters in a pantomime. 'I didn't know he dished it out.'

'Not to us, he doesn't. But he does to the lower forms. He didn't when we were juniors but *apparently* he does now. Two of them told me, separately, which is how I know. If any kid fools about in singing class he makes them stay behind after the others have gone. Then he makes them pull their shorts and pants down, pulls them across his lap and spanks their bums – I mean their bottoms, sir – with his hand. The thing is, I don't know if he's supposed to. I've been thinking I ought to tell someone, sir, but I didn't quite know how to – or who. Whom. Then Moyse told me what you'd said.' Abelard stopped and looked into Tom's eyes with the satisfied expression of someone who has successfully carried out a difficult duty.

'Thank you for coming to see me,' Tom said. 'I'm glad you did. It does sound – what you tell me – a bit unorthodox, I agree. But I'm sure there's no harm in it. Father Claude is a long way from being what you might call a man of the world. He probably doesn't realise that other people might find – er – might read something into a punishment like that that really isn't there.'

'I see what you mean, sir,' said Abelard thoughtfully. 'But that isn't quite all. The two boys who told me this also said that, as they were getting up again after he'd smacked them, Father Claude brushed his hand against their – er – against their penises, like an accident. And he said, 'Sorry, I didn't mean to do that'. But he said it to both of them. On both occasions. So it seemed to me that perhaps it wasn't an accident.'

'I see. These two boys – did they tell anyone else besides you? Dexter? Rickman? Moyse?'

'I don't think so, sir. They were nervous enough just telling me. I don't think they'd have gone to the house captains. And I'm sure they wouldn't have told Moyse. Everyone knows Moyse is the apple of Father Claude's eye, being his star pupil and all. He's going to do Grade Eight next year, which most people don't do till they're sixteen at least. And he's got a lot of respect for Father

Claude as a music teacher. So I haven't told Moyse about this either, you see. He might be disilluded, you see, and then that might affect his playing. Which would be a shame.'

Tom thought he was learning more about the goings-on at Star of the Sea today than he had in the whole six and a half weeks he'd been here. He said, 'Again, thank you for coming to see me. I'll need to think about this. I'll have to tell this to Father Matthew, but I'll need to choose a moment when he's a bit less pressured than he is today. But I won't need to mention your name if you'd rather I didn't.'

'Thank you, sir.'

'And I don't think you and I need discuss this further. OK? And perhaps – no, I'm sure – you'll be sensitive enough to keep this discussion we've just had confidential. You still won't need to tell Moyse.'

'No, I won't, sir. You can rely on me. And thank you for listening.'

'Any time,' Tom said. 'Don't forget that.' And now, just as John Moyse had done half an hour earlier, Abelard nodded, turned on his heel, and took himself off at a brisk walk, looking very important.

It certainly wasn't the day for talking to Father Matthew about Father Claude. Not after the interview they'd had with him that morning. Though, a little before supper time, Father Matthew came looking for Tom. Fortunately, Tom was in his room preparing lessons for the next morning, alone. Christopher was doing exactly the same thing in his own room. It was a piece of luck. They could not have given the acting headmaster a better impression of conscientious diligence and propriety if they'd engineered it on purpose. Father Matthew had still not got back his customary smile, and the twinkle was still absent from his eye, but he seemed more affable than earlier, which was something.

'I'd been meaning to say thank you to you, Tom – and to Christopher too when I find him – for your extra work recently, covering for Father Louis's absence. If I didn't do so this morning, well, I think you'll understand I was a bit preoccupied with other things. You won't need to do dormitory duties again, at least not in the foreseeable future. So your evenings will be your own again from now on. About this evening, though...' The priest stopped, and looked almost embarrassed. 'I think it might be best if you didn't come to staff supper. Just for tonight. The women are ... well, in a bit of a state about things. You know how it is with women.' A wisp of doubt clouded his face for an instant, then went away. 'At least, I suppose you do. In the circumstances I think it might be better if you two young men gave them a bit of breathing space just for tonight. And since I don't want you to forgo your supper, or to feel inconvenienced by this, I'd like to give you both a couple of pounds out of petty cash, which should enable you to afford a reasonably decent meal in town – or at least, better than we can offer here – and a drink to go with it. I hope you'll find that acceptable?'

Tom was a bit surprised, but the terms sounded very reasonable, so he accepted, said he was sure that Christopher would also be agreeable, and Father Matthew thanked him for his understanding, before going along to Christopher's room to have a re-run of the same conversation.

They collected their cash from Father Matthew, in his office, on their way out. Two pound notes and a ten-shilling note each. It might not buy them dinner with wine at Marchesis', but they would be able to eat quite well all the same. As he handed over the money Father Matthew said, choosing his words rather slowly and carefully, 'I imagine you feel we were heavy-handed in our treatment of those two boys. To be honest, I feel much the same. Unfortunately it was one of the women who made the discovery.' He paused. He looked very tired now. 'Perhaps if it had been me, or one of you... Well, we all know the story of Pandora's box... All right, there's no more to be said. And now I still have to go and tell Father Louis what's happened to his two best henchmen.' He jerked his eyes towards the ceiling and then dismissed them with a wave that they could imagine stood in for a white flag.

They left by the front door. There was no need to use their special side gate tonight as they were going out with Father Matthew's blessing, almost at his command. As they left they could hear the assembly hall piano being played. John Moyse – presumably it was he – was practising, or simply playing over and again, a little wisp of a melody, infinitely sad, that seemed to lose its way as it threaded from one minor key arpeggio to another. Like Rachel weeping for her children, it seemed like a lament for the loss of a whole world.

***

From John Moyse's New Journal: Friday June 22ⁿᵈ 1962

This was the day that Angelo and Simon got expelled and I became a house captain. (So did Edward.)

What they did was simply what a lot of teenage boys do together before they get interested in girls or if there aren't any girls about. Or so I've read. It's just one step on from play-fighting, isn't it? And nobody makes a song and dance about that. Then someone gets caught and it's all back to the five sins that cry to heaven for vengeance and all hell breaks out. But it's not as if anyone can get pregnant when it's two boys – even if they do <u>that</u>, which I'm pretty certain they never went as far as.

So. You make a new best friend and then immediately you lose him. I doubt he'll be going to Downside now. I went and saw Simon, then Angelo as they waited to be taken home. I never saw anyone more upset than Simon – till I saw Angelo. Angelo wanted to hold me and I let him. I admit it felt nice, but I've never wanted to go further with him even if he did. Save that for a girl one day.

Christopher also went to see Angelo, which made me wonder, but Tom said no, it wasn't like that, he was just being friendly and decent, and I believe him. Tom and Christopher have stopped even pretending to talk like schoolmasters. They're both good chaps who seem today like two kids a bit older than Angelo and me but just as mixed up. One reason for this: the Kent Messenger arrived in the table games room with most of page 11 neatly cut away, and the Times also had a small piece missing from page 19. I went to see Cathy. She doesn't take the Times, obviously, but she had the Messenger rolled up in her bag and let me borrow it. Page 11 had a review – I suppose by that woman who Angelo knows – of Miss O's picture. Wow, wow, and thrice wow! No wonder all the staff have been going about with long faces all day. But it proves Angelo and I were right all along.

When I first came here the place seemed very big and frightening and very lonely. Hard punishments and cold classrooms in the winter. Compulsory sport even in hailstorms. Bullying by older boys and endlessly the cane from Father L. But then it got better. There's nobody big enough to bully me here now, and prefects hardly ever get caned and if we do it doesn't hurt. Perhaps it never did really hurt: it just felt like it. In the procession yesterday everything seemed to be ending beautifully, and me and Angelo would be together next term too, and Star of the Sea began to seem a cosy little place – only the thought of Downside a little frightening, but with Angelo there it'd be alright. Now all that's changed and this place seems as hard and cold and lonely as it ever did. Me a house captain for my last six weeks. What a sick joke!

NINETEEN

The Admiral Digby didn't do food. In those days most pubs didn't. All you could get were packets of Smith's Crisps with a little screw of blue paper inside which contained salt. So Tom and Christopher walked along the cliff a little way towards the town, to where the built-up sea-front promenade optimistically began, some two miles before you got to the town centre itself. There they found a modest café-restaurant where you could get prawn cocktail, chicken and chips with peas and a grilled tomato, followed by Black Forest gateau and with a glass of wine included, all comfortably within the budget Father Matthew had given them. There was even enough left over to buy them a pint in the pub afterwards.

They talked all through the meal about the events of the day, repeating and repeating, in their shocked state, the same things endlessly to each other. About the expulsions, about the reviews in the newspapers, about Tom's conversations with John Moyse and Edward Abelard. About the need to tell Father Matthew at some point what Abelard had told Tom about Father Claude, about the problem of finding the right moment to do that now that it seemed their own positions were so precarious that the female members of staff wouldn't even eat an evening meal with them. At least the chicken and chips were a consolation.

The sea was a pattern of turquoise and cobalt as they walked back along the cliff towards the Admiral Digby, the sun still in the sky above the power station, the lights at the airfield's runway threshold gleaming like tiny red beads in rows of three.

'You lads look a trifle agitated tonight, if I might say so,' Roger told them as he drew their pints. 'Anything been happening?'

Tom grimaced. 'Quite a lot, actually.'

Roger got the message. 'Find a seat in the garden. I'll be out as soon as I can.'

Ten minutes later he was. They poured out the whole story – or stories. Christopher concluded, 'So we feel a very long way from being safe. Safe in our jobs I suppose I mean. Too many people know too much about us now.'

'Well, hold on to your hats, and it may all blow over,' said Roger reassuringly. 'Malcolm and I have weathered it all these years. He's at home with his parents tonight, by the way, but he'll be over tomorrow. But if anything goes wrong and you need a friend or two ... well, you know where to find us.'

They thanked him, but for once declined his offer of a second pint. Memories of this morning's hangovers were still too raw.

They hadn't got beyond removing their ties, which was something. Tom was sitting on Christopher's bed and Christopher was by the window, about to draw the curtains shut, when the knock came. An urgent fistful of knocks. A similar salvo could be heard two doors away as someone else tried to get an answer from Tom's empty room. Tom got to his feet as Christopher turned and said, 'Come in.'

John Moyse stood there, in pyjamas, slippers and dressing-gown. He was joined at once by Edward Abelard, similarly dressed, who, seeing Christopher's door opening, had quickly abandoned his attack on Tom's. If the boys were surprised to find the two young teachers together at nearly midnight they gave no sign of it. They had bigger surprises than that to report.

'It's Father Louis,' said Moyse. 'I think he's gone completely round the bend.'

Abelard continued seamlessly. 'He arrived in the dormitory just minutes ago and switched on all the lights. He was wearing his hood up over his head like he does on cold winter mornings. He told everyone to get up, and that there was going to be a fire.'

'Fire?' Tom was seriously alarmed.

'Not that sort of fire,' said Moyse. 'He started quoting from the Apocalypse again, I think it was. "God sent fire from Heaven to consume them. Death and Hell were thrown into the lake of fire." You know the sort of thing.'

'Go on,' said Tom.

Abelard continued. 'A bonfire of all Angelo's and Simon's things. He told Smith and Bowood to fetch their old sheets from Room Fifteen and Kellaway and Easton to strip the blankets off their beds and carry them downstairs.'

'Where to?' Christopher asked, running his fingers through his hair as if that might make him look more prepared for action.

'Down the main staircase. Then out of the front door, I imagine,' said Moyse.

'We didn't wait to see,' Abelard explained. 'We thought we'd better come and tell you straight away.'

Tom just remembered to say thank you for that as the four of them left Christopher's bedroom and hurried along the corridor. They leapt down the chapel stairs and then ran the length of the chapel cloister before turning left into the main cloister towards the front door. The main cloister was filling up with boys, all running the same way. Boys were pouring down the main staircase, and the back staircase and the school cloister staircase too. They were pyjama-clad, some struggling into their dressing-gowns as they ran. The whole place swarmed like an ants' nest turned up by a spade.

The four of them waded through the throng and got to the front door, which stood open, its wide Gothic arch framing a spectacle that made some speechless and caused others to gasp out loud. For those who had seen Renaissance depictions of the Bonfire of the Vanities that was the first thing that came to mind. With his pointed hood up, Father Louis even looked like Savonarola as he threw into the flames the items that some of the youngest boys were handing up to him: clothing and books. Sheets and blankets were already well alight, causing an orange pillar of fire to rise almost vertically – for there was no wind – from the fierce blaze on the lawn in the centre of the front courtyard. Its light shone flickering around a ring of young faces; they seemed mesmerised, like faces in a cinema. Other boys were coming round the corner from the classroom end, carrying armfuls of books. There seemed far too many to have all belonged to the two disgraced boys: too many books and too many clothes. Christopher remembered seeing Dexter's suitcase full of all his things. There would be a dreadful price to pay for this orgy in the morning. Christopher remembered that Savonarola had later perished in Florentine flames himself.

It was Christopher who moved first. Out through the door and into the crowd. He reached Father Louis, put out a hand and touched his shoulder. Father Louis turned quickly and peered out of the depths of his hood at him as though trying to remember who he was. He looked less angry than perplexed.

'Father,' Christopher said. 'Dear Father Louis. You shouldn't be down here in the night. I think we should get you up to bed.' He looked around for support. It was already at his side in the shape of Tom. Then Father Louis spoke.

'We've been too soft. Too lax. It was discipline we needed. We'll have no more hot water, no hot baths. Cold showers at night and morning. As we did in the old days in France. We must repair the damage. All of us must atone. As I did. I had a mistress at fifteen, I did. Oh yes, you look at me surprised. You didn't know that, did you? Though why should you know?' He looked out at them with hollow staring eyes wire-rimmed with spectacles: the eyes of a drowned man, seen through water. 'It was wrong. So very wrong. Yet not the Sin of Sodom. Still I had to go away. Atone, as we all must. Atone with a lifetime of the taming of the self, the mortification of the flesh, the subjugation of the will. We are not put on Earth to please ourselves or pleasure each other, but to be pleasing to God alone. Only in the next life are we to be happy, and then only through sacrifice in this one. Promise me...'

Whatever he might have been asking them to promise was drowned out by the whoosh of a fire extinguisher, deployed by Abelard, and then another one – to make assurance double sure? – wielded by John Moyse. Then came Father Matthew's voice from the doorway, calmly restoring order. 'That's it now. Everybody back to bed. Quietly and no running. In an orderly fashion, back to your dormitories.' Father Matthew was in pyjamas and dressing-gown like everyone else. But Sister, when she arrived on the scene a few seconds later, was already in full uniform, complete with starched headdress. Did she sleep in the thing? She was at Father Louis's side in an instant. She took his hand but then turned to look at Christopher and Tom. 'You did well,' she said. 'You may have gone a little way towards redeeming yourselves. Now help me get him back to bed.'

Tom and Christopher spent the rest of the night in the same bed. But they did not make love. They barely slept. They talked over the event they had witnessed, and the things Father Louis had said. 'Do you think he really had a mistress at fifteen?' Christopher asked Tom. 'Or was that just another of the tricks his mind's playing on him?'

'It was probably real enough,' said Tom. 'Since we know he really did leave home at fifteen to join a tough seminary in France. But, my God... You screw a girl as a teenager – maybe get her pregnant, maybe not. But either way ... to feel you have to spend the next sixty years making amends... Change your country. Become a priest. An ambulance driver on a battlefield. A monk. Ending up here. It's hard – I mean it hurts – to think of it.'

'Miss Coyle too, perhaps,' said Christopher. 'Do you think they know each other's stories?'

'I doubt it very much,' said Tom. 'There's fellowship in Heaven, or so we're told, but none in Hell.'

In the morning a car came all the way from Chartham, the place near Canterbury for those who laughed at nothing, to take Father Louis away. Staff breakfast that Saturday would be remembered as the one at which nobody said a word to anyone else. Even the necessary pass-the-toast requests were muttered, almost whispered. It was inconceivable that Moyse and Abelard would have told the three women that they'd gone to Christopher's room and found him and Tom preparing for bed together, yet it was as if everyone knew. None of them could imagine how they would face a class at twenty past nine and teach.

Father Matthew had said the morning Mass. At the end he had tacked on a decade of the Rosary for the intention of Father Louis, and asked the boys to remember their headmaster in their private prayers as well. After breakfast in the refectory he climbed the stairs and went towards the staff dining room, where he met the two people he was looking for just coming out. 'My office. Now please, gentlemen.' In grim silence he led the way. Never had the main and chapel cloisters seemed so long, nor so uncountable their vaulted bays.

Tom and Christopher did not know what was coming when Father Matthew led them into his office and firmly shut the door behind them, but they knew that it was bad. Father Matthew took his usual seat behind the desk, facing them, but did not invite them to sit down. 'I've had a letter,' he began. 'From Mr Stephen Dexter. You may or may not know that he's a barrister and a QC. I have to inform you both – and it's very painful for me to have to do so – that very big trouble lies ahead. His letter claims that one or both of you told his son there had been no element of wrong-doing in his conduct with Rickman. That their behaviour was perfectly normal. Not only that but – with what motive in mind I can not imagine – you told him that you indulged in similar behaviour yourselves.'

Tom couldn't hide the shock on his face as he turned to look at Christopher. His open mouth began to make a sound but Father Matthew's upraised hand stopped him from turning it into words. 'Please don't, Tom. It's better that you stay silent. I am not going to ask you if any of this is true or not. One of the prefects has already told me that he found you last night in a situation which appeared to him surprising, not to say compromising.' Please don't let that prefect have been John, thought Christopher. Let it have been Abelard. 'I am aware that there could be any number of perfectly innocent reasons why the two of you might have been in the same room at eleven o'clock at night. It might have been to borrow a book, for example, or to verify a doubt about the constitutional status of Hong-Kong. But I'm afraid that Mr Dexter goes on to say that he feels duty-bound to ask the police to investigate, and we may expect a visit from them soon.'

Father Matthew paused, gave them an indeterminate look, neither hostile nor supportive, and swallowed. Then he said, 'I am not going to ask you if you are in fact...' His lips clenched for a moment and his head shook, fractionally, involuntarily. 'I won't try to go groping after words. You already understand what I mean. I will not ask you that because I can not take the risk that the answer might be yes. I really must not know. But the police will ask you that question. Make no mistake about that. Mr Dexter ends his letter by saying, as one gentleman to another, he felt an obligation of courtesy to let me know in advance of his intention to contact the police.' Father Matthew checked his watch. 'The letter was written yesterday at the end of the afternoon. I would imagine that Mr Dexter will be contacting the police this morning. Quite possibly around now.

'The only thing I can do to limit the damage is this. I propose to release you from your contracts with immediate effect. But your choice to leave Star of the Sea will be yours and yours alone. Agree?' He didn't pause long enough for them not to. 'You will not enter your classrooms this morning except if, during assembly in a few minutes' time, you need to retrieve any personal effects. The balance of your pay will be sent to you by cheque, care of your parents' addresses. We will say, truthfully, that you chose to leave for private reasons which were not explained to us. In your own interests I think it would be advisable for you to be gone within the half hour. There is a phone number for a local taxi firm here on my desk. I shall leave the room now and leave the phone at your disposal for the next few minutes. I will not ask you, or enquire from others where you decide to go, and I think it would be wise of you not to attempt to contact me or anyone else at Star of the Sea again.'

He stood up and walked round the desk towards them. To their surprise he gave both of them his hand to shake. They took it and mumbled their stunned goodbyes. Then the acting headmaster left his office and closed the door on them, leaving them alone with the taxi firm's number and the telephone on the desk. They stared at them numbly, with the kind of horror with which they might have contemplated a loaded pistol and a bottle of Scotch.

They didn't use them. Thirty minutes later, while the sound of the final Assembly hymn swam in the air behind him, Tom let himself out of the side gate by the oil tanks for the last time, carrying his small suitcase. He left the key in the lock on the inside for Mr Barker to reclaim, remembering his promise to him to 'return it before you leave'. He walked down the hill, un-accosted, though probably not unobserved – net curtains such useful things in streets like these – and then round the corner to the Admiral Digby. There was really nowhere else to go.

Tom didn't know whether anybody would be up, his experience of pubs at nine in the morning being as limited as that of most people's, saving cleaners and draymen. But when he came round to the seaward, garden, side of the building, he was relieved to see Roger among the flowerbeds with a watering can. And equally if not more relieved to see that he was talking to Christopher, who had just that moment arrived from the other direction, having trailed his own small suitcase across the sports field and through the grounds of St Ursula's to reach the lane that led past the pub.

Among the worst of nightmares, that of friends arriving unannounced, with suitcases and long faces, must rank quite high. But Roger simply said, 'Better get you inside. We'll talk in there.'

'You remember that pilot,' Christopher said abruptly, as soon as they had updated Roger on the events of the last night and this morning. 'Captain Jimmie whatever his name was. Maybe he could fly us out of the country. Is that a thought?'

'Don't be daft,' Tom jumped in at once, partly to spare Roger the embarrassment of having to reply in the same terms. 'He didn't think he'd even be able to wangle us a flight around the block. He can't just fly one of the BEA fleet into some foreign airfield and hope no-one'll notice.'

They hadn't talked through to the next step as they hurriedly packed their things half an hour before. It was as much as they could manage just to agree on the idea of getting to the Admiral Digby with a view to holing up there for a time, if Roger permitted. Though Tom had given some gloomy thought, on his luggage-encumbered walk down the road, to the cautionary tale of Oscar Wilde, waiting fatalistically at the Cadogan Hotel, drinking hock and seltzer while his friends consulted the boat-train timetables, until the police came and grabbed him.

'You're seriously thinking of going to France, then?' Roger said. Tom was startled that there was no sign of surprise in Roger's voice. Though that was explained by what Roger said next. 'We talked about that. Malcolm and I. We thought you might decide to do that. If things got tough, I mean. Knowing you've got friends there.'

'Friends, yes,' said Tom. 'But you'd be testing friendship to its limits if you turned up on someone's doorstep in a foreign country without money or prospects of any kind and asked them to take you in...' He stopped, aware of the irony.

Luckily, Roger laughed. 'But they do, you know,' he said, gesturing down at their two suitcases, which still stood on the floor beside them, where they sat, in the morning-empty saloon bar. 'Take you in, without question, I mean. If they're good friends, that is.'

'Thank you,' Christopher made the only possible reply.

'We're already geared up for a mackerel-fishing trip tonight,' Roger said. 'Though you might have forgotten that in all the excitement. We could decide to go a bit farther a-field if that suited you.' He stopped, giving them time to take this in.

'Jesus Christ,' Tom said. He thought, they've discussed this already, Roger and Malcolm. Planned their next cross-Channel adventure around us. How weird life is. How tangled and twisted.

'Think about it. But I'll phone Malcolm right away anyway. Put him in the picture at least, whatever you decide.' He got up and made his way behind the bar to where the phone was.

'This is all happening so quickly,' said Christopher. 'I don't know.'

'You thought a bloody aeroplane,' said Tom. 'In your dreams. Now it looks like getting real, you feel a bit different.'

'An open boat...' Christopher was beginning to feel sick. It was Saturday. They couldn't even get money from their accounts at the bank. Contact parents? What could Christopher possibly say to them? But tear himself away, uproot himself from his whole world of home and family – cut the ties of parental love. Break not only the past but the future too. No going to Oxford in the autumn... 'Tom, I don't think I can.'

'And the alternative?' Tom said softly. Perhaps there was an alternative for Christopher. Christopher, at nineteen, was still a minor. If all this came to court a picture would be painted of the seduction and corruption, by Tom, of an innocent boy. Witnesses from Bellhurst would be brought to rake over the causes of his departure from there just months ago. You didn't have to look as far back as Oscar Wilde to find a precedent. The

Montagu case was only eight years before. On the flimsiest of evidence, two men had gone to prison for eighteen months, another, a peer of the realm, for twelve. It wasn't what had happened that was the point; it was how people would see it. There was nothing in view but horizons of ruin and desolation. A big sea and a small boat at the mercy of the waves, a destination where nothing awaited of any kind, except the uncertain haven of very new and untested friendships. Prison. The abomination of desolation. Tom too was feeling sick. Yes, there was an alternative for Christopher. He'd stay behind. Tom would have to go alone.

Roger came back from the phone. 'Malcolm says yes, if you decide you want to,' he said. 'He's re-checked the shipping forecast already. Tides and wind will be perfect tonight during darkness. Even a moon.'

'When does he need to know by?' asked Tom weakly.

'I think you'll be surprised how soon you decide, one way or the other,' said Roger, from the vantage-point of his extra twenty years.

***

From John Moyse's New Journal: Saturday June 23rd 1962

After Thursday night and Friday morning who would have thought more possible? But... Last night Father Louis came madly into the dormitory long after lights-out, with a band of junior boys who he must have rounded up from the babies' dorms. They looked scared stiff as he made them strip Angelo's and Simon's beds and take the blankets, mattresses and pillows downstairs. The sheets had already gone to Room 15, presumably, but he made people go there too and fetch them out. He talked of bonfires and vanities. Edward and I tried to talk to him but he pushed us away roughly and it threatened to turn into a scrap, which wd have made matters worse. Edward and I then ran to find either Tom or Christopher. We found them both in Christopher's room, which I should have forseen, and kicked myself for taking Edward with me. At least they weren't actually doing anything unlike Angelo and Simon.

Medieval scene when we got to the front quad. Father L throwing things into the flames like Savonarola. Ed (his best idea so far) got a fire extinguisher, so I got another and we put the fire out. Sister, Tom and Christopher led Father L back indoors and upstairs. He seemed to be in a daze or a dream. I really don't think he knew what was happening or where he was. Father Matthew told everyone to go to bed and we helped him do the rounds and make sure everyone did.

That was that until this morning. And this is where I kick myself. Ed must have told Fr M about Tom and Christopher being together last night. I saw him leading them towards his office very silently after breakfast. Then they were gone. Just like that. Not at assembly. Father Claude and Father Matthew took their classes this morning. Meanwhile Fr L was taken away to Chartham. It's hard to believe that he survived the Somme, body and mind intact, but the mere thought – not even the sight but the mere thought – of two boys playing with each other in bed brings the roof of his world crashing down.

At lunchtime the police arrived, on the trail of Tom and Christopher but nobody seems to know where they've gone. I don't know what I feel about them. I've known, since we saw the David and Jonathan picture – and Angelo had guessed before because of Bouloygne. But couldn't have guessed it would cause the rumpus it did all round. And I knew about Angelo and Simon too of course. But isn't it supposed to be one of those things you grow out of and doesn't do anyone any harm? Apparantly not. Tom's not a teenager any more even if Christopher is. I suppose they were teachers and supposed to set an example, but then their bedrooms are private, and they always behaved correctly when we were around, and never pushed themselves towards any of the boys in that way. It's as if sex wrecks everything. Like a bull in a china shop. Or – I've just thought, like a dog in a chapel – remembering the curious incident earlier this term. Maybe that's what Father L was thinking, in his crazy way, when he shouted at Miss O'Deere to get out of mass. It's always all about sex.

The police took Father Matthew away. They released him later without charge, but he went straight to the abbey, didn't come back here. I found that out from Cathy, who got it from Miss O'Deere who was told by the abbot himself They were accusing him of conceiling the whereabouts of suspects, but had to let him go because there was no proof.

Ed and I had to get everyone into the assembly hall after tea. The abbot arrived and made some announcements. He said Father Louis had retired (a funny way of putting it, esp. as everyone knows exactly what did happen) and that Father Matthew was being transferred to another monastery in the west of England that had a great and urgent need of his financhial skills. We all know he used to be the abbey's bursar, but you could see everyone saw through that one. Then he said that an announcement about a new head teacher would be made tomorrow. He said head teacher, not headmaster, and everyone noticed that. There was a sort of ripple went round. It means he's thinking of possibly a woman. My guess (and Ed thinks so too) is that it'll be Miss O'Deere. Maybe not a bad idea, though it won't affect me very much. Another five weeks and I'm gone from here.

TWENTY

They would set off at eleven that night, Malcolm said: an hour and forty minutes after sunset. It wouldn't be dark, though; there would be little cloud and a nearly full moon, which would set a little time before dawn. They would take advantage not only of the night but of an hour of slack water at the beginning, then they'd have the tide going in their direction for a good five hours. 'By which time we'll be nearly there.' With the wind blowing from the east, Malcolm said, they could sail on a beam reach almost all the way.

He showed them the route he'd plotted on the chart: English Channel, eastern section; Tom clutched at the words like straws. 'Almost due south. Through the Downs where you've already been. South Foreland to starboard and the South Goodwin light to port. Due south to pass the Varne light a couple of miles to starboard, then south east across the shipping lanes. We'll have raised the Gris Nez lighthouse by then, dead ahead, all being well. Steer a bit clear of the Cape itself – cross-tides – so a bit of a dog's leg round the corner, but then straight into Boulogne. Wind's at three: means gentle breeze. We'll be there for breakfast. Sunrise about four forty-five.'

He seemed very well prepared, Tom thought. Almost uncannily so. In addition to passage and harbour charts he'd brought oilskin coats and trousers and sea-boots, torches, full tool-kit and first aid. A compass was lashed to the thwart plank. There were distress flares, though no radio. Biscuits, cold sausage and chocolate, and flasks of tea and soup came down to the cove from the pub. Their suitcases, double wrapped in tarpaulins, went into the hold. Tom had an idea that Malcolm had been planning this for much longer than just a couple of days. At least

– he clutched at a positive thought – they wouldn't be crossing the horse-whipped seas of winter.

Before Malcolm's arrival with the Orca in the late afternoon they'd spent the day in hiding on the beach. A day on the beach in summer was an idyll when it was yours by choice. But how changed that all was when the cove became your prison, the sun your stern-faced guard and time hung on you like a fetter. They sought out bits of shade where they could find it, behind the higher rocks, and breathed that sour and disconcerting smell of weed-grown beach in shade. Roger brought them sandwiches and beer at lunchtime, and then tea. Each ventured up the tunnel once, to the back areas of the pub, to move his bowels.

They had no phone numbers for their friends in France. It was too late to write – though they still owed them a letter – and although a telegram would have been a possibility, what on earth could they say? They would arrive like thieves in the night, like the bridegroom in the parable of the wise and foolish virgins, like prodigal sons. They'd deal with the reception they got when the moment came.

When eleven o'clock arrived at last, the Orca wouldn't sail. The 'gentle breeze' out in the bay and Channel did not make its way into the cove. They attempted to haul her, body-breakingly, along the jetty to get her under way but that didn't work either. In the end they had to break with their original plan to leave the cove in total silence. Malcolm used the engine for the few minutes it took them to reach the open sea. Then the sails at last began to fill, were sheeted in, and the engine could be switched off. As if to redeem his failure to leave the shore unheard as well as unseen Malcolm left the navigation lights unlit for a further half hour. Malcolm usually deferred to Roger when decisions were being made on land, but it was different when they were at sea in Malcolm's own boat. Roger might call him Skipper with a laugh in his voice, but he never queried or disagreed with his decisions on board the Orca. If he ever doubted the wisdom of his lover-captain's decisions he kept that to himself.

Roger fished inside his oilskin coat and brought a wallet out. 'I want you to have this,' he said to Tom, and handed him four five-pound notes.

'We can't take that,' Tom said. 'That's a week's wages and more.'

'That's why you must accept it,' Roger said. 'Think of it as a loan. To be paid back if and when you can, one day.'

Malcolm also rummaged in a pocket. A paper money-bag came out. 'French coins left from our last trip. Might get you through Sunday, till you can change the notes when banks open next day.' There was no point arguing again. They both thanked him, and Roger, instead.

Malcolm suggested that, at least for the quiet first part of the trip they should stand alternate watches each two hours, giving the off-watch pair a chance to rest – up to a point. There was little comfort to be found below the deck among the stowage in the old fish hold, with the bilge all wet and reeking underneath. 'Meant to put bunks down there years ago,' Malcolm said, and not for the first time, 'but never did.' But on a moonlit, starry summer night you could sit or even lie on deck, at least for now, riding on the gentle swell of the bay and then the Downs.

Malcolm and Tom had the first watch. Malcolm was helmsman, Tom the lookout, adjusting very occasionally the trim of the jib or foresail when Malcolm instructed him to. Roger and Christopher sat on the forward hatch cover. After a while they both lay back on it, swaddled in their oilskins, and keeping their boots firmly planted on the deck in front of them. Though the hatch cover was the size of a very small double bed it was only about as comfortable as the shallow-pitched roof of a garden shed. Christopher lay looking up at the stars as they appeared to float, weaving and bobbing between the shrouds, and trying to imagine pillows where his head found only coils of rope.

Neither pair of men felt much desire for conversation. Each was preoccupied with his own thoughts, and weighed down by the magnitude of their undertaking. Tom and Christopher faced the bigger challenges – new life, no cash, new country, no job, the loss of family, home and friends. But the other two were not without anxieties of their own. Not only the journey out but the voyage back to face, with just the two of them as crew. If they avoided mishap on the way, would they escape detection? Would they be intercepted, boarded by the British or French coast guard? They didn't know yet whether their departure had gone unnoticed or unreported. Earlier Malcolm had said, 'You can't sail unseen in these days of radar. All we can hope is to go unquestioned, unremarked.' When they got home, would the police come knocking on the Admiral Digby's door in connection with the two disappeared young men? What was the charge: aiding and abetting the escape of suspects? Something like that.

Christopher hadn't known he'd been asleep, but here was Tom shaking him awake. It was after one o'clock. The lights of Dover shone from a few miles away on the starboard beam. The South Goodwin lightship flashed its regular message of warning a little way behind them on the port side. The breeze was a little more brisk. The moon had crossed a quarter of the sky.

Roger was a more relaxed helmsman than Malcolm had been. Before Malcolm and Tom went to lie down on the hard hatch cover, and Roger took the tiller into his hand, he lit a cigarette. It glowed like an extra, miniature, navigation light. He told Christopher, 'Just look out for the Varne light on the starboard bow. We pass it a couple of miles wide and we'll be about right. One flash every five seconds. It's red by the way. We turn a little bit east after that and with any luck a lighthouse should eventually pop up ahead. If it's Gris Nez we'll go on round to Boulogne. If we've got it wrong and it's the Calais light we'll drop you off there and put you on the train.'

That sounded very reassuring to Christopher. The sea was not quite so gentle now that they were heading into the middle of the Strait. He asked himself if he was beginning to feel seasick but told himself he wasn't. He was delighted when the Varne light began to flash, just where Roger said it would, and he called out the flashes. He was so intent on getting this absolutely right that he went on calling them every five seconds for about a minute, until Roger had to ask him to stop. After they came abeam the light, then passed it, and Roger adjusted the helm, Christopher peered intently ahead, willing the French light to appear at once. But it wouldn't show itself just yet. The distance you could see from little more than your own height above the waves was much less than from the deck of a ferry. And Dover meanwhile had disappeared astern.

There began to be ships. There was no drive on the right rule in the Dover Strait back then. Small craft crossed the Channel like cats crossing a busy road junction, never quite knowing if the vehicle they sprinted in front of or dodged behind concealed another, faster one behind it, going the other way. Cargo ships and tankers, looking as big as cathedrals from Christopher's viewpoint just above the water, came charging past from all directions, some well lit up, others with just their navigation lights and a dull glow from the bridge. Christopher alerted Roger to the approach of each one, not always sure which of them Roger could see and which would be hidden from him by the sails. A surprisingly long time after the passage of each one – so long that you'd almost forgotten about it – the nearside wave of its wake would hit, and cause the Orca to rear and plunge, until she met the further edge of the turbulent water and came out the other side. Whenever this happened, Tom and Malcolm, lying on the hatch cover, jerked up into a sitting position. Being thrown around, and drenched with spray was somehow even less pleasant when you were lying on your back.

At one point a night ferry, ablaze with lights like a palace on a party night, sailed across their path. Roger said it was going from Dover to Zeebrugge or Ostend. Now the sea was agitated even in the intervals between the ships. Spray came over the bulwarks all the time now and in as well as out through the scupper holes; the deck was permanently awash. Tom and Malcolm had given up any hope of resting on the hatch covers till the official start of their watch: Malcolm perched on the bulwark near Roger at the stern, and Tom kept Christopher, still the lookout, company in the bows.

The light appeared, almost miraculously, dead ahead, and white. Christopher called the flashes. Every fifteen seconds they came. Roger was satisfied after four. 'That's Gris Nez,' Roger said. 'Old Grey Nose. We're nearly there.'

Christopher had lost all track of time. He couldn't say if his spell on watch had passed slowly or fast. The moon was bobbing and ducking among the westward waves. Making out the hands of his wristwatch with some difficulty in what was left of the moon's light he was surprised to see it was already three o'clock. His two-hour look-out was ended.

There would be no question of lying back down on the hatch covers now, let alone going to sleep. The waves were growing in height. From an unthreatening, if bouncy, three feet they had risen to four. Some were five feet high and burst over the bow with the noise of small explosions. It was when Christopher estimated their height at six feet, nearly half a foot taller than he stood himself, that he began to be seriously afraid. Roger still stood on the deck, setting an example, Christopher guessed, and wanting to reassure, but he held on with one hand to the forward shroud. Christopher and Tom crouched tight on the bulwarks, facing each other, each clutching for safety and comfort at the backstay on his side. Malcolm was between them, at the tiller again, and holding tight. The waves detonated with increasing ferocity, like mines; the sky and the sails were loud with noise. The light of Cap Gris Nez, though they were closing on it fast, and despite its eminence on the cliff, sometimes dipped out of sight among the wave crests, and then popped up and startled you, like a long-necked diving bird.

And behold, a great tempest arose in the sea, so that the boat was covered with waves... And his disciples went to him and waked him, saying, 'Lord save us, or we perish.'

The words of hymns began to sound through Christopher's head, the tunes and the words a bit mixed up, and ghosting in and out with the wind.

Hail, Queen of Heav'n, the ocean star,
Guide of the wand'rer here below.
Thrown on life's surge, we claim thy care;
Save us from peril and from woe
Mother of Christ, star of the sea,
Pray for the wanderer, pray for me.
Bang went another wave.
O gentle, chaste, and spotless Maid,
We sinners make our prayers through thee;
Remind thy Son that he has paid

The price of our iniquity.
Virgin most pure, star of the sea,
Pray for the sinner, pray for me.

Christopher remembered that since meeting Tom he hadn't been to Confession.

Pity our sorrows, calm our fears,
And soothe with hope our misery...
...Pray for the mourner, pray for me.

And for Tom. For Roger. For Malcolm...

Dark night hath come down on us, Mother, and we
Look out for thy shining, sweet star of the sea.

The lighthouse popped its head up out of the water, flashed once, then went below again.

Dark night hath come down on this rough-spoken world.

And the banners of darkness are boldly unfurled;

And the tempest-tossed Church – all her eyes are on thee;

They look to thy shining, sweet star of the sea.

The moon had nearly gone. The boat plunged downwards yet again. Something went over with a crash in the hold below. Suitcases. What a time to be thinking about suitcases.

Tom and Roger saw it first, behind Christopher's back. It looked like a wall approaching, or an express train coming at them sideways from out of the darkness. It gleamed darkly like engine oil. Their two voices rose in a tangle of words – though the words were approximately the same. 'Wave. Massive. Enormous wave. Starboard, starboard bow, bow.'

Malcolm bent his head, peered under the boom and saw it. 'Jesus fucking Christ,' he said. It was the first time either Tom or Christopher had heard him sound alarmed, or even surprised, by anything. But he reacted at once, doing what his years' experience of sailing had made second nature. He pulled hard on the tiller to bring the Orca's head round to face the wave full square. And because he knew what would happen next he also shouted, 'Gybing. Heads,' and made a grab for the mainsheet as the boat's stern swung past the eye of the wind. He missed, and the boom, unfettered, slammed across the deck like a scythe, till it took up the mainsheet's slack on the other side, stopped dead, and the wind punched into the new side of the mainsail with a bang.

The Orca was climbing the water wall. In what faint light there was you could see the crest begin to fray into raggy plumes of grey and dirty white. Reaching the top the Orca began to fall straight down, as the footfall of someone who walks on firm snow plunges deep into the fragile, knife-edge crest of a drift.

Christopher just managed to miss decapitation by the swinging boom. He was rising, turning to see the wave, when Roger and Tom had shouted out and, hearing Malcolm's warning, half fell, half threw himself, face downward on the deck. The breaking wave reared over him then crashed deafeningly, drenchingly, around and onto him with enormous weight. The breath was crushed out of him. As if there might be a requirement for more water on the scene, he burst into tears.

Now the boat was tipping steeply, headfirst, into the trough. Too overwrought to notice they'd ridden the wave crest without capsizing, and that he was still alive, Christopher clawed and scrabbled his way uphill to where Malcolm, water streaming from his hair and oilskins, crouched over the tiller a foot or two away. Lord save us, or we perish. He threw himself across the tiller and around the helmsman's neck. He wailed, 'I need my home. Take me back.' It wasn't really Malcolm he wanted: it was his mother; though he didn't know that then.

Tom was upon him, in a fury, pulling him away from Malcolm. Roger was anchoring Tom with one hand in the waist-strap of his oilskin, the other wrapped tightly round the backstay. Tom yelled at Christopher. 'Let go of him. I've got you. He's got enough to do without you. Let him sail the bloody boat.'

They crested another wave. It was less than half the height of the last one. A little of it came aboard and splashed around them. They hardly noticed it. Between them, Tom and Roger managed to unclasp Christopher from Malcolm and to hold onto him themselves. 'I want to go back,' Christopher gibbered. 'All of this was wrong.'

He'd rather be with Malcolm than with me, thought Tom, the bottom falling out of his world as precipitously as the boat was this moment falling into yet another trough. I should have seen the signs. They were all around me. Now he'll leave me alone in France and go back with the others in the daylight. He'll let Malcolm take him home.

Surprising Tom, Malcolm spoke. To Christopher. 'I'm taking you to France, kid. If you love Tom that's where you'll want to be.' The boat was under control now, heading, albeit bumpily, south west.

A mad voice in Christopher's head was screaming, 'I don't love Tom, I love you.' Luckily, something wiser up there stopped him shouting it aloud.

This is all about Malcolm, Tom thought suddenly. This whole bloody, mad adventure. It's because Malcolm didn't go to Dunkirk as a ten-year-old and the eighteen-year-old Roger did. He's been looking all his life to make up for that, to prove himself in his own eyes and to Roger – and we've provided his opportunity. Simple as that. And he may yet kill us all in the process. We could have stayed in England and sat things out. There never any need for this.

Malcolm no longer had the look of a contented cat. He looked uncertain and upset. He was saying something to Christopher, almost shouting at him. Tom tuned in.

'Take the bloody helm.'

'I can't.'

'Christopher, take the fucking helm. You've done it before.'

'That was...'

'Just do it. I'm skipper here. Just do it. I'll be beside you all the way. Take it.'

In the end Christopher was too surprised, too overcome by everything to argue any more. Obediently he slid round Malcolm and took hold of the tiller. Malcolm crouched beside him. 'Look at the compass. Keep the heading south south west for another ten minutes. I'll help you in the turn. Got that?'

Christopher nodded. To his surprise he could read the compass quite easily without a torch. He looked behind him for a second. The sky was light beyond the crags of Gris Nez: the absurdly early midsummer dawn. The Cape, its lighthouse, and the turbulent criss-cross currents were receding astern. In a state of shock Christopher gripped the tiller like a vice. The boat held her course. Soon Malcolm was telling him to turn south, then south south east, and helping him re-trim the sails. Tom was never more than a foot away, while Roger peered ahead.

Christopher began to feel a sense of exhilaration, mixed with calm. Things had the unreality of dreams. Roger's call that the cathedral of Boulogne was in sight and dead ahead. The sun, half an hour after that, swarming up over the French hills. The smell of those hills as the early warmth scalded the dew: the smell of fresh-cut grass turning to hay.

Inspiration came to Malcolm one more time. As they approached the north breakwater of Boulogne, he got

Tom to take over the helm and steer them in. A colony of cormorants on an old fort by the entrance welcomed them with fish-eyed stares and a flapping of their dark wings.

'I'm sorry I had to do that, Christopher,' said Malcolm. 'Shout at you, I mean. But putting you at the helm was all I could think to do.' They were sitting over steaming bowls of coffee and chicory in an early-opening fishermen's bar on the quayside.

'Best thing you could have done,' said Tom. His feelings about Malcolm had changed magically as he'd steered them into harbour. Adrenalin had pumped afresh as he'd taken the tiller from Christopher and then followed Malcolm's instructions to take them past the preening cormorants and through the outer harbour towards the port. Malcolm had seemed to be snatching Christopher from him, just as the sea had nearly done, but then, like the sea, had as quickly given him back. If he still wanted him.

They had walked past this bar on their walk to the end of the jetty just a few weeks ago. Back then they wouldn't have dreamed of going in. But this time it had been right opposite the point where they moored the Orca – Roger asking a group of fishermen, in unexpectedly fluent French, if they'd be OK there for twenty minutes while they had a coffee before sailing home.

'I'm sorry if anyone got frightened back there,' Malcolm said, sounding a bit uncomfortable about it. Frightened was an understatement. Christopher had disappeared immediately to the *toilettes* when they'd come in. The others, not much less urgently, had followed suit. 'It was my fault though. I shouldn't have gone in so close to the Cape. Old Grey Nose can give you a nasty welcome even in the best weather. I was in too much of a hurry. Should have steered a wider course. Sincere apologies to all'

'You did a brilliant job,' Tom said, his voice breaking a little as his mind went back to what he'd just been through. 'That was some tidal wave you got us over.'

'Must have been a good eleven feet,' Malcolm agreed. Christopher felt somehow let down by this. His wave had had an epic, mythic quality about it that he didn't want to hear measured in prosaic feet.

'Yes, he did a good job,' said Roger, who hadn't said much since they'd sat at their Formica-topped table among the smoking, breakfasting fisher-folk.

'He's sailed the Channel before,' Tom said.

'Not in the Orca, he hasn't. Not as skipper. And certainly never at night. I'm proud of him.' He said this seriously, without smiling, but he pulled Malcolm's head towards him and kissed his cheek. Some heads turned in their direction but there was no judgement in anybody's look. The grizzled heads around them knew more than most about dangers shared. And Malcolm began to look a bit more like a contented cat again – for the first time in many hours.

When Christopher did open his mouth to speak it was almost to beg Roger and Malcolm not to sail away so soon. He wanted them to meet their French friends... He couldn't bear to imagine them sailing back through the big waves around the Cape. They needed to catch the returning tide, they told him. They'd have it with them for five hours, then slack water, and then they'd be nearly there. But they had to go now. The pub was staffed for lunchtime but Roger would need to be there this evening. Malcolm had work to go to on Monday morning... 'I'll make you a promise, though,' Malcolm said to Christopher. 'We'll take a long route round Gris Nez, even if it adds an hour or two. Then you don't have to imagine us going through all that.' He gave him a serious smile. 'Anyway, it's daylight and the sun's shining.' Outside the café windows it was painting the whole town white.

They returned to the Orca and hauled suitcases from the hold. Unwrapping them from their tarpaulins they found them dryer than their owners were. It was agreed that Tom and Christopher would find a way to phone the Admiral Digby that evening, no matter what the cost. Tom and Christopher helped cast off. They watched the boat go, exchanging a wave with its crew from time to time while they were still big enough to see, then simply watching until the north breakwater, two miles offshore, hid the russet sails from sight.

They were alone. Two young men, one damp, one soaking, with suitcases, on a foreign quayside. The drunk monk had been closer to the truth than Tom had realised, he now thought. Tom had joined him in exile. He was indeed like Paul Verlaine, wandering Europe with a boy in tow. It might have been David. He could as well have slept with David when he wanted to, then brought him here. The situation would have been no more desperate than this, the catastrophe no more complete. David was a schoolboy, Christopher a teacher, but they were the same age. And David had at least been constant in his affections during their brief four months. Instead, here he was with Christopher who, though intelligent, beautiful and sweet-natured, had shown himself as ready as Titania, or Prospero's daughter – whatever her name was – to fall in love with everyone he met.

Christopher was thinking how unforeseeable the last twenty-four hours had been, how unimaginable the next. He had lost everything: parents, family, friends and belongings, bright future at university, the lot. All he had was Tom, handsome but somehow rudderless, goal-less, and now destitute – penniless and without prospects –

and a bit of a bully at times. He said, coldly, 'I'm sorry. I was frightened by a wave. That's not how I mean to go on.'

Tom said, 'I was frightened too. Even Malcolm was for a second or two.'

'I lost my head,' said Christopher.

'You lost your footing, that was all.' Tom felt sorry for him now, though he still wasn't sure if he liked him.

'In the Southern Ocean the waves are high as three-storey houses: fifty, sixty feet. Troughs half a mile long in between.'

'Nobody takes a fishing smack across the Southern Ocean.' Tom remembered something. 'And nobody manages to be brave all the time. Two mornings ago, when you went to talk to Dexter, I wasn't brave enough to comfort him. You were.' Though that bravery had cost them dear. Two mornings ago!

'I suppose it's practice for what lies ahead.'

'All big waves from now on, you mean?' said Tom. 'At the beginning, maybe. But only at first.'

They turned and walked towards the town. Suitcases had no wheels in those days. You carried them till radius and ulna threatened to tear from their fastenings, then you changed sides. The quayside seemed very long. They had their passports ready, in damp pockets: they expected to be stopped at any moment by some official or gendarme. But no-one took any notice of them at all. The Rue Faidherbe, when they got to it – the street that led to Michel's studio – was a seriously steep hill. That was odd, Tom thought. He'd remembered it as being almost flat.

Christopher said suddenly, 'Are you OK with me? Will I do?'

Tom turned and looked at him for a moment as if considering the question very seriously. Then he surprised himself by smiling broadly. 'You'll do,' he said, and continued to smile at him.

'You can call me Chris if you want to,' his lover told him.

Together they began to climb the hill.

***

From John Moyse's New Journal: Sunday June 24th 1962

Saint John's day. To be exact, the feast of the nativity of John the Baptist. The other Saint John, the apostle, has his feast on December 27th. So I have two name days if I want them. I don't know if I was named after the Baptist or the Apostle, and I don't suppose my parents do either. For all I know they might have named me after St John of the Cross, St John Chrysostom or one of the twelve other St Johns in the Church calendar. But today is the one everyone thinks of as St John's day, because of all the legends around it. Ghosts and crusading armies coming alive on St John's eve and it being midsummer and all that stuff. So I tend to think of this one as my name day.

A young priest from the abbey who nobody'd seen before said Mass. There was no sermon. Sister invigilated breakfast, and Mr Charteris came in for letter writing. There's a massive shortage of resident staff. Then at lunch the abbot walked into the refectory and said we'd have a new headmaster starting tomorrow morning. This time he said headmaster, not head teacher, and everyone pricked up their ears.

It's going to be Father Claude. You could kind of hear the surprise and nobody clapped. It's an odd choice, it seems to me. He's a very shy man, OK with kids but not good around adults and a headmaster has to deal with both. I don't know how he'll cope with discipline and the rough and tumble of it all. I saw Ed shaking his head when the announcement was being made, but afterwards he didn't want to talk about it. Might be good for school music, I suppose, but as I say, it's an odd choice. But anyway, I'm out of here in a few weeks and – when it comes to adults making decisions about other adults – what do I know?

After lunch I walked to the end of the playing fields and looked out beyond the veg gardens and the houses in the dip below. Like I used to sometimes when I was new and wanted to be alone. I felt like that today. Like Garbo. I just wanted to be alone. I miss Angelo a lot. I also discovered that I miss Christopher too. I didn't know I'd come to like him as much as that. But I did like him, and he liked me – in a perfectly innocent way.

The landscape looks as bleak today as it ever did when I was new, although it's midsummer now. Beyond the bay lies the whole expanse of Kent like a long thick charcoal line, with home 60 miles away the other side of the North Downs. In the bay the river Stour lies like a curled dead snake, its mouth agape in the mud. And on the hill the airfield sits. An Argosy on a training flight today. I suddenly realised that when we kids used to come here and look over the fence we were looking at means of escape from here. The way out. By air, by the London road following along beside the runway, and by boat and ship in the channel and the bay.

I wondered if Tom and Christopher had made their escape by boat – like James II, fleeing to France in a fishing boat. Perhaps by night. They had friends with a sailing boat after all, and other friends in France, according to Angelo. Perhaps they'd gone there. I watched the sea a long time, remembered there was a protestant hymn that goes 'For those in peril on the sea.' I said a prayer for them. Then I said one for Angelo too.

Couldn't do any harm. Praying's about the only thing you can do in this world that never does any harm to anyone.

Then suddenly a boat appeared from behind Deal pier. It was a sailing boat. I watched it coming very slowly. Couldn't see which way it was headed at first, it was tacking this way and that because of the northern breeze. But it was coming this way, I saw in the end. I could see its red sails – sorry, tan – and realised it was the boat that T and C used to sail on. I watched it coming nearer for over an hour, till the sun shone through the sails and made them glow like fire. Could see it very clearly but not near enough to count the crew. So my guess might have been right. It had taken T and C across to France in the night and was now coming back. I wonder who its owners are. Suppose I'll never know. At last it turned away and made for the mouth of the Stour. It went on up into the river and then disappeared behind buildings and against the dark land. I remembered the painting Angelo did of it – I'd let him use my rough sketch to jog his memory. That got him the art prize, and that got him invited to Canterbury where he saw the David and Jonathan ... and then all the rest. I went on standing there until I suddenly realised that I was crying. I made myself stop. It's something a house captain, even if he's only going to be in the job a month or so, must never be seen to do.

THE END

****

The Dog In The Chapel is the first book in the Dog in the Chapel Trilogy. It is now also available as an audiobook, read by the author. The second book is **Tom & Christopher And Their Kind.** The third is **Dog Roses.**

About the Author

Anthony McDonald is the author of thirty-one books. He studied modern history at Durham University, then worked briefly as a musical instrument maker and as a farmhand before moving into the theatre, where he has worked in every capacity except director and electrician. He has also spent several years teaching English in Paris and London. He now lives in rural East Sussex.

Novels by Anthony McDonald

TENERIFE
THE DOG IN THE CHAPEL
TOM & CHRISTOPHER AND THEIR KIND
DOG ROSES
THE RAVEN AND THE JACKDAW
SILVER CITY
IVOR'S GHOSTS
ADAM
BLUE SKY ADAM
GETTING ORLANDO
ORANGE BITTER, ORANGE SWEET
ALONG THE STARS
WOODCOCK FLIGHT

Short stories
MATCHES IN THE DARK

<u>Diary</u>

RALPH: DIARY OF A GAY TEEN

Comedy

THE GULLIVER MOB

Gay Romance Series:

Sweet Nineteen
Gay Romance on Garda
Gay Romance in Majorca
Gay Tartan
Cocker and I
Cam Cox
The Paris Novel
The Van Gogh Window
Tibidabo
Spring Sonata
Touching Fifty
Romance on the Orient Express

‒‒‒‒

And, writing as 'Adam Wye'

Boy Next Door
Love in Venice
Gay in Moscow

All titles are available as Kindle ebooks and as paperbacks from Amazon.

<u>www.anthonymcdonald.co.uk</u>

Made in the USA
Middletown, DE
20 October 2020